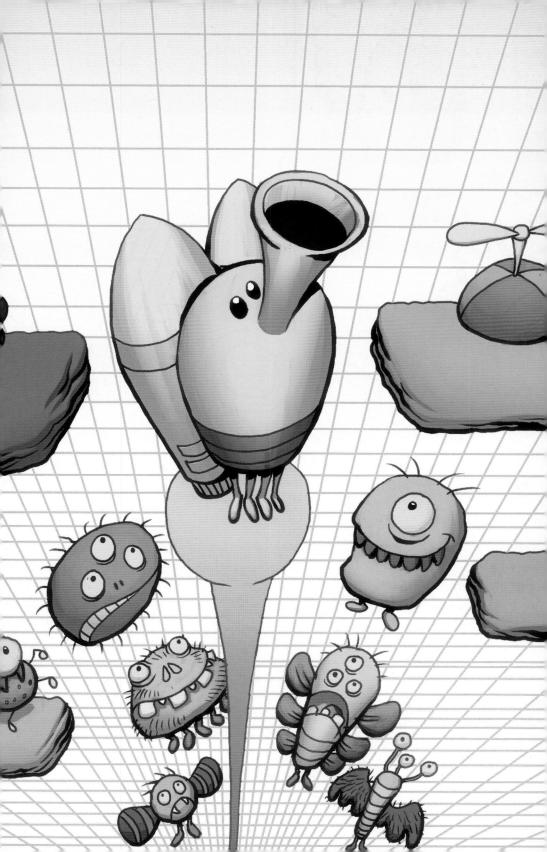

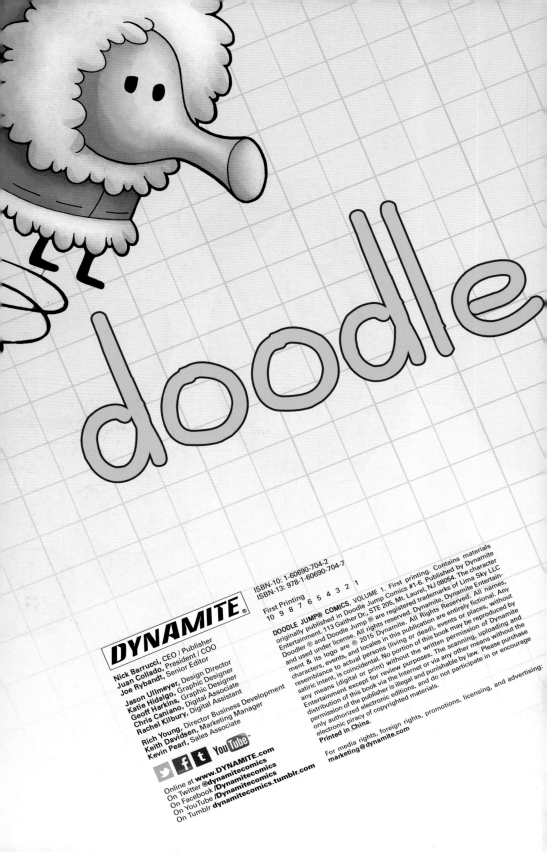

doodle

ISBN-10: 1-60690-704-2
ISBN-13: 978-1-60690-704-7

First Printing
10 9 8 7 6 5 4 3 2 1

DOODLE JUMP® COMICS, VOLUME 1. First printing. Contains materials originally published in Doodle Jump Comics #1-6. Published by Dynamite Entertainment. 113 Gaither Dr., STE 205, Mt. Laurel, NJ 08054. The character Doodler ® and Doodle Jump ® are registered trademarks of Lima Sky LLC and used under license. All rights reserved. Dynamite, Dynamite Entertainment & its logo are ® 2015 Dynamite. All Rights Reserved. All names, characters, events, and locales in this publication are entirely fictional. Any resemblance to actual persons (living or dead), events or places, without satiric intent, is coincidental. No portion of this book may be reproduced by any means (digital or print) without the written permission of Dynamite Entertainment except for review purposes. The scanning, uploading and distribution of this book via the Internet or via any other means without the permission of the publisher is illegal and punishable by law. Please purchase only authorized electronic editions, and do not participate in or encourage electronic piracy of copyrighted materials.
Printed in China.

For media rights, foreign rights, promotions, licensing, and advertising: marketing@dynamite.com

DYNAMITE®

Nick Barrucci, CEO / Publisher
Juan Collado, President / COO
Joe Rybandt, Senior Editor

Jason Ullmeyer, Design Director
Katie Hidalgo, Graphic Designer
Geoff Harkins, Graphic Designer
Chris Caniano, Digital Associate
Rachel Kilbury, Digital Assistant

Rich Young, Director Business Development
Keith Davidsen, Marketing Manager
Kevin Pearl, Sales Associate

Online at www.DYNAMITE.com
On Twitter @dynamitecomics
On Facebook /Dynamitecomics
On YouTube /Dynamitecomics
On Tumblr dynamitecomics.tumblr.com

jump®

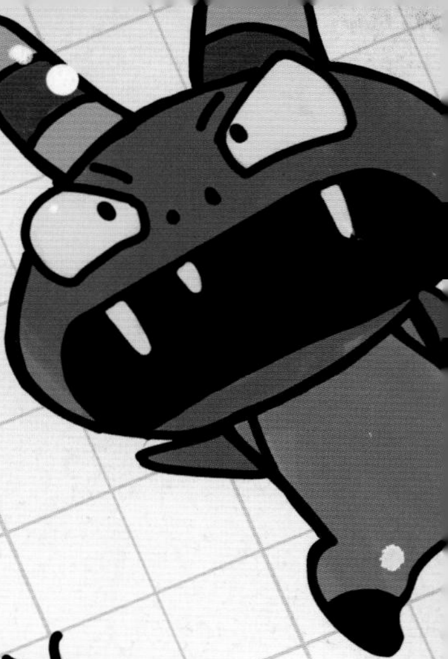

written by MEREDITH GRAN
and MARIO UDZENIJA
art by STEVE UY
letters by BILL TORTOLINI
collection cover by REBEKIE BENNINGTON
book design by JASON ULLMEYER
consulting editor RICH YOUNG

special thanks to ERIC KARP at lima sky

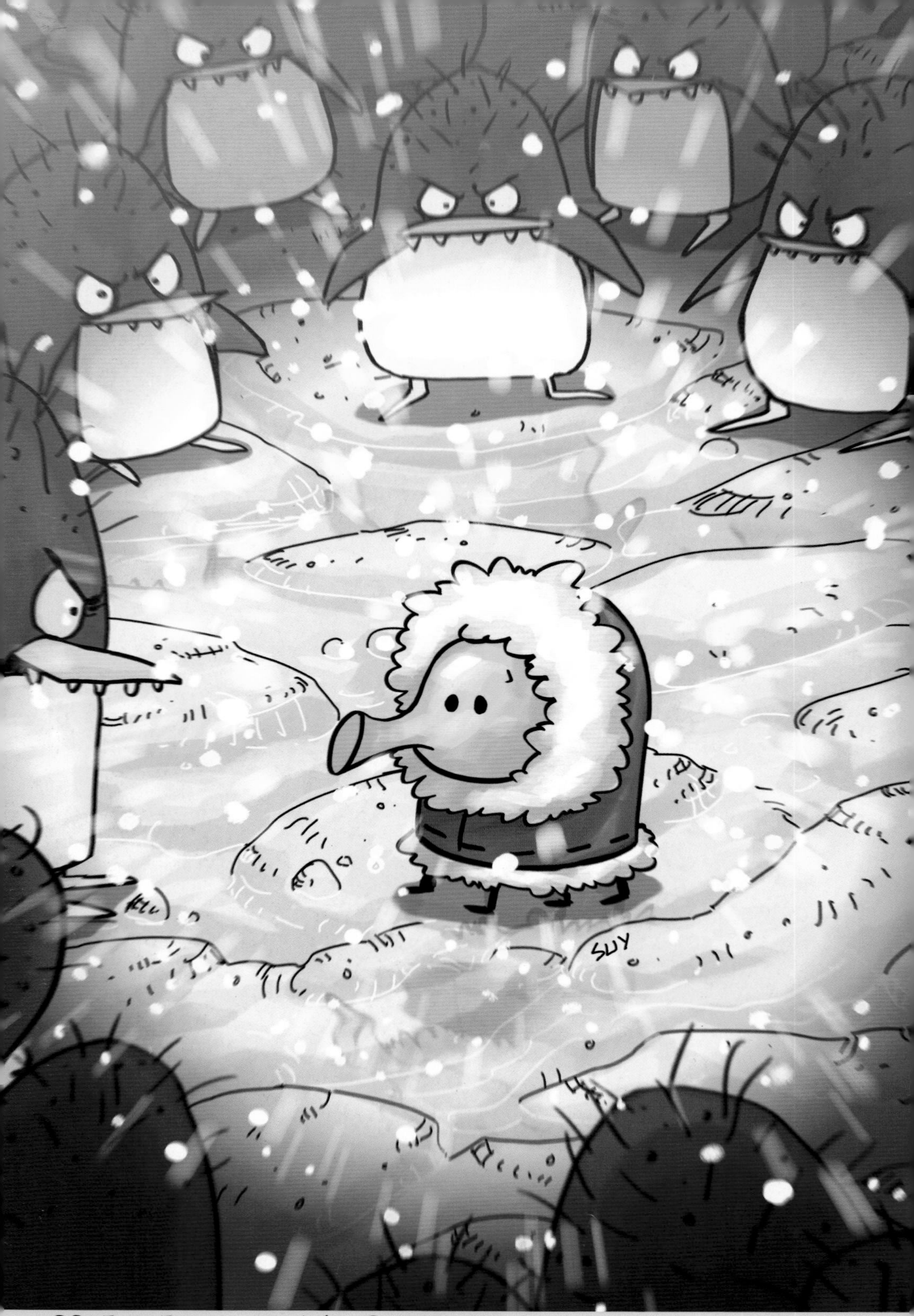
SUY

ISSUE ONE cover art by STEVE UY

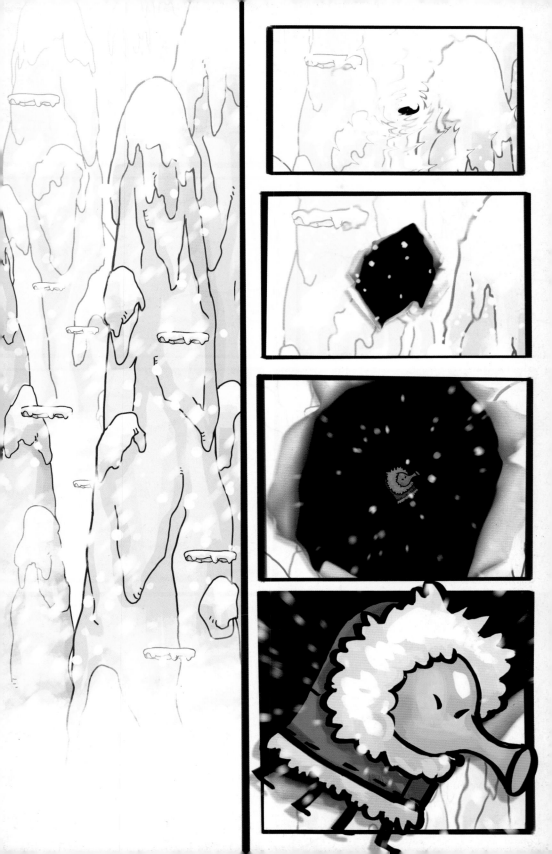

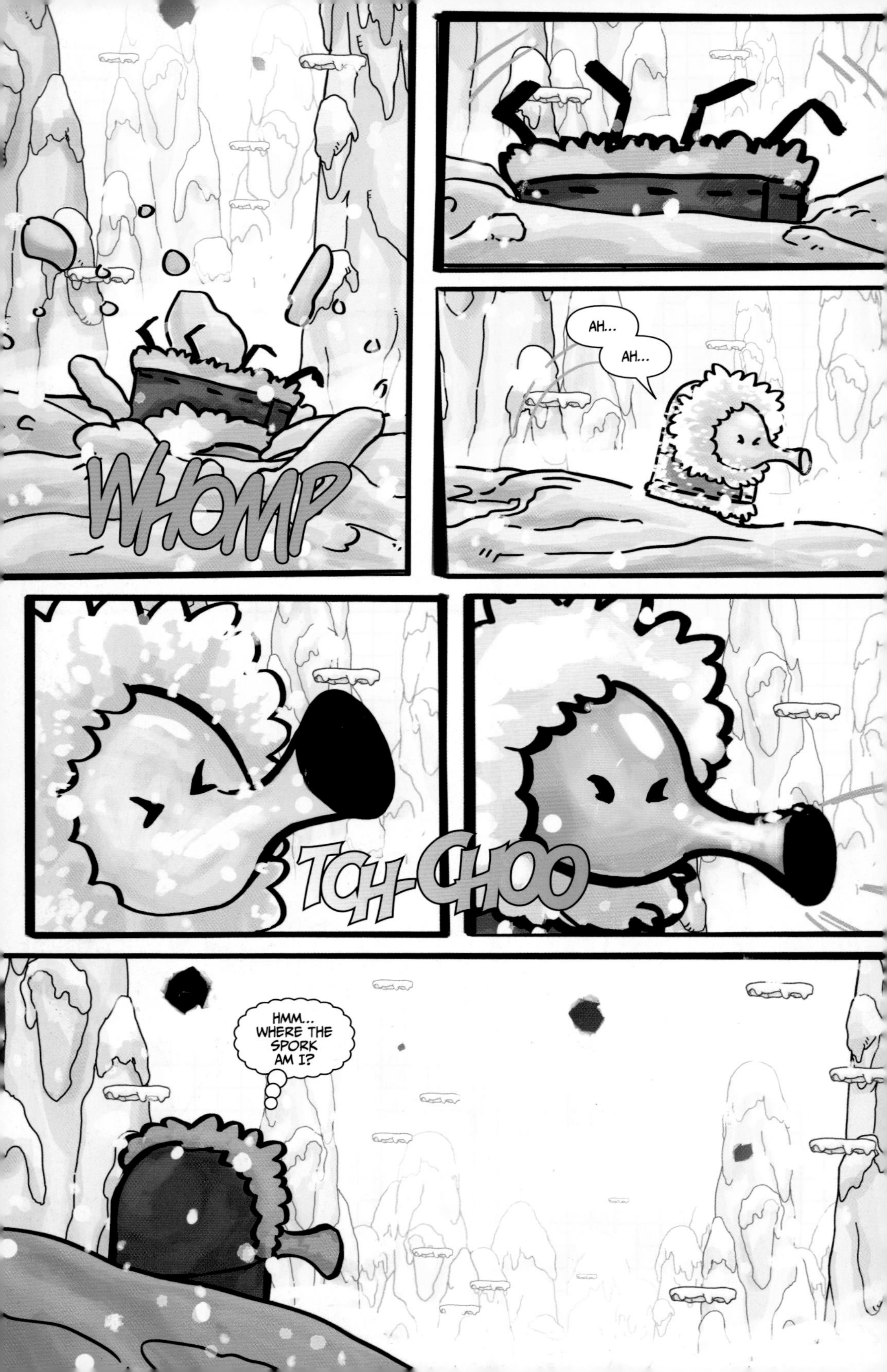
WHOMP
AH...
AH...
TCH-CHOO
HMM... WHERE THE SPORK AM I?

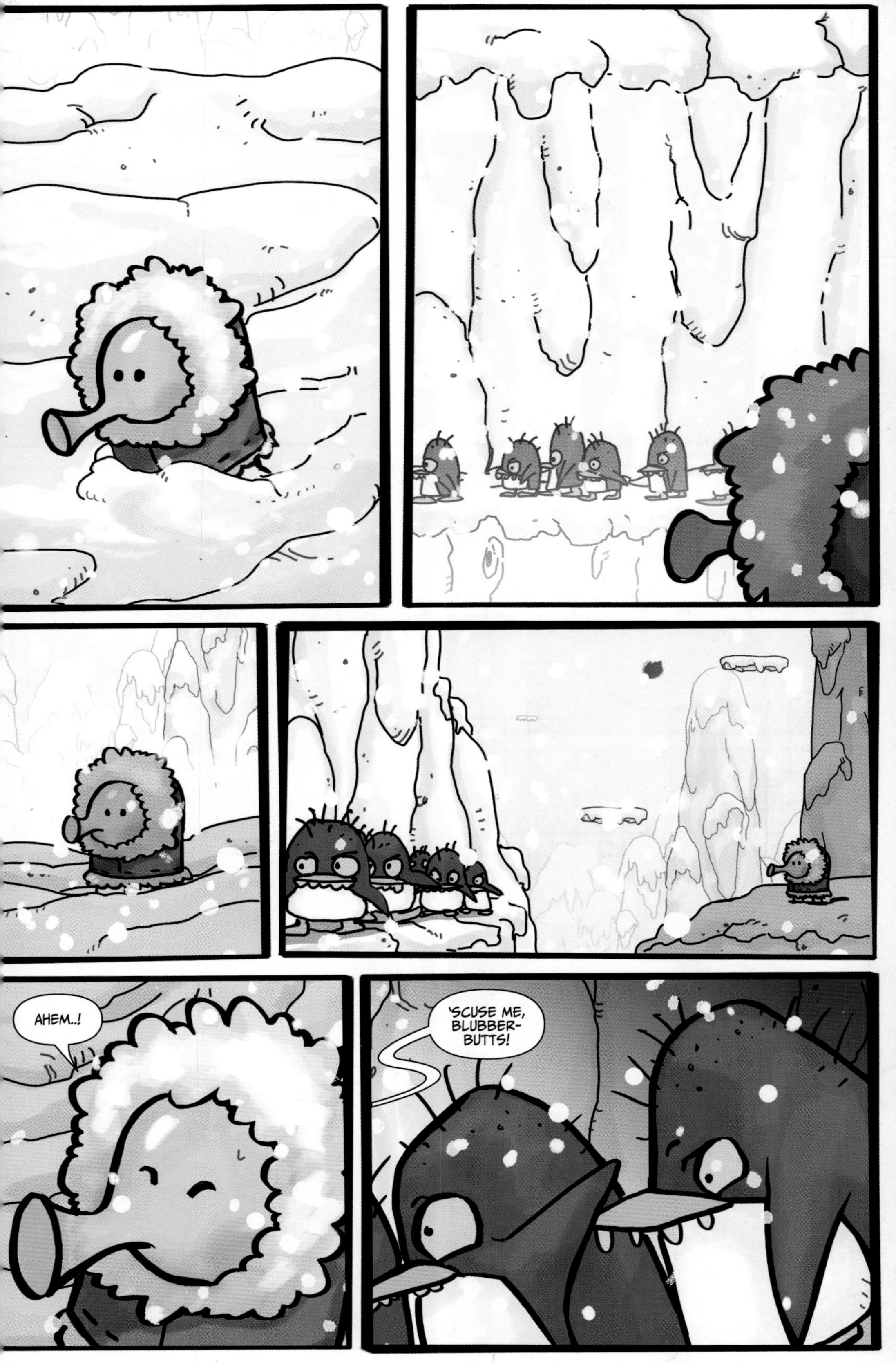
AHEM..!
'SCUSE ME, BLUBBER-BUTTS!

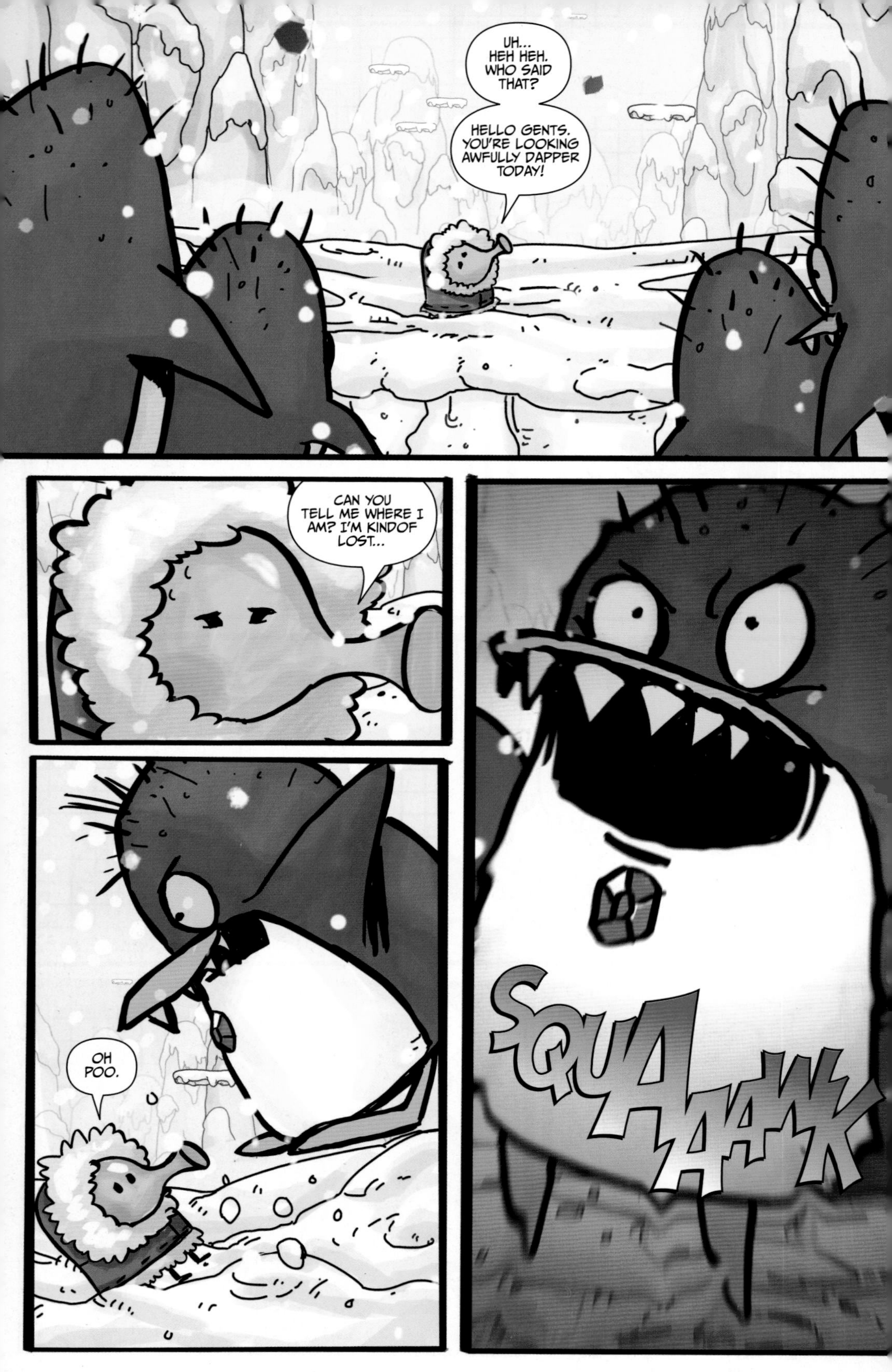
UH... HEH HEH. WHO SAID THAT?
HELLO GENTS. YOU'RE LOOKING AWFULLY DAPPER TODAY!
CAN YOU TELL ME WHERE I AM? I'M KINDOF LOST...
OH POO.
SQUAAAAWK

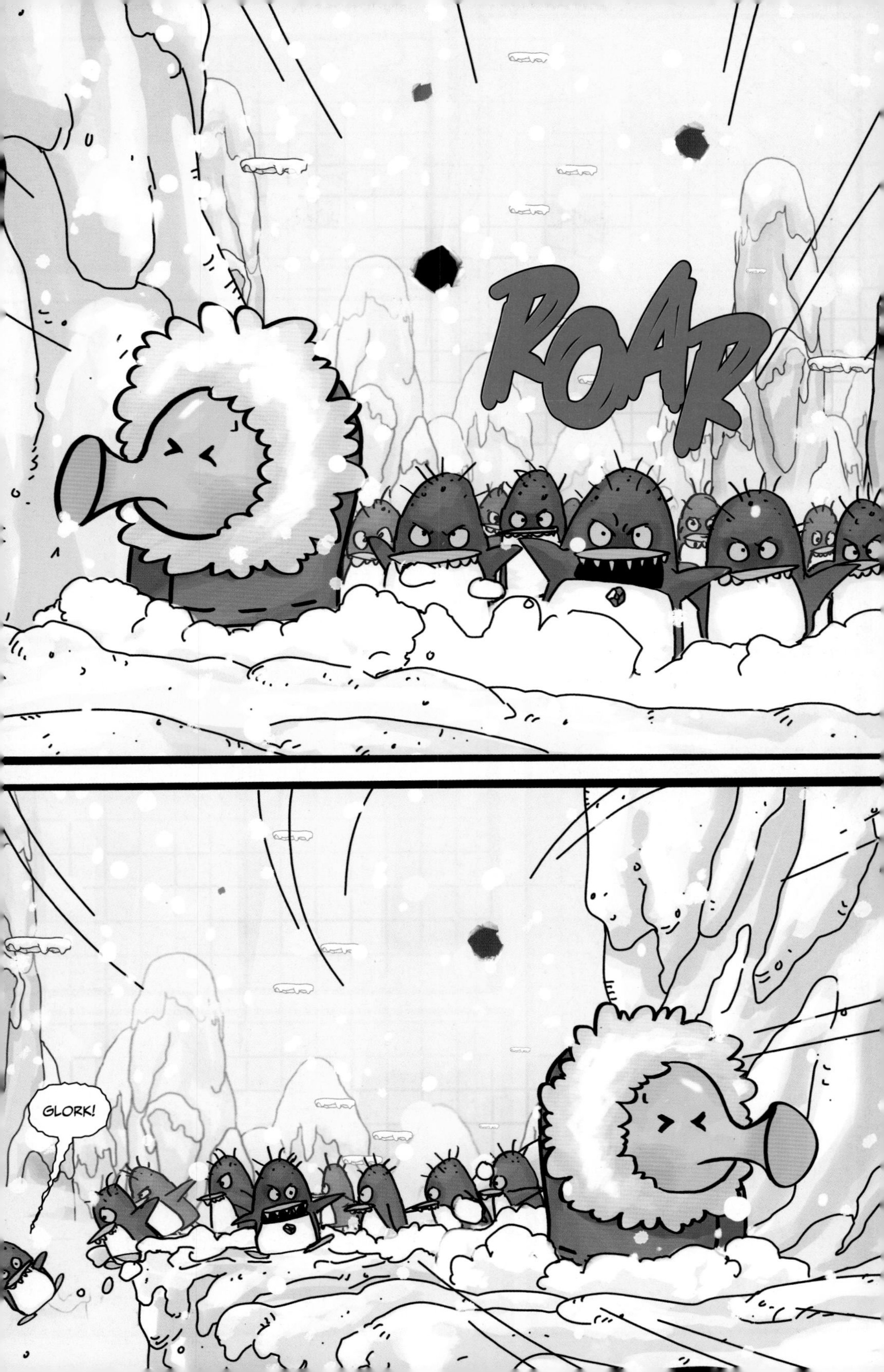
ROAR
GLORK!

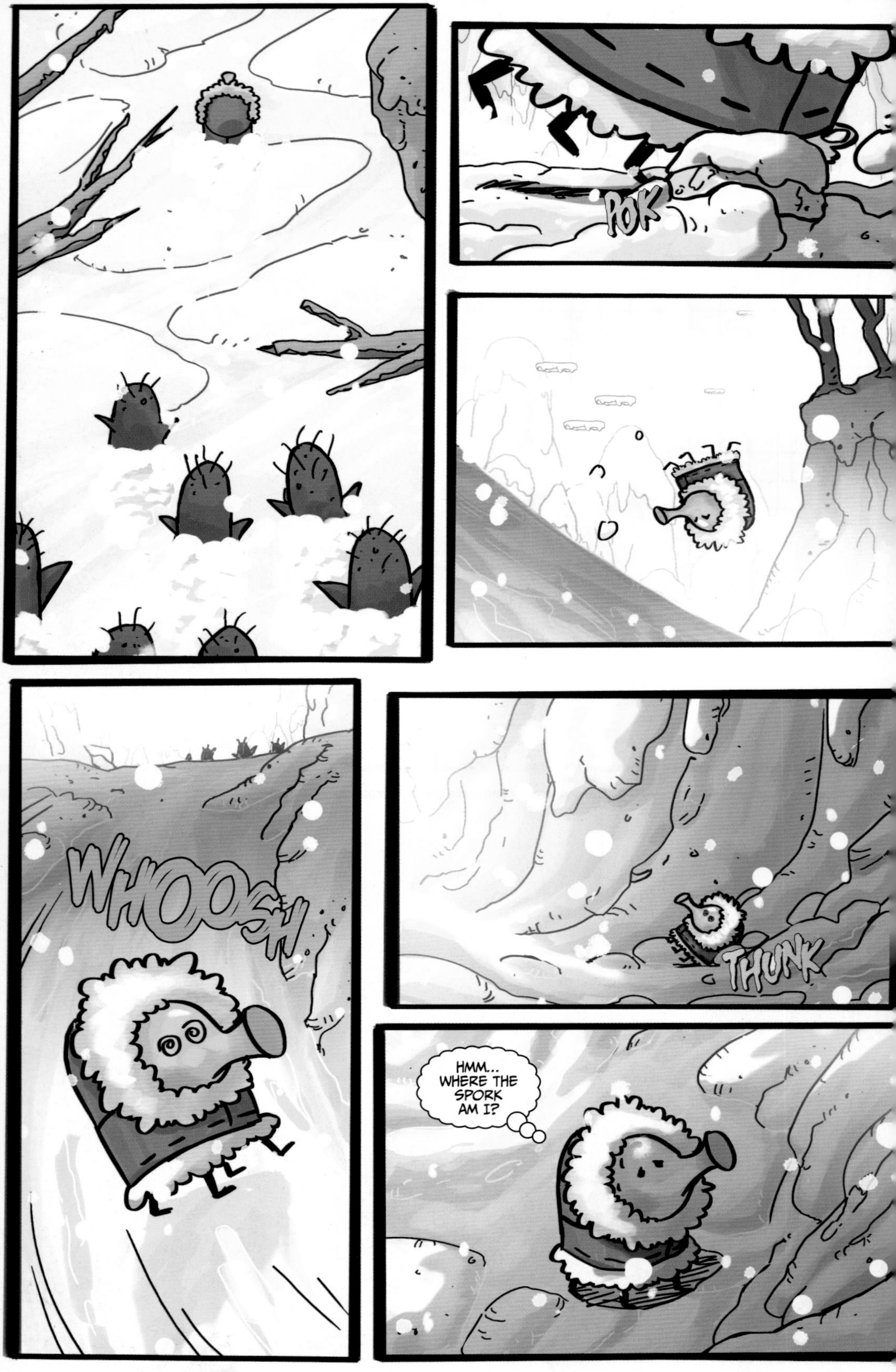
POK
WHOOSH
THUNK
HMM... WHERE THE SPORK AM I?

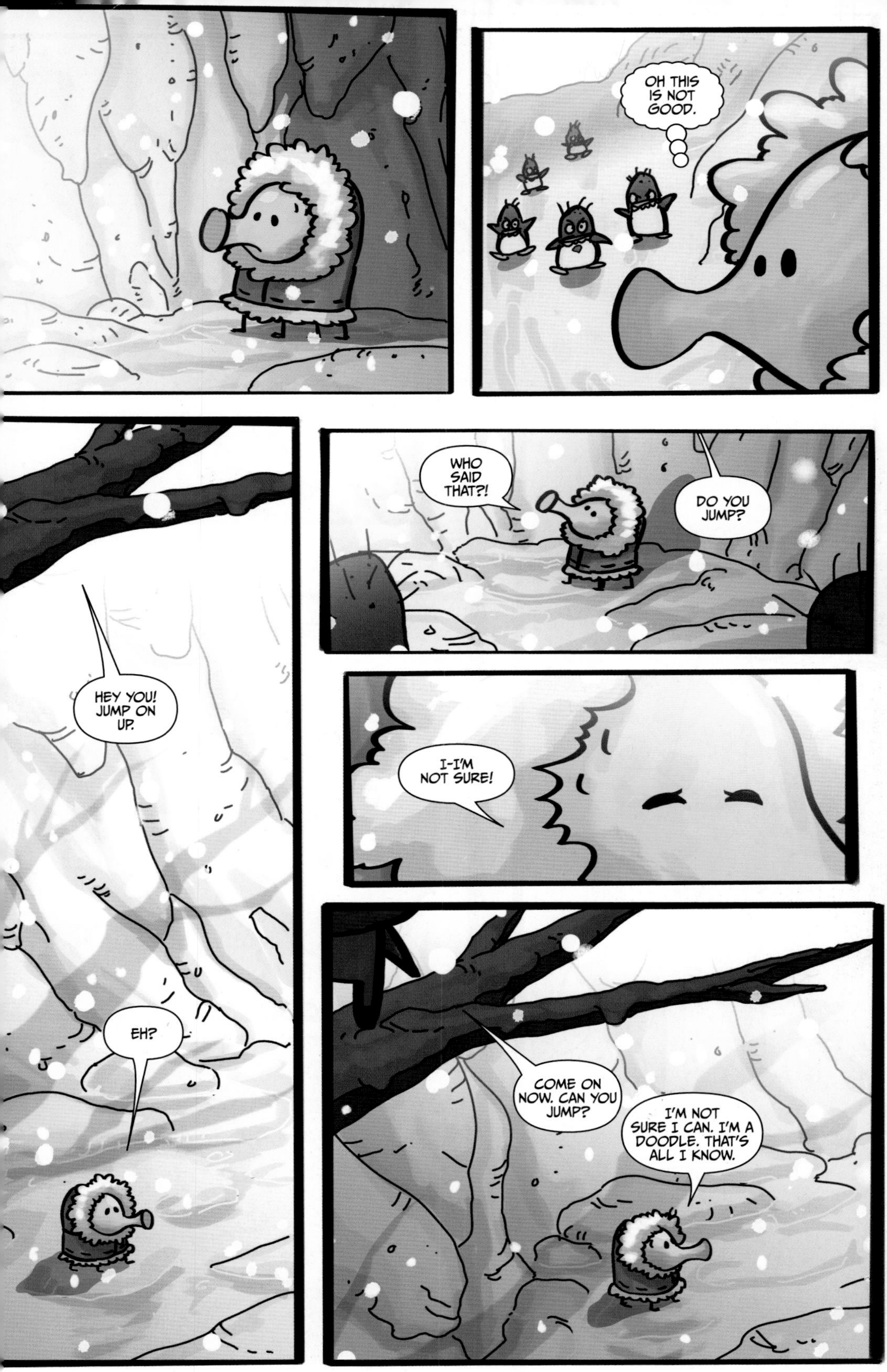
OH THIS IS NOT GOOD.
HEY YOU! JUMP ON UP.
EH?
WHO SAID THAT?!
DO YOU JUMP?
I-I'M NOT SURE!
COME ON NOW. CAN YOU JUMP?
I'M NOT SURE I CAN. I'M A DOODLE. THAT'S ALL I KNOW.

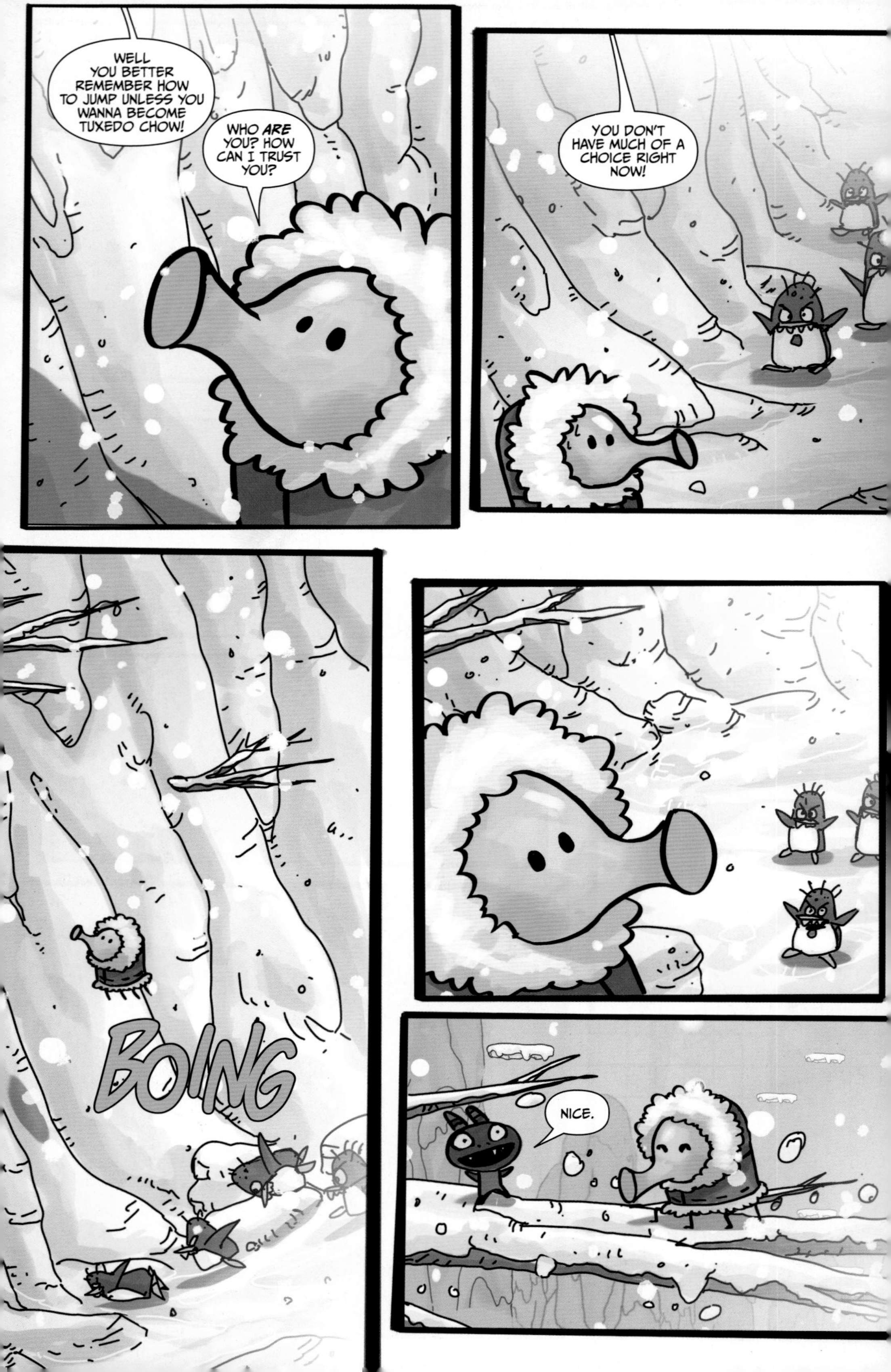
WELL YOU BETTER REMEMBER HOW TO JUMP UNLESS YOU WANNA BECOME TUXEDO CHOW!
WHO ARE YOU? HOW CAN I TRUST YOU?
YOU DON'T HAVE MUCH OF A CHOICE RIGHT NOW!
BOING
NICE.

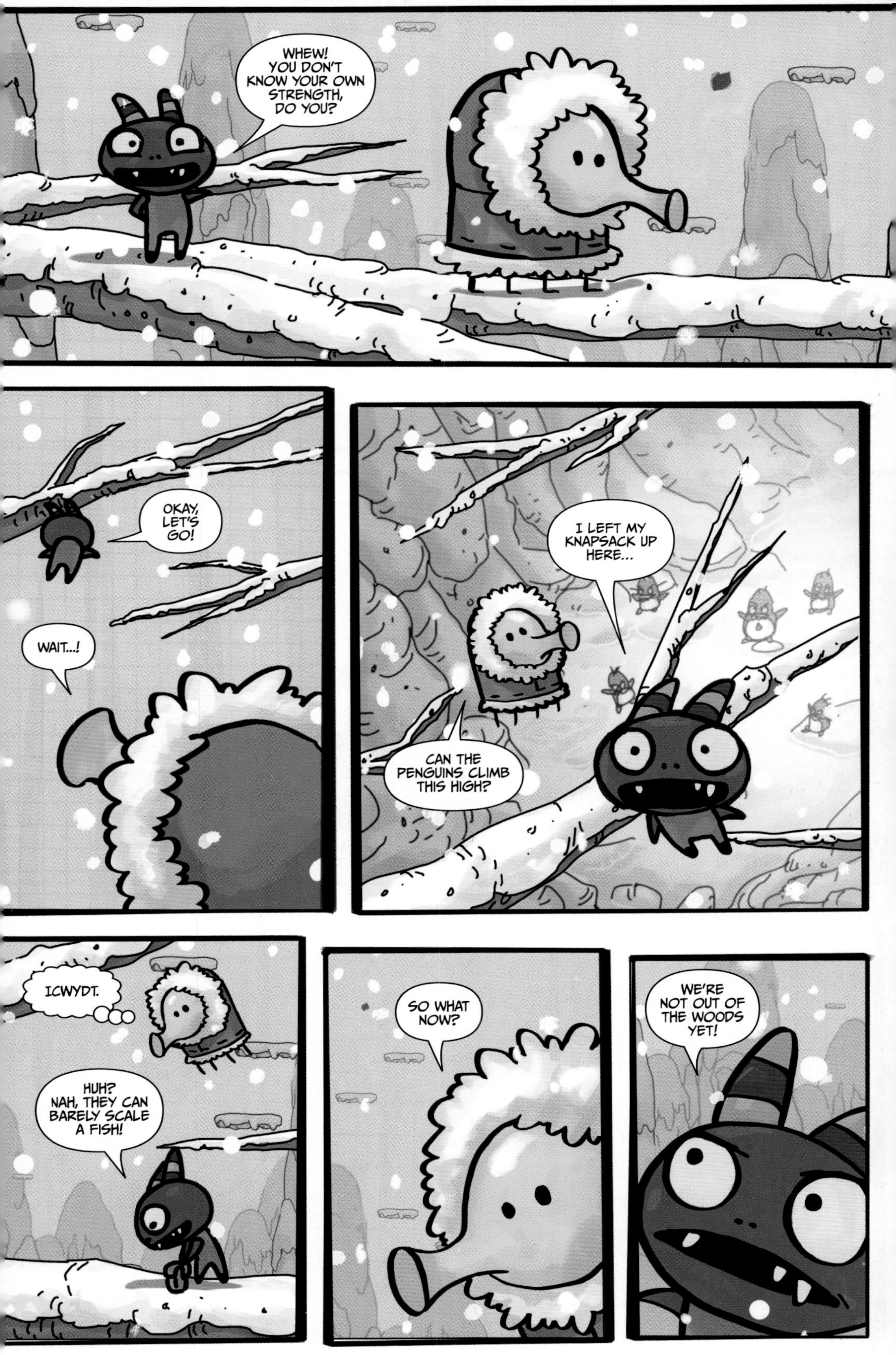
WHEW! YOU DON'T KNOW YOUR OWN STRENGTH, DO YOU?
OKAY, LET'S GO!
WAIT...!
I LEFT MY KNAPSACK UP HERE...
CAN THE PENGUINS CLIMB THIS HIGH?
ICWYDT.
HUH? NAH, THEY CAN BARELY SCALE A FISH!
SO WHAT NOW?
WE'RE NOT OUT OF THE WOODS YET!

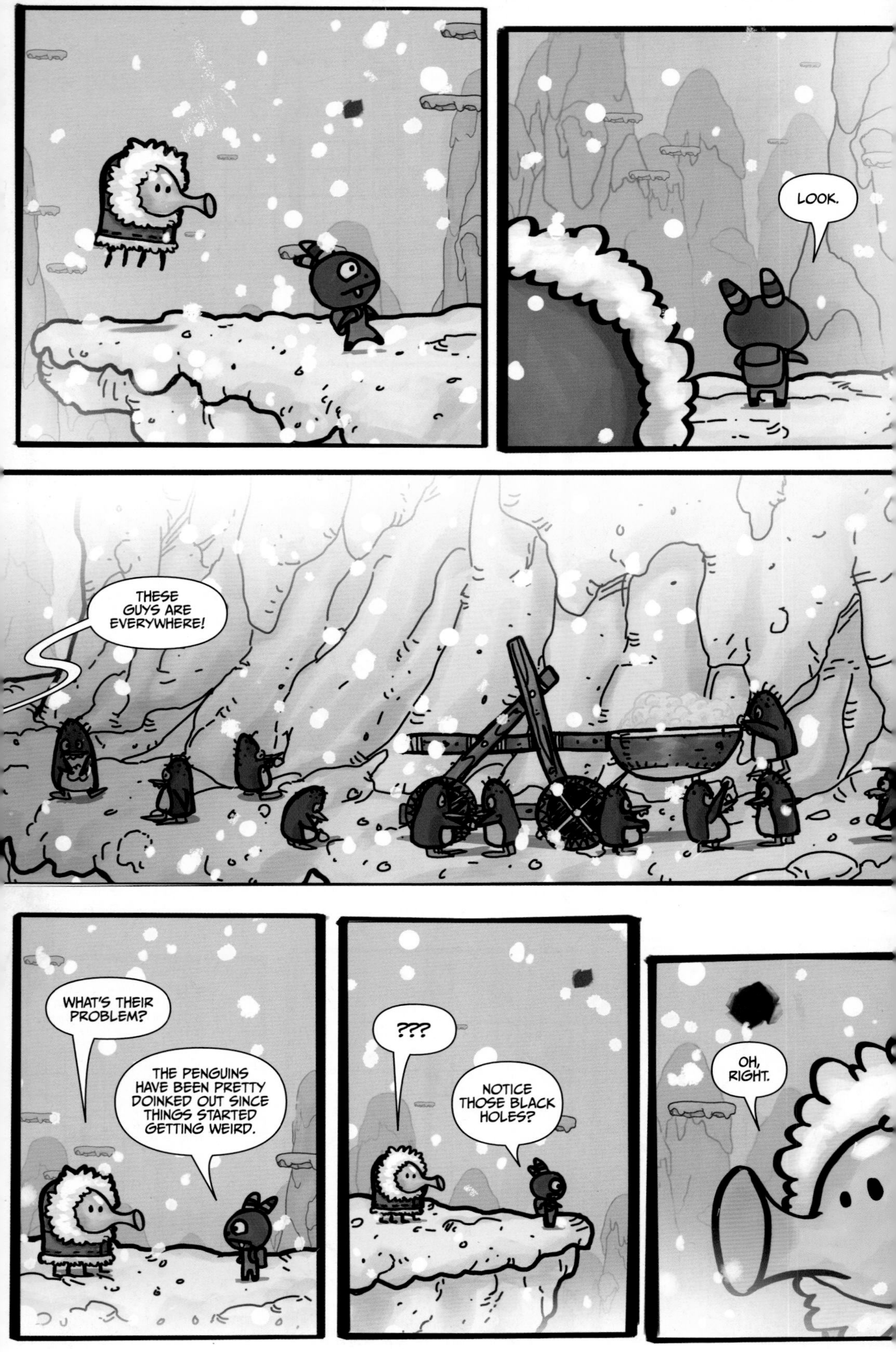
LOOK.
THESE GUYS ARE EVERYWHERE!
WHAT'S THEIR PROBLEM?
THE PENGUINS HAVE BEEN PRETTY DOINKED OUT SINCE THINGS STARTED GETTING WEIRD.
???
NOTICE THOSE BLACK HOLES?
OH, RIGHT.

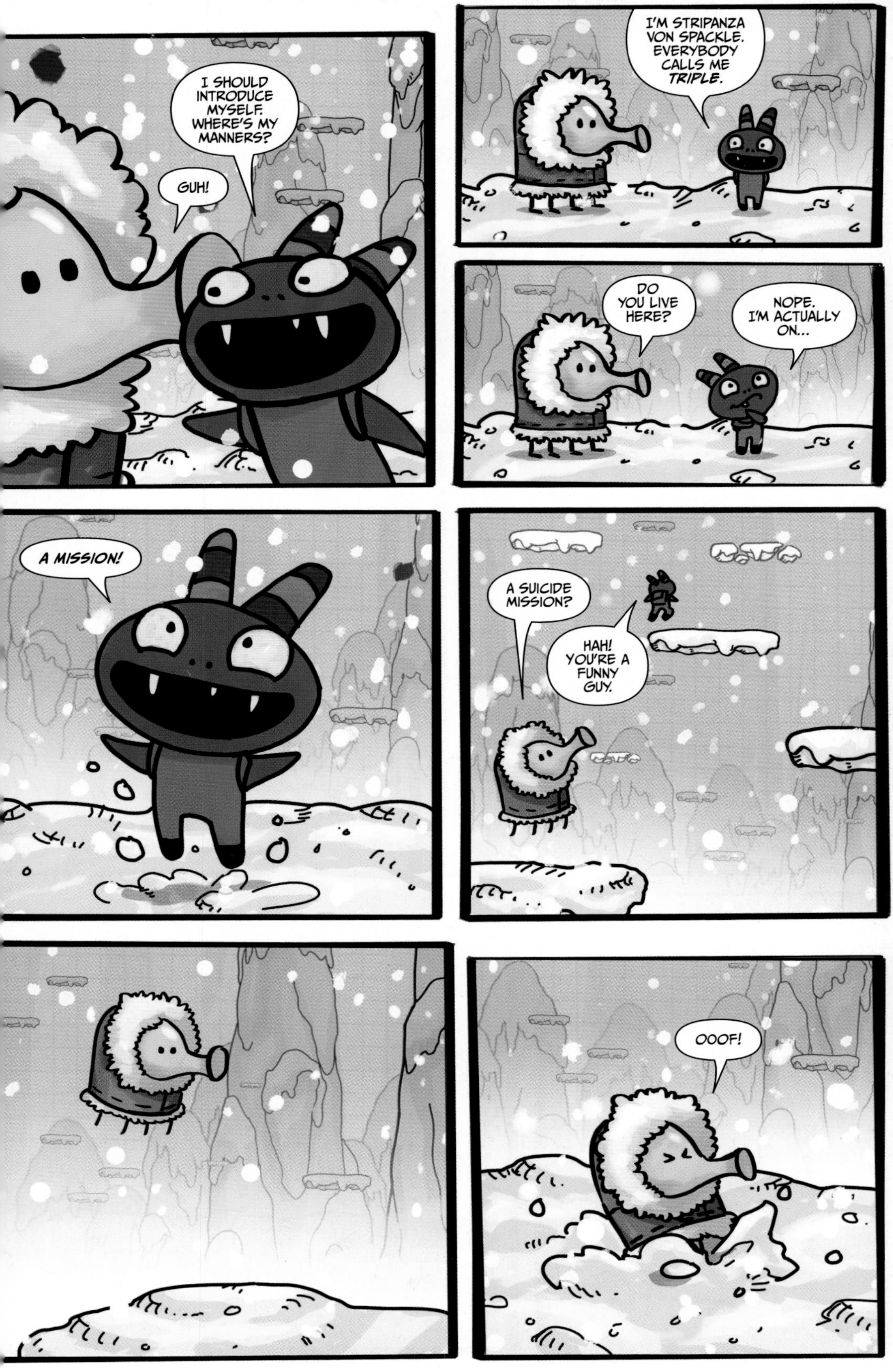
I SHOULD INTRODUCE MYSELF. WHERE'S MY MANNERS?
GUH!
I'M STRIPANZA VON SPACKLE. EVERYBODY CALLS ME *TRIPLE*.
DO YOU LIVE HERE?
NOPE. I'M ACTUALLY ON...
A MISSION!
A SUICIDE MISSION?
HAH! YOU'RE A FUNNY GUY.
OOOF!

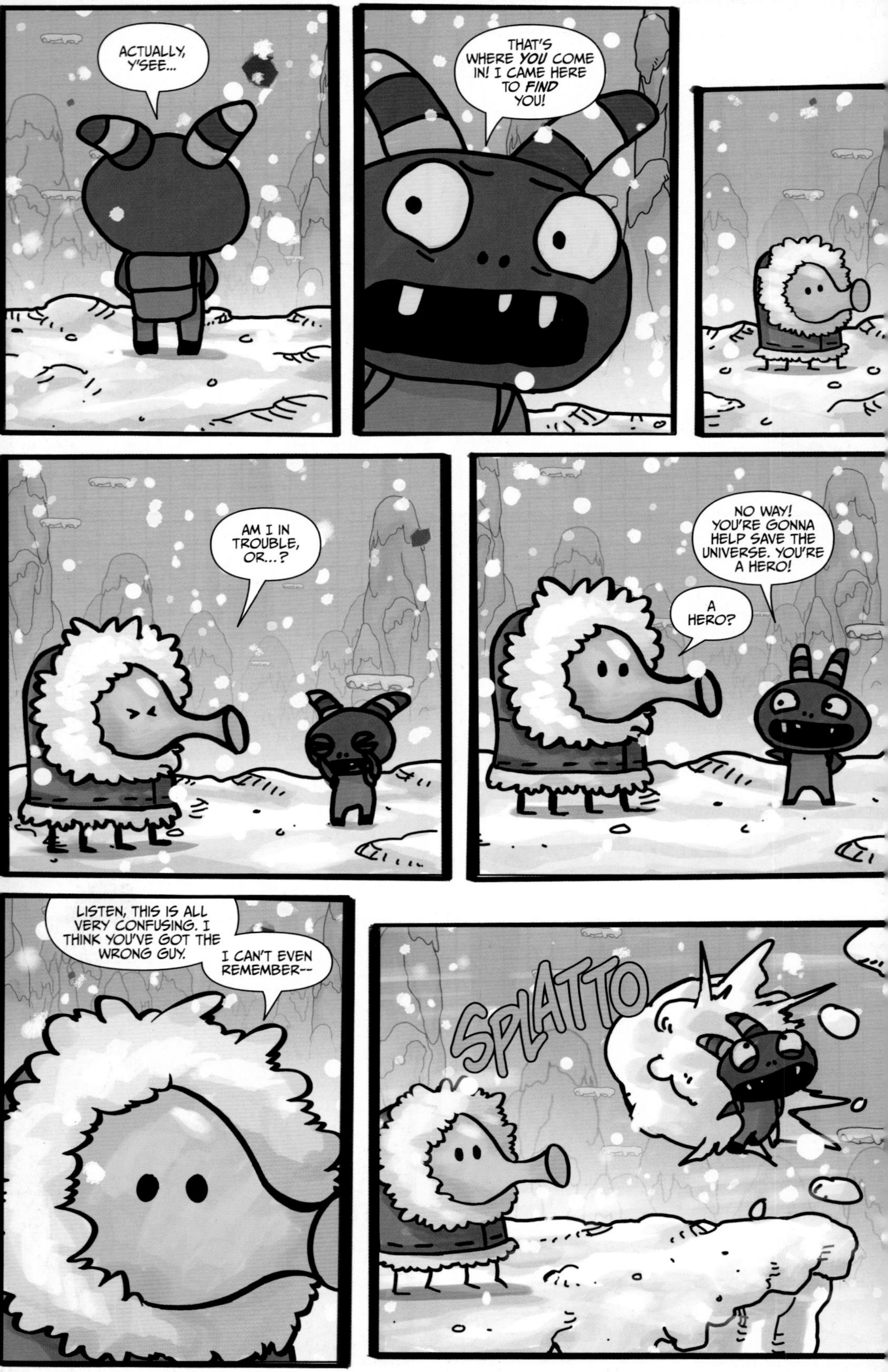
ACTUALLY, Y'SEE...
THAT'S WHERE YOU COME IN! I CAME HERE TO FIND YOU!
AM I IN TROUBLE, OR...?
A HERO?
NO WAY! YOU'RE GONNA HELP SAVE THE UNIVERSE. YOU'RE A HERO!
LISTEN, THIS IS ALL VERY CONFUSING. I THINK YOU'VE GOT THE WRONG GUY.
I CAN'T EVEN REMEMBER--
SPLATTO

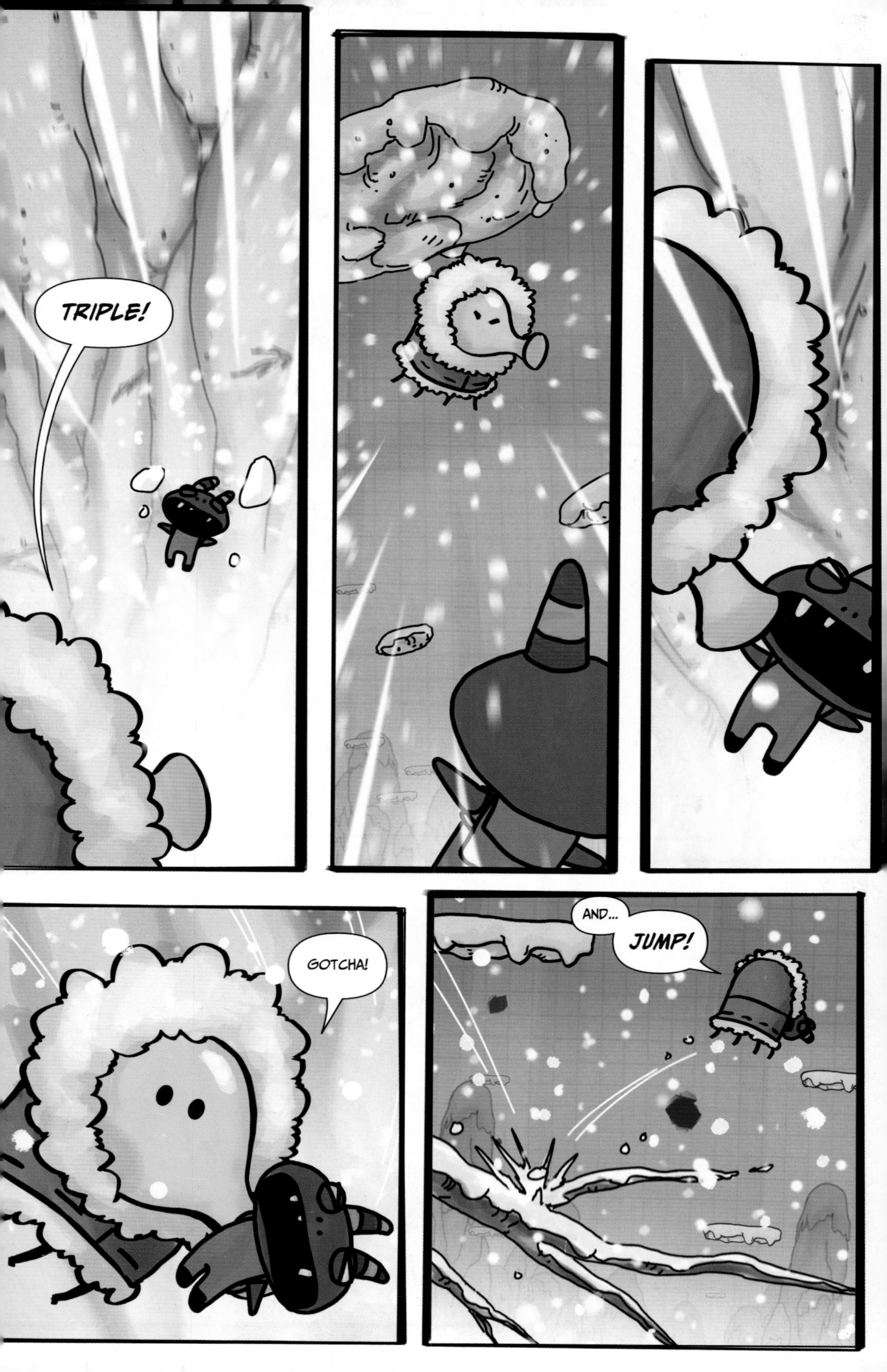
TRIPLE!
GOTCHA!
AND...
JUMP!

PENGUINS..!

HEY! ARE YOU OKAY?

YEAH... JUST A LITTLE FROSTY!

DANG PENGUINS!

WE CAN'T GET AROUND THEM. THERE'S ONLY ONE WAY.

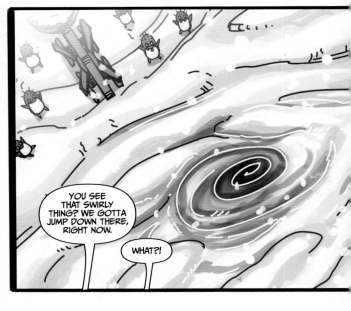

YOU SEE THAT SWIRLY THING? WE GOTTA JUMP DOWN THERE, RIGHT NOW.

WHAT?!

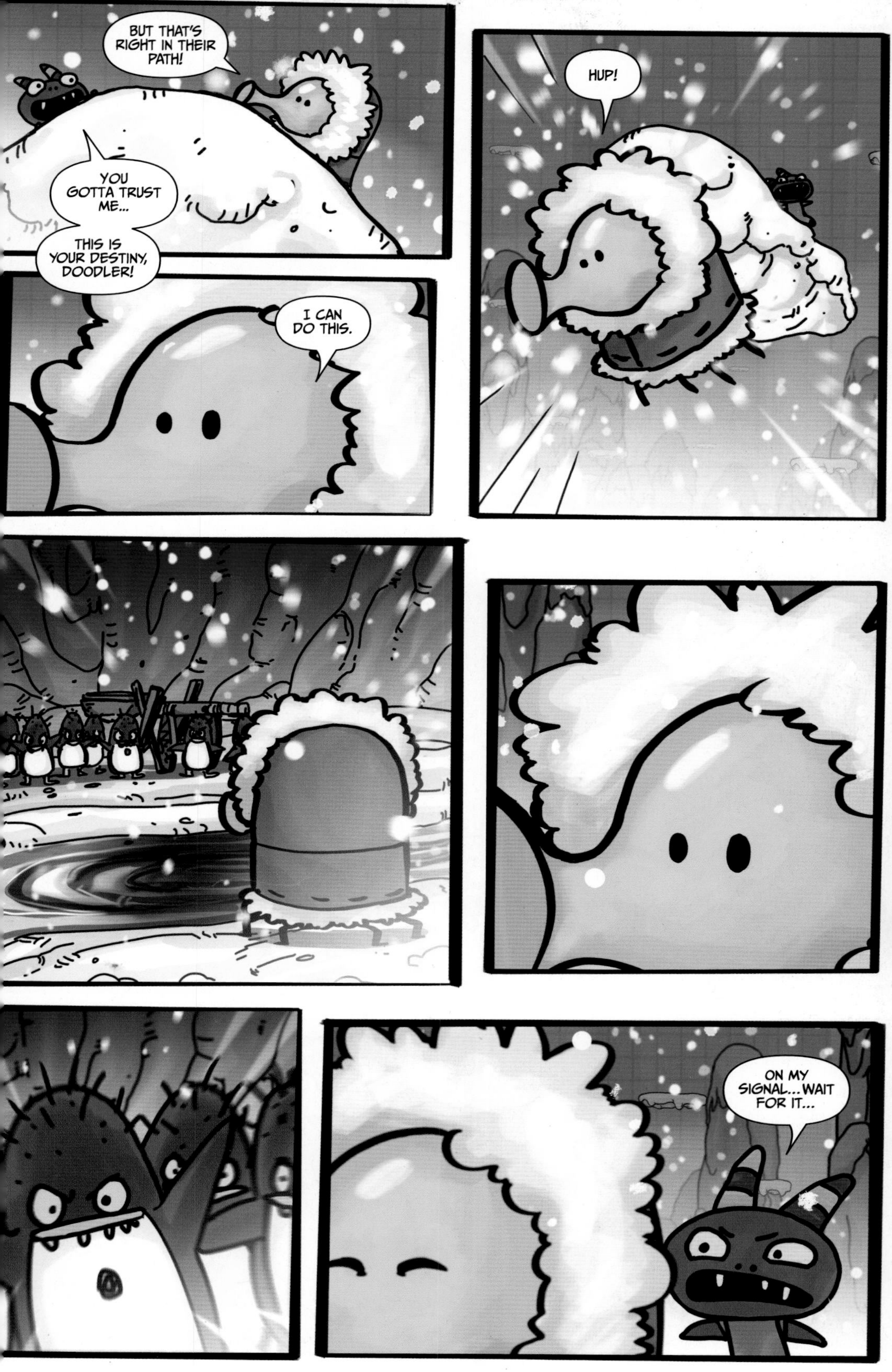
BUT THAT'S RIGHT IN THEIR PATH!
YOU GOTTA TRUST ME...
THIS IS YOUR DESTINY, DOODLER!
HUP!
I CAN DO THIS.
ON MY SIGNAL... WAIT FOR IT...

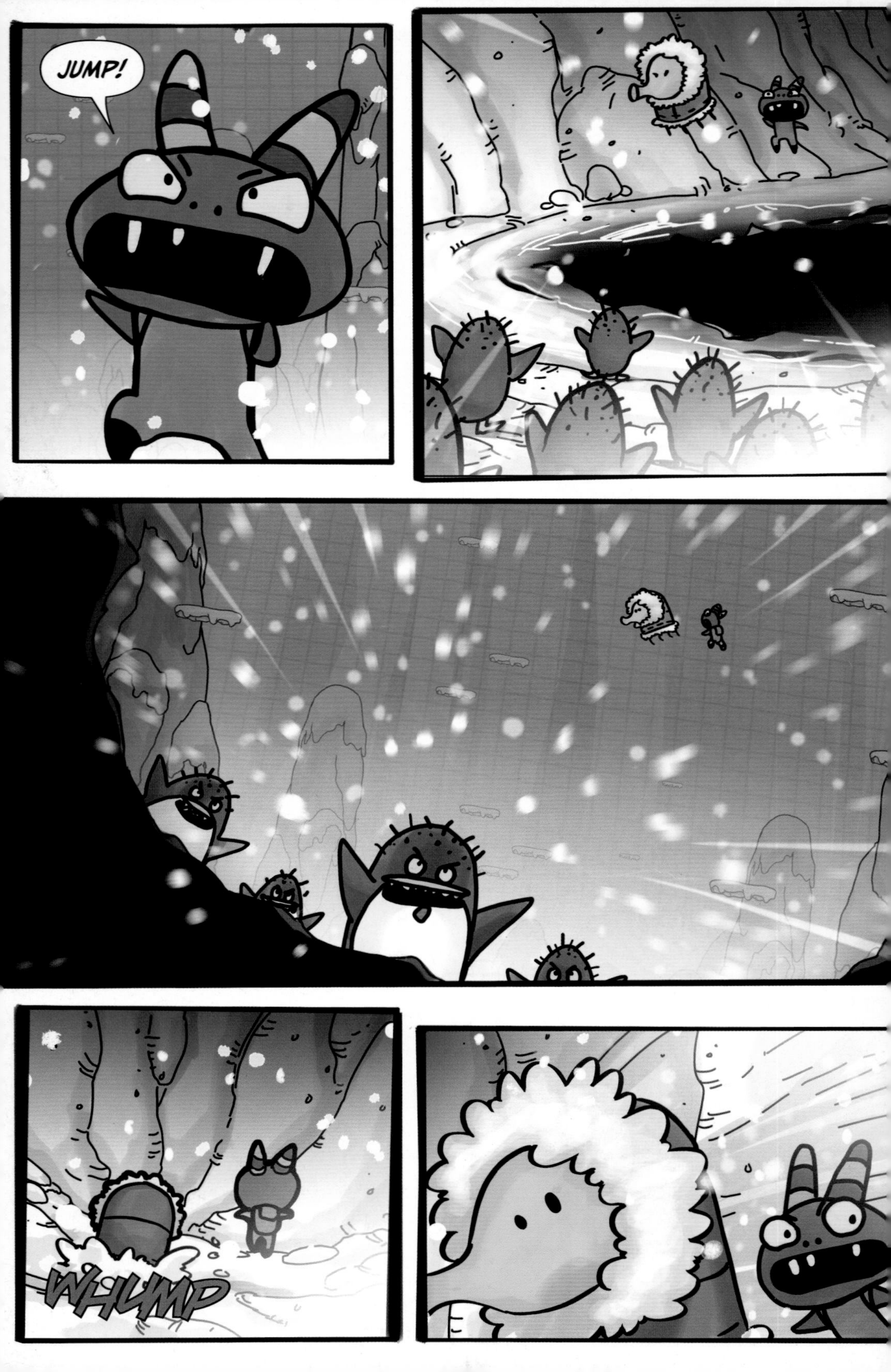
JUMP!
WHUMP

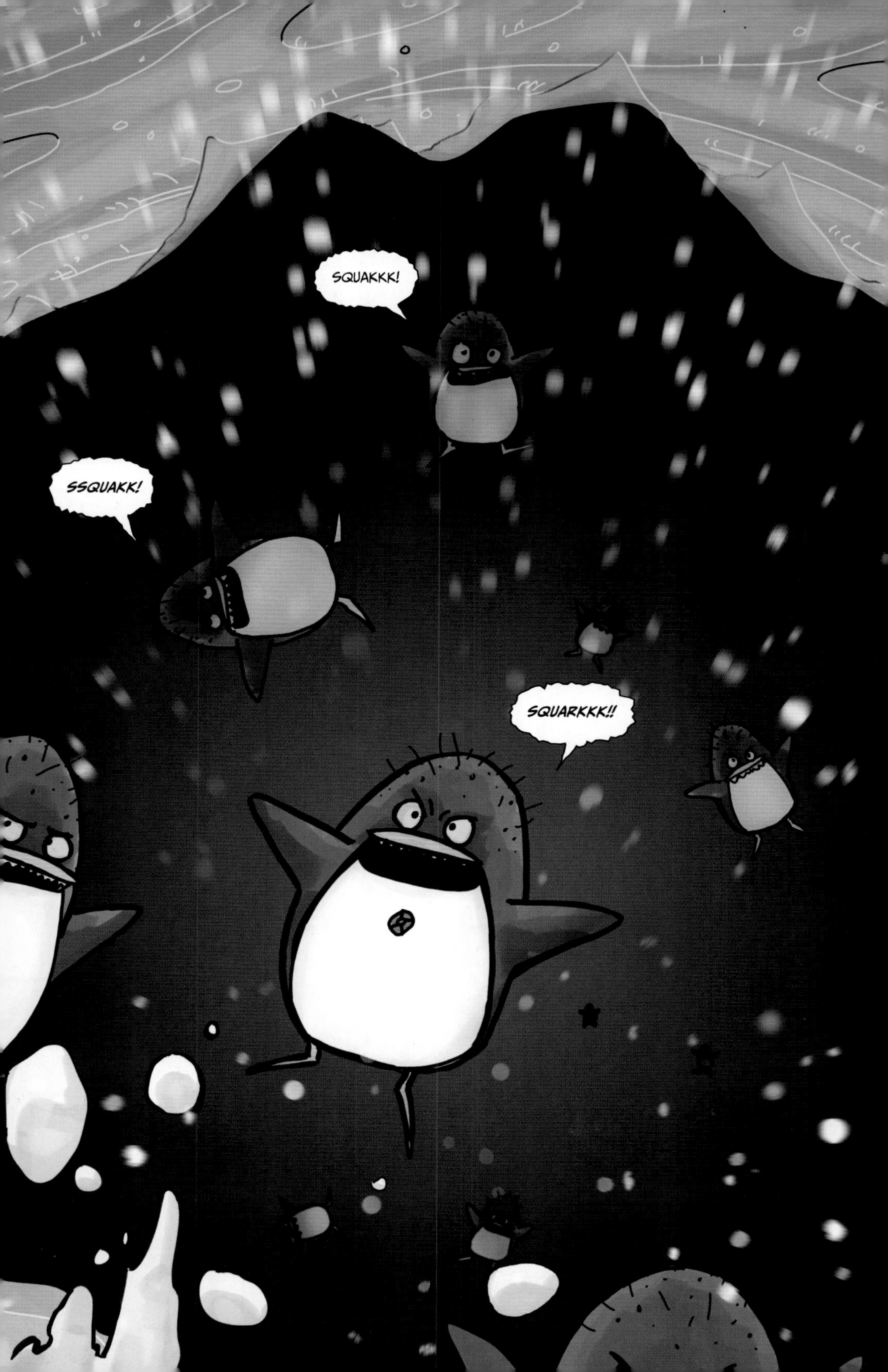
SQUAKKK!
SSQUAKK!
SQUARKKK!!

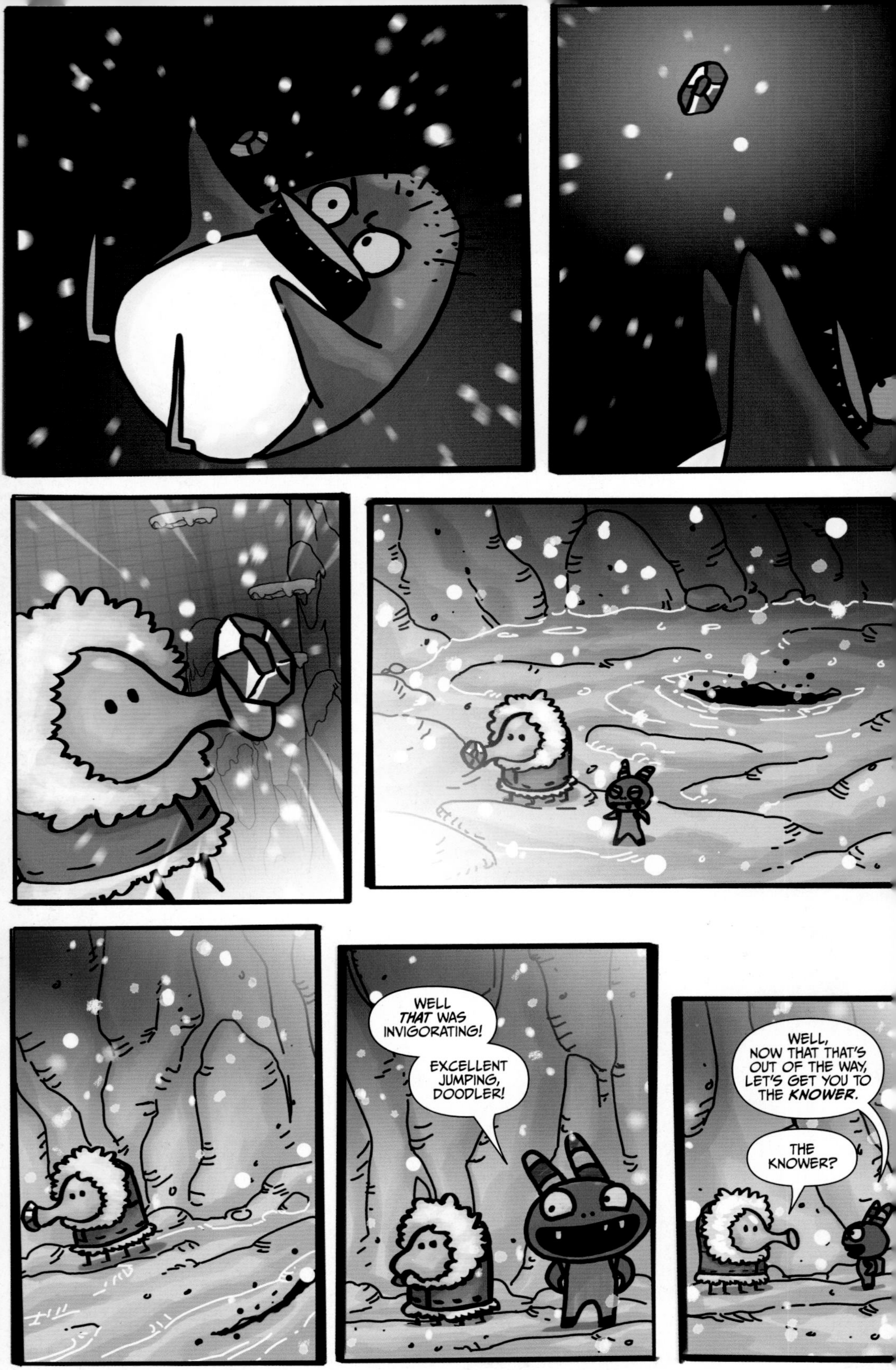
WELL THAT WAS INVIGORATING!
EXCELLENT JUMPING, DOODLER!
WELL, NOW THAT THAT'S OUT OF THE WAY, LET'S GET YOU TO THE KNOWER.
THE KNOWER?

OH, COME ON!

THE KNOWER (OF ALL THINGS WORTH KNOWING)! DON'T YOU KNOW HIM?

NO!

WELL HE KNOWS EVERYTHING. AND HE'LL GET YOU ON TRACK FOR THE NEXT PART OF YOUR QUEST!

LOOK, I KNOW THIS IS HARD TO TAKE IN ALL AT ONCE...

AND I PROBABLY SEEM LIKE SOME KINDA CREEP TO YOU.

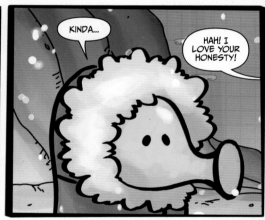

KINDA...

HAH! I LOVE YOUR HONESTY!

BUT I PROMISE I ONLY WANT TO HELP YOU!

BESIDES, DO I LOOK LIKE I COULD TAKE YOU IN A FIGHT?

NOPE.

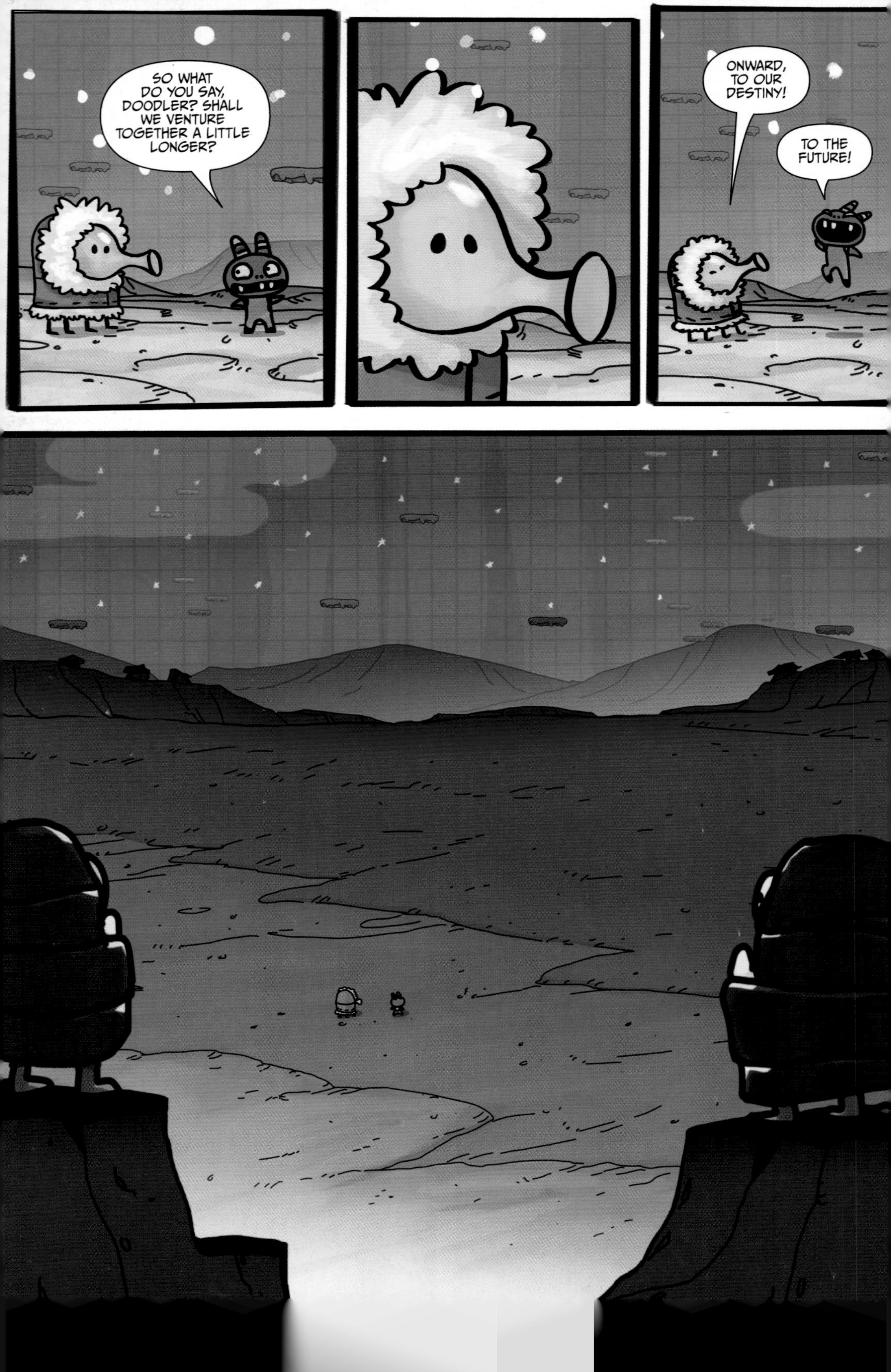
SO WHAT DO YOU SAY, DOODLER? SHALL WE VENTURE TOGETHER A LITTLE LONGER?
ONWARD, TO OUR DESTINY!
TO THE FUTURE!

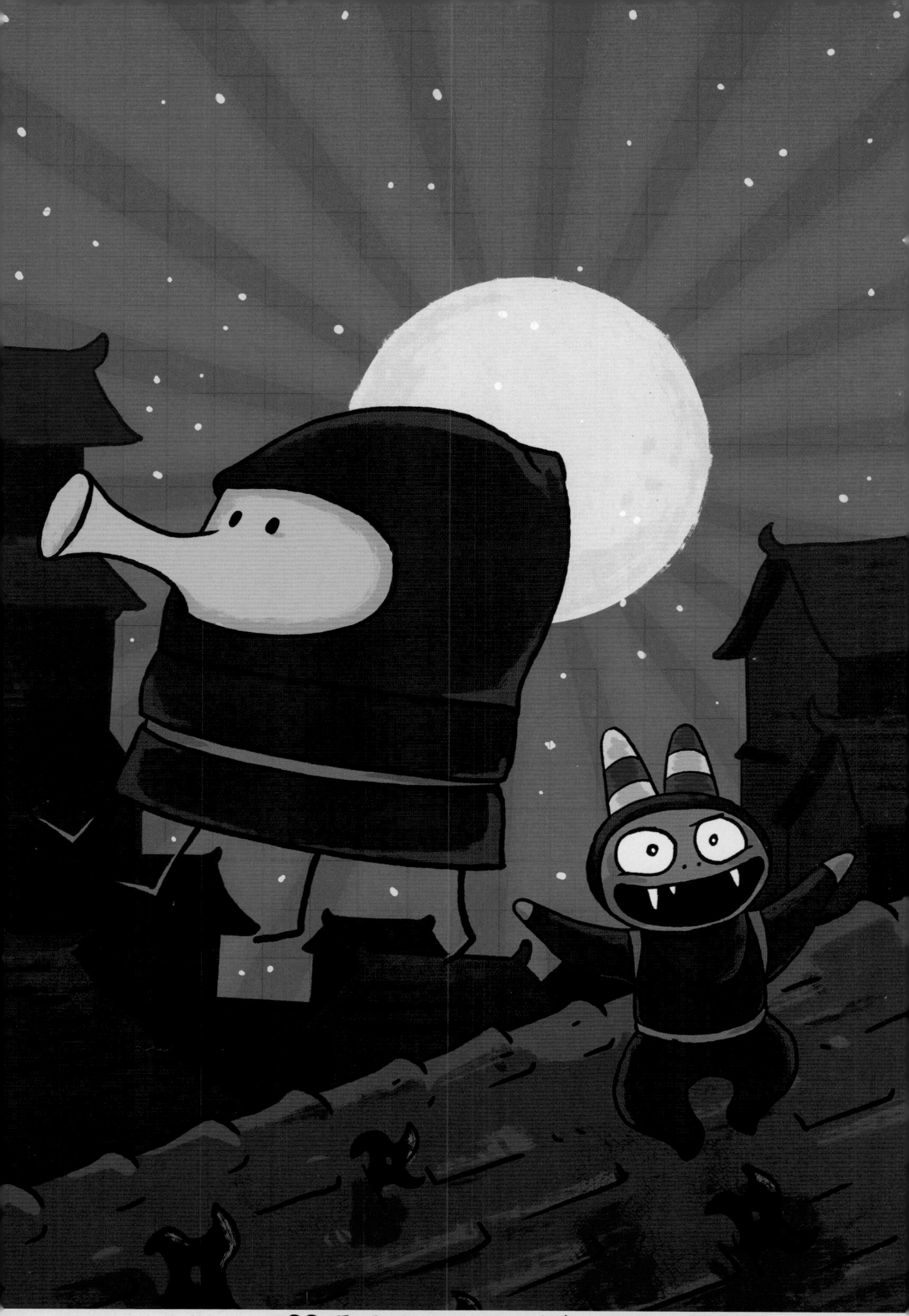

ISSUE TWO cover art by REBEKIE BENNINGTON

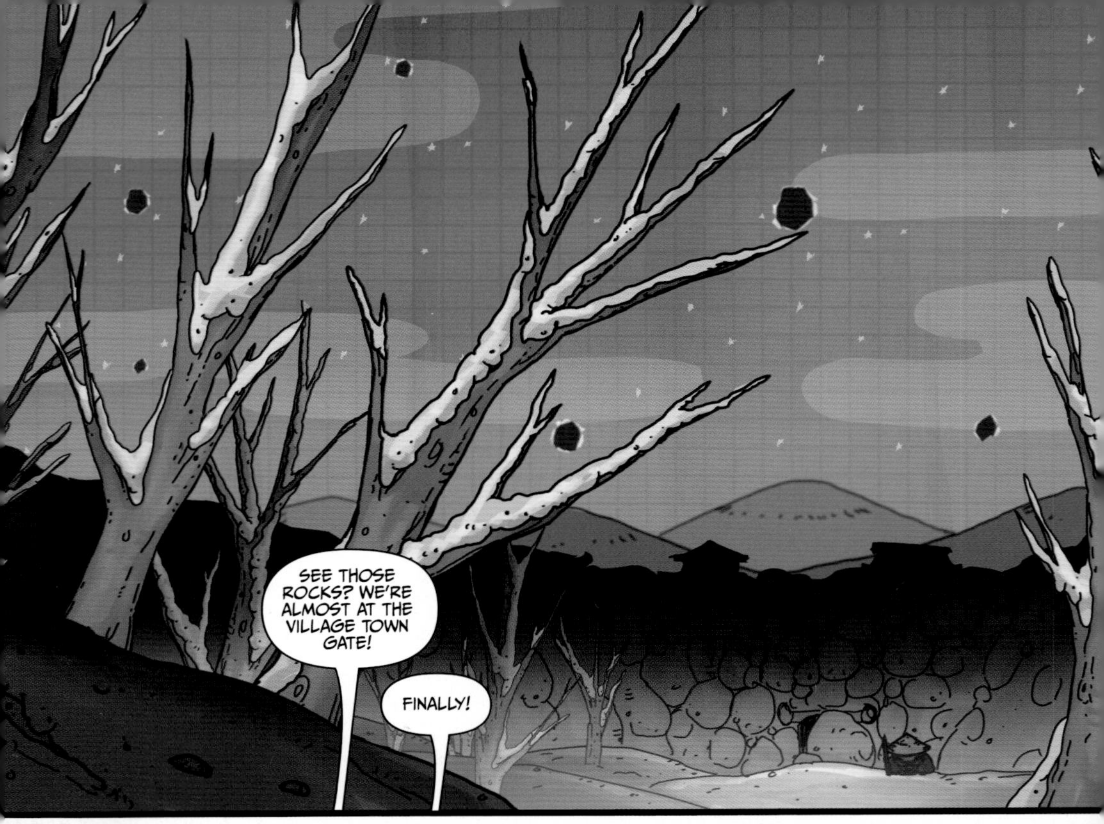
SEE THOSE ROCKS? WE'RE ALMOST AT THE VILLAGE TOWN GATE!
FINALLY!

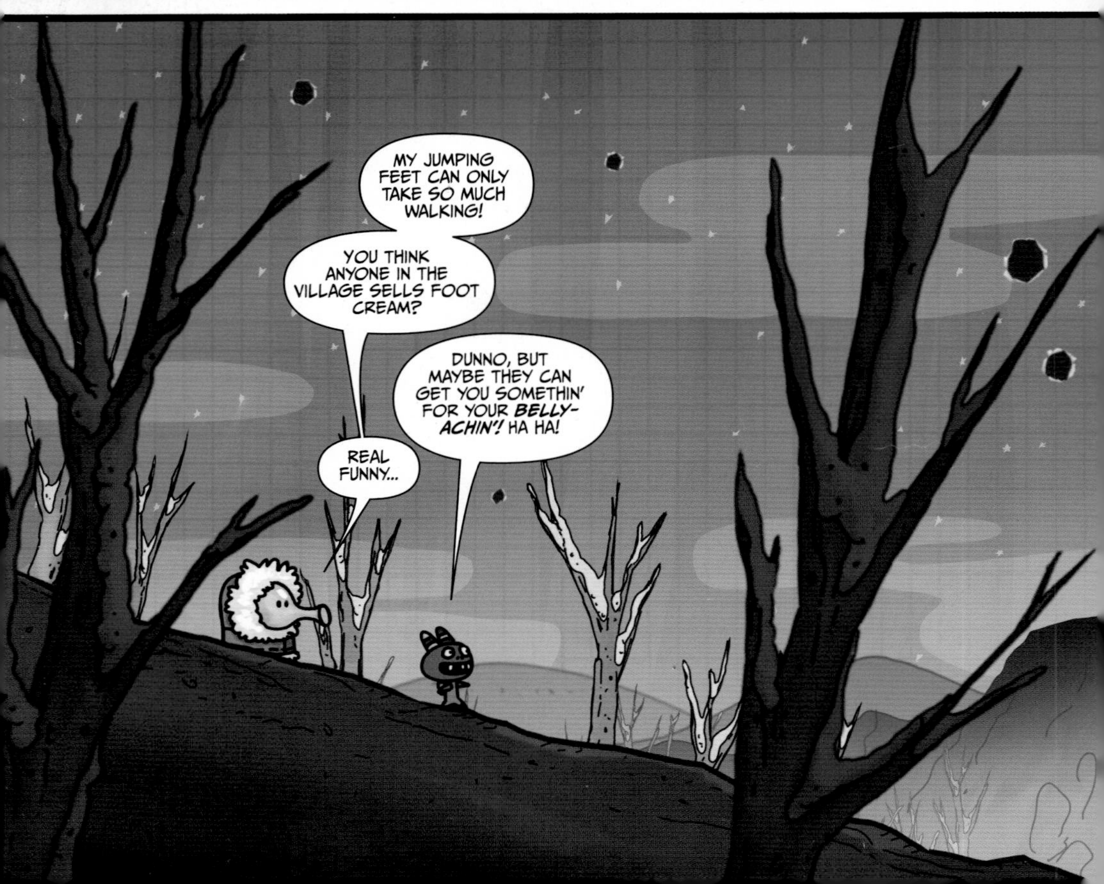
MY JUMPING FEET CAN ONLY TAKE SO MUCH WALKING!
YOU THINK ANYONE IN THE VILLAGE SELLS FOOT CREAM?
DUNNO, BUT MAYBE THEY CAN GET YOU SOMETHIN' FOR YOUR **BELLY-ACHIN'!** HA HA!
REAL FUNNY...

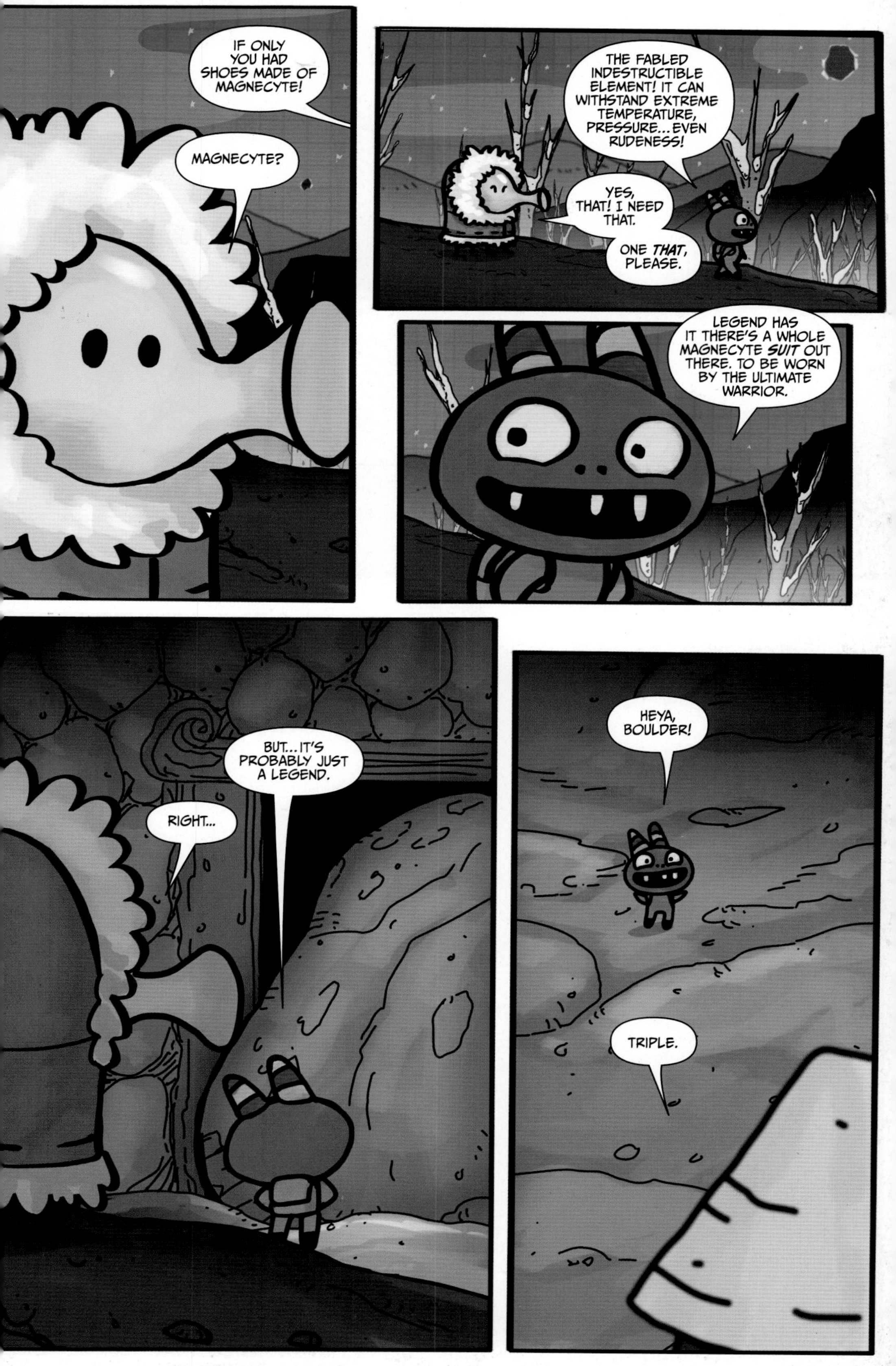
IF ONLY YOU HAD SHOES MADE OF MAGNECYTE!
MAGNECYTE?
THE FABLED INDESTRUCTIBLE ELEMENT! IT CAN WITHSTAND EXTREME TEMPERATURE, PRESSURE... EVEN RUDENESS!
YES, THAT! I NEED THAT.
ONE *THAT*, PLEASE.
LEGEND HAS IT THERE'S A WHOLE MAGNECYTE ***SUIT*** OUT THERE. TO BE WORN BY THE ULTIMATE WARRIOR.
BUT... IT'S PROBABLY JUST A LEGEND.
RIGHT...
HEYA, BOULDER!
TRIPLE.

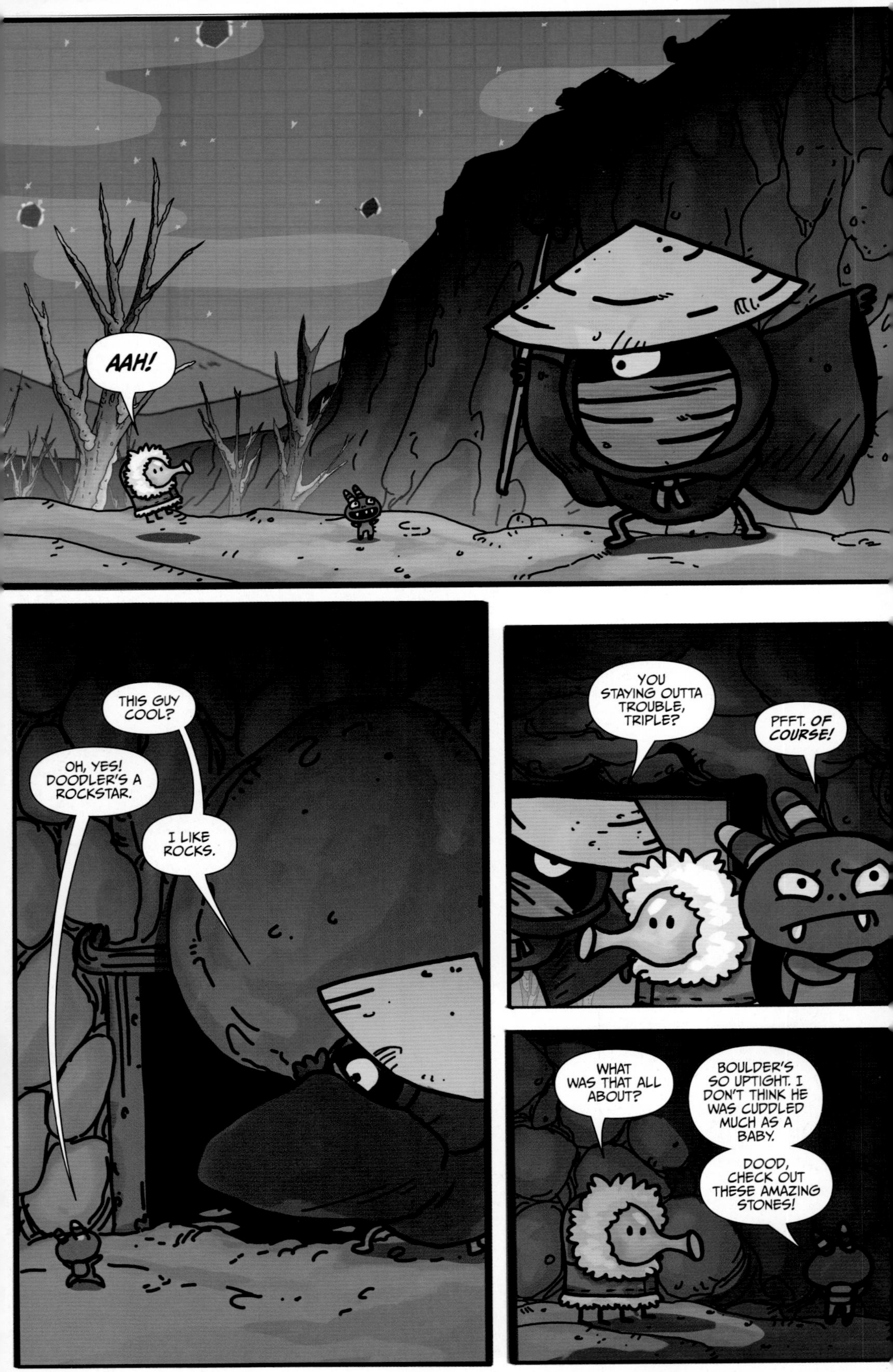

AAH!
THIS GUY COOL?
OH, YES! DOODLER'S A ROCKSTAR.
I LIKE ROCKS.
YOU STAYING OUTTA TROUBLE, TRIPLE?
PFFT. OF COURSE!
WHAT WAS THAT ALL ABOUT?
BOULDER'S SO UPTIGHT. I DON'T THINK HE WAS CUDDLED MUCH AS A BABY.
DOOD, CHECK OUT THESE AMAZING STONES!

ALL RIGHT DOODLER!

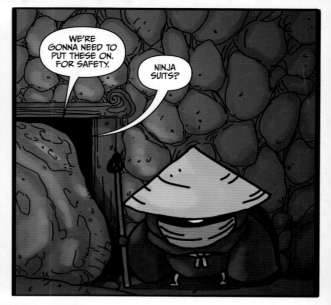

WE'RE GONNA NEED TO PUT THESE ON. FOR SAFETY.

NINJA SUITS?

PRETTY CLASSY, EH?

HOW IS THIS FOR SAFETY EXACTLY?

IF YOU DON'T LISTEN TO ME, YOU'LL FIND OUT FAST.

YOU BETTER NOT BE PRANKING ME.

HA HA! NEVER!

WOW, TALK ABOUT WHO WORE IT BEST!

REALLY?

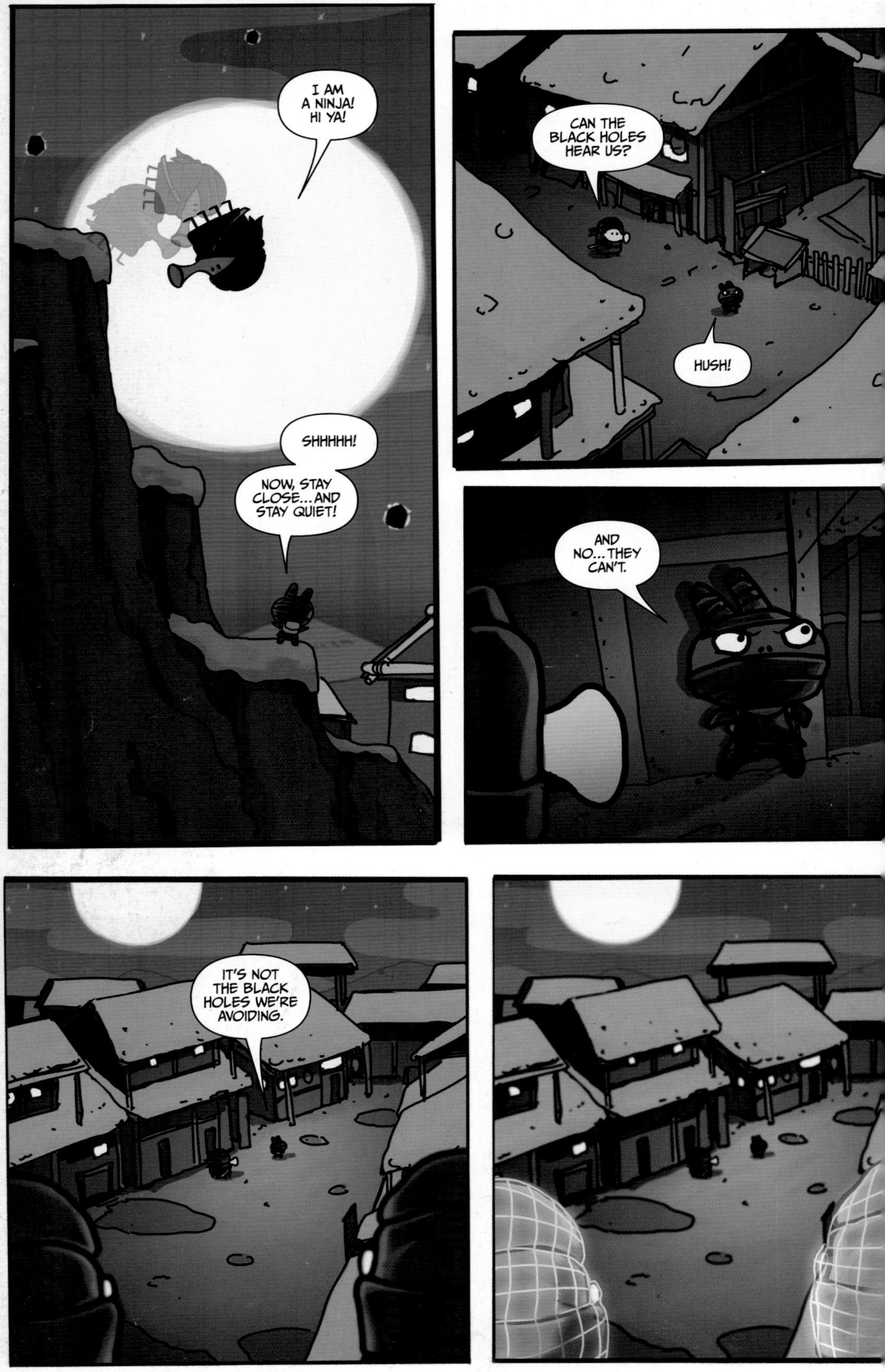
I AM A NINJA! HI YA!
SHHHHH!
NOW, STAY CLOSE... AND STAY QUIET!
CAN THE BLACK HOLES HEAR US?
HUSH!
AND NO... THEY CAN'T.
IT'S NOT THE BLACK HOLES WE'RE AVOIDING.

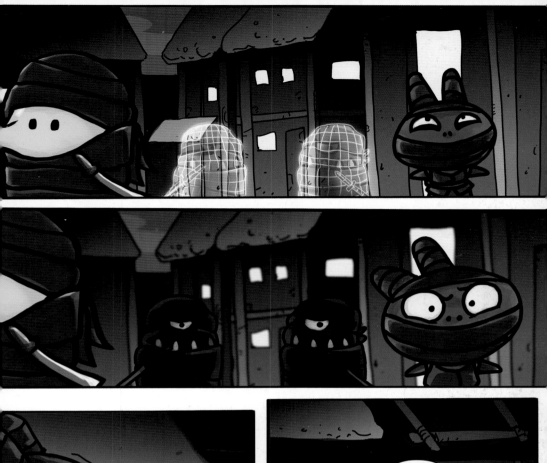

DOODLER, RU--

SSWACK

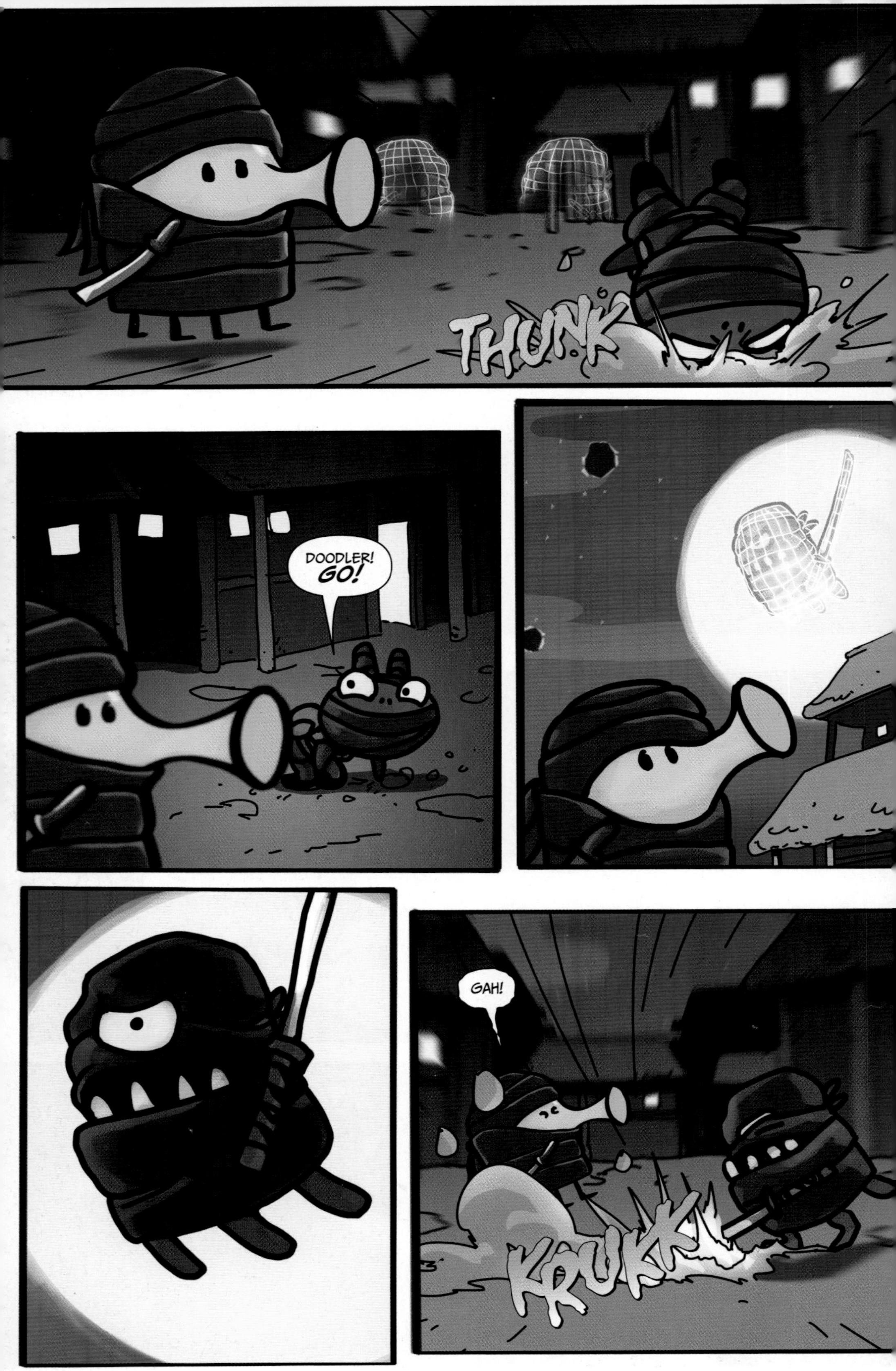

THUNK
DOODLER! GO!
GAH!
KRUKK

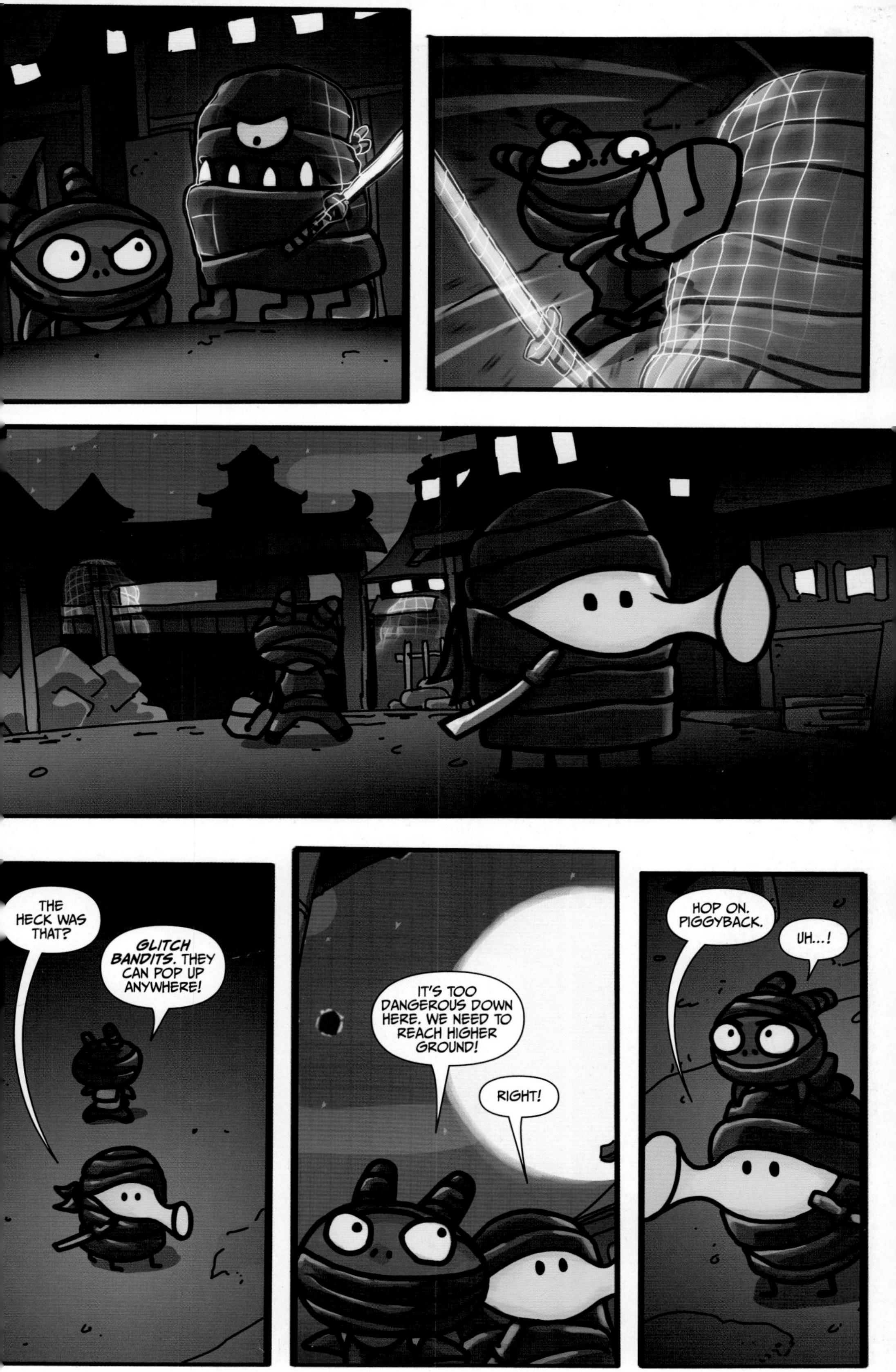
THE HECK WAS THAT?
GLITCH BANDITS. THEY CAN POP UP ANYWHERE!
IT'S TOO DANGEROUS DOWN HERE. WE NEED TO REACH HIGHER GROUND!
RIGHT!
HOP ON. PIGGYBACK.
UH...!

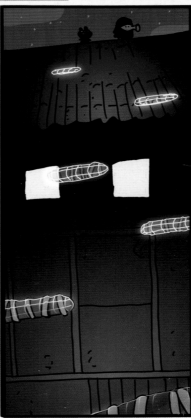

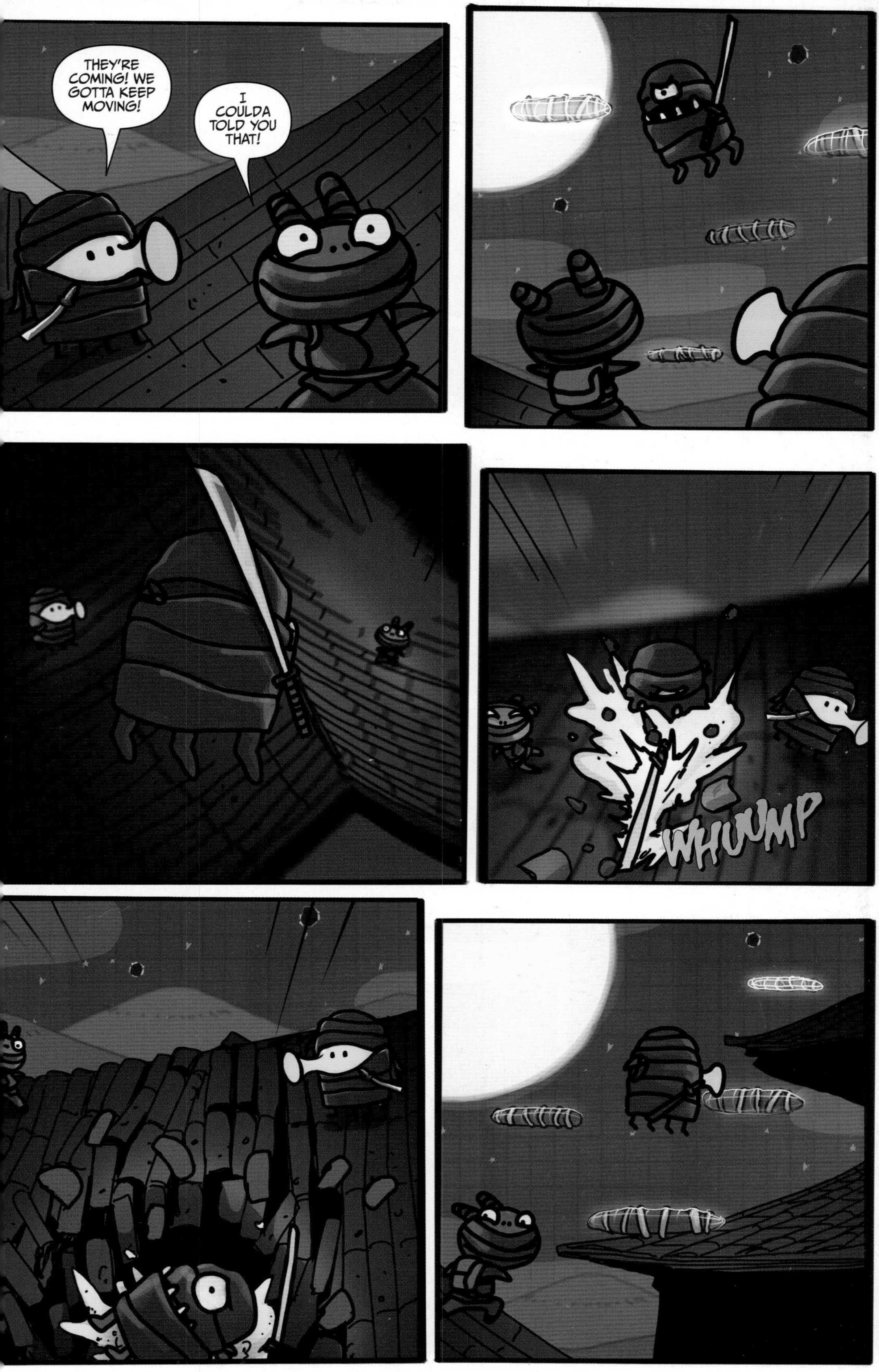
THEY'RE COMING! WE GOTTA KEEP MOVING!
I COULDA TOLD YOU THAT!
WHUUMP

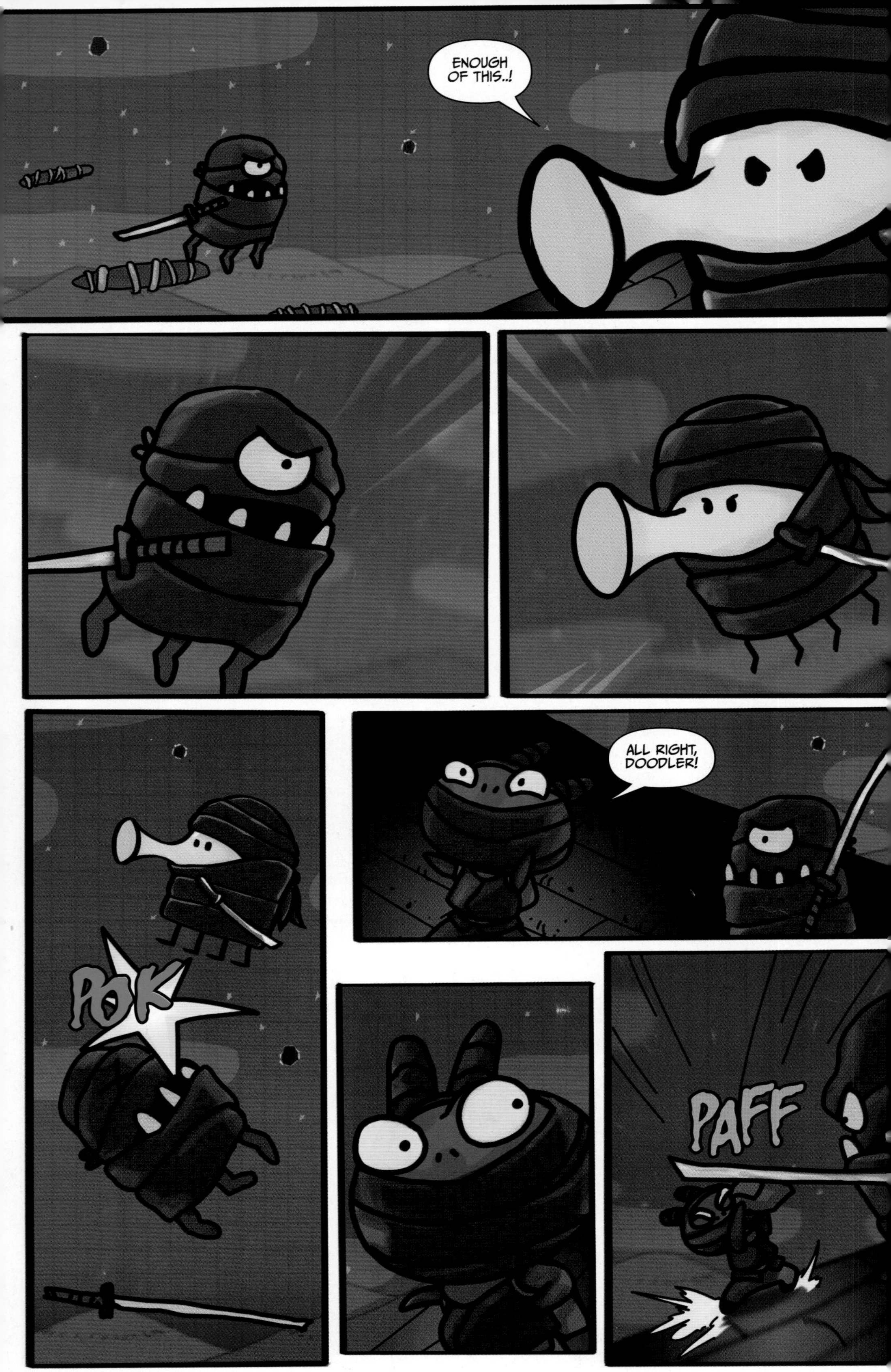
ENOUGH OF THIS..!
POK
ALL RIGHT, DOODLER!
PAFF

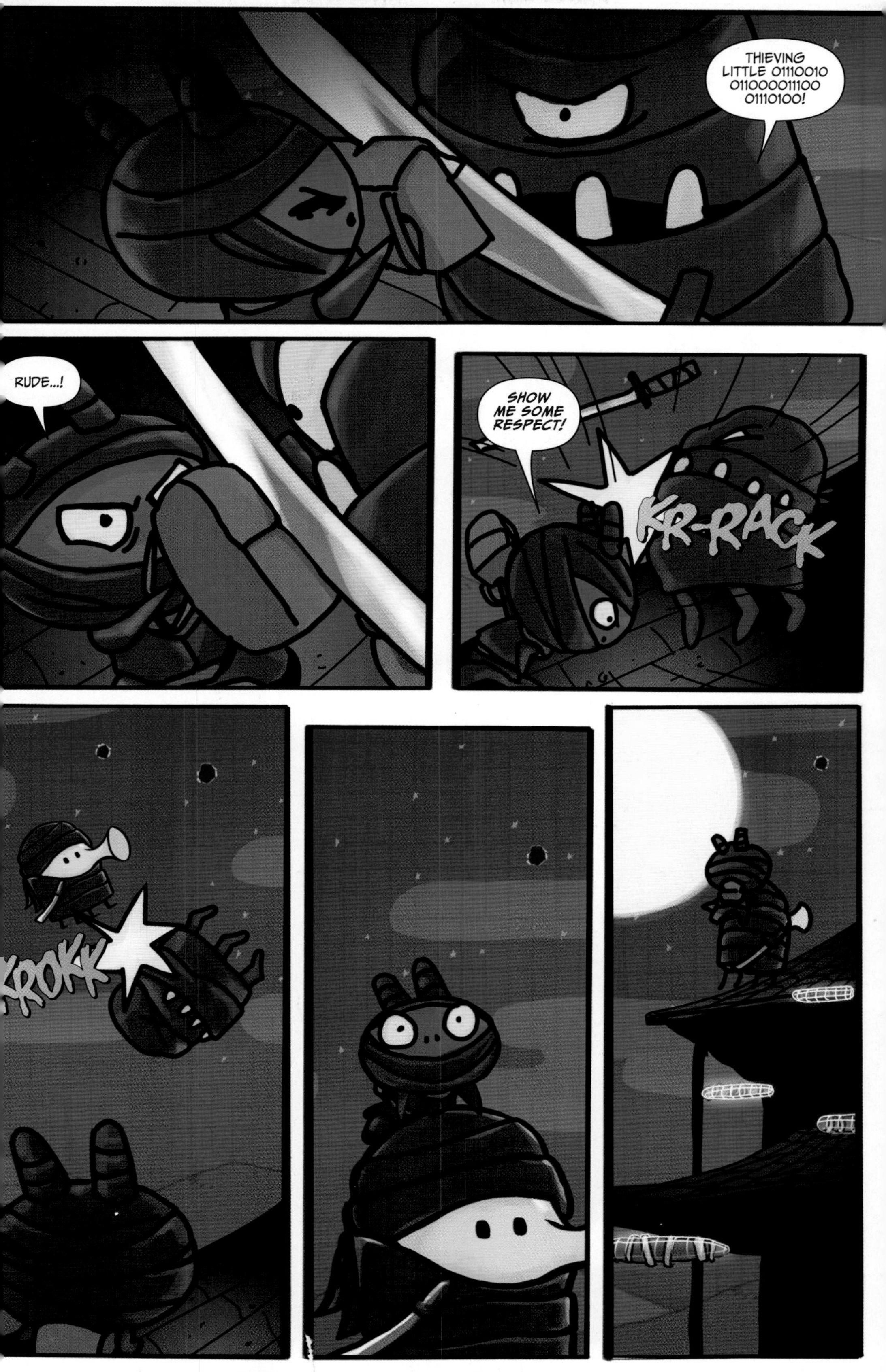
THIEVING LITTLE 01110010 011000011100 01110100!
RUDE...!
SHOW ME SOME RESPECT!
KR-RACK
KROKK

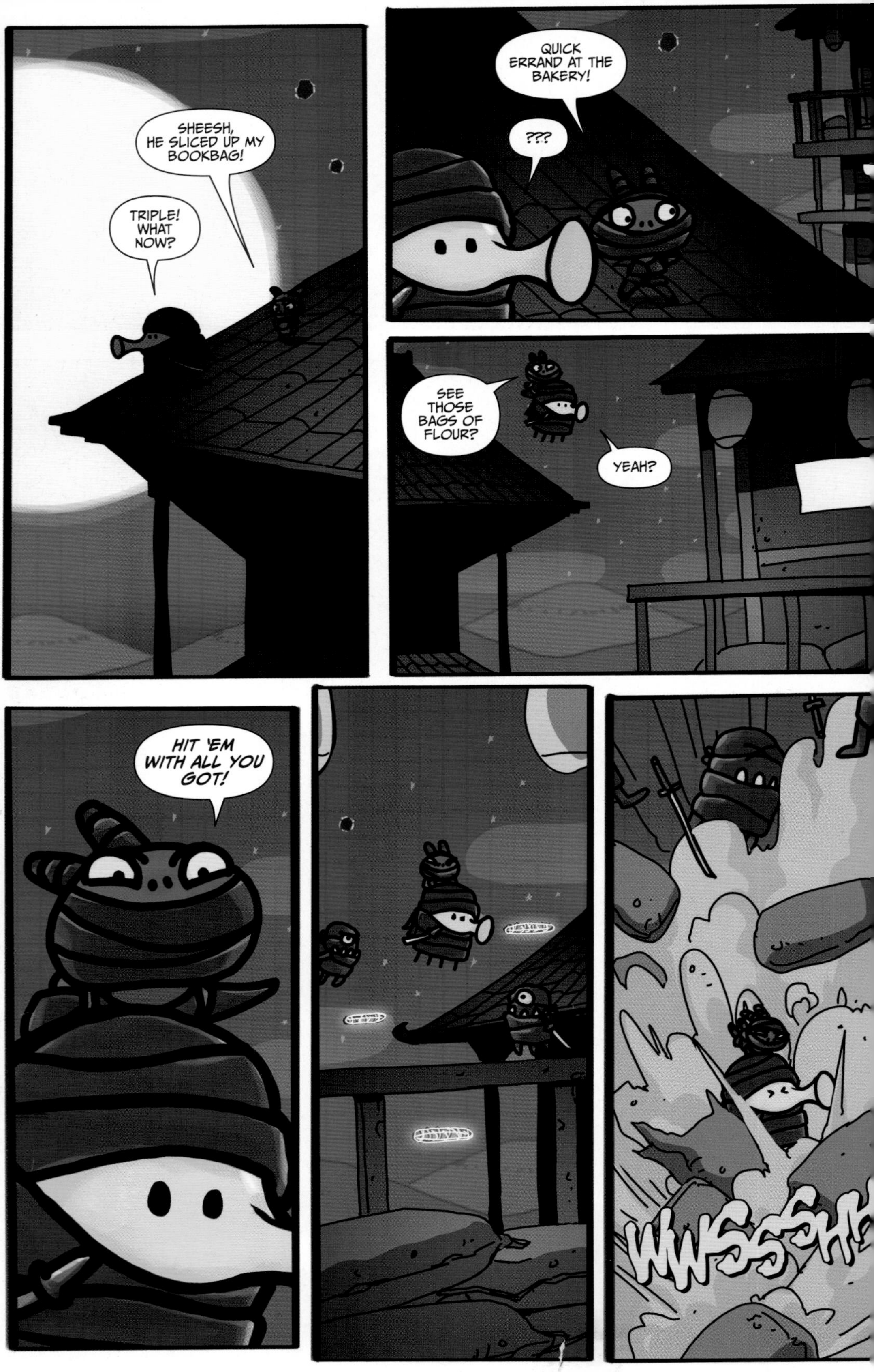

SHEESH, HE SLICED UP MY BOOKBAG!
TRIPLE! WHAT NOW?
QUICK ERRAND AT THE BAKERY!
???
SEE THOSE BAGS OF FLOUR?
YEAH?
HIT 'EM WITH ALL YOU GOT!

WOOO!!!

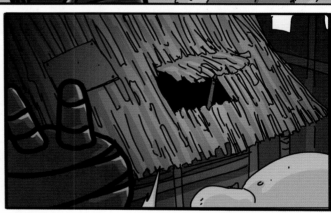

SLAM

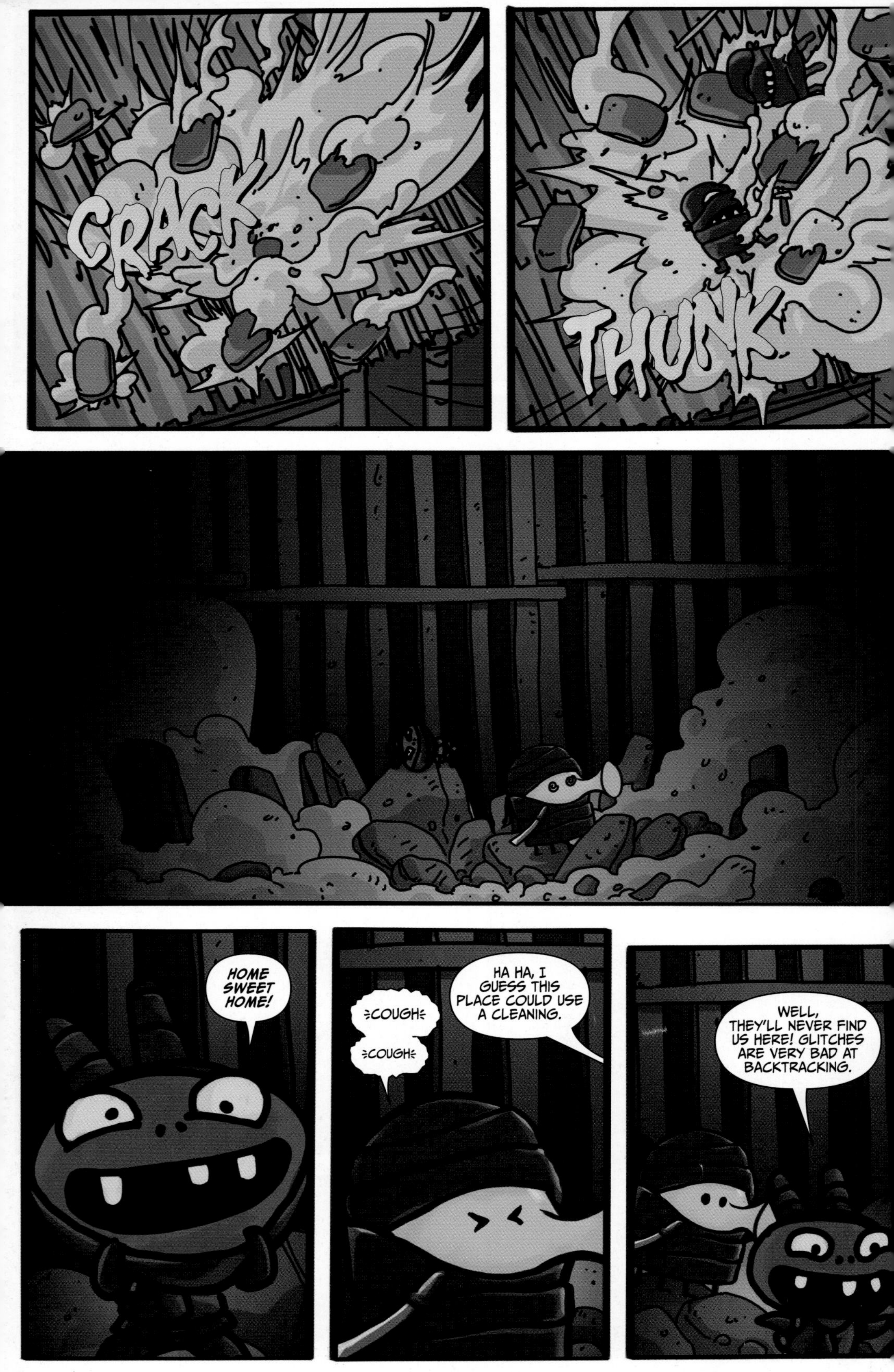
CRACK
THUNK
HOME SWEET HOME!
COUGH
COUGH
HA HA, I GUESS THIS PLACE COULD USE A CLEANING.
WELL, THEY'LL NEVER FIND US HERE! GLITCHES ARE VERY BAD AT BACKTRACKING.

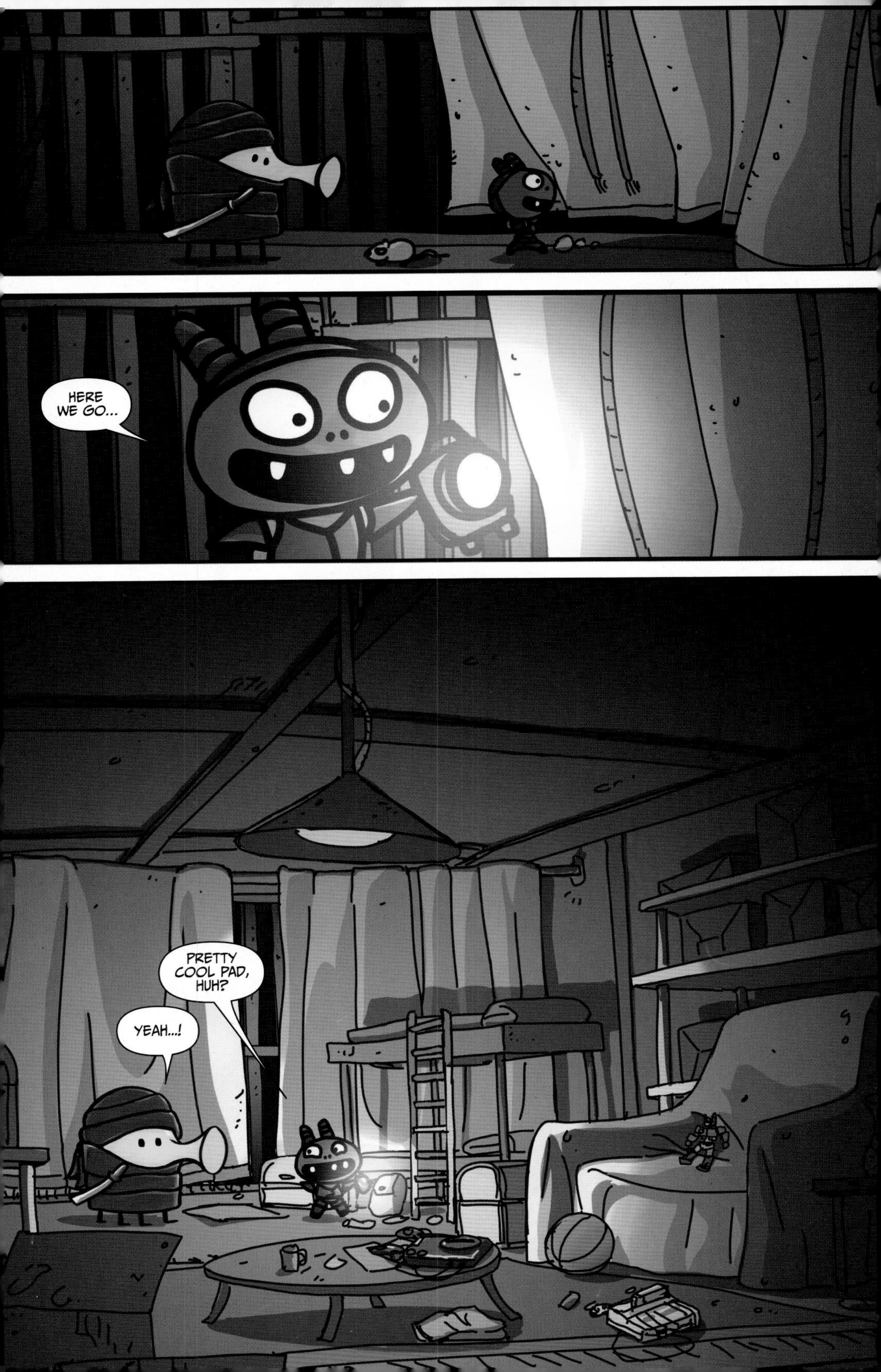
HERE WE GO...
PRETTY COOL PAD, HUH?
YEAH...!

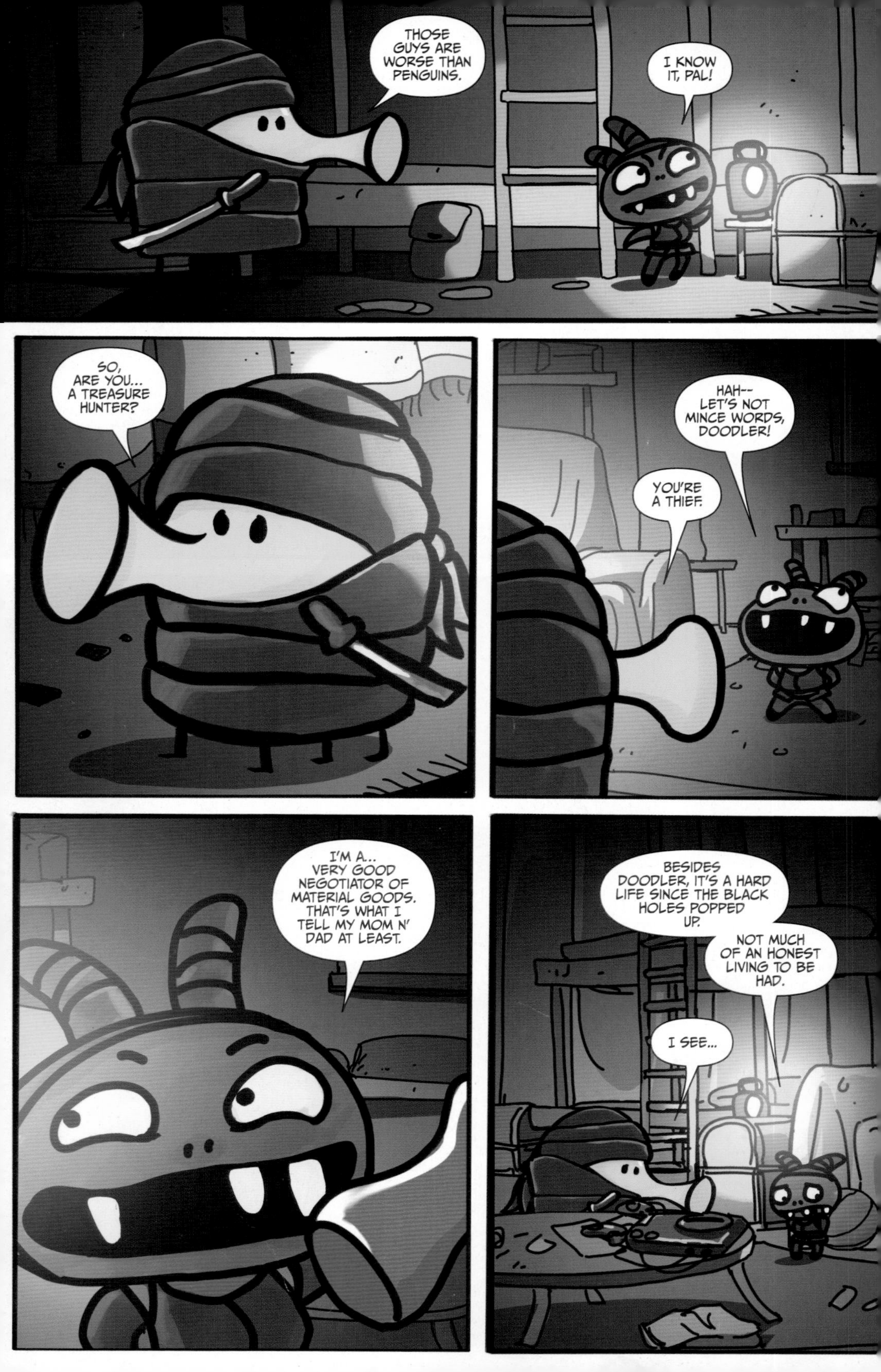
THOSE GUYS ARE WORSE THAN PENGUINS.
I KNOW IT, PAL!
SO, ARE YOU... A TREASURE HUNTER?
HAH-- LET'S NOT MINCE WORDS, DOODLER!
YOU'RE A THIEF.
I'M A... VERY GOOD NEGOTIATOR OF MATERIAL GOODS. THAT'S WHAT I TELL MY MOM N' DAD AT LEAST.
BESIDES DOODLER, IT'S A HARD LIFE SINCE THE BLACK HOLES POPPED UP.
NOT MUCH OF AN HONEST LIVING TO BE HAD.
I SEE...

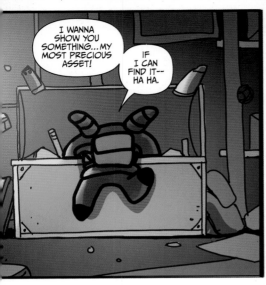

I WANNA SHOW YOU SOMETHING...MY MOST PRECIOUS ASSET!

IF I CAN FIND IT-- HA HA.

THE GLITCH SCROLL!

WOW..!

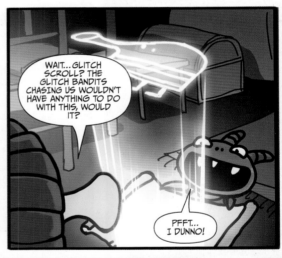

WAIT...GLITCH SCROLL? THE GLITCH BANDITS CHASING US WOULDN'T HAVE ANYTHING TO DO WITH THIS, WOULD IT?

PFFT... I DUNNO!

A PRETTY FLATTERING PICTURE, IN MY OPINION!

TRIPLE, WHY IS THERE AN IMAGE OF ME ON THE SCROLL?

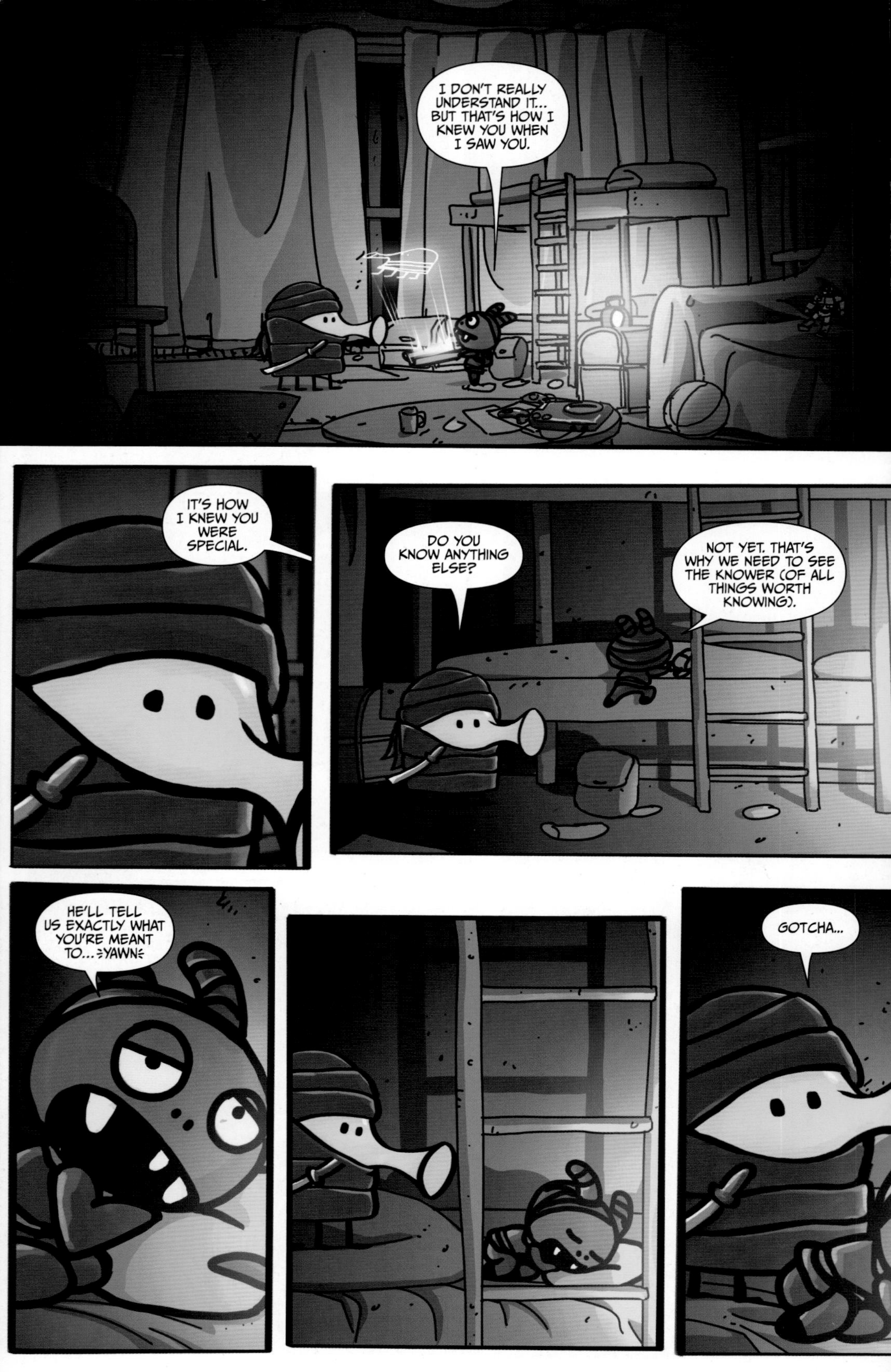
I DON'T REALLY UNDERSTAND IT... BUT THAT'S HOW I KNEW YOU WHEN I SAW YOU.
IT'S HOW I KNEW YOU WERE SPECIAL.
DO YOU KNOW ANYTHING ELSE?
NOT YET. THAT'S WHY WE NEED TO SEE THE KNOWER (OF ALL THINGS WORTH KNOWING).
HE'LL TELL US EXACTLY WHAT YOU'RE MEANT TO... ≶YAWN≶
GOTCHA...

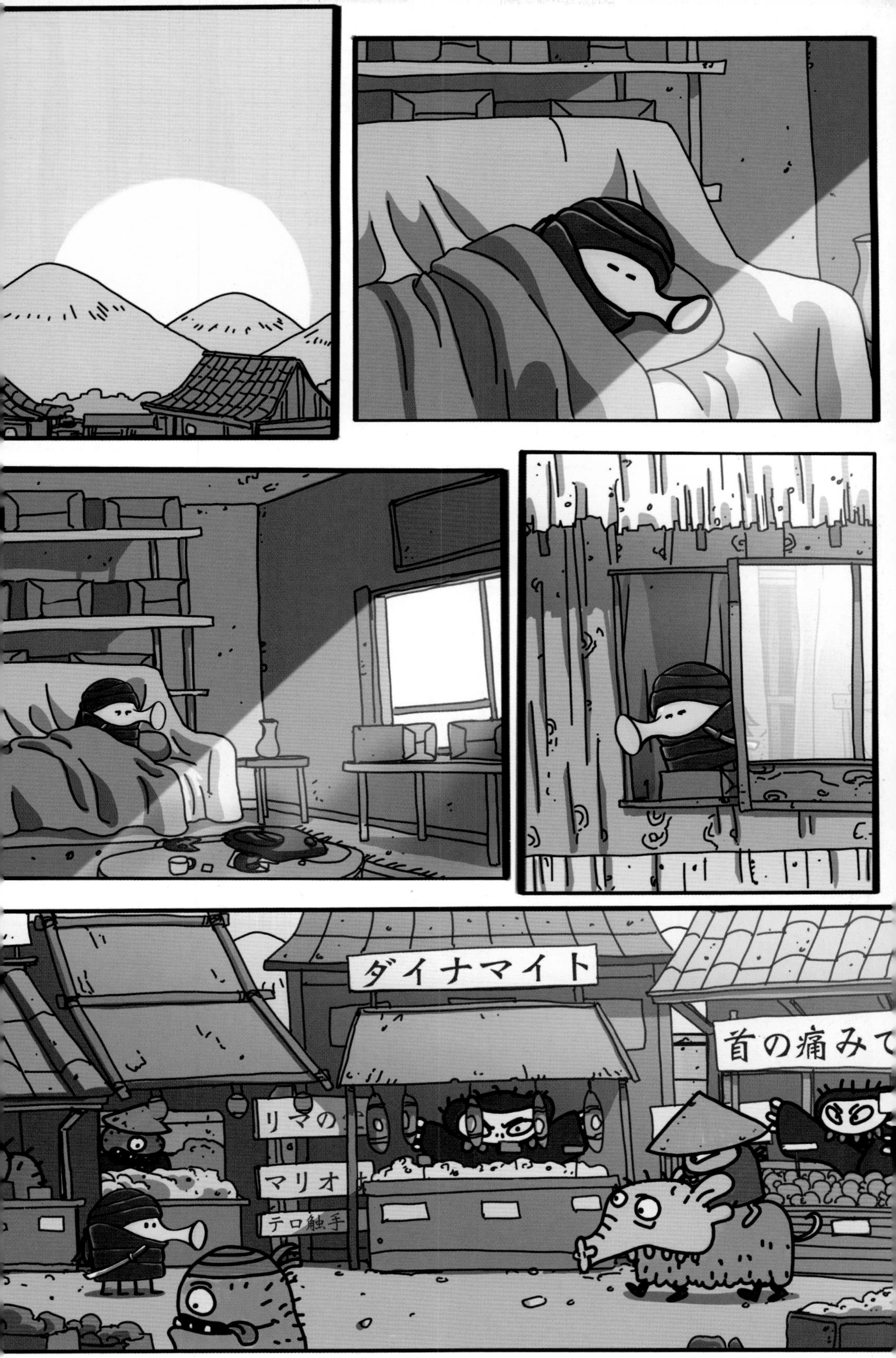
ダイナマイト
首の痛みて
リマの
マリオ
テロ触手

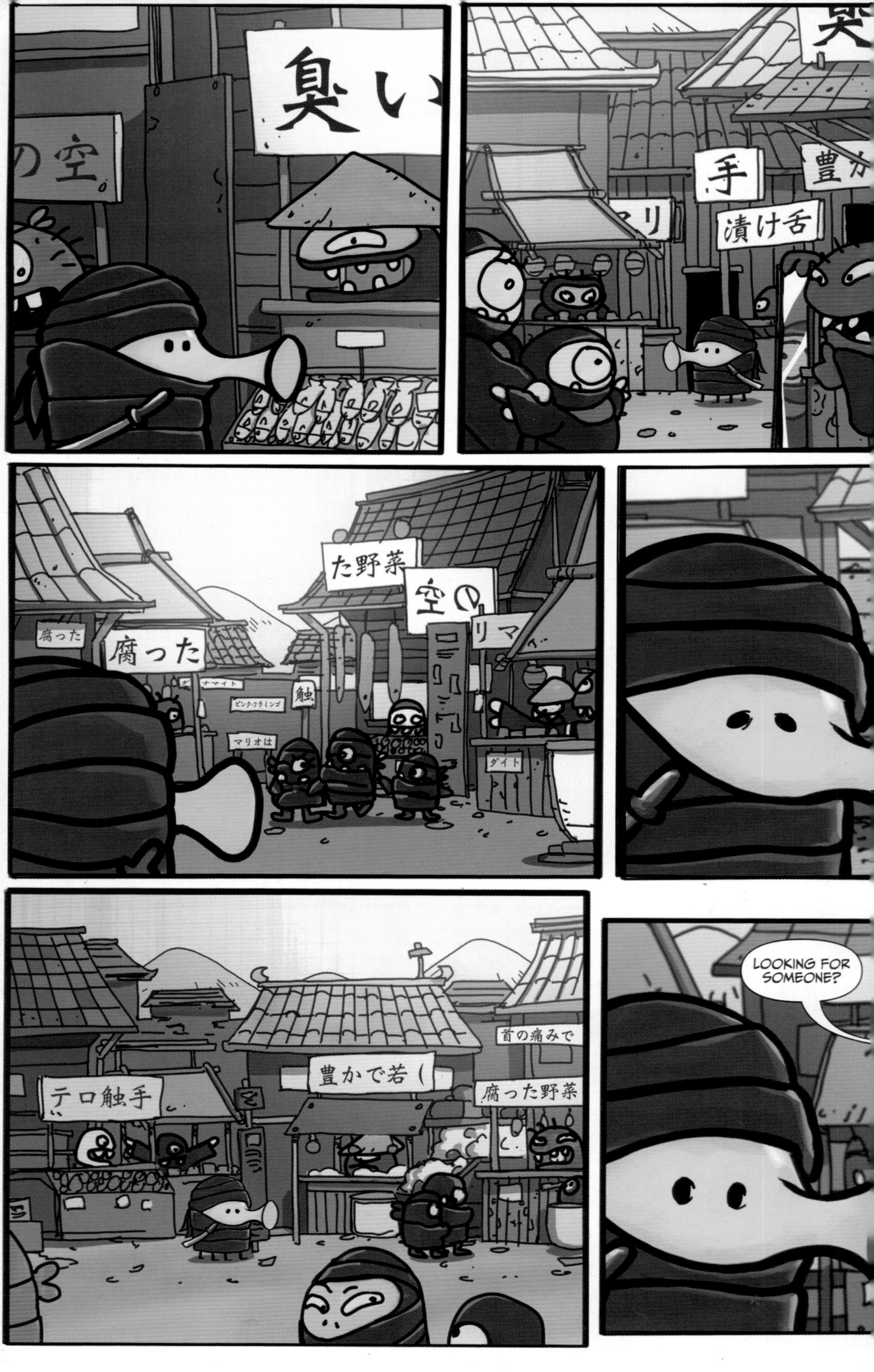

臭い
の空
手
豊か
漬け舌
リ
た野菜
空の
リマ
腐った
腐った
触
マリオは
ダイト
テロ触手
豊かで若
首の痛みで
腐った野菜
LOOKING FOR SOMEONE?

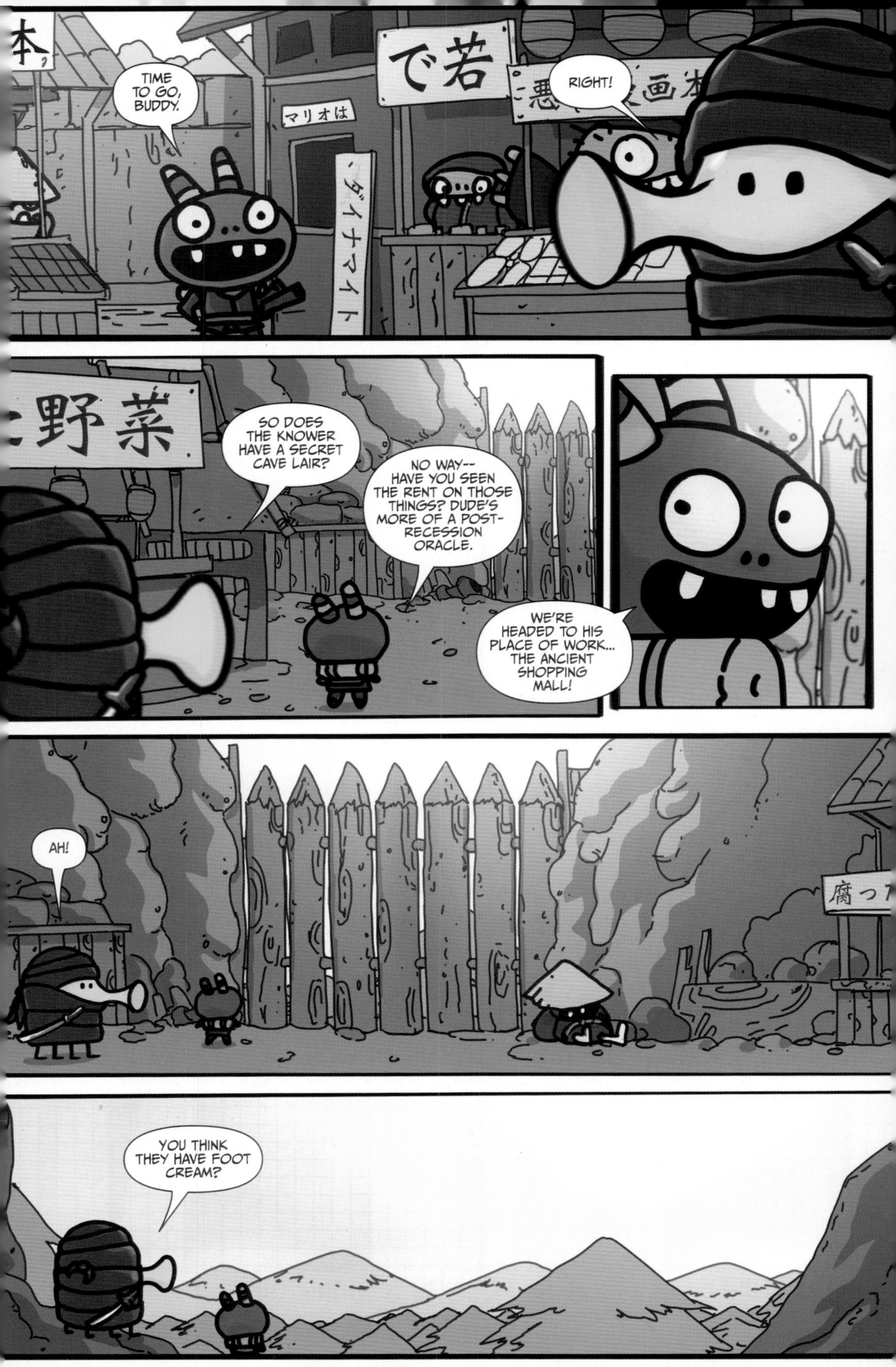

で若
マリオは
TIME TO GO, BUDDY.
ダイナマイト
RIGHT!
野菜
SO DOES THE KNOWER HAVE A SECRET CAVE LAIR?
NO WAY-- HAVE YOU SEEN THE RENT ON THOSE THINGS? DUDE'S MORE OF A POST-RECESSION ORACLE.
WE'RE HEADED TO HIS PLACE OF WORK... THE ANCIENT SHOPPING MALL!
AH!
YOU THINK THEY HAVE FOOT CREAM?

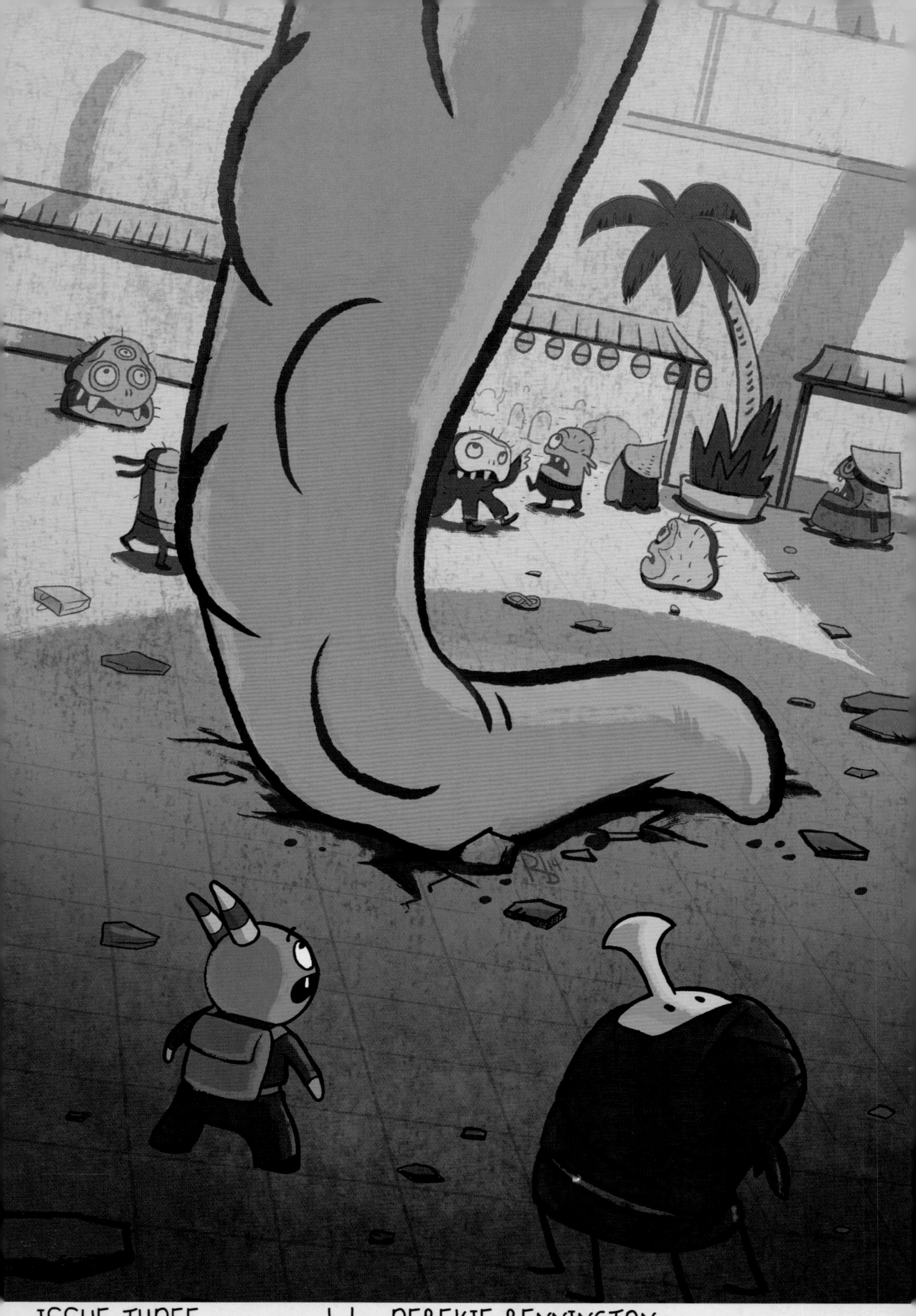

ISSUE THREE cover art by REBEKIE BENNINGTON

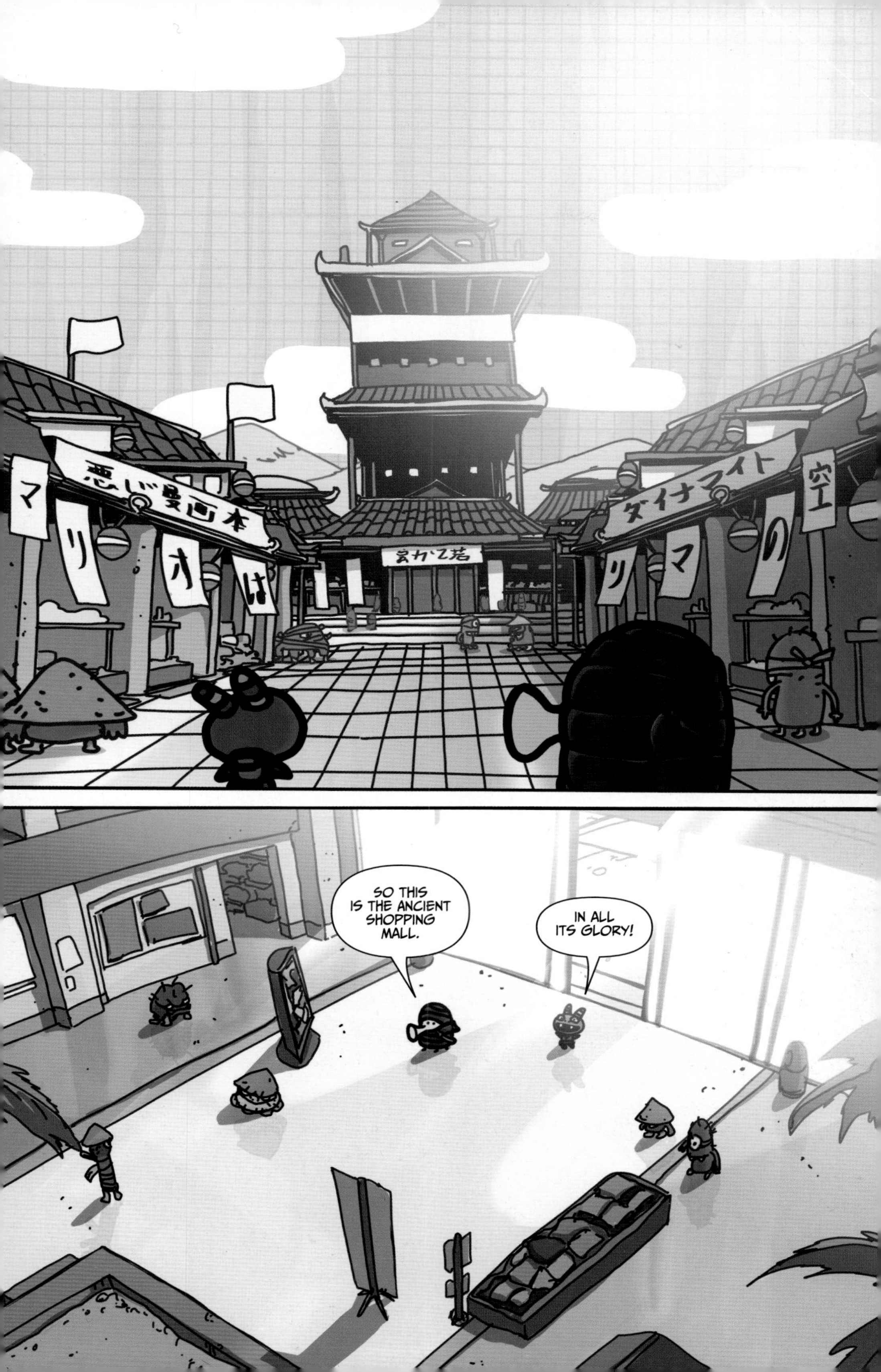
SO THIS IS THE ANCIENT SHOPPING MALL.
IN ALL ITS GLORY!

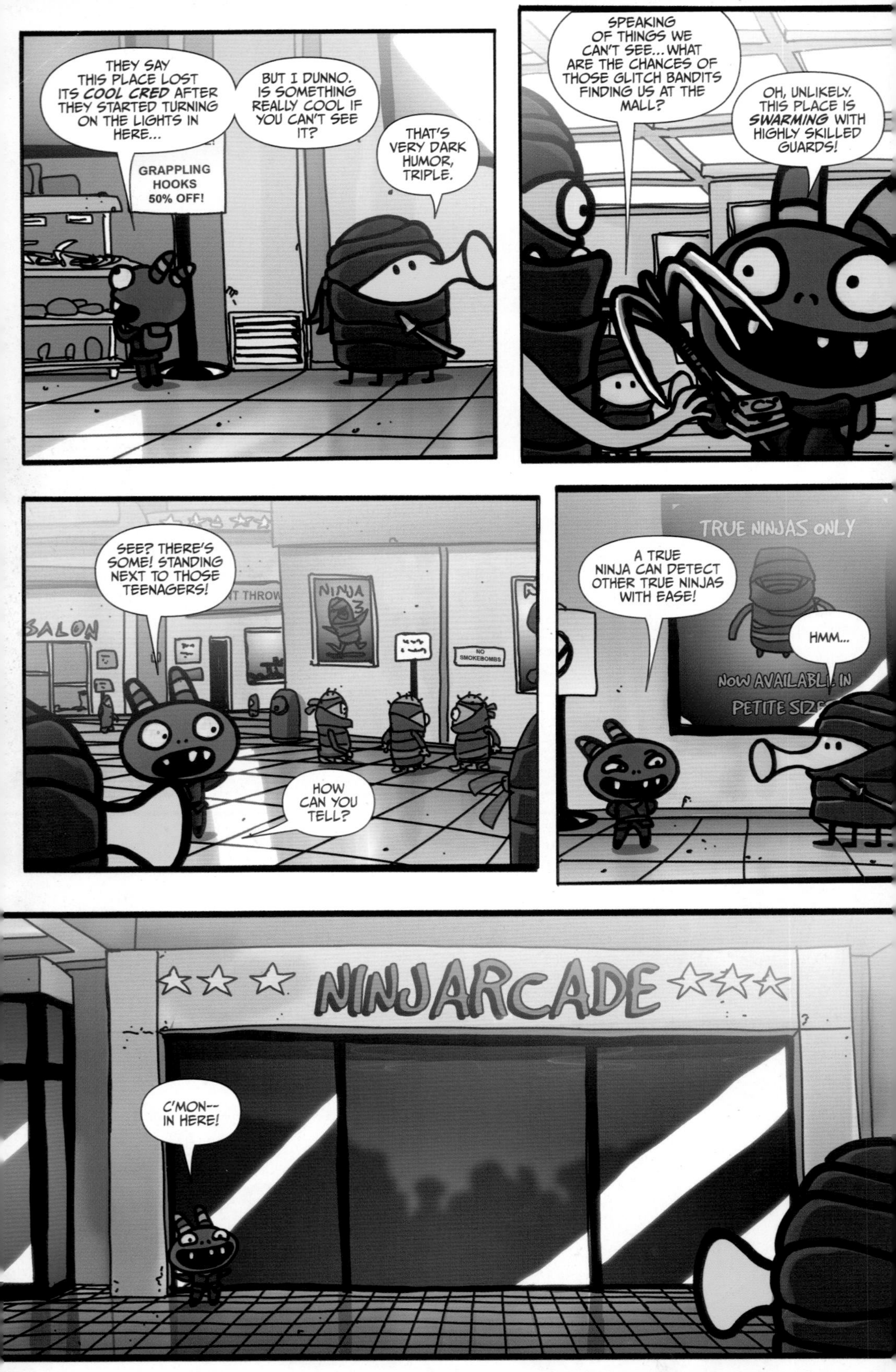
THEY SAY THIS PLACE LOST ITS COOL CRED AFTER THEY STARTED TURNING ON THE LIGHTS IN HERE...
GRAPPLING HOOKS 50% OFF!
BUT I DUNNO. IS SOMETHING REALLY COOL IF YOU CAN'T SEE IT?
THAT'S VERY DARK HUMOR, TRIPLE.
SPEAKING OF THINGS WE CAN'T SEE... WHAT ARE THE CHANCES OF THOSE GLITCH BANDITS FINDING US AT THE MALL?
OH, UNLIKELY. THIS PLACE IS SWARMING WITH HIGHLY SKILLED GUARDS!
SEE? THERE'S SOME! STANDING NEXT TO THOSE TEENAGERS!
SALON
NT THROW
NINJA 3
NO SMOKEBOMBS
HOW CAN YOU TELL?
TRUE NINJAS ONLY
A TRUE NINJA CAN DETECT OTHER TRUE NINJAS WITH EASE!
HMM...
NOW AVAILABL IN PETITE SIZ
NINJARCADE
C'MON-- IN HERE!

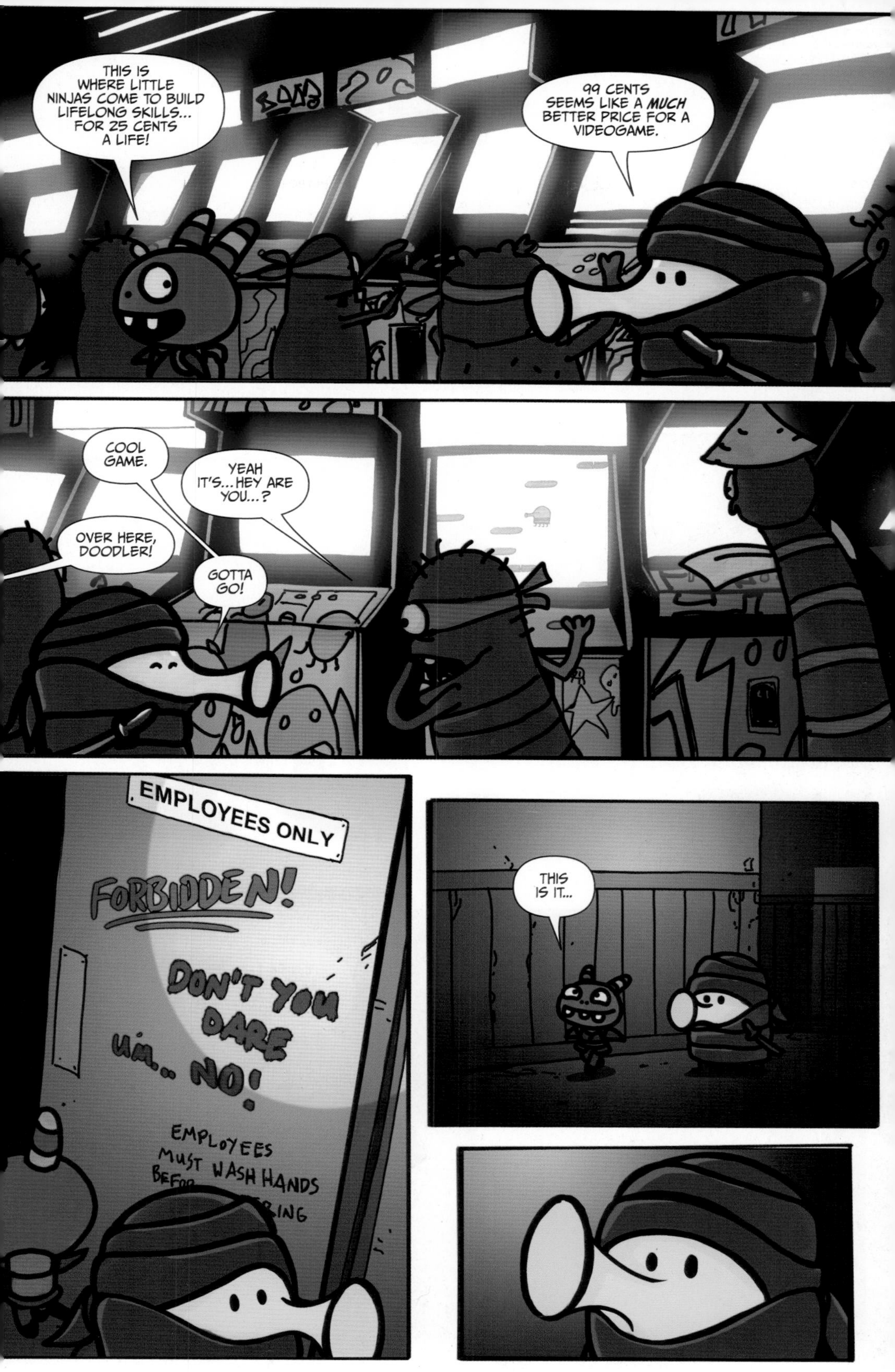
THIS IS WHERE LITTLE NINJAS COME TO BUILD LIFELONG SKILLS... FOR 25 CENTS A LIFE!
99 CENTS SEEMS LIKE A *MUCH* BETTER PRICE FOR A VIDEOGAME.
COOL GAME.
YEAH IT'S... HEY ARE YOU...?
OVER HERE, DOODLER!
GOTTA GO!
EMPLOYEES ONLY
FORBIDDEN!
DON'T YOU DARE
UM... NO!
EMPLOYEES MUST WASH HANDS
THIS IS IT...

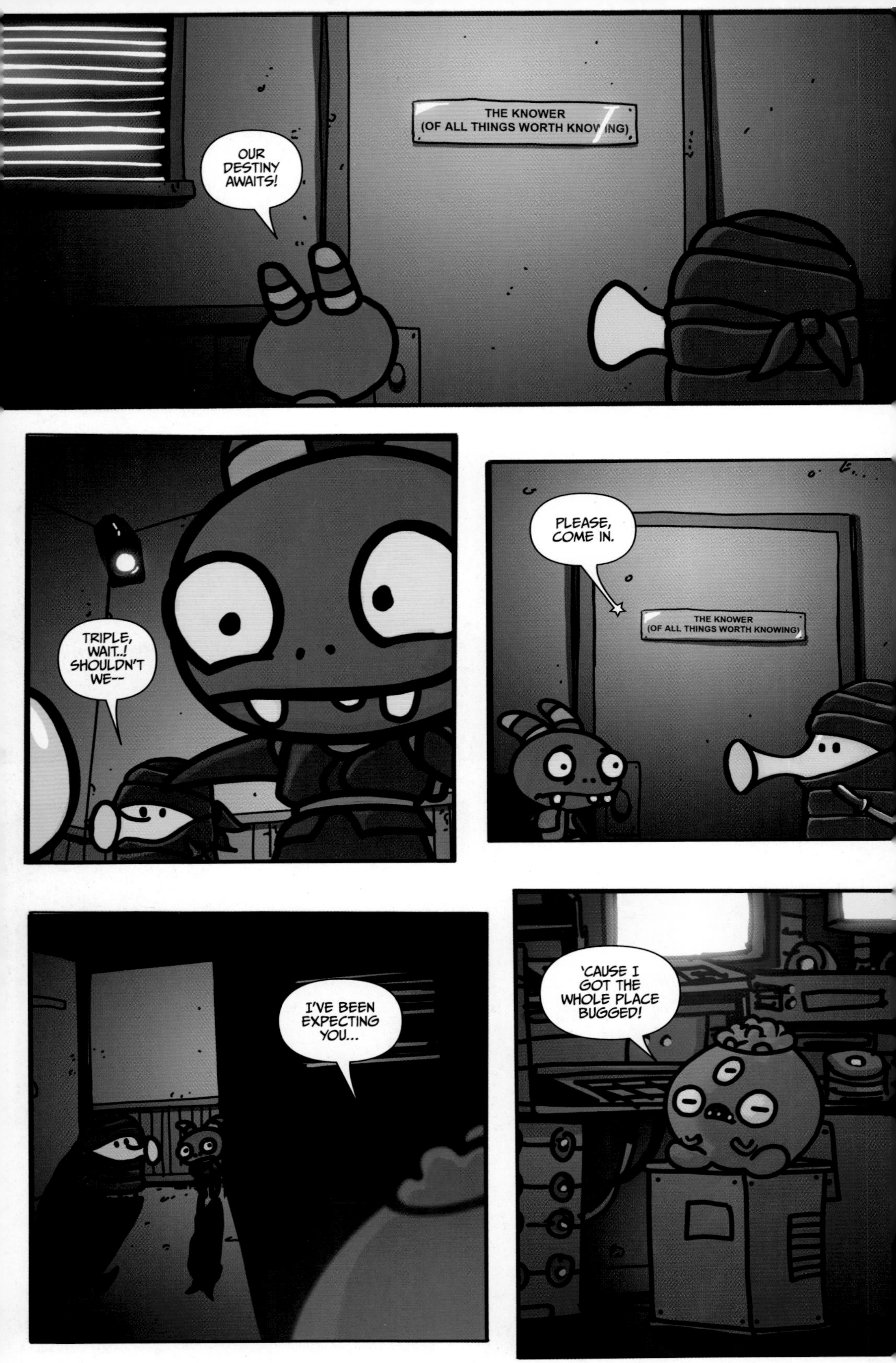
THE KNOWER
(OF ALL THINGS WORTH KNOWING)
OUR DESTINY AWAITS!
TRIPLE, WAIT..! SHOULDN'T WE--
PLEASE, COME IN.
THE KNOWER
(OF ALL THINGS WORTH KNOWING)
I'VE BEEN EXPECTING YOU...
'CAUSE I GOT THE WHOLE PLACE BUGGED!

PRETTY NEAT, HUH? IT WASN'T HARD, REALLY... NINJAS EXPECT EVERYTHING EXCEPT VIDEO CAMERAS!
THAT IS SOME AMAZING TECHNOLOGY, MR. KNOWER!
YES, IT REALLY IS. ANYWAY, I'M BUSY TODAY, SO GET OUT.
NO, PLEASE-- WE CAME A LONG WAY TO BE HERE!
UH HUH.
TRUST ME, THIS IS WORTH YOUR TIME. IT HAS TO DO WITH THE PROPHESY!
HAVE YOU EVER SEEN ONE OF TH--
NO WAY-- A MINT CONDITION, FIRST EDITION DATA SCROLL!!
GIVE IT HERE! WHY ARE YOU HOLDING IT LIKE THAT? YOU'LL RUIN IT!
YOU PROMISE TO HELP US, RIGHT?
SURE, OF COURSE! ANYTHING! JUST LET ME SEE IT!
HERE YA GO.

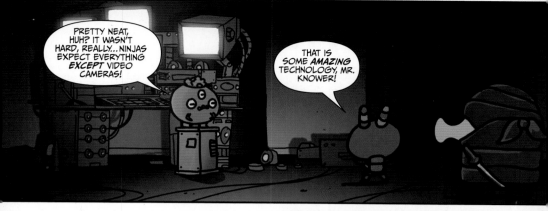

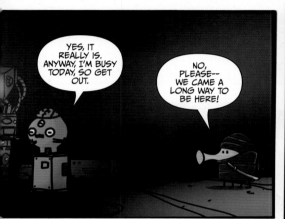

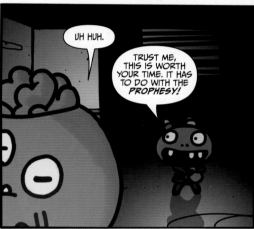

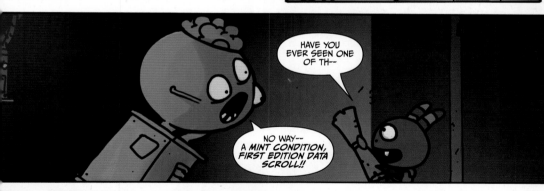

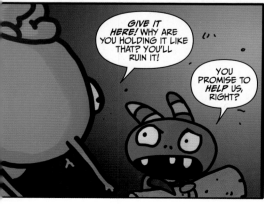

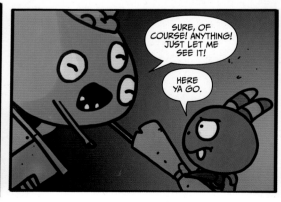

AMAZING... IT'S JUST LIKE I'VE READ ABOUT... SUCH PERFECTION!

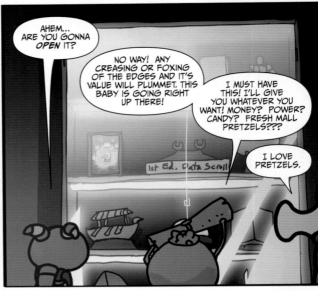

AHEM... ARE YOU GONNA *OPEN* IT?

NO WAY! ANY CREASING OR FOXING OF THE EDGES AND IT'S VALUE WILL PLUMMET. THIS BABY IS GOING RIGHT UP THERE!

I MUST HAVE THIS! I'LL GIVE YOU WHATEVER YOU WANT! MONEY? POWER? CANDY? FRESH MALL PRETZELS???

I LOVE PRETZELS.

1st Ed. Data Scroll

UGH, *LOOK* YOU IDIOT!

HMM... WHO'S THAT?

OH.

HEY.

SO YOUR FRIEND HERE REALLY IS PROPHESIZED IN THE SCROLL? WHY DIDN'T YOU TELL ME?

SRSLY?!?

OK YOU GUYS ARE LEGIT LET'S TAKE A LOOK.

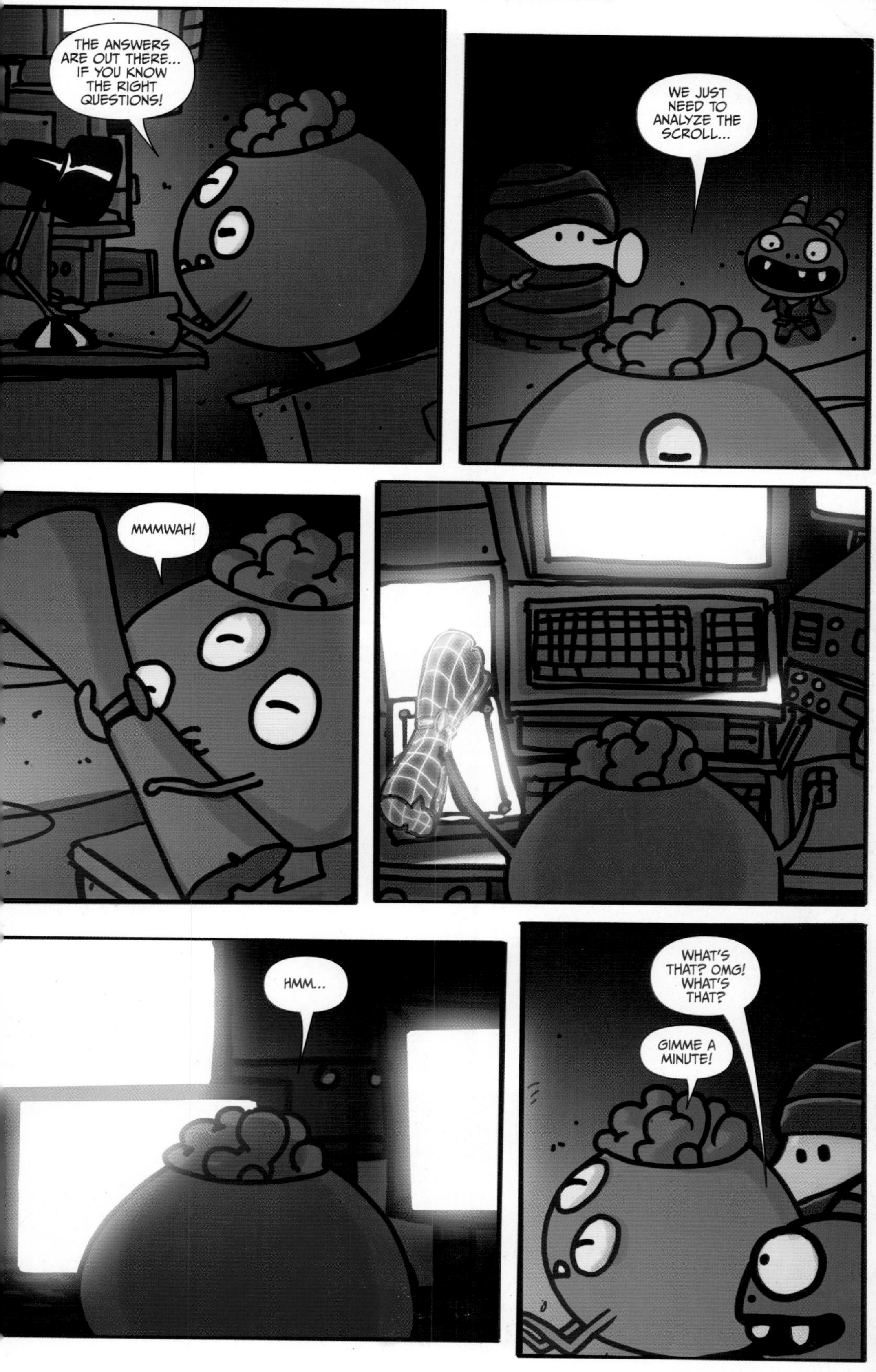
THE ANSWERS ARE OUT THERE... IF YOU KNOW THE RIGHT QUESTIONS!
WE JUST NEED TO ANALYZE THE SCROLL...
MMMWAH!
HMM...
WHAT'S THAT? OMG! WHAT'S THAT?
GIMME A MINUTE!

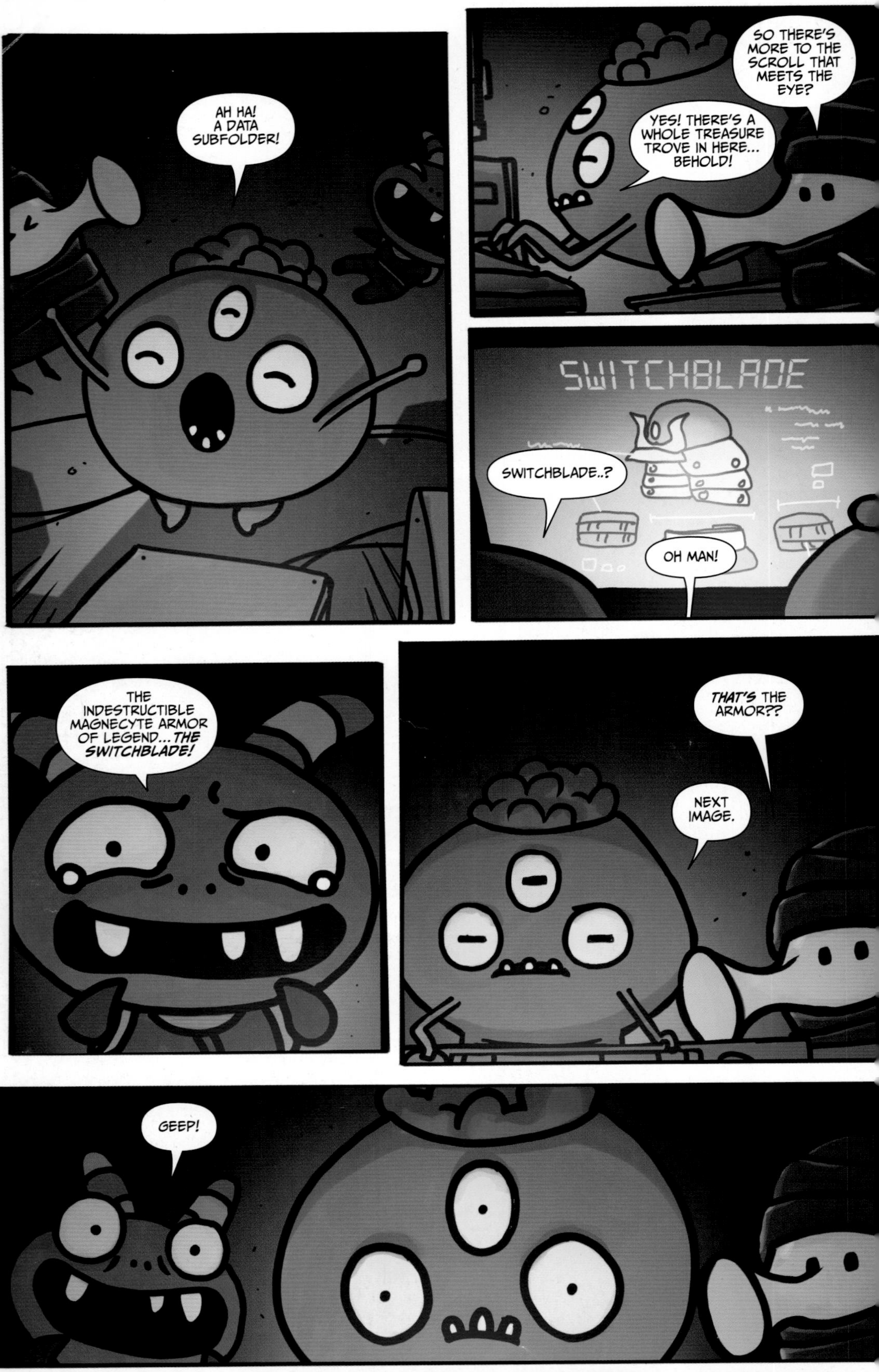
AH HA! A DATA SUBFOLDER!
SO THERE'S MORE TO THE SCROLL THAT MEETS THE EYE?
YES! THERE'S A WHOLE TREASURE TROVE IN HERE... BEHOLD!
SWITCHBLADE
SWITCHBLADE..?
OH MAN!
THE INDESTRUCTIBLE MAGNECYTE ARMOR OF LEGEND...*THE SWITCHBLADE!*
THAT'S THE ARMOR??
NEXT IMAGE.
GEEP!

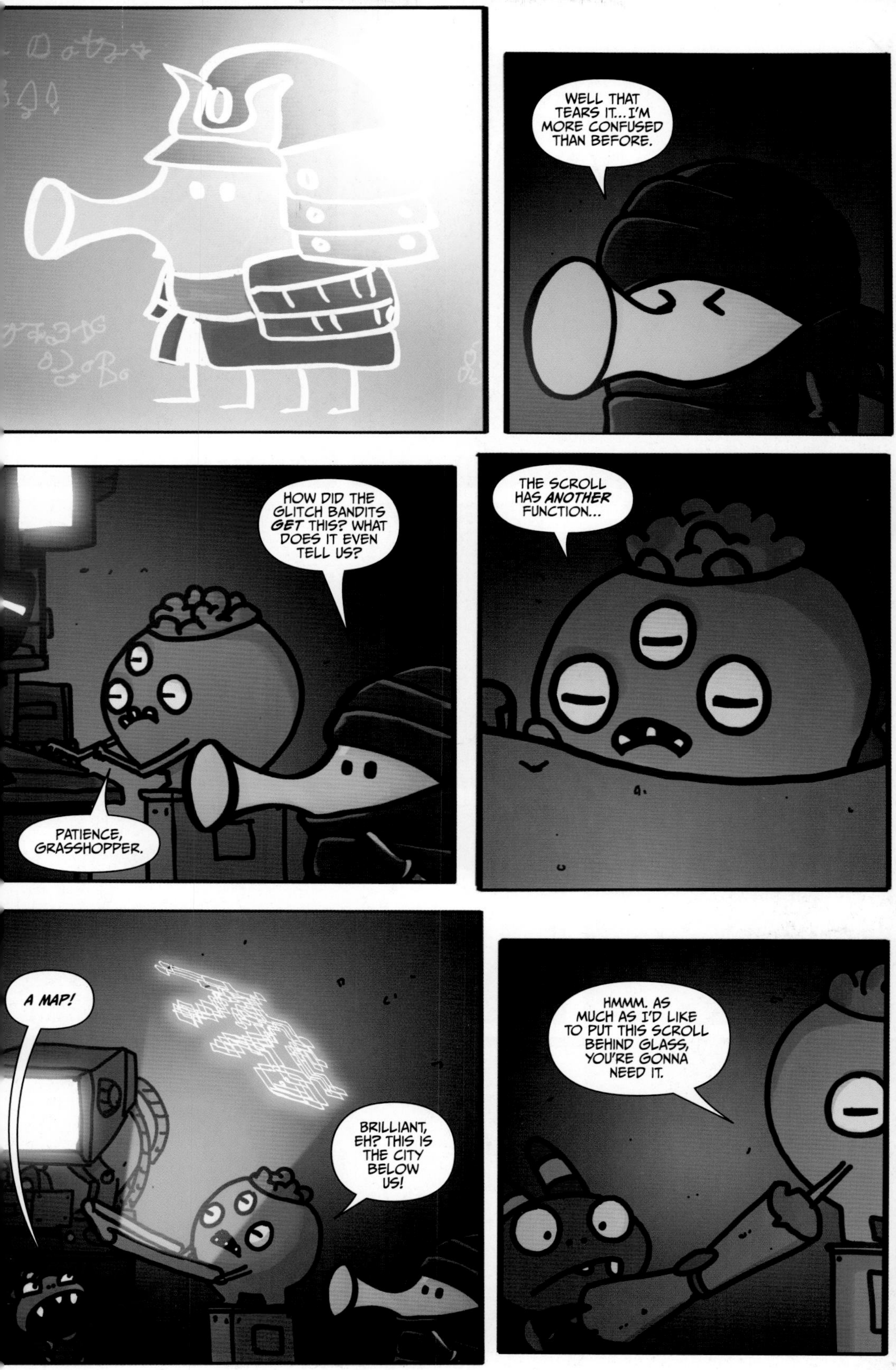
WELL THAT TEARS IT...I'M MORE CONFUSED THAN BEFORE.
HOW DID THE GLITCH BANDITS GET THIS? WHAT DOES IT EVEN TELL US?
PATIENCE, GRASSHOPPER.
THE SCROLL HAS ANOTHER FUNCTION...
A MAP!
BRILLIANT, EH? THIS IS THE CITY BELOW US!
HMMM. AS MUCH AS I'D LIKE TO PUT THIS SCROLL BEHIND GLASS, YOU'RE GONNA NEED IT.

THANK YOU, MR. KNOWER.

NOW GET OUTTA HERE, AND FIND SOME COOL--

RRRMMMBBLLSHH

WH-WHAT THE HECK?!

IT'S...

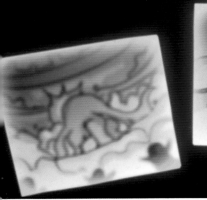

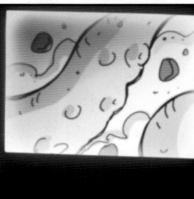

A MONSTER??
IT'S COMING FROM UNDERGROUND..!
THE MALL IS DOOMED! THERE'S NO WAY THE GUARDS WILL RISK THEIR NECKS ON THAT!
THEN WE HAVE TO FIGHT IT!
HA HA HA HA... REALLY THOUGH?
IT'S IN THE PROPHECY., REMEMBER! YOU'RE THE HERO!
EASY FOR YOU TO SAY...
DOODLER, LET'S GO!
ONE LAST THING, DOODLER!
WHEN IN DOUBT, GO FOR HIGHER GROUND!
WHEW... IT'S HARD BEING SO SMART.

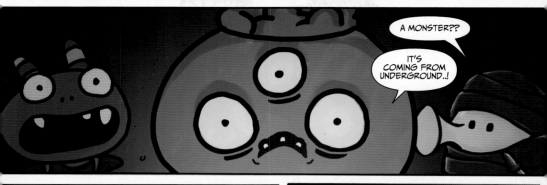

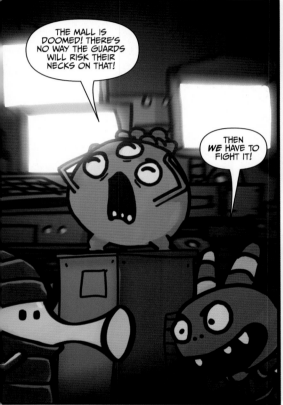

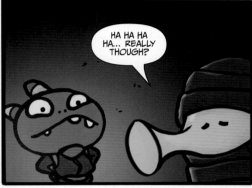

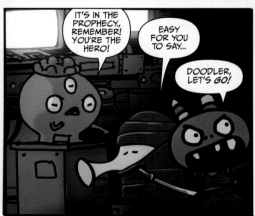

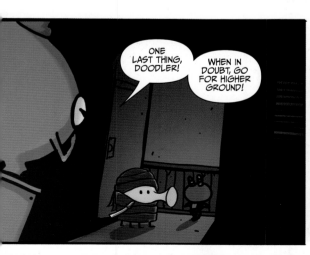

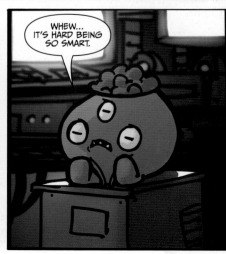

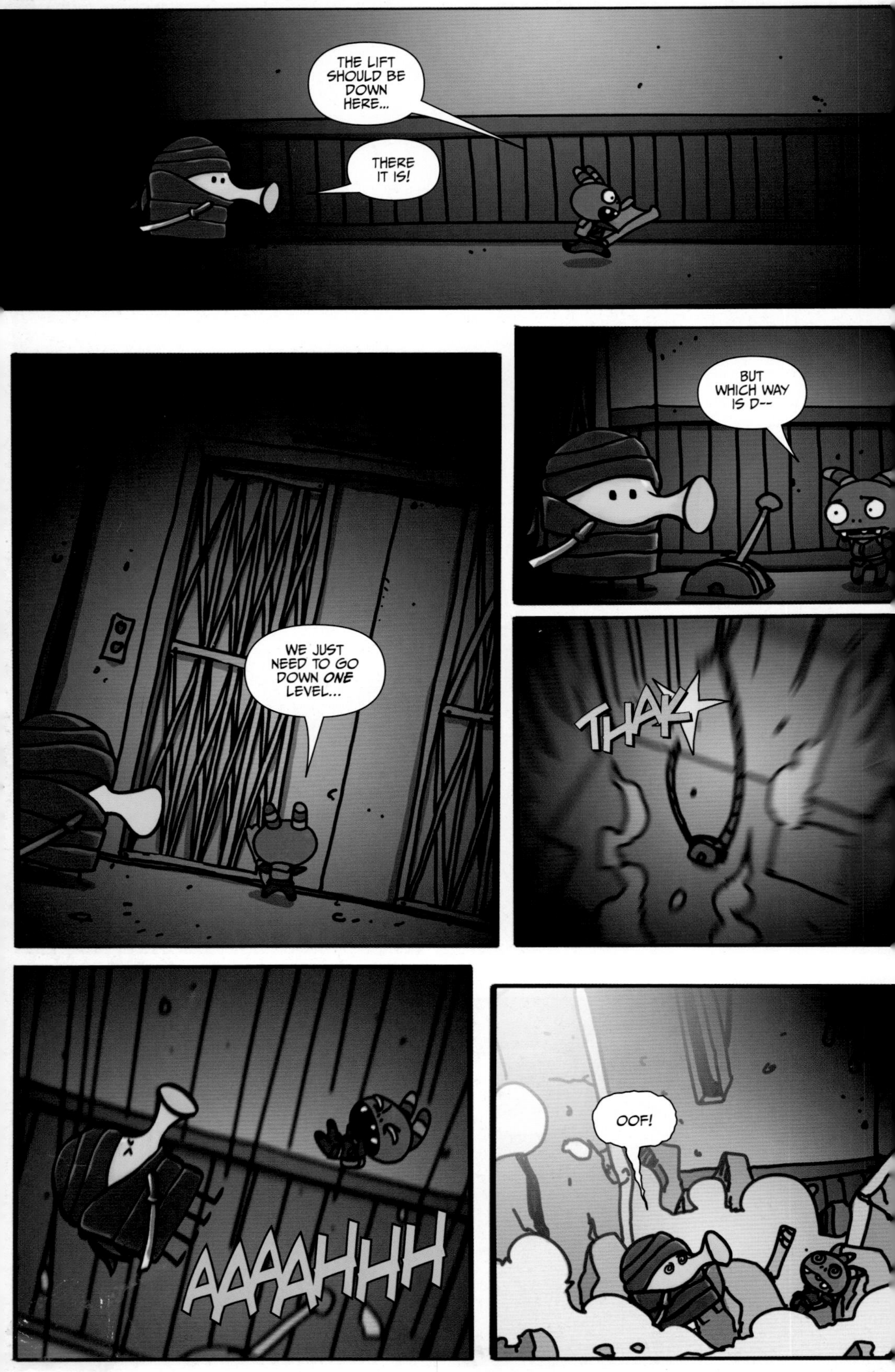
THE LIFT SHOULD BE DOWN HERE...
THERE IT IS!
WE JUST NEED TO GO DOWN ONE LEVEL...
BUT WHICH WAY IS D--
THAK
AAAAHHH
OOF!

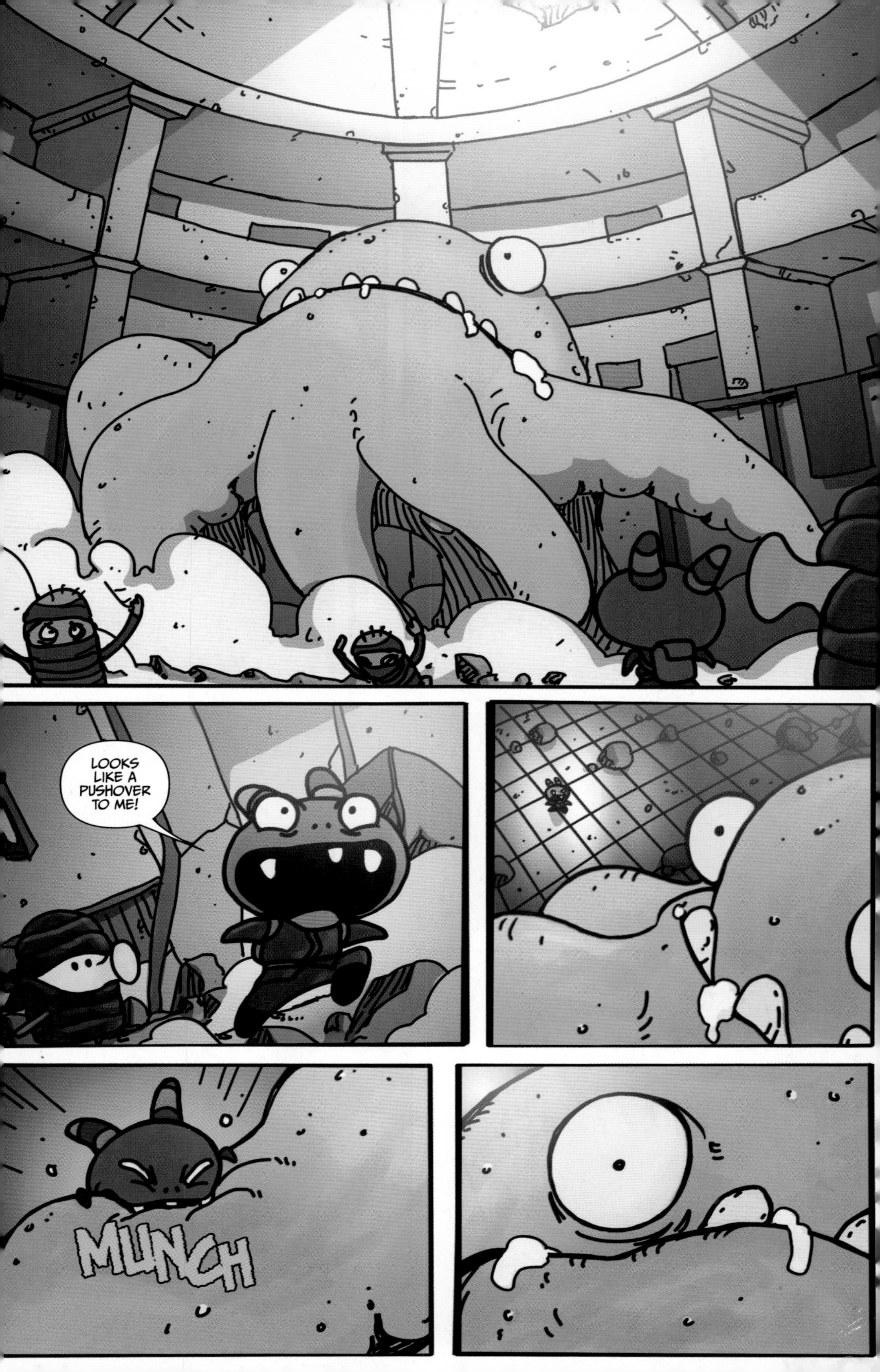
LOOKS LIKE A PUSHOVER TO ME!
MUNCH

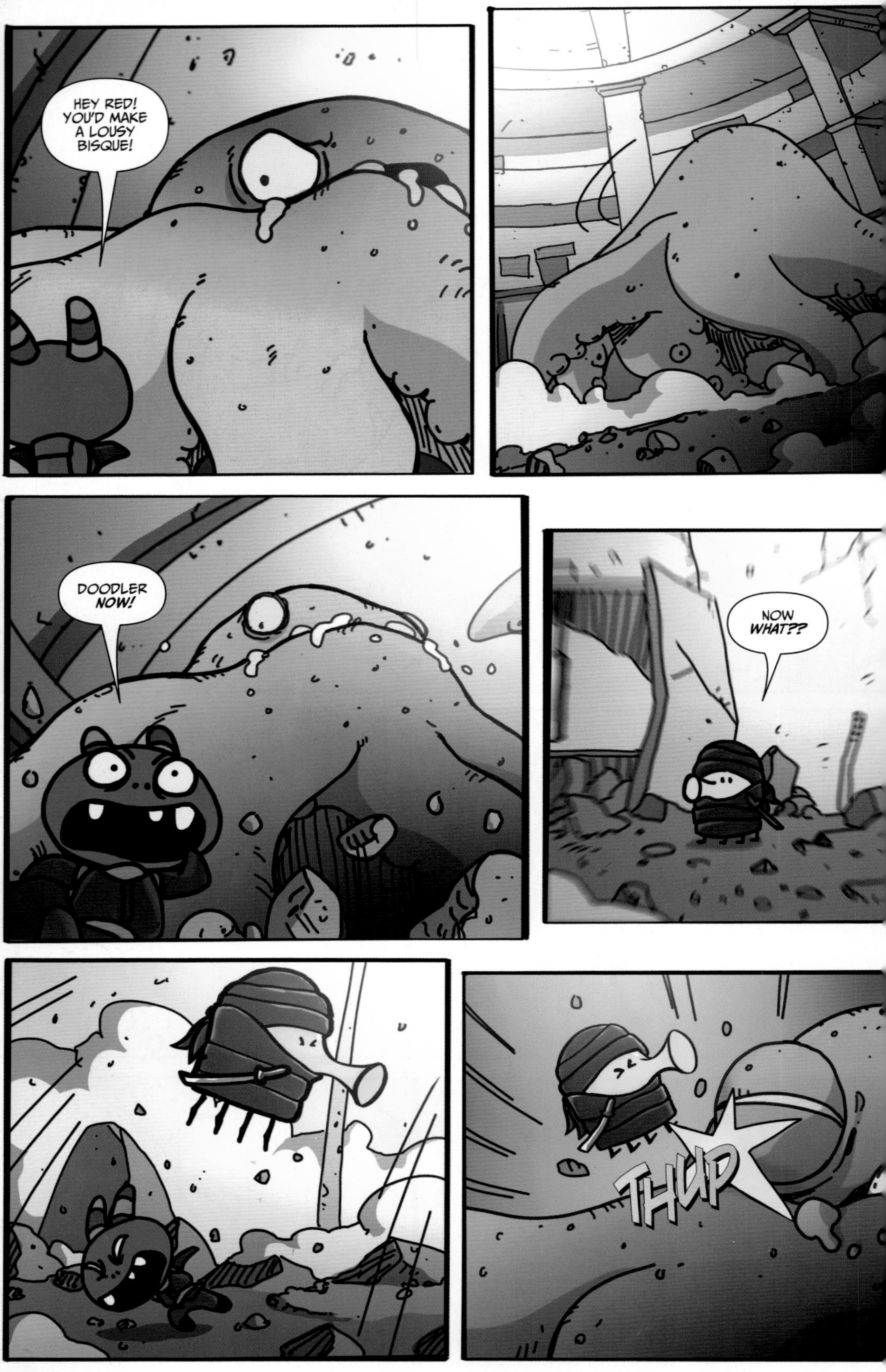
HEY RED! YOU'D MAKE A LOUSY BISQUE!
DOODLER NOW!
NOW WHAT??
THUP

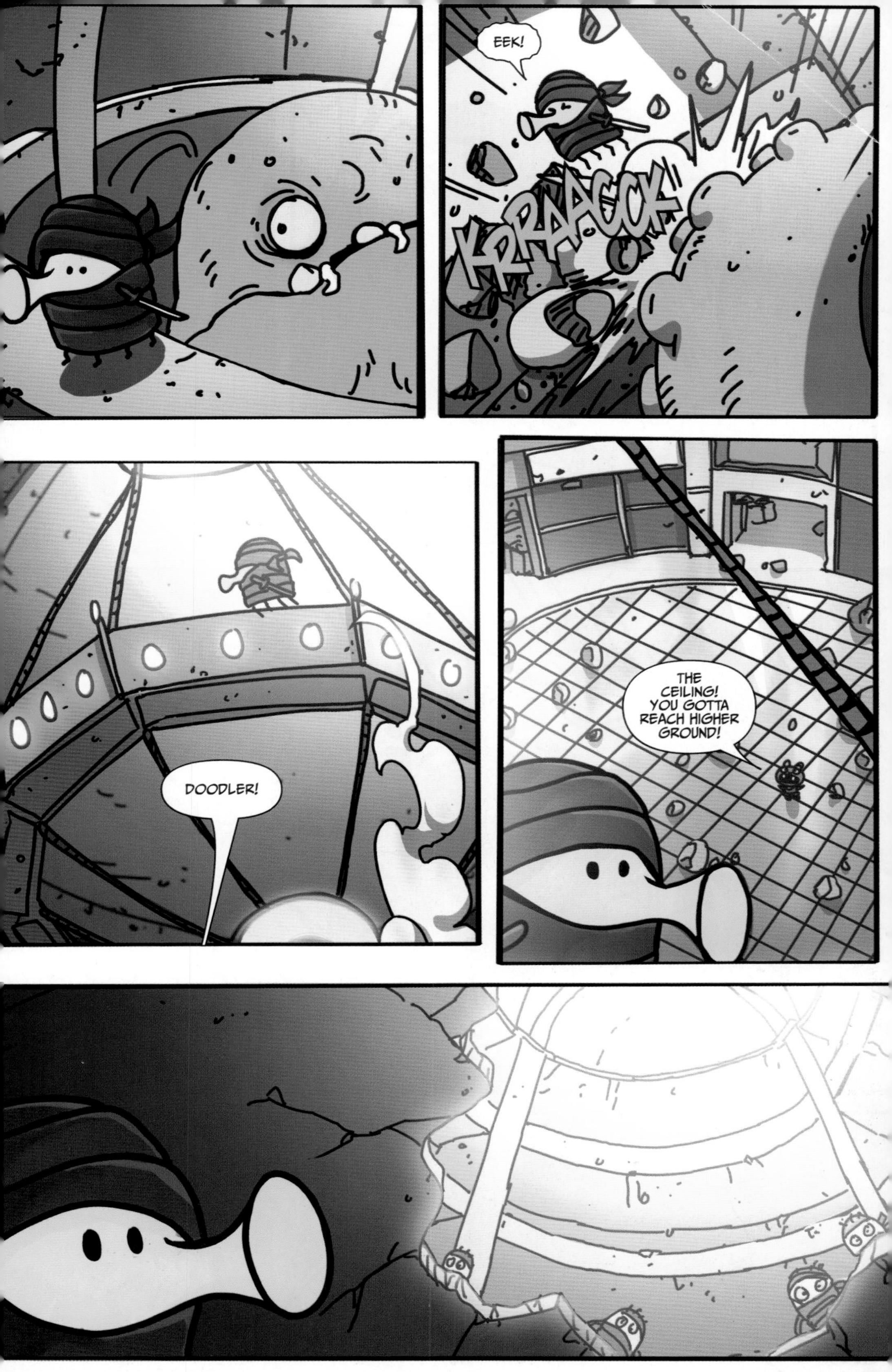
EEK!
KRRAACCK
DOODLER!
THE CEILING! YOU GOTTA REACH HIGHER GROUND!

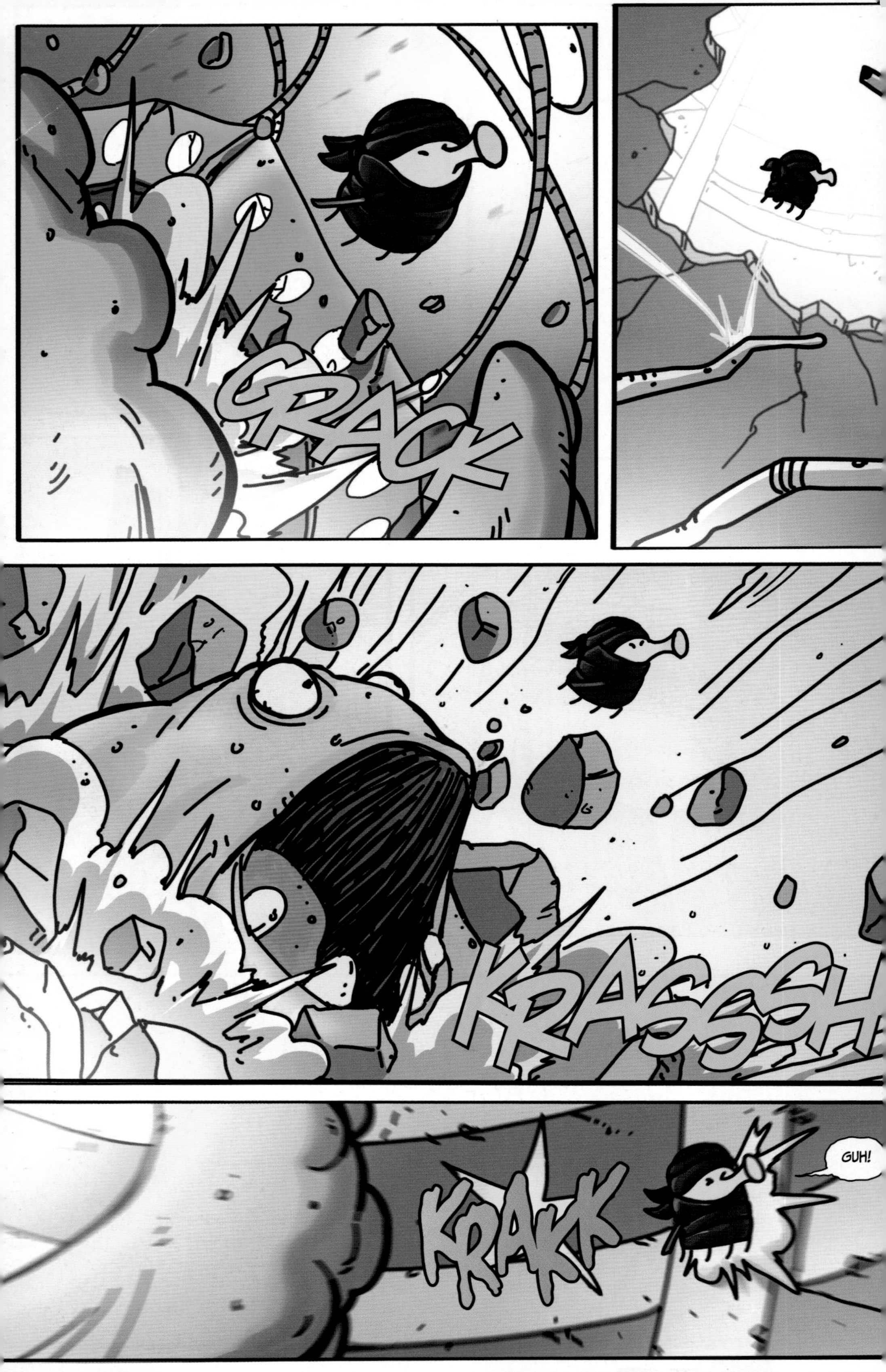
CRACK
KRASSSH
KRAKK
GUH!

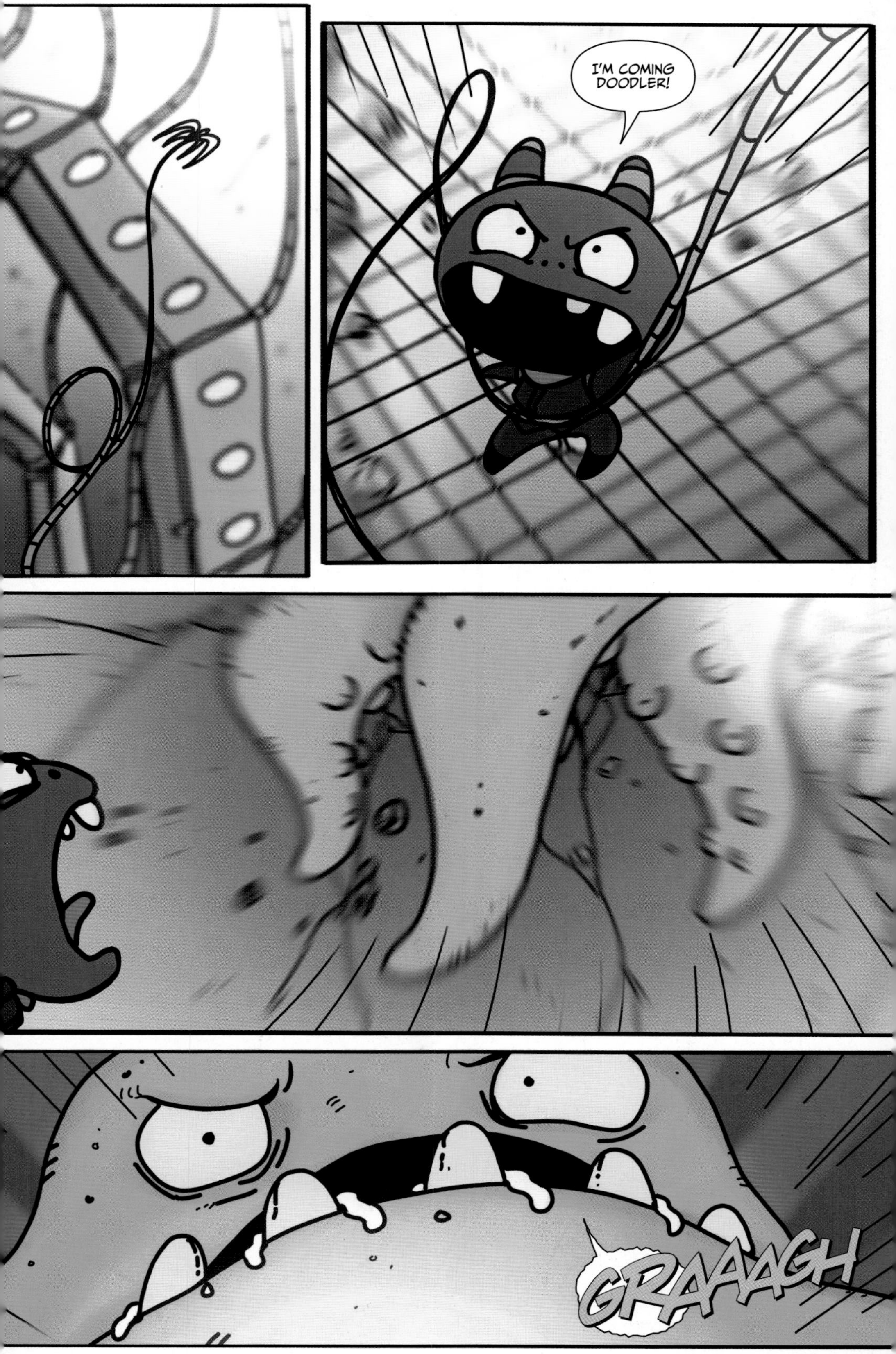
I'M COMING DOODLER!
GRAAAGH

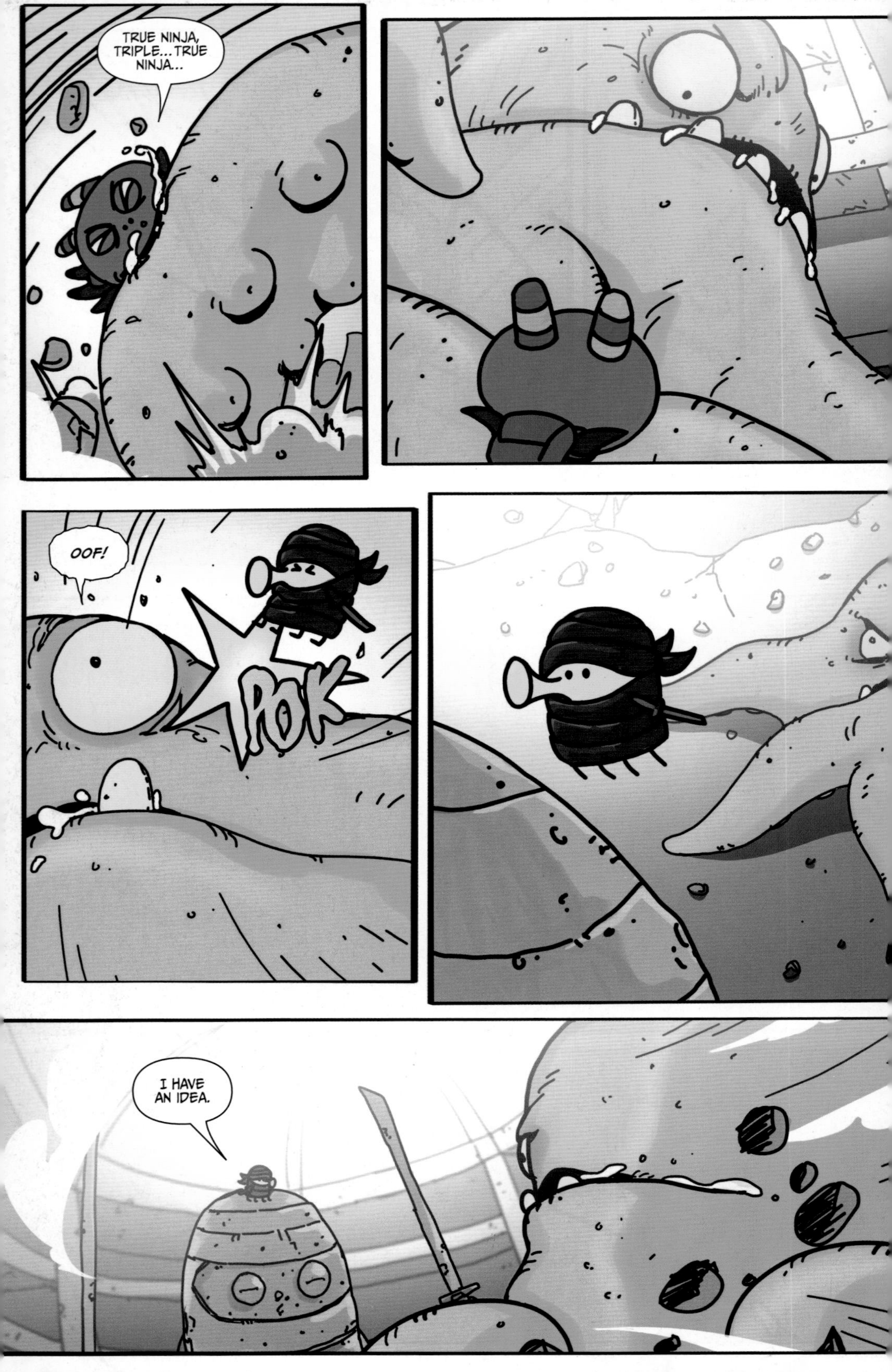
TRUE NINJA, TRIPLE...TRUE NINJA...
OOF!
POK
I HAVE AN IDEA.

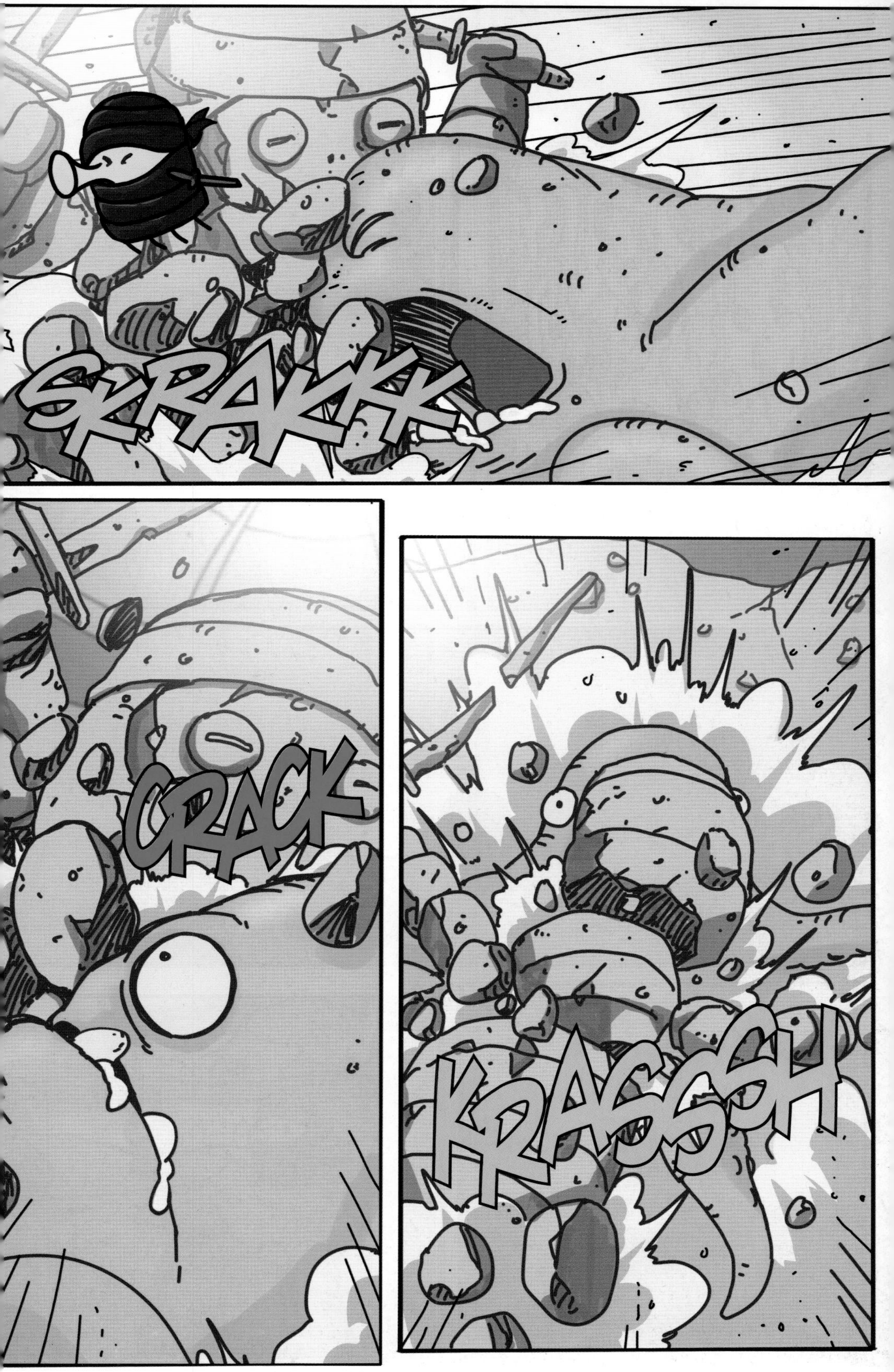
SKRAKKK
CRACK
KRASSSH

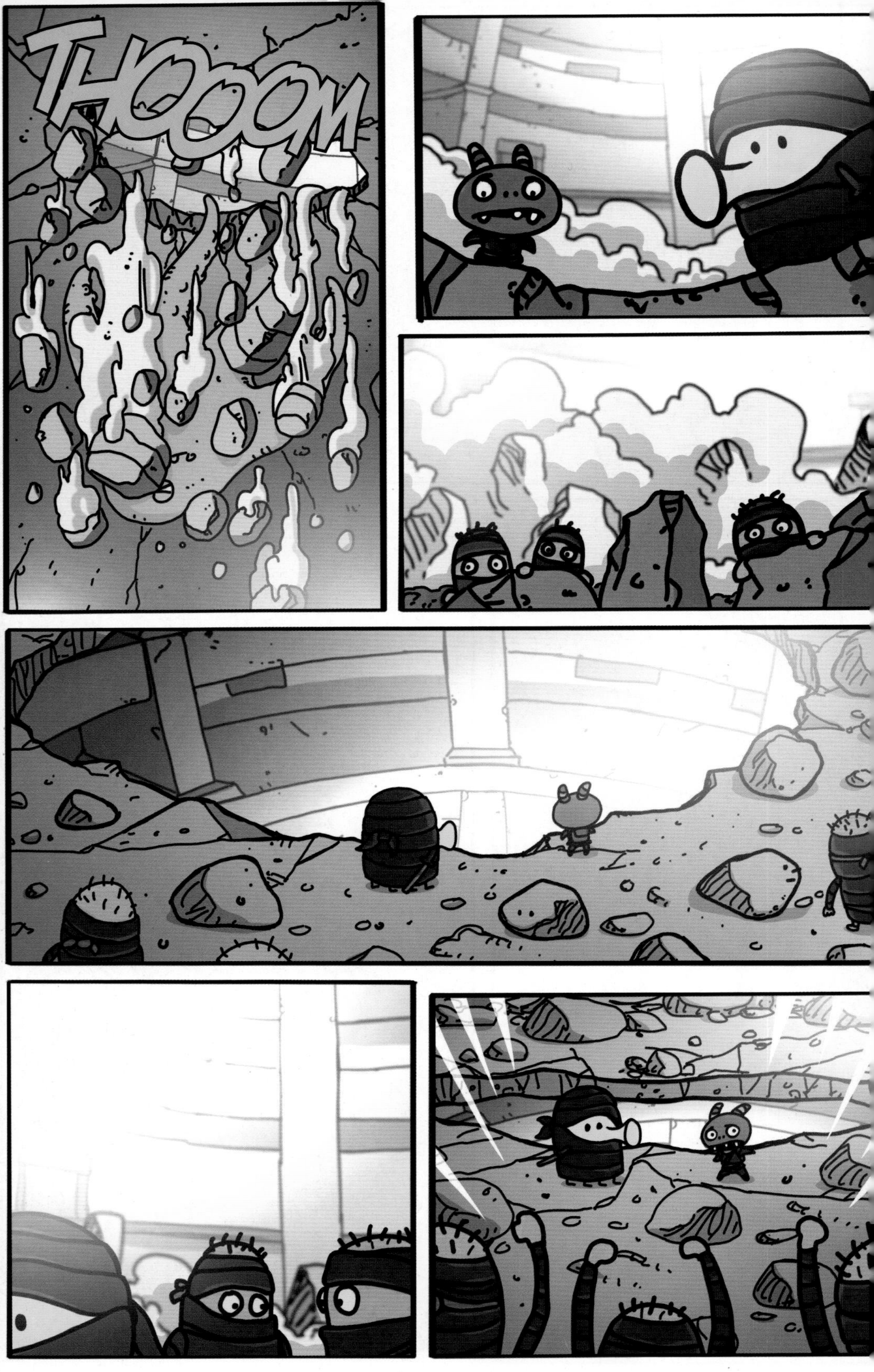
THOOOM

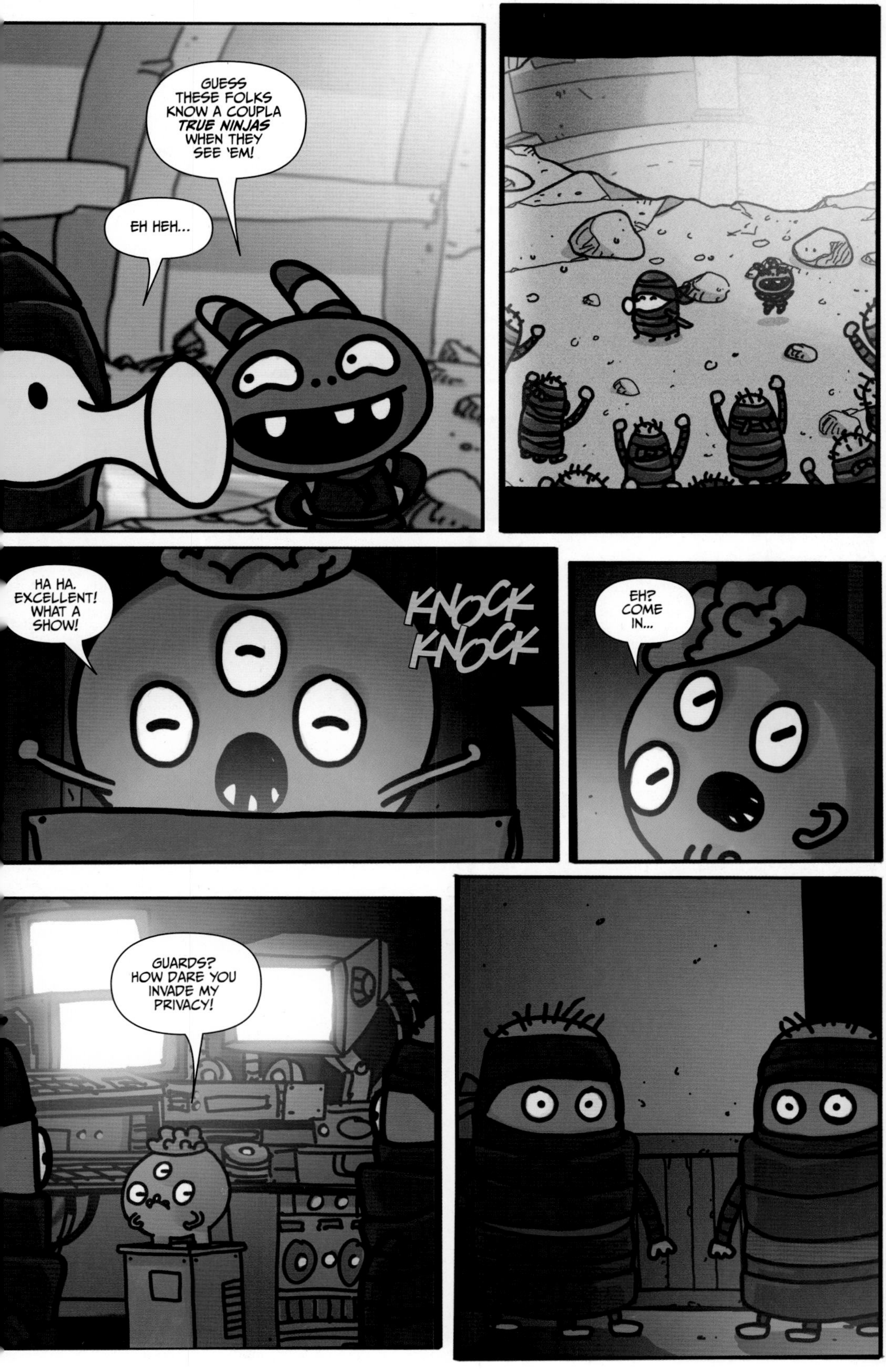
GUESS THESE FOLKS KNOW A COUPLA TRUE NINJAS WHEN THEY SEE 'EM!
EH HEH...
HA HA. EXCELLENT! WHAT A SHOW!
KNOCK KNOCK
EH? COME IN...
GUARDS? HOW DARE YOU INVADE MY PRIVACY!

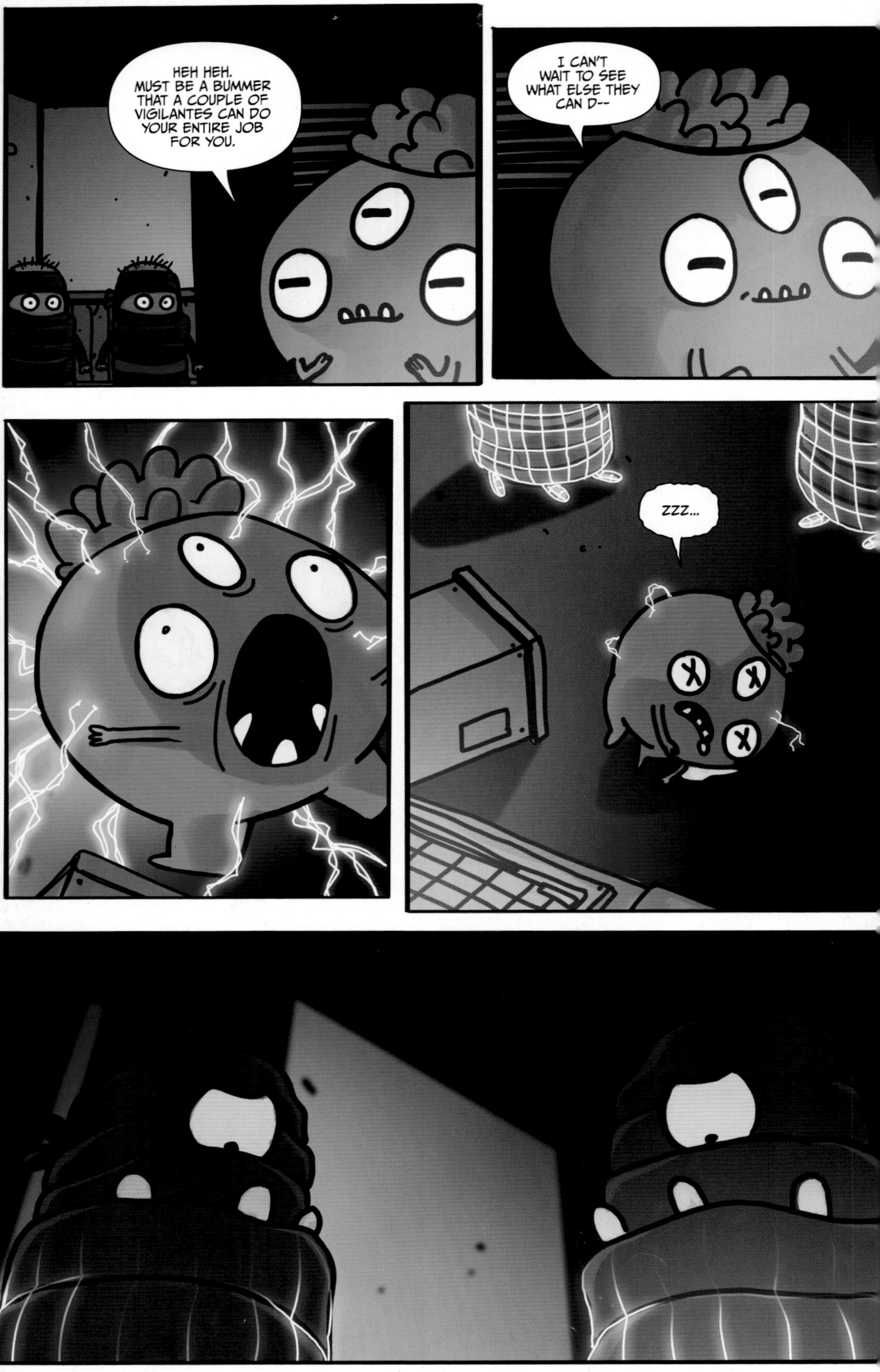
HEH HEH.
MUST BE A BUMMER THAT A COUPLE OF VIGILANTES CAN DO YOUR ENTIRE JOB FOR YOU.
I CAN'T WAIT TO SEE WHAT ELSE THEY CAN D--
ZZZ...

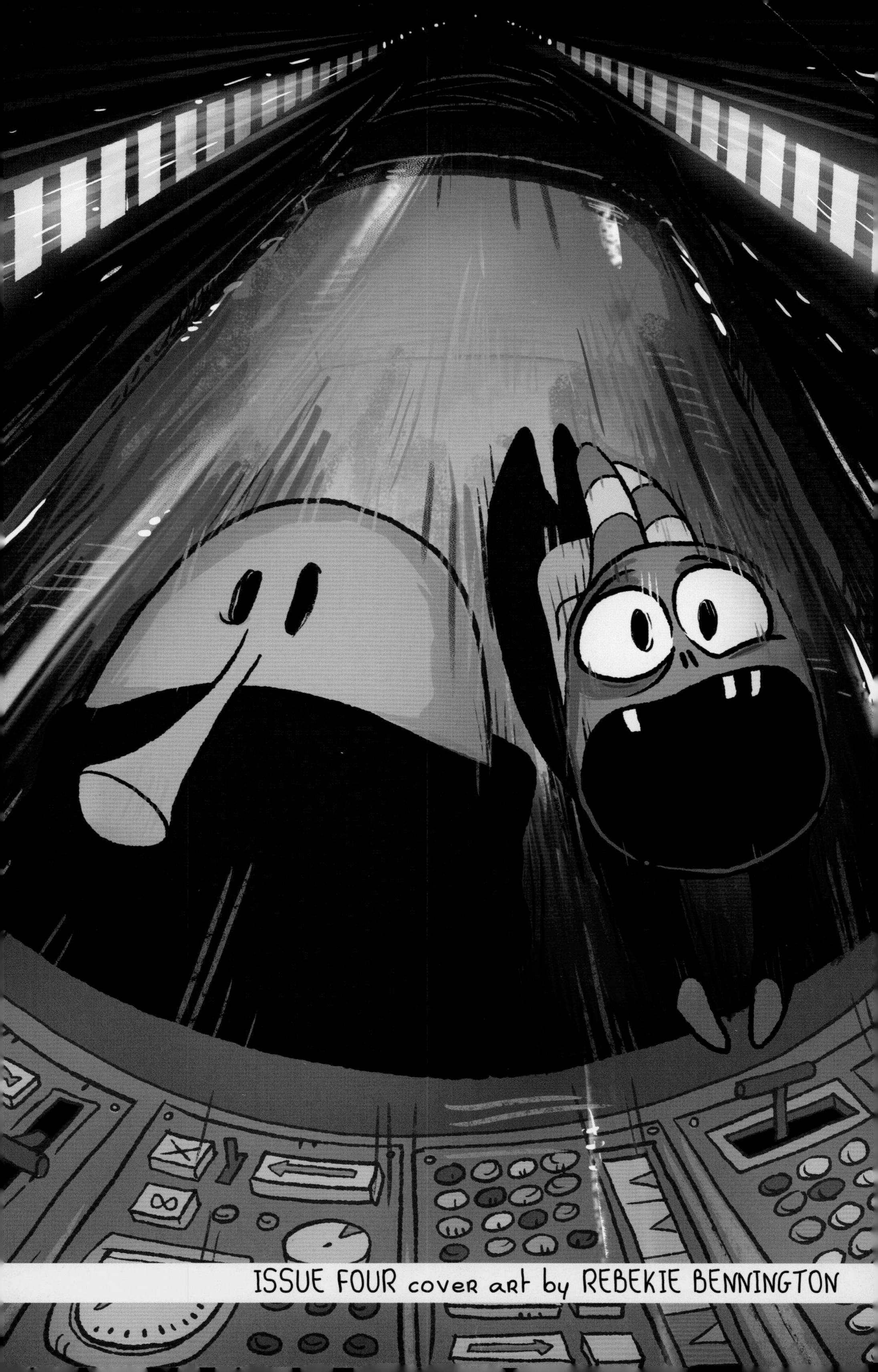

ISSUE FOUR cover art by REBEKIE BENNINGTON

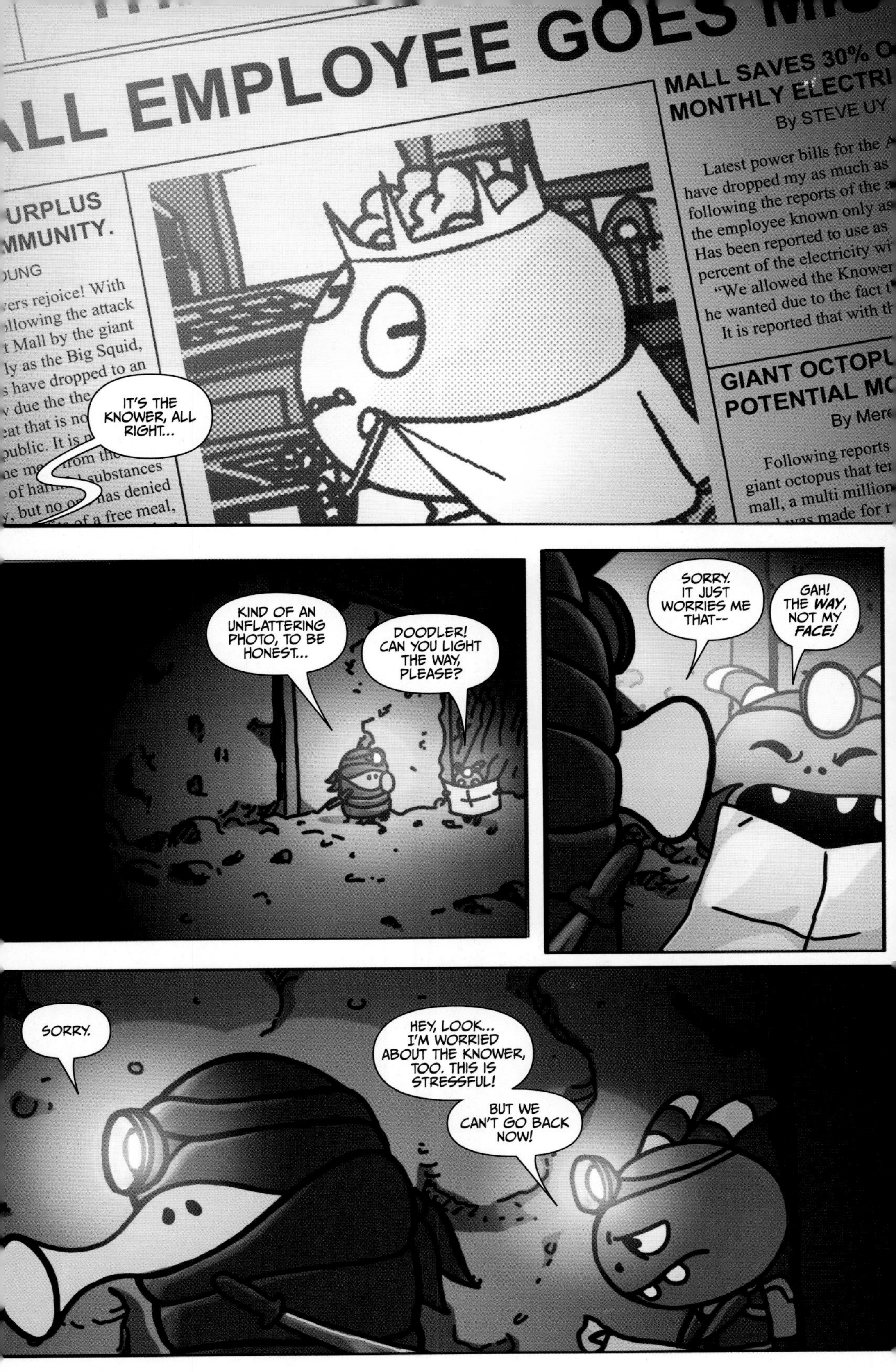
ALL EMPLOYEE GOES MIS
MALL SAVES 30% O
MONTHLY ELECTRI
By STEVE UY
URPLUS
MMUNITY.
GIANT OCTOPU
POTENTIAL MO
IT'S THE KNOWER, ALL RIGHT...
KIND OF AN UNFLATTERING PHOTO, TO BE HONEST...
DOODLER! CAN YOU LIGHT THE WAY, PLEASE?
SORRY. IT JUST WORRIES ME THAT--
GAH! THE *WAY*, NOT MY *FACE!*
SORRY.
HEY, LOOK... I'M WORRIED ABOUT THE KNOWER, TOO. THIS IS STRESSFUL!
BUT WE CAN'T GO BACK NOW!

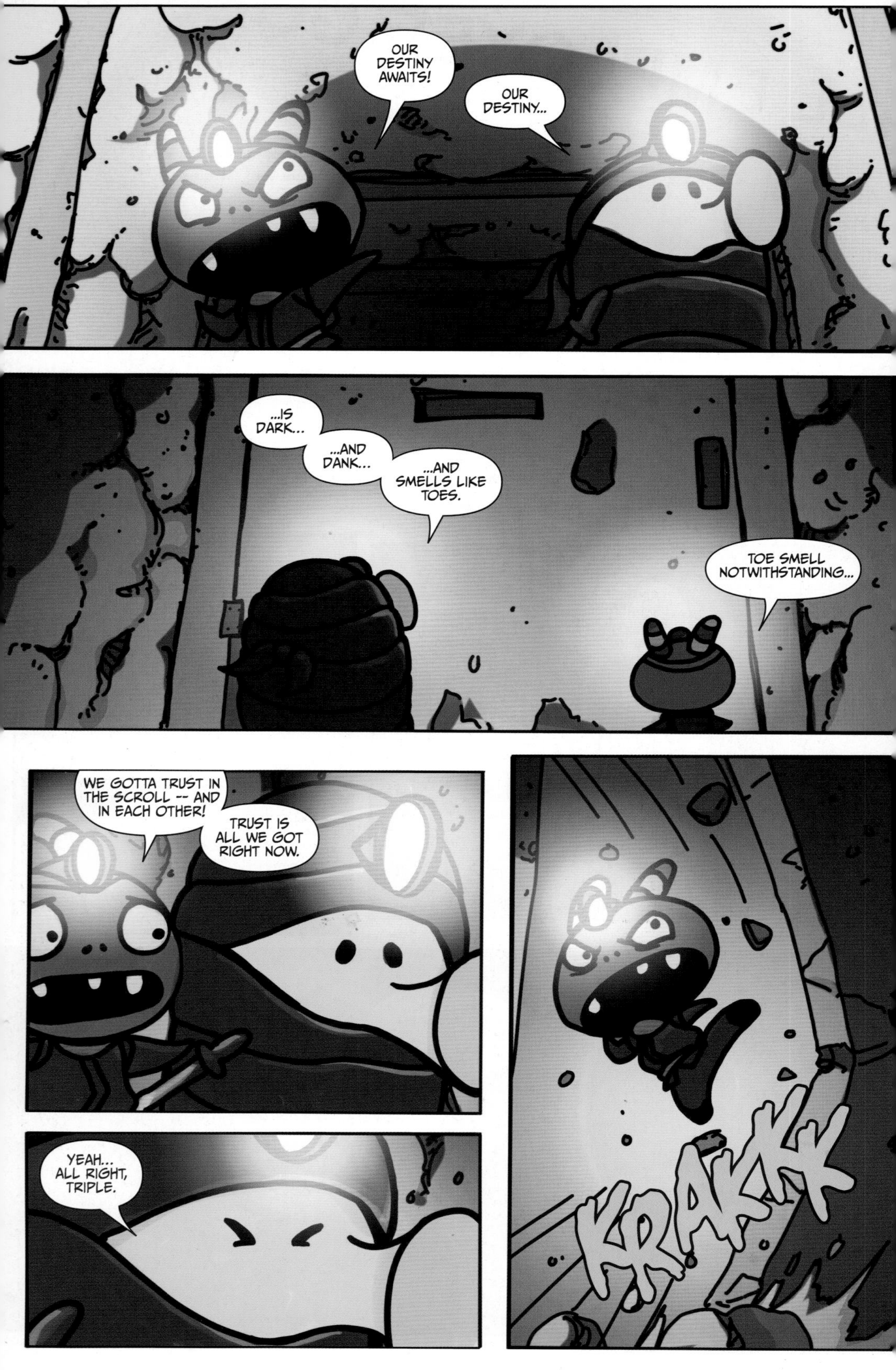
OUR DESTINY AWAITS!
OUR DESTINY...
...IS DARK...
...AND DANK...
...AND SMELLS LIKE TOES.
TOE SMELL NOTWITHSTANDING...
WE GOTTA TRUST IN THE SCROLL -- AND IN EACH OTHER!
TRUST IS ALL WE GOT RIGHT NOW.
YEAH... ALL RIGHT, TRIPLE.
KRAKKK

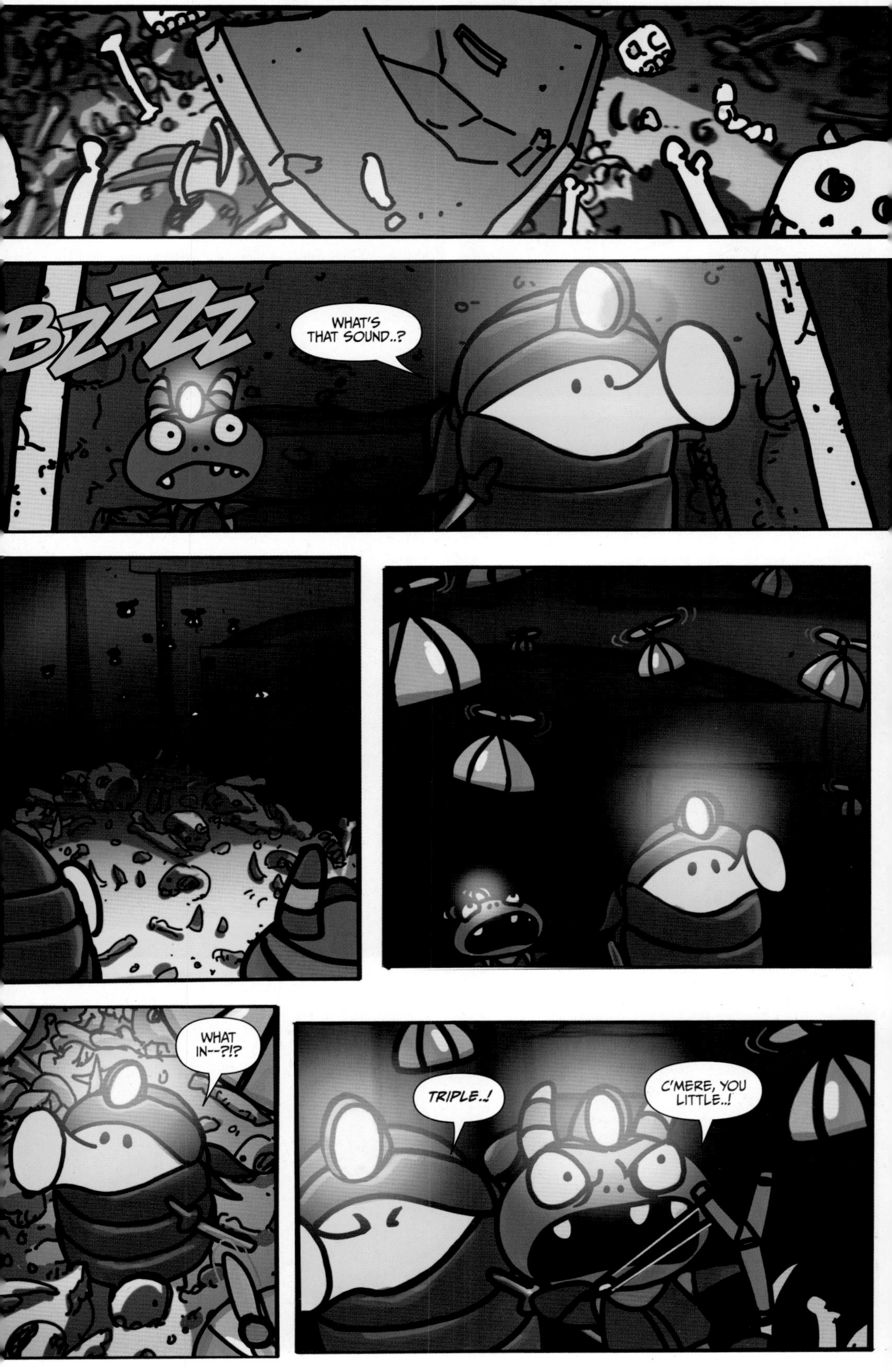
BZZZZZ
WHAT'S THAT SOUND..?
WHAT IN--?!?
TRIPLE..!
C'MERE, YOU LITTLE..!

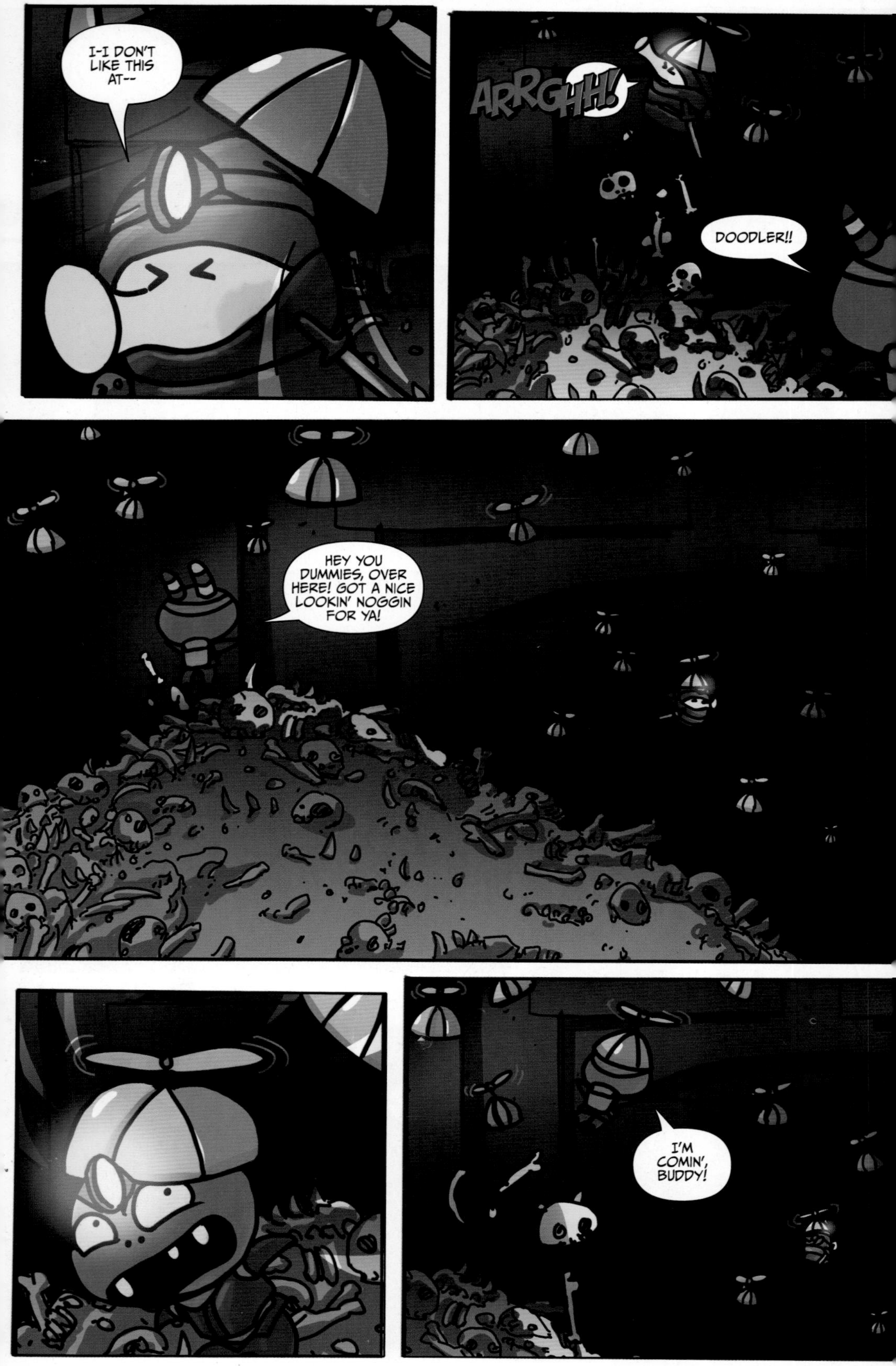
I-I DON'T LIKE THIS AT--
ARRGHH!
DOODLER!!
HEY YOU DUMMIES, OVER HERE! GOT A NICE LOOKIN' NOGGIN FOR YA!
I'M COMIN', BUDDY!

WHOA! HEY!
TRIPLE! YOU FOLLOWED ME!
OF COURSE! Y'THINK I'D LEAVE YOU *BEHIND?*
GUH!

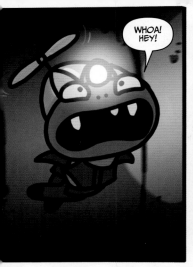

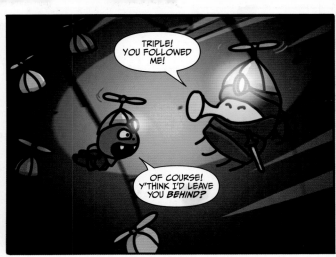

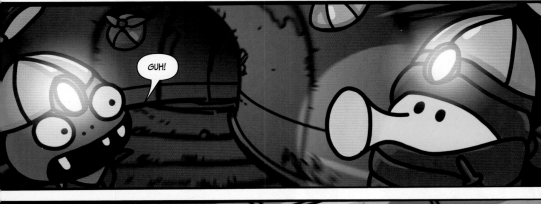

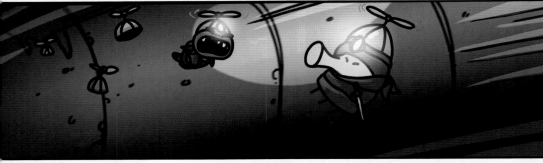

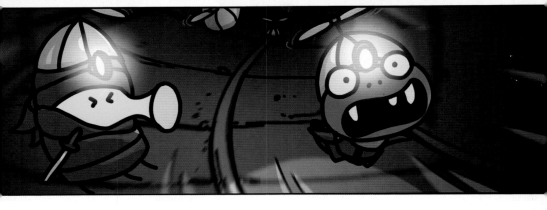

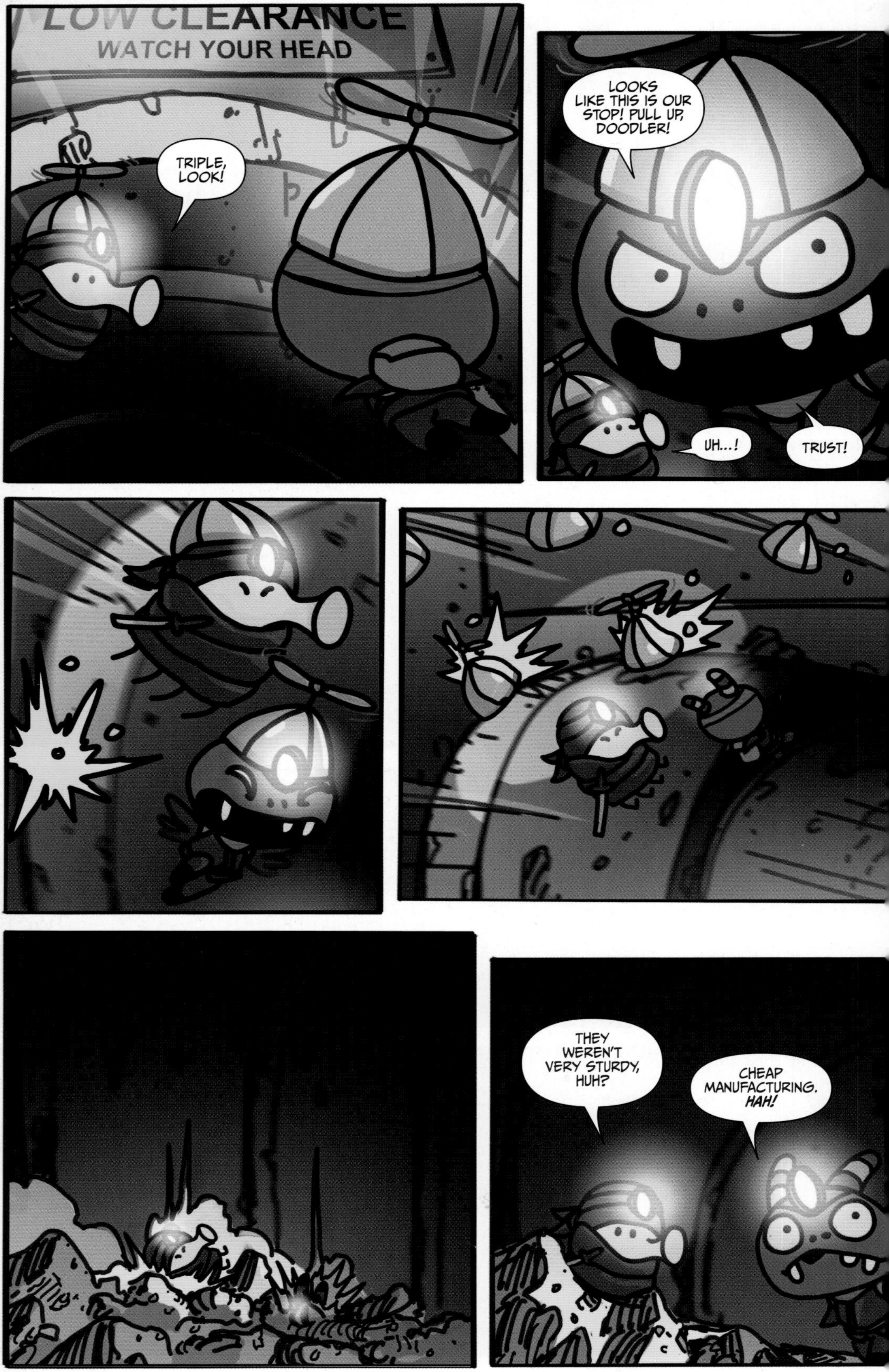
LOW CLEARANCE
WATCH YOUR HEAD
TRIPLE, LOOK!
LOOKS LIKE THIS IS OUR STOP! PULL UP, DOODLER!
UH...!
TRUST!
THEY WEREN'T VERY STURDY, HUH?
CHEAP MANUFACTURING. HAH!

ACCORDING TO THE SCROLL, WE'RE EVEN CLOSER THAN BEFORE!

WHOEVER SENT THOSE FLYING HATS, HE DIDN'T WANT US TO COME HERE. ACCORDING TO THE SCROLL, WE'RE GETTING REALLY CLOSE.

THE FACTORY... I WONDER WHAT THEY MAKE THERE.

THAT'S THE PLACE!

DO YOU THINK THESE TRACKS ARE FOR TRAINS?

THEY AIN'T FOR SWIMMING IN.

NOT TRAINS, DOODLER. CAPSULES!

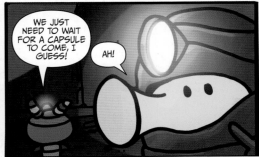

WE JUST NEED TO WAIT FOR A CAPSULE TO COME, I GUESS!

AH!

OVER HERE!
YOINKS! THAT WAS FAST!
HOLD IT, DOODLER!
YOU GOTTA KNOW WHAT TO *DO* WITH THESE THINGS, PAL!
I'M DRIVING!
GOOD THING YOU'RE TRAVELING WITH A LEVEL THREE CERTIFIED CAPSULE CADETTE!
WE'LL BE COASTING AT THE SPEED OF HOWEVER-FAST-THESE-GO...
...*ZOOM* IN NO TIME.
OKAY...
HMM, ALL RIGHT... FORWARD... MY SIMULATOR'S BUTTON WAS RIGHT HERE...WHERE'S THE DANG GO BUTTON?

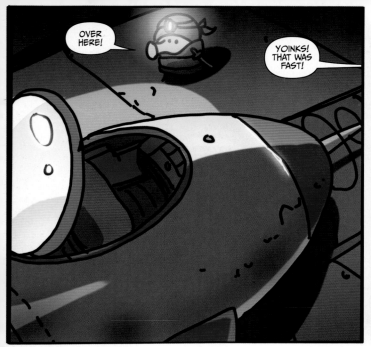

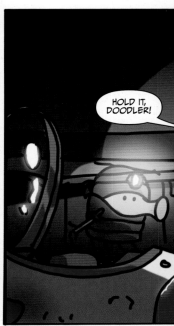

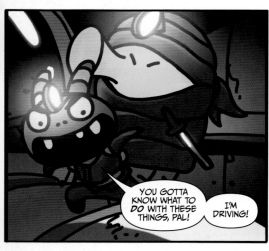

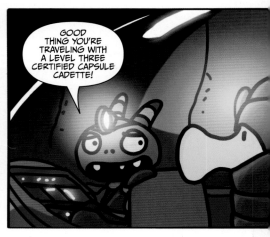

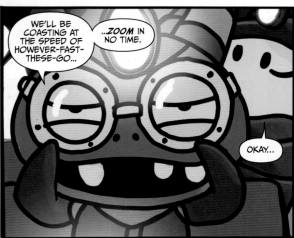

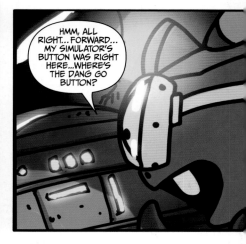

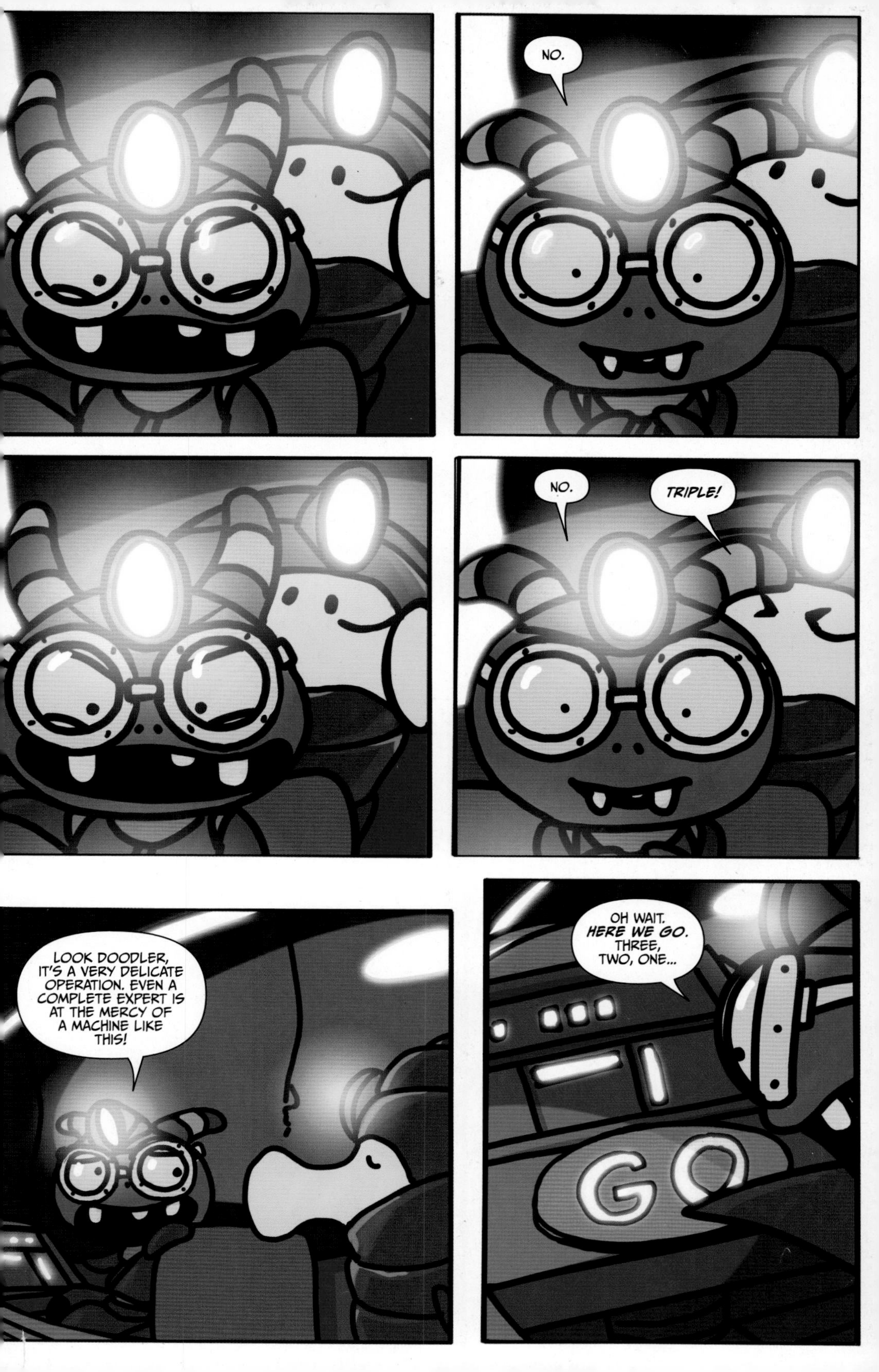
NO.
NO.
TRIPLE!
LOOK DOODLER, IT'S A VERY DELICATE OPERATION. EVEN A COMPLETE EXPERT IS AT THE MERCY OF A MACHINE LIKE THIS!
OH WAIT. HERE WE GO. THREE, TWO, ONE...
GO

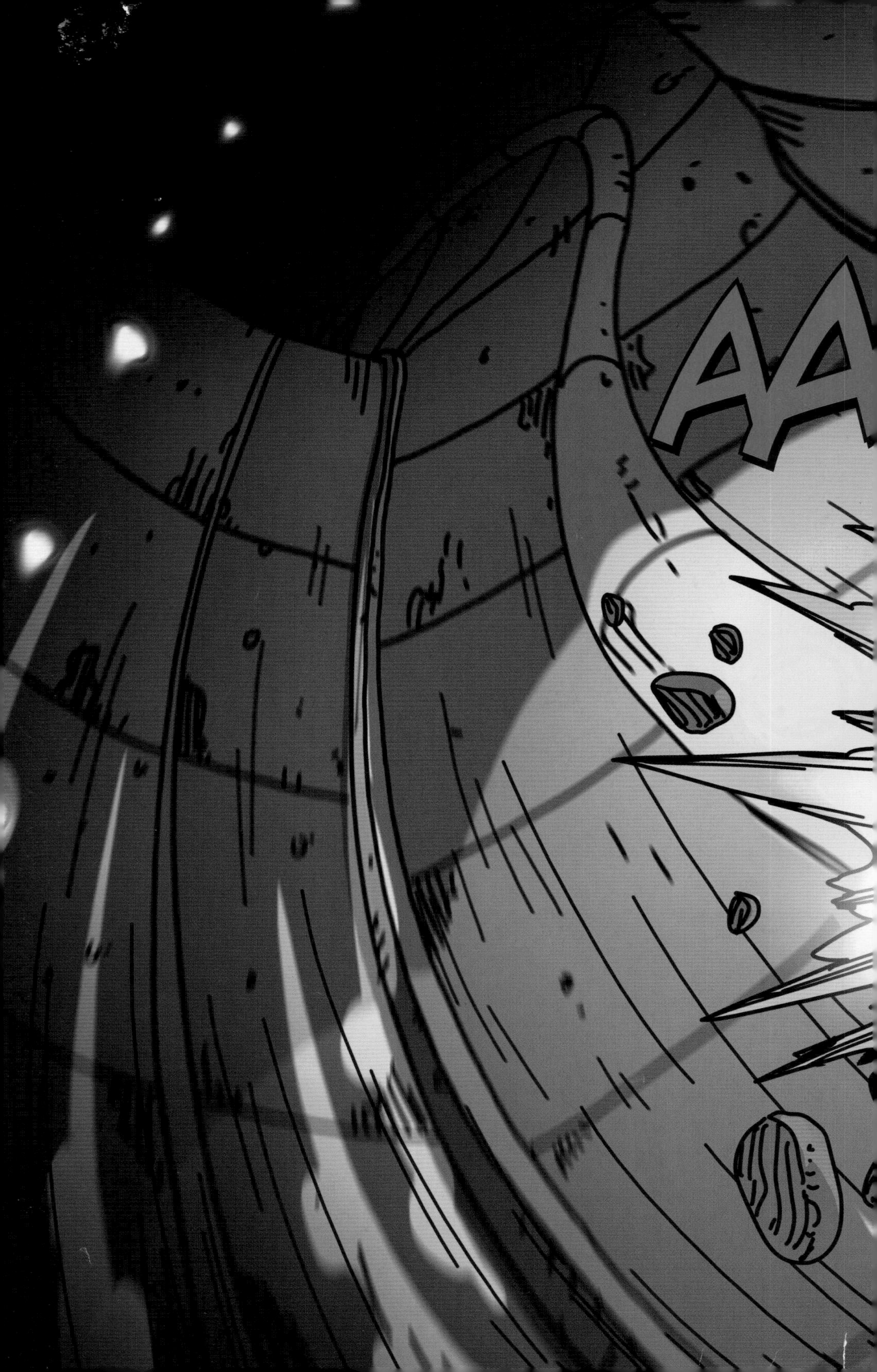
AA

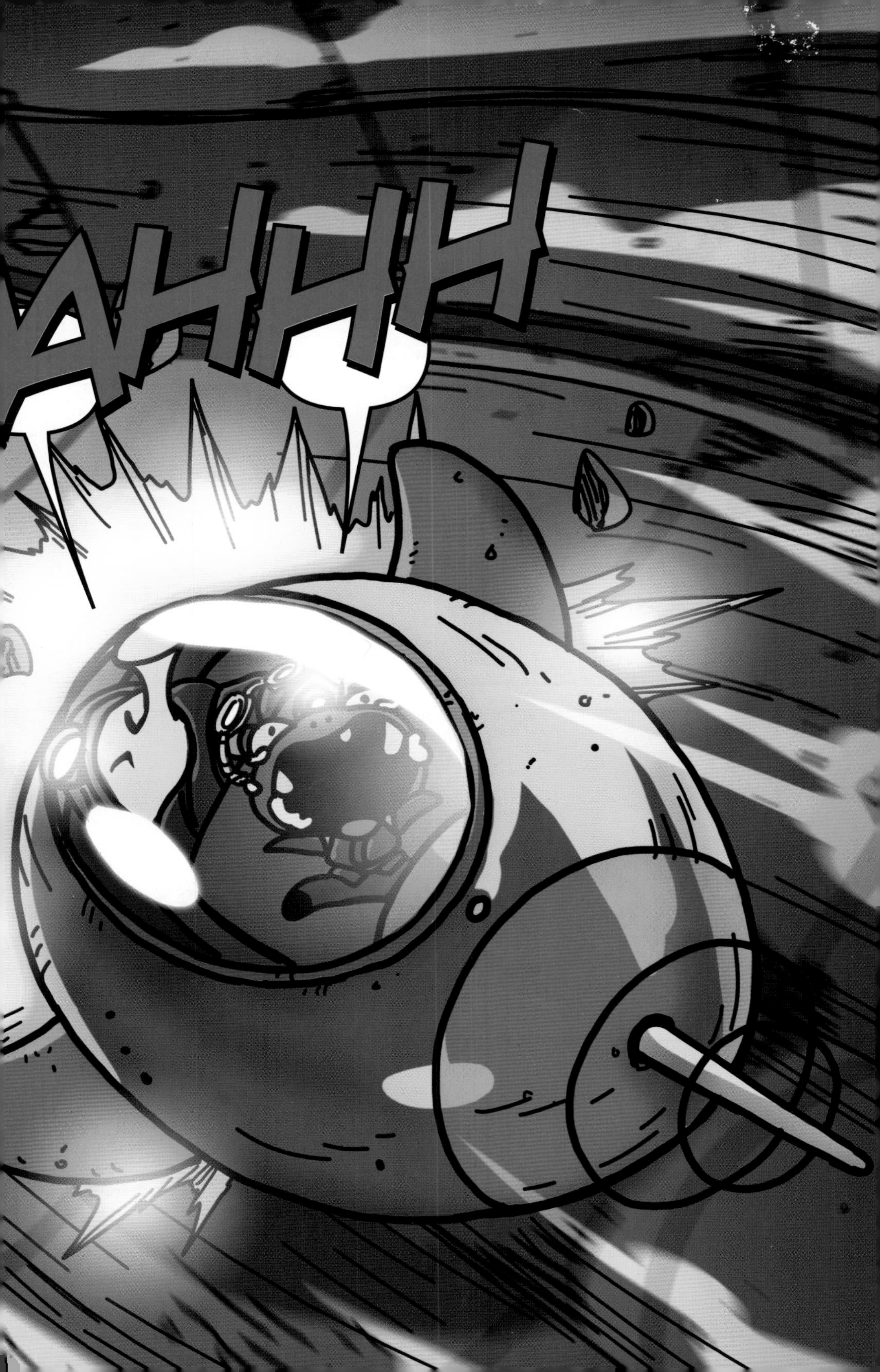
AHHHH

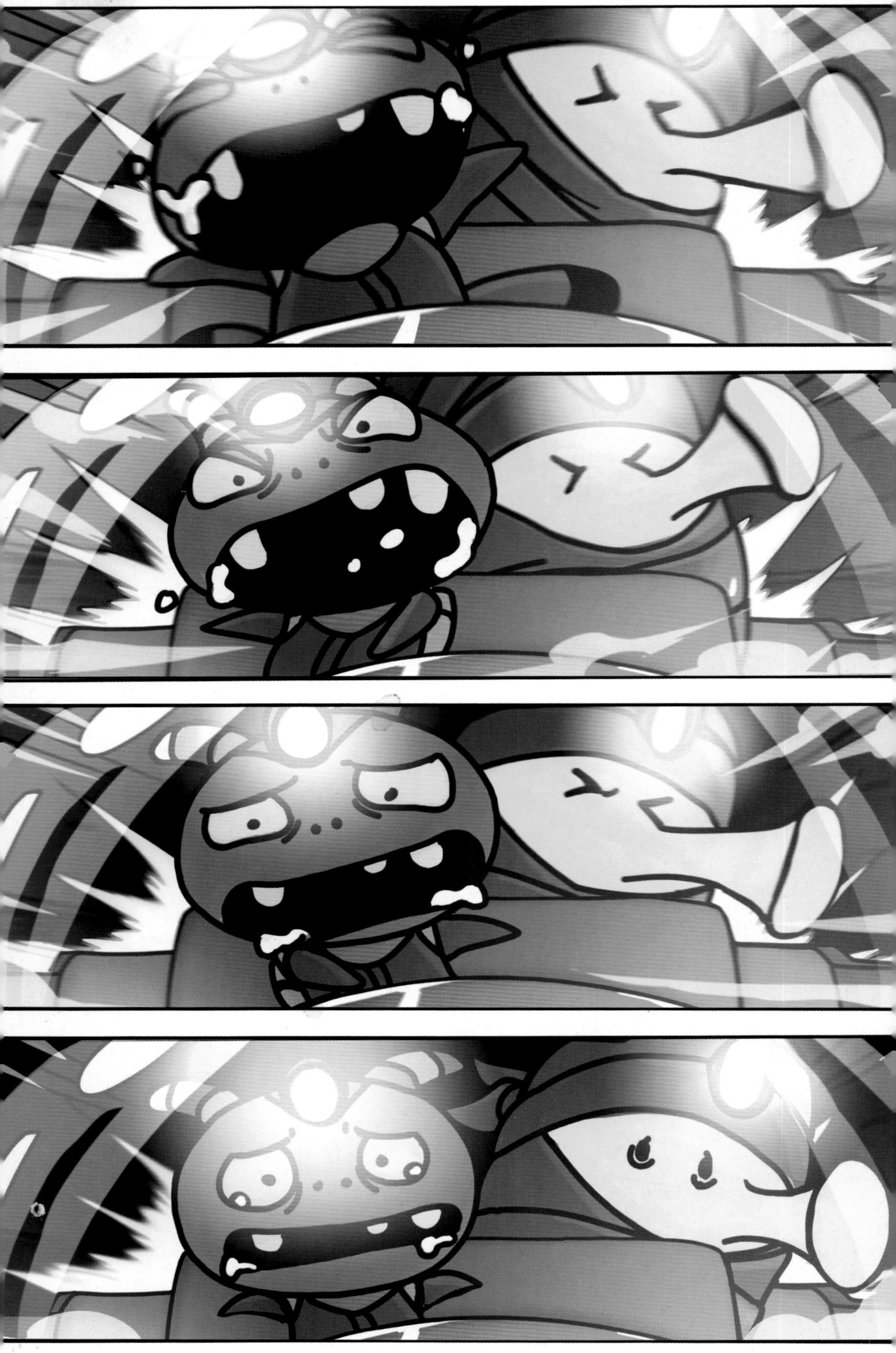

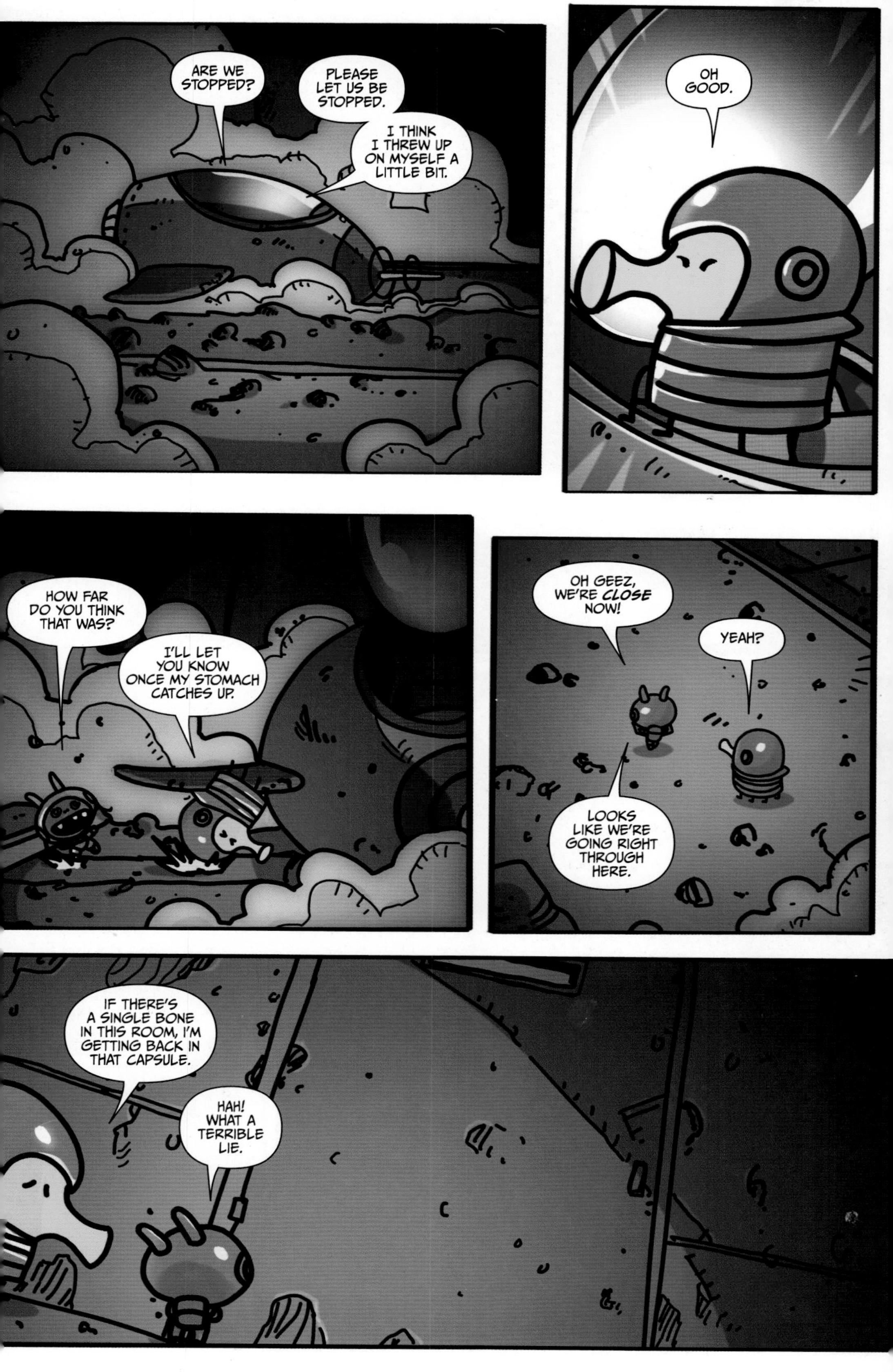
ARE WE STOPPED?
PLEASE LET US BE STOPPED.
I THINK I THREW UP ON MYSELF A LITTLE BIT.
OH GOOD.
HOW FAR DO YOU THINK THAT WAS?
I'LL LET YOU KNOW ONCE MY STOMACH CATCHES UP.
OH GEEZ, WE'RE *CLOSE* NOW!
YEAH?
LOOKS LIKE WE'RE GOING RIGHT THROUGH HERE.
IF THERE'S A SINGLE BONE IN THIS ROOM, I'M GETTING BACK IN THAT CAPSULE.
HAH! WHAT A TERRIBLE LIE.

HELLOOOOO!

GOSH... SOME KIND OF CONTROL ROOM!

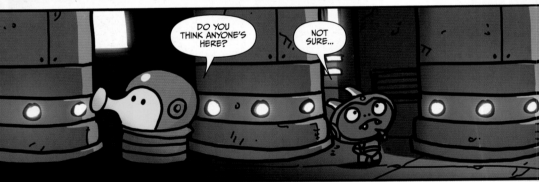

DO YOU THINK ANYONE'S HERE?

NOT SURE...

HEY!!

ANY NERDS IN HERE?!

TRIPLE...!

JUST WONDERING...

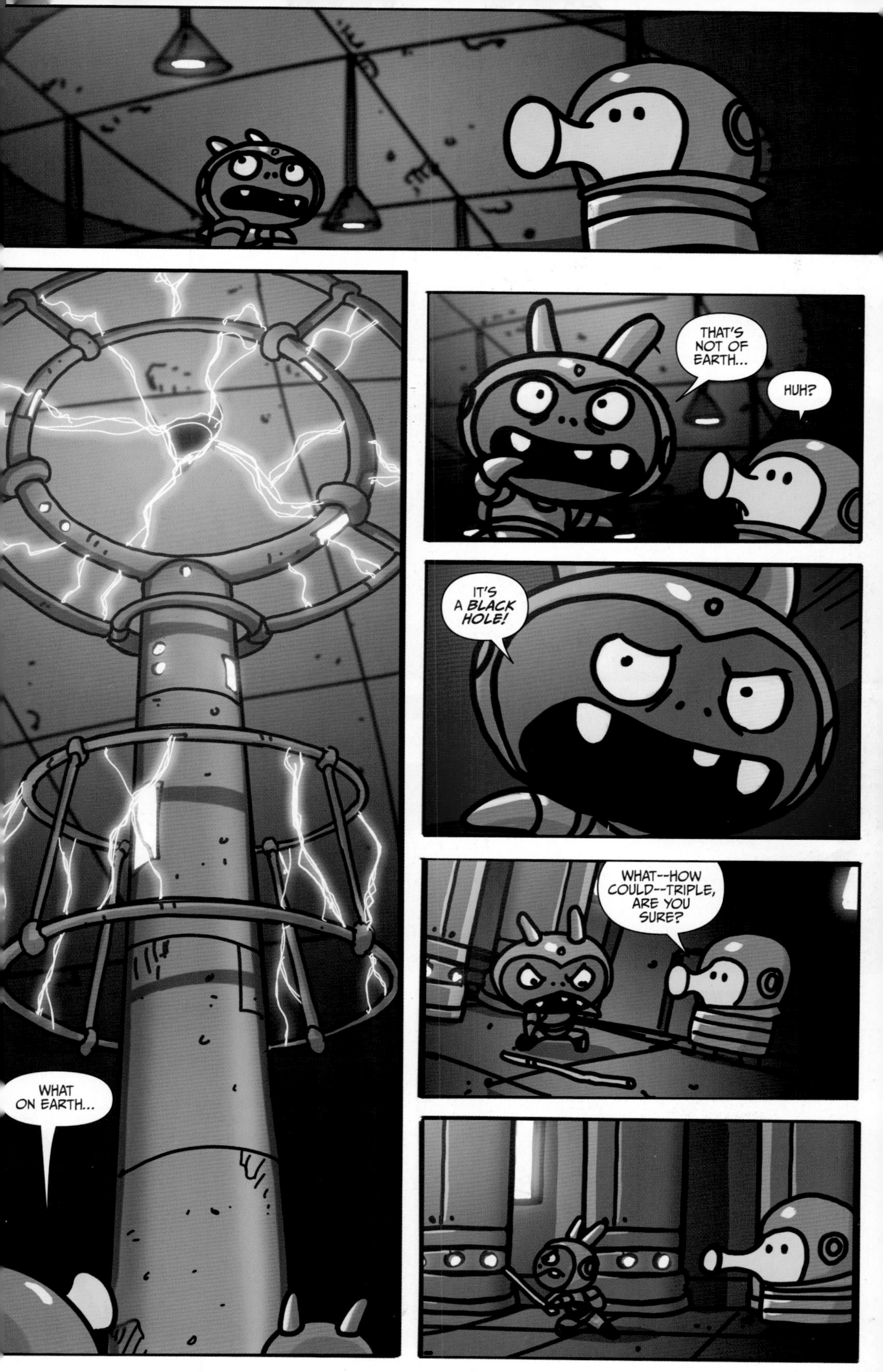
WHAT ON EARTH...
THAT'S NOT OF EARTH...
HUH?
IT'S A *BLACK HOLE!*
WHAT--HOW COULD--TRIPLE, ARE YOU SURE?

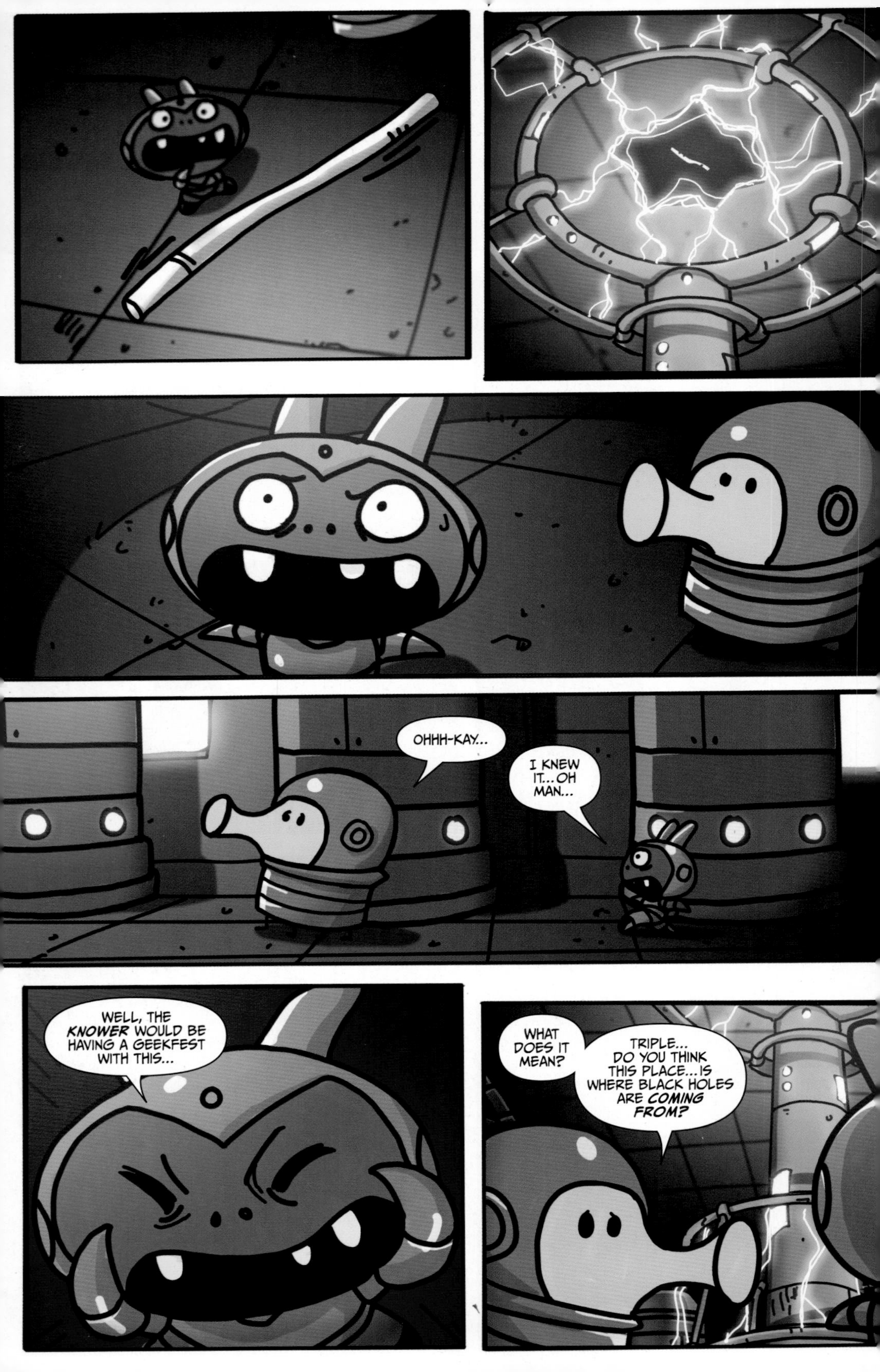
OHHH-KAY...
I KNEW IT...OH MAN...
WELL, THE *KNOWER* WOULD BE HAVING A GEEKFEST WITH THIS...
WHAT DOES IT MEAN?
TRIPLE... DO YOU THINK THIS PLACE...IS WHERE BLACK HOLES ARE *COMING FROM?*

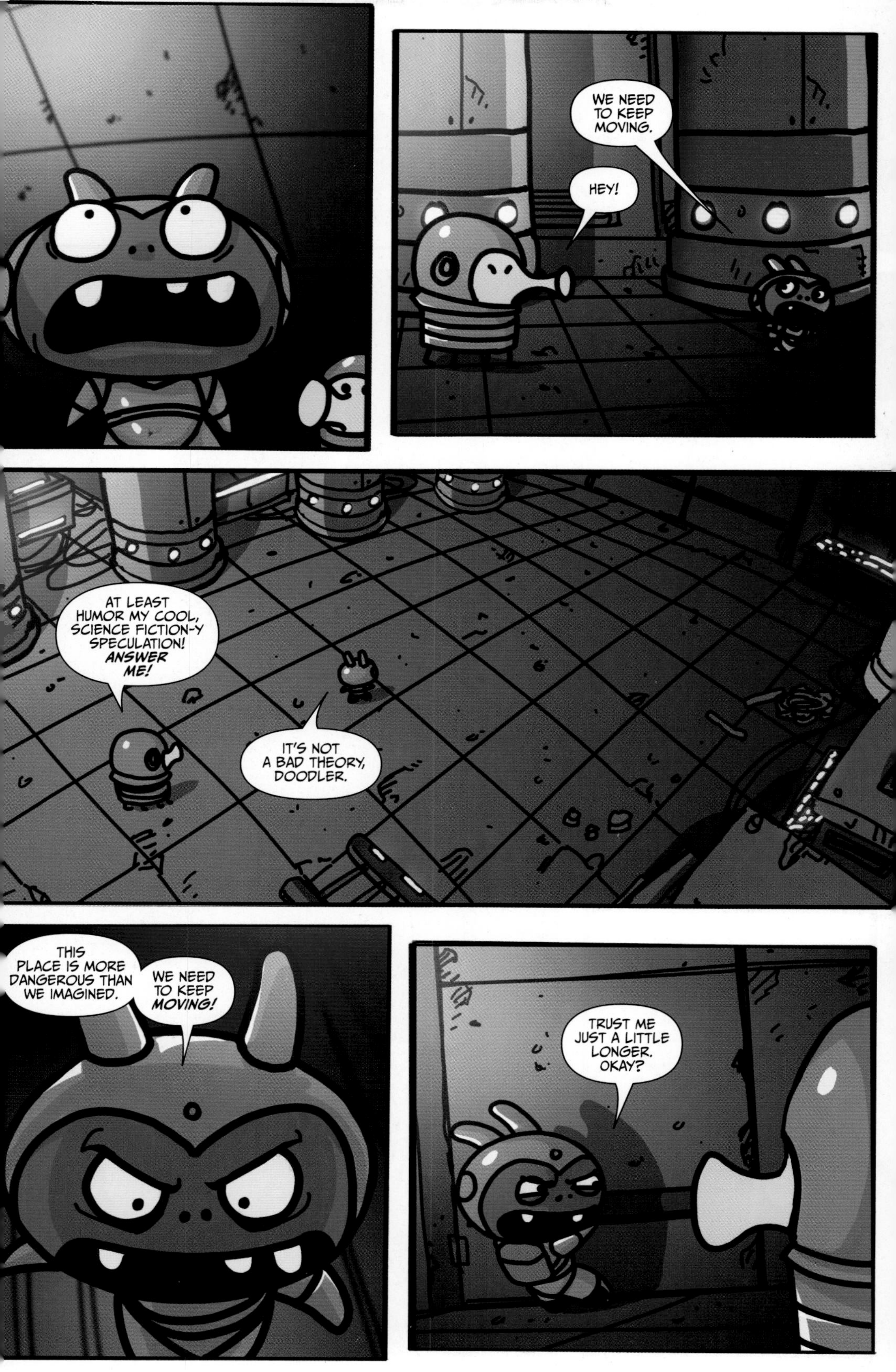

WE NEED TO KEEP MOVING.
HEY!
AT LEAST HUMOR MY COOL, SCIENCE FICTION-Y SPECULATION! *ANSWER ME!*
IT'S NOT A BAD THEORY, DOODLER.
THIS PLACE IS MORE DANGEROUS THAN WE IMAGINED.
WE NEED TO KEEP *MOVING!*
TRUST ME JUST A LITTLE LONGER. OKAY?

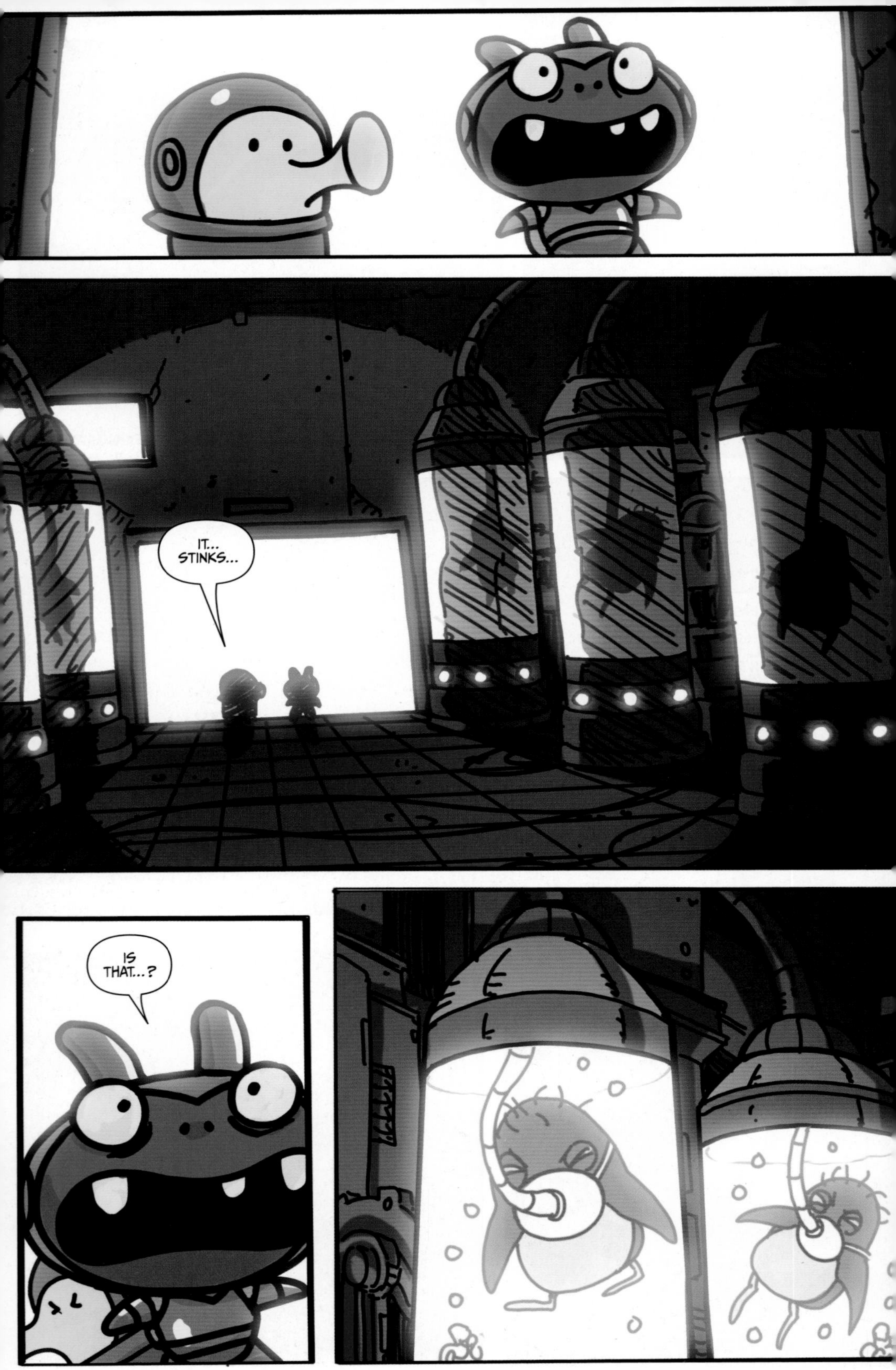
IT... STINKS...
IS THAT...?

THIS... IS...

SICK!!

WHO *DID* THIS TO YOU?!

I DON'T *CARE* HOW DOPEY YOU PENGUINS ARE... NO ONE DESERVES *THIS!*

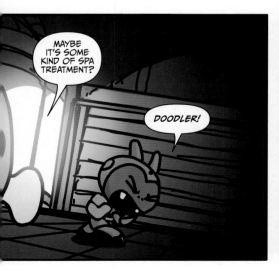

MAYBE IT'S SOME KIND OF SPA TREATMENT?

DOODLER!

WHATEVER'S GOING ON HERE IS PURE, FACTORY SEALED EVIL!

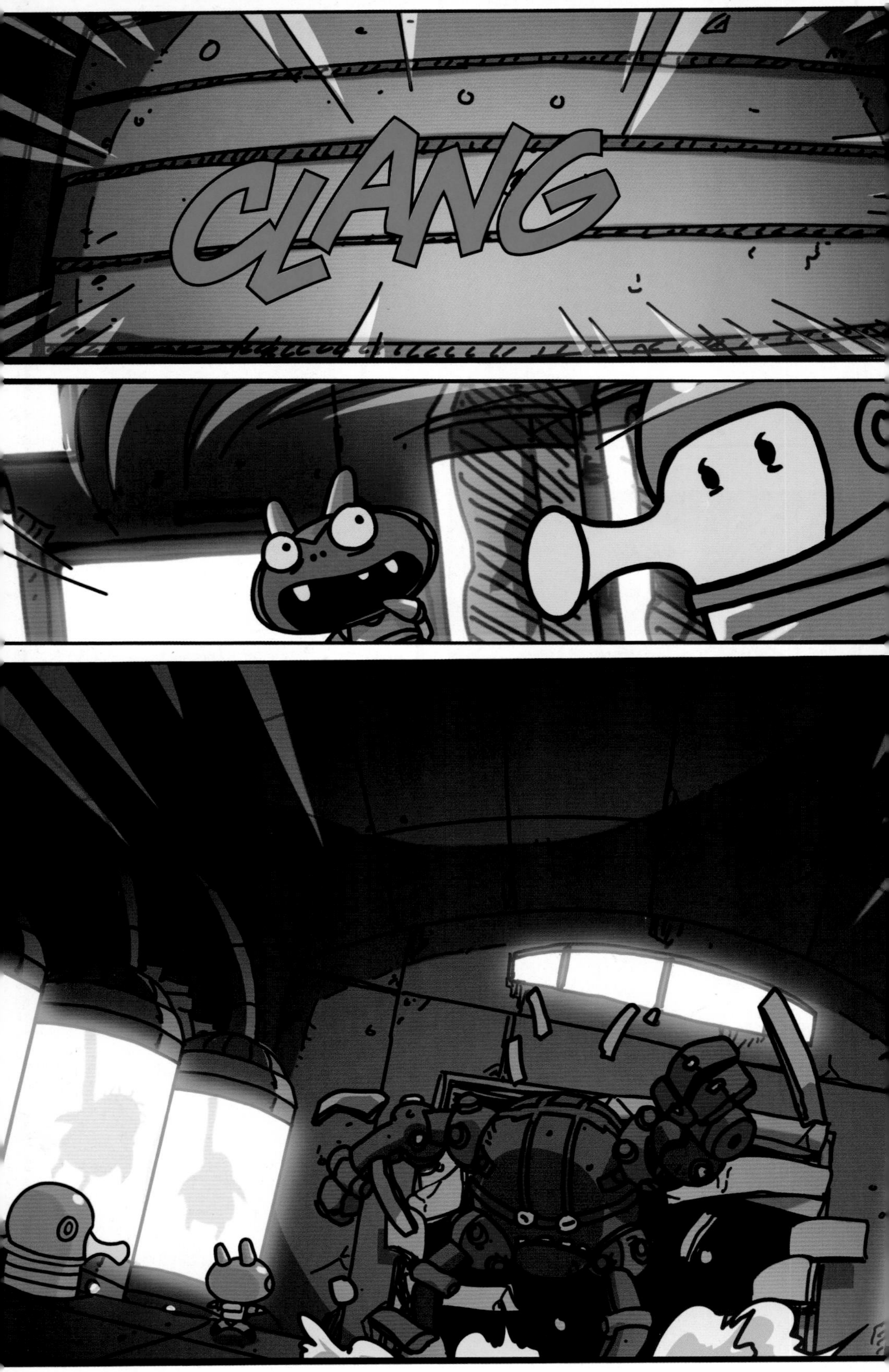
CLANG

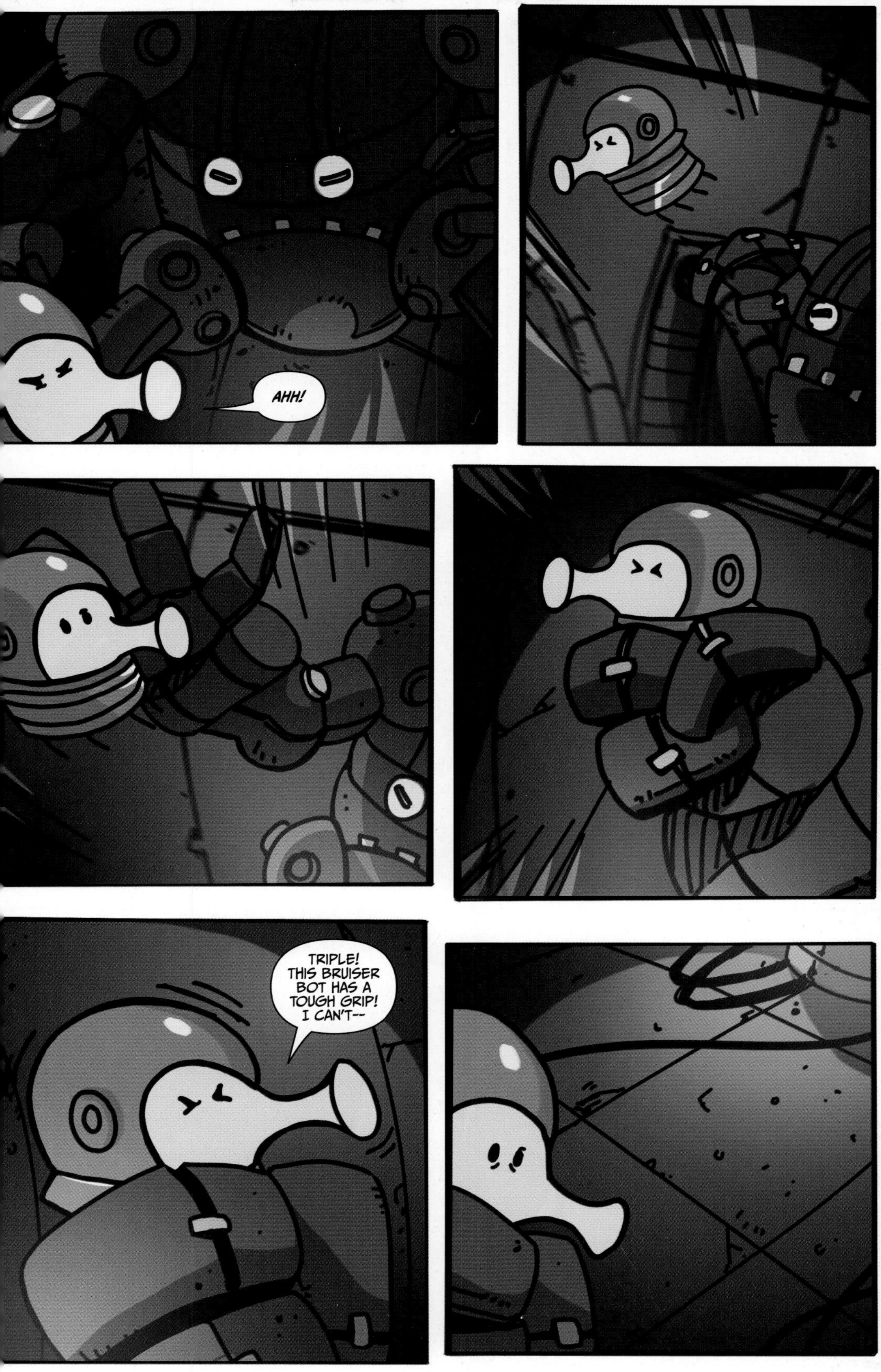
AHH!
TRIPLE! THIS BRUISER BOT HAS A TOUGH GRIP! I CAN'T--

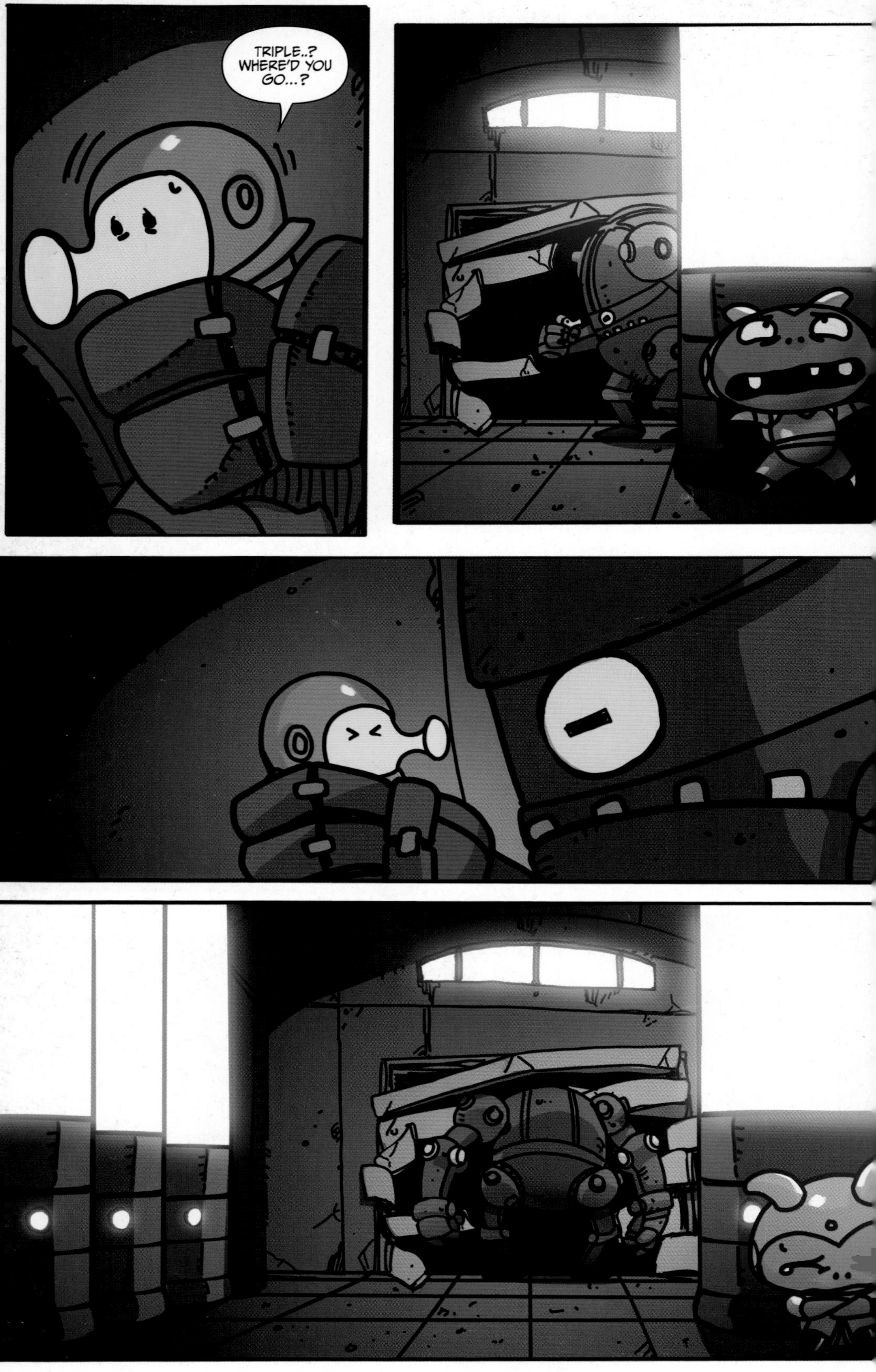
TRIPLE..? WHERE'D YOU GO...?

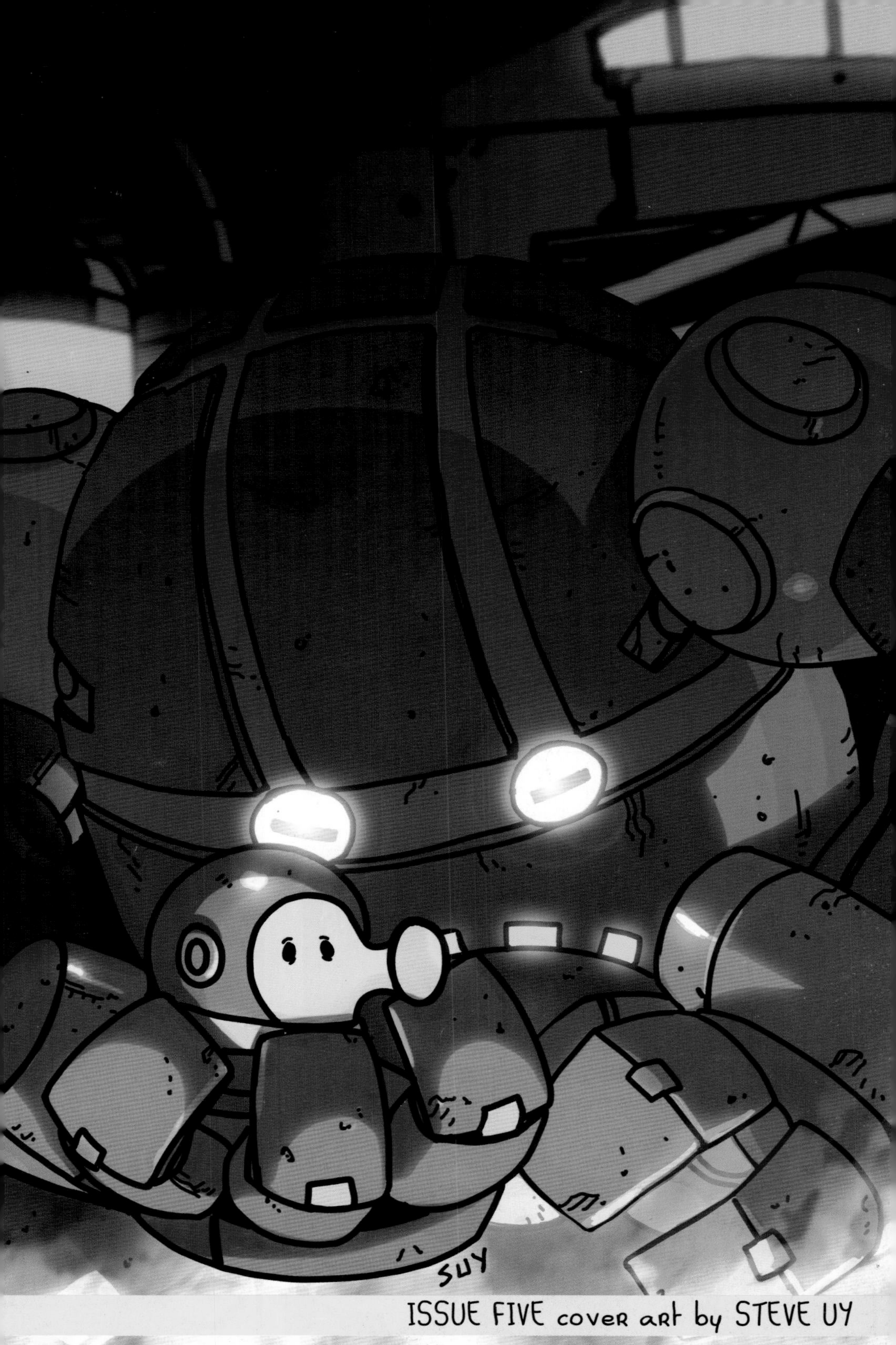
SUY

ISSUE FIVE cover art by STEVE UY

RIGHT THIS WAY.

MIND THE DUST PLEASE. DECORATING IS JUST ONE OF MOMBOT'S MANY JOBS.

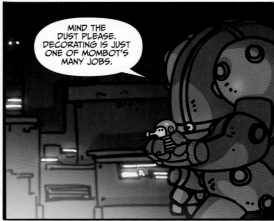

CLANG CLANG CLANG

TRIPLE...HOW COULD YOU JUST... *ABANDON* ME?

I THOUGHT SHE WAS MY FRIEND, AT LEAST...

MOMBOT WILL NEVER ABANDON YOU. I WILL LOVE YOU UNTIL YOUR DEATH.

NOT *YOU*, YOU METAL DUNCE! I'M TALKING ABOUT MY FRIEND!

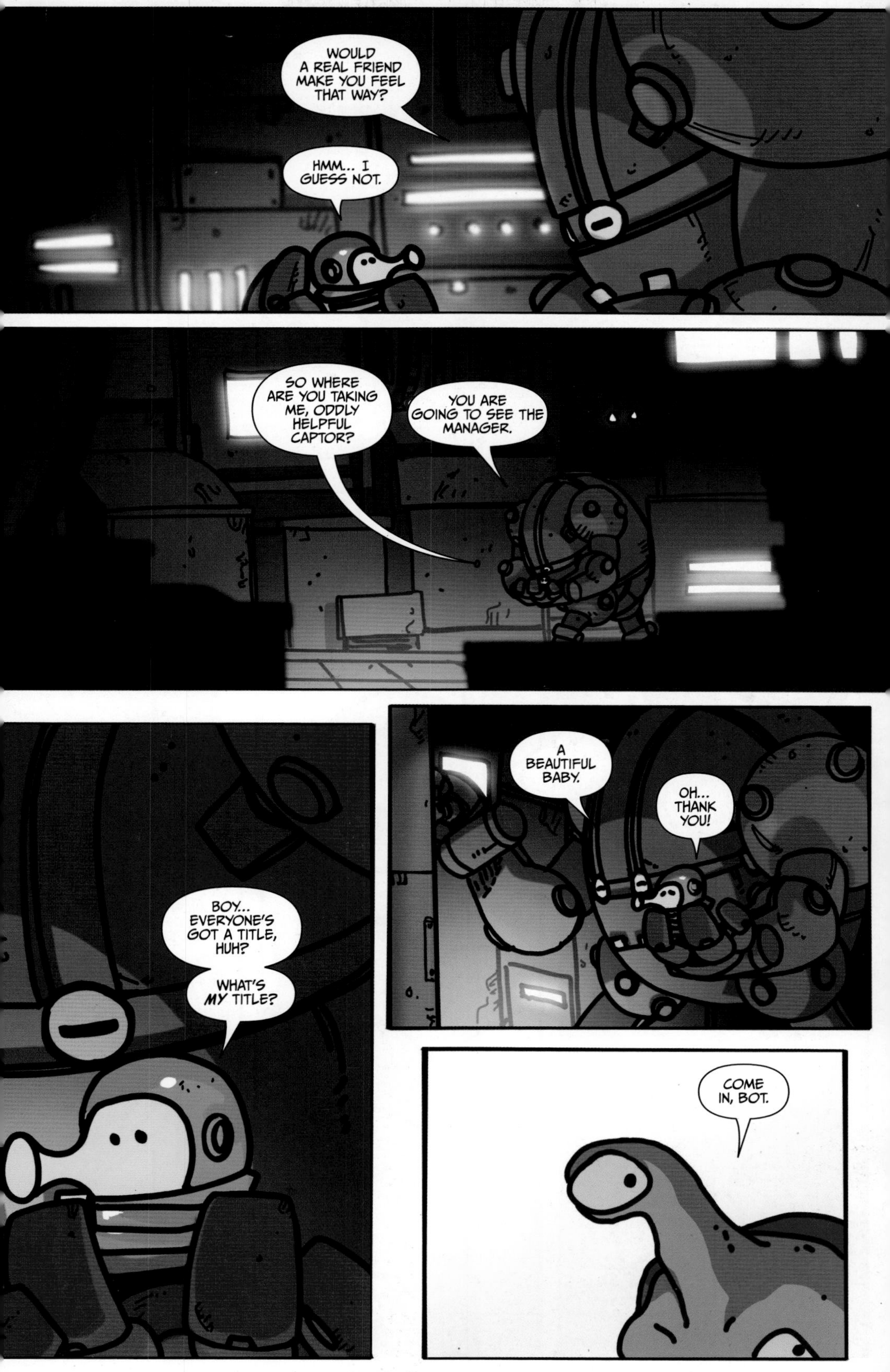
WOULD A REAL FRIEND MAKE YOU FEEL THAT WAY?
HMM... I GUESS NOT.
SO WHERE ARE YOU TAKING ME, ODDLY HELPFUL CAPTOR?
YOU ARE GOING TO SEE THE MANAGER.
BOY... EVERYONE'S GOT A TITLE, HUH?
WHAT'S *MY* TITLE?
A BEAUTIFUL BABY.
OH... THANK YOU!
COME IN, BOT.

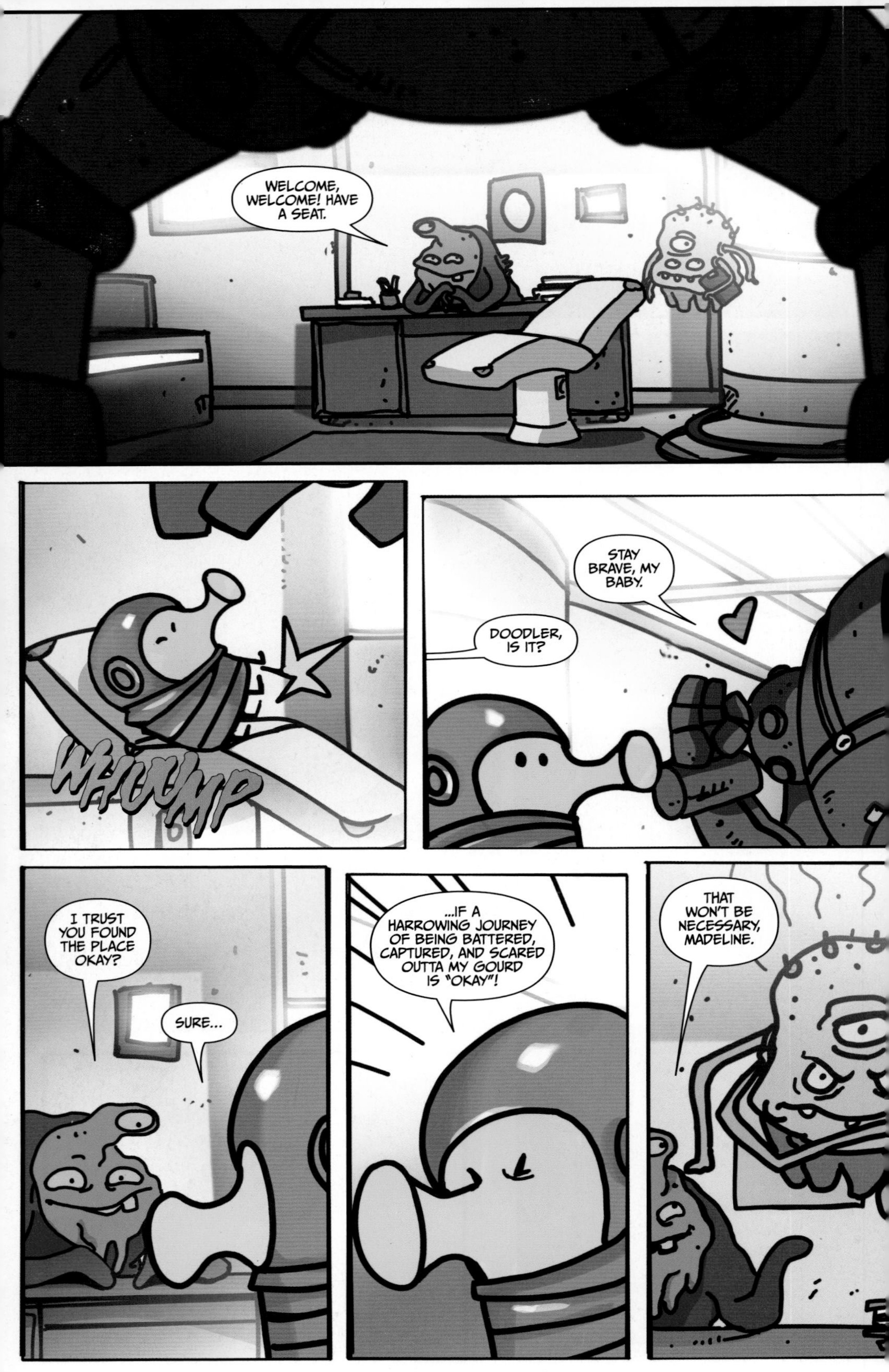
WELCOME, WELCOME! HAVE A SEAT.
WHUUMP
STAY BRAVE, MY BABY.
DOODLER, IS IT?
I TRUST YOU FOUND THE PLACE OKAY?
SURE...
...IF A HARROWING JOURNEY OF BEING BATTERED, CAPTURED, AND SCARED OUTTA MY GOURD IS "OKAY"!
THAT WON'T BE NECESSARY, MADELINE.

I'M CERTAINLY SORRY TO HEAR THAT, DOODLER! MY GOAL IS TO MAKE YOU AS COMFORTABLE AS POSSIBLE.

WHAT'S WITH ALL THE PENGUINS BACK THERE? WHY ARE THEY IN *JARS?*

LIKE BLUBBERY LITTLE *PICKLES?*

ARE YOU THE REASON THE PENGUINS HAVE GONE CRAZY?

THE "CRAZY", AS YOU SAY, WAS AN UNFORTUNATE SIDE EFFECT.

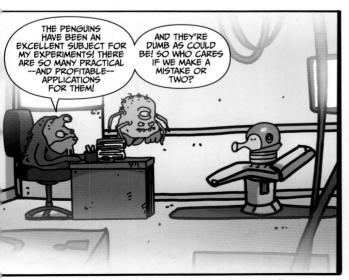

THE PENGUINS HAVE BEEN AN EXCELLENT SUBJECT FOR MY EXPERIMENTS! THERE ARE SO MANY PRACTICAL --AND PROFITABLE-- APPLICATIONS FOR THEM!

AND THEY'RE DUMB AS COULD BE! SO WHO CARES IF WE MAKE A MISTAKE OR TWO?

BUT I WON'T MAKE THE SAME MISTAKES AGAIN. NOT WITH YOU.

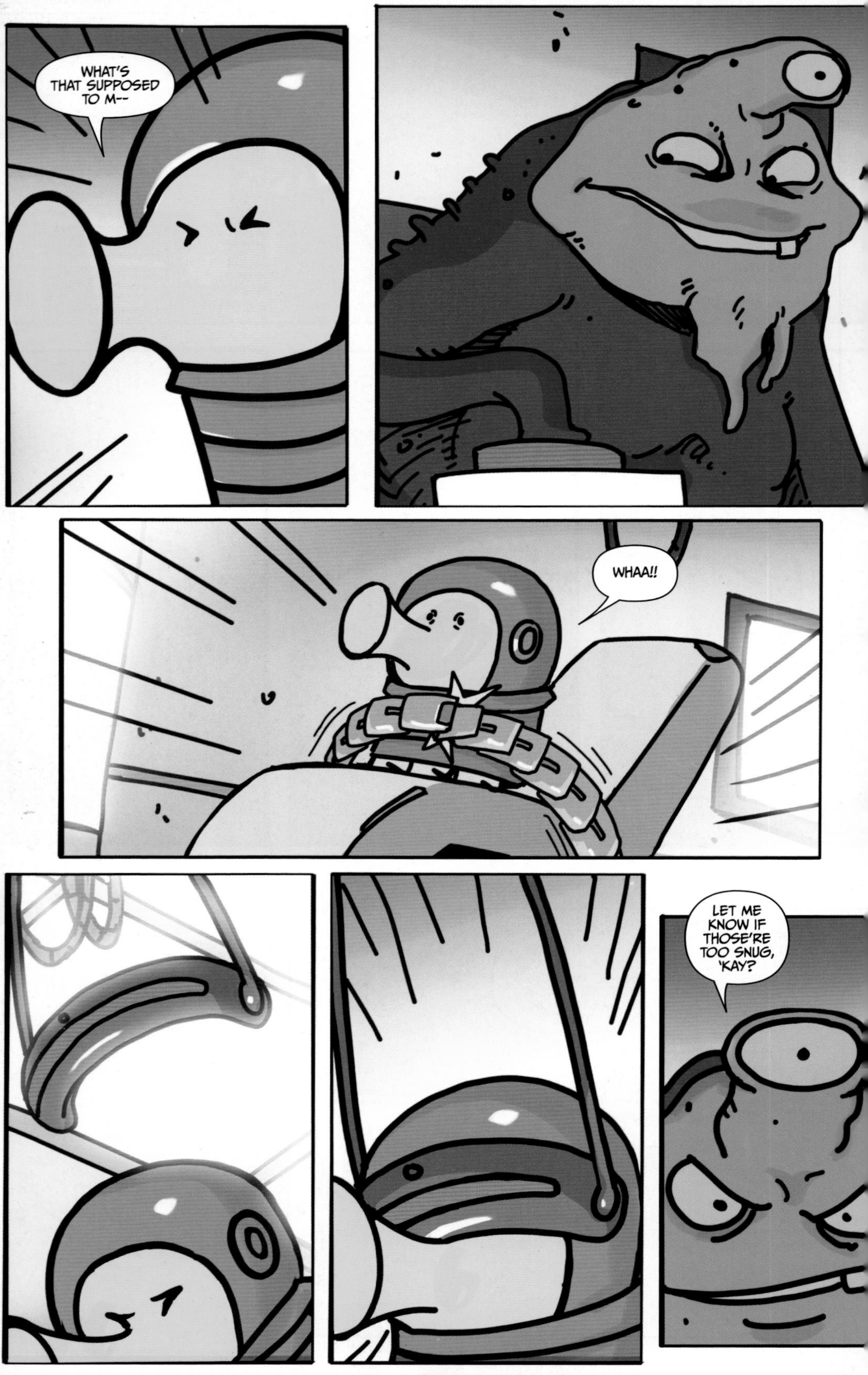
WHAT'S THAT SUPPOSED TO M--
WHAA!!
LET ME KNOW IF THOSE'RE TOO SNUG, 'KAY?

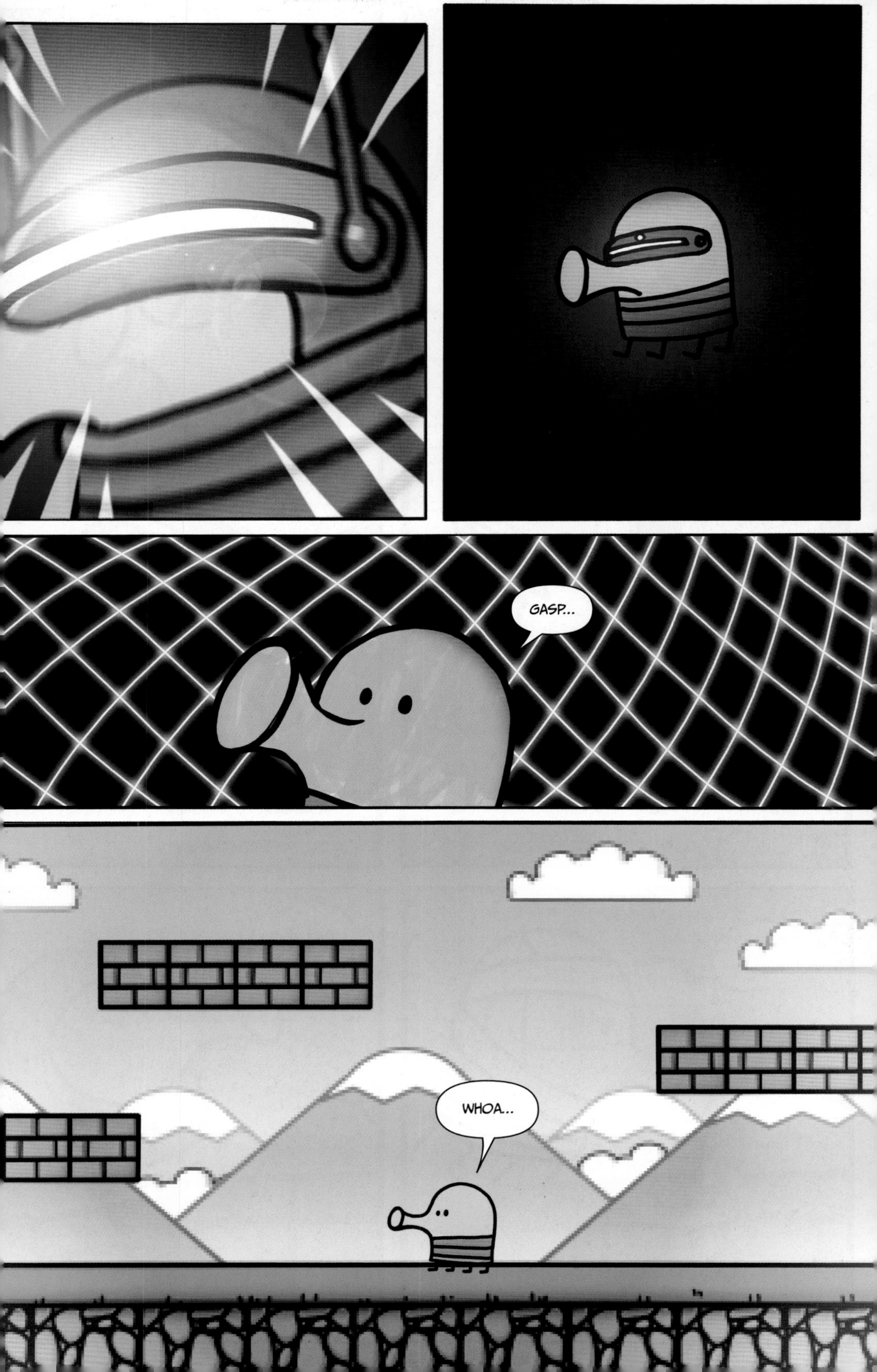
GASP...
WHOA...

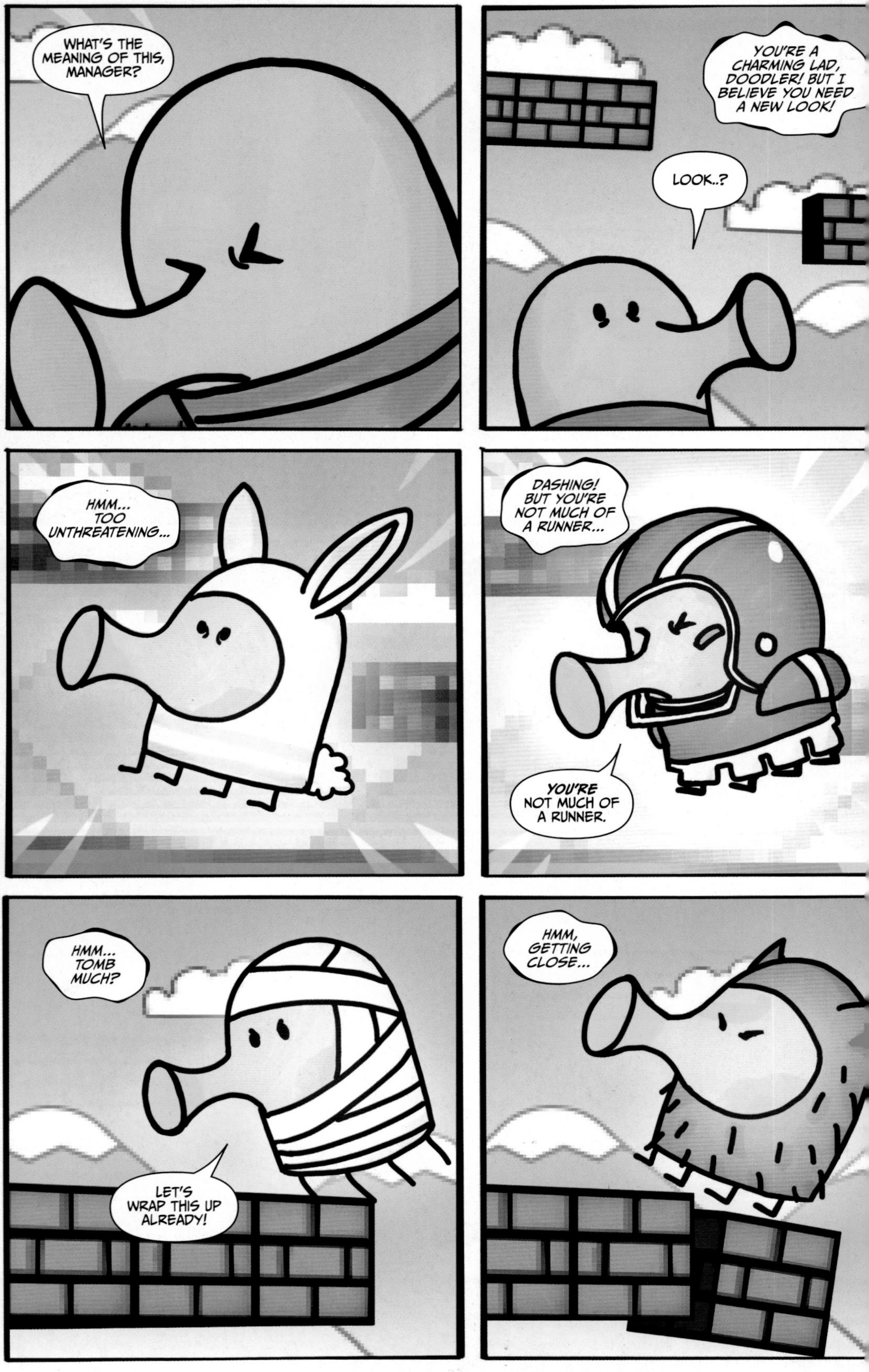
WHAT'S THE MEANING OF THIS, MANAGER?
YOU'RE A CHARMING LAD, DOODLER! BUT I BELIEVE YOU NEED A NEW LOOK!
LOOK..?
HMM... TOO UNTHREATENING...
DASHING! BUT YOU'RE NOT MUCH OF A RUNNER...
YOU'RE NOT MUCH OF A RUNNER.
HMM... TOMB MUCH?
LET'S WRAP THIS UP ALREADY!
HMM, GETTING CLOSE...

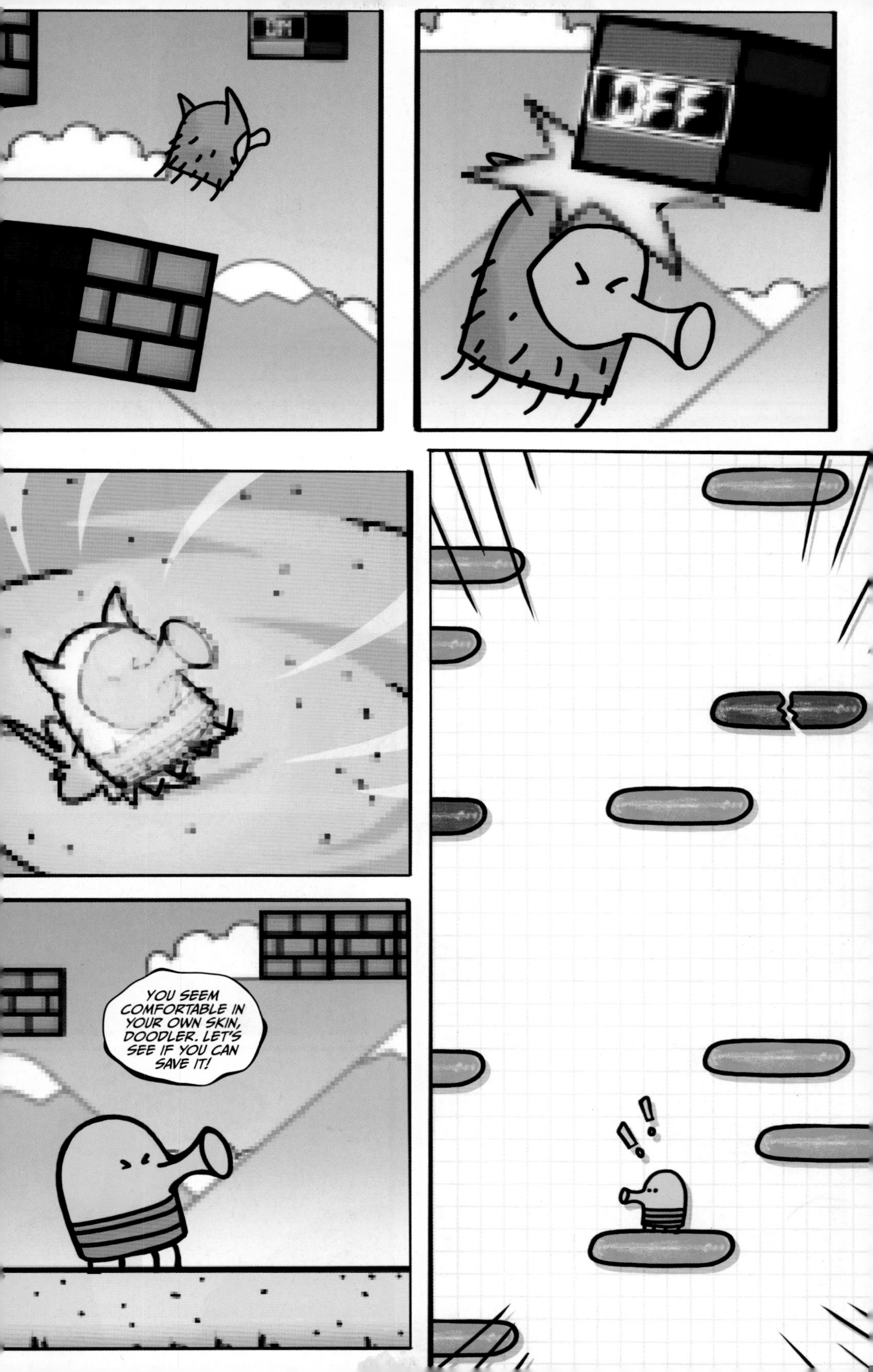
OFF
YOU SEEM COMFORTABLE IN YOUR OWN SKIN, DOODLER. LET'S SEE IF YOU CAN SAVE IT!

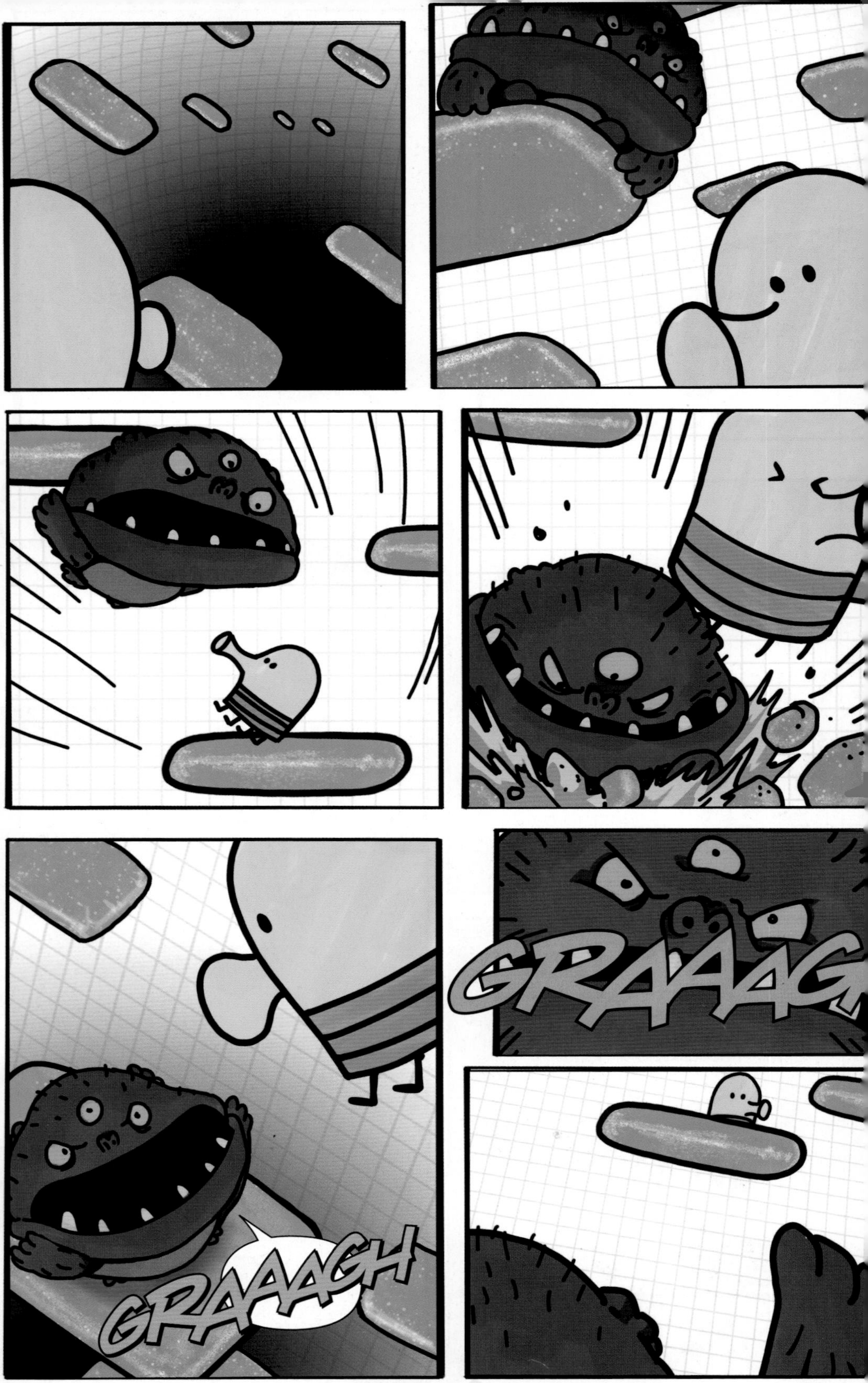
GRAAAGH
GRAAAGH

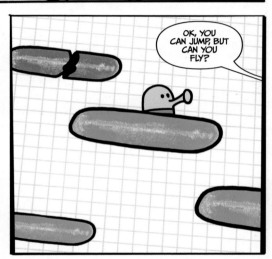

OK, YOU CAN JUMP, BUT CAN YOU FLY?

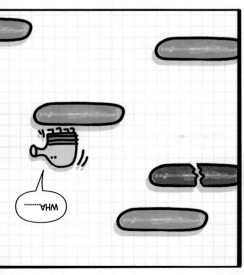

.........WHA

AAAAHHHH

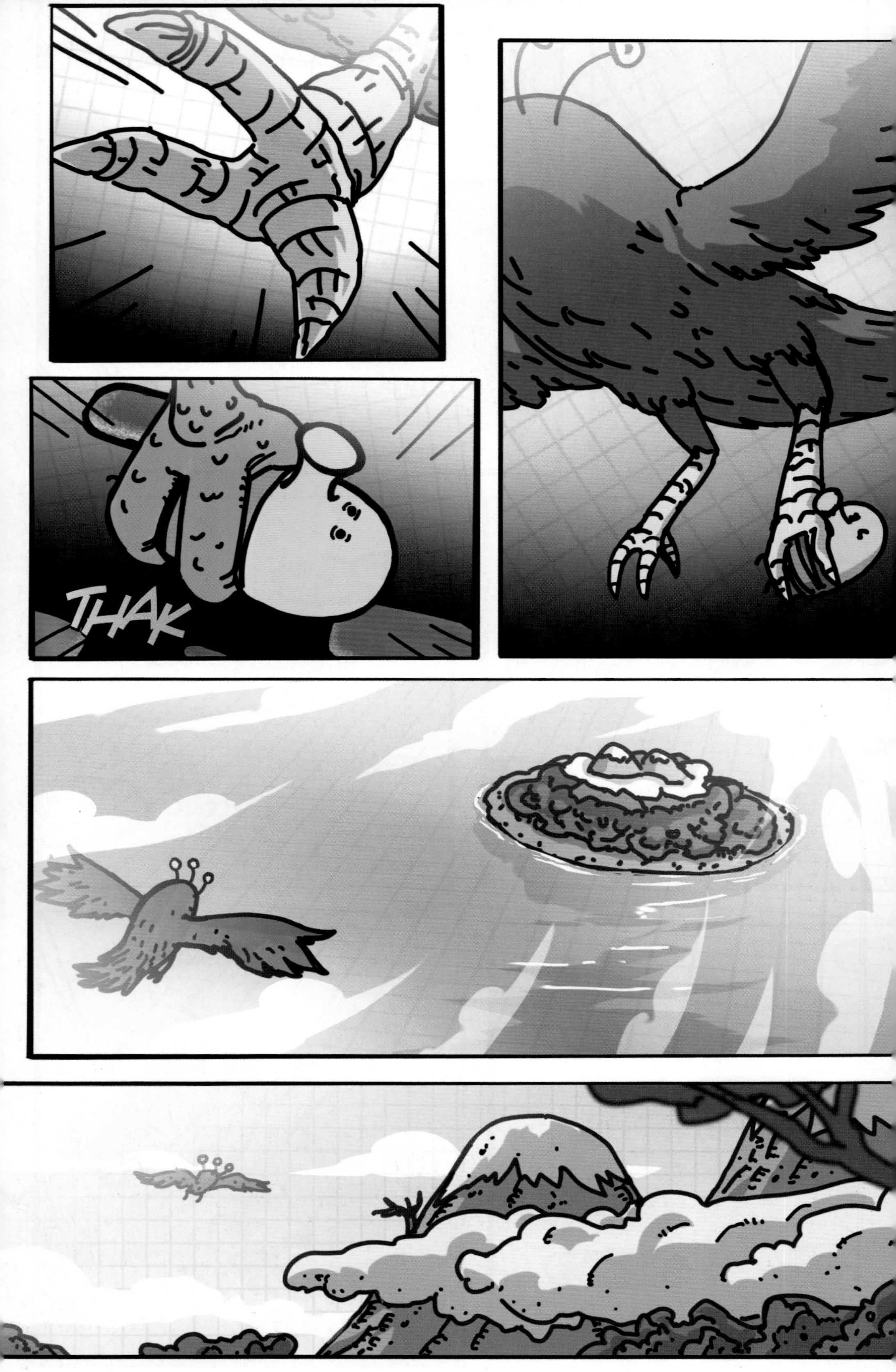
THAK

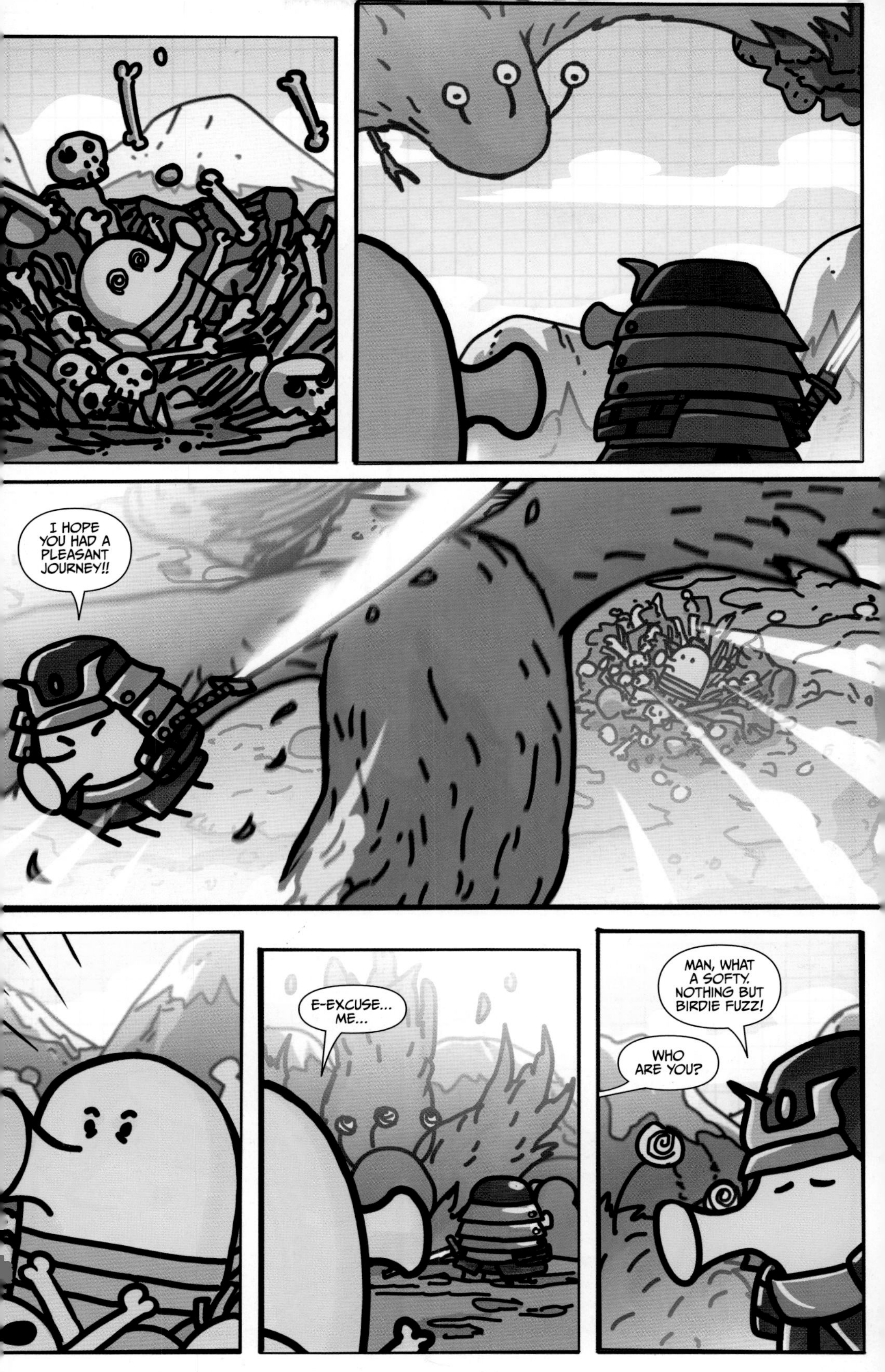
I HOPE YOU HAD A PLEASANT JOURNEY!!
E-EXCUSE... ME...
MAN, WHAT A SOFTY. NOTHING BUT BIRDIE FUZZ!
WHO ARE YOU?

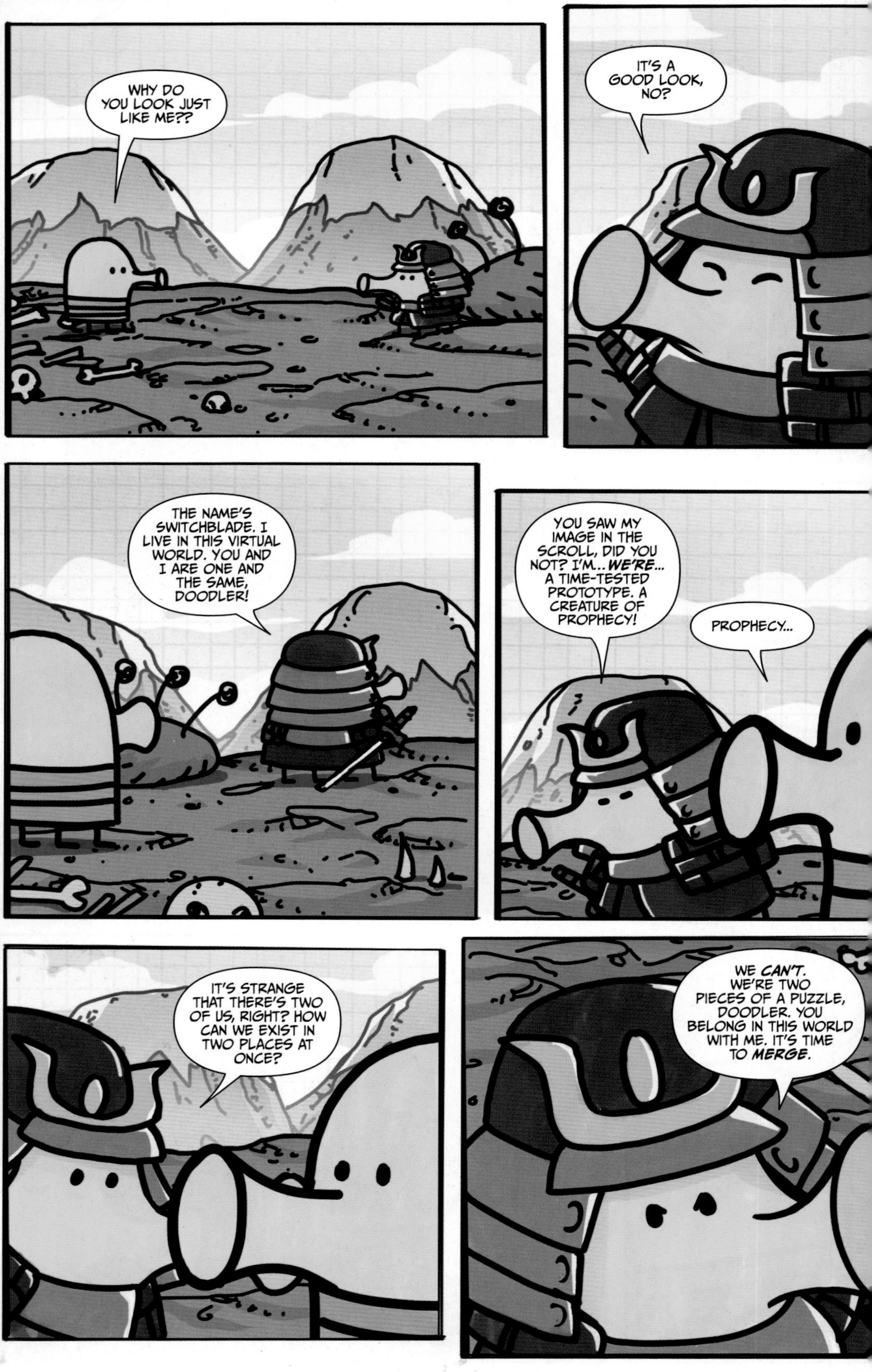
WHY DO YOU LOOK JUST LIKE ME??
IT'S A GOOD LOOK, NO?
THE NAME'S SWITCHBLADE. I LIVE IN THIS VIRTUAL WORLD. YOU AND I ARE ONE AND THE SAME, DOODLER!
YOU SAW MY IMAGE IN THE SCROLL, DID YOU NOT? I'M... *WE'RE*... A TIME-TESTED PROTOTYPE. A CREATURE OF PROPHECY!
PROPHECY...
IT'S STRANGE THAT THERE'S TWO OF US, RIGHT? HOW CAN WE EXIST IN TWO PLACES AT ONCE?
WE *CAN'T*. WE'RE TWO PIECES OF A PUZZLE, DOODLER. YOU BELONG IN THIS WORLD WITH ME. IT'S TIME TO *MERGE*.

MUH-MERGE..?

NO... I CAN'T-- THAT WOULDN'T--

DON'T BE AFRAID. IT'S COMPLETELY PAINLESS.

NO...!

I DON'T EXACTLY HAVE *TIME* FOR YOU TO THINK IT OVER...

NO!

GET BACK HERE!!!

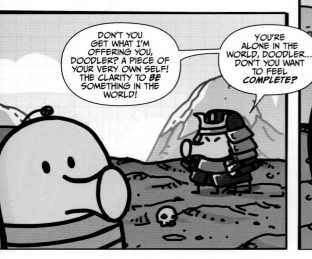

DON'T YOU GET WHAT I'M OFFERING YOU, DOODLER? A PIECE OF YOUR VERY OWN SELF! THE CLARITY TO *BE* SOMETHING IN THE WORLD!

YOU'RE ALONE IN THE WORLD, DOODLER... DON'T YOU WANT TO FEEL *COMPLETE?*

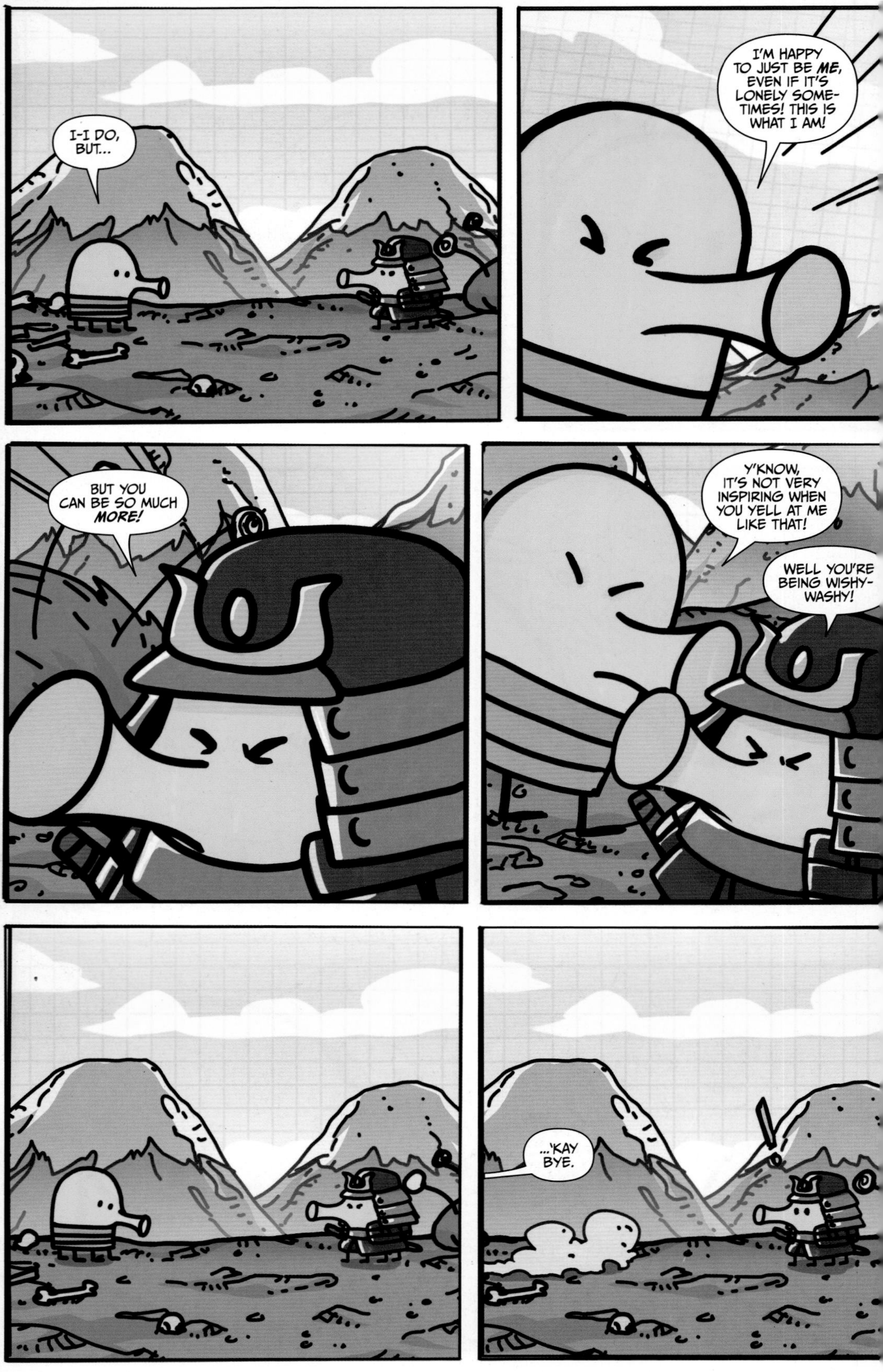
I-I DO, BUT...
I'M HAPPY TO JUST BE *ME*, EVEN IF IT'S LONELY SOME-TIMES! THIS IS WHAT I AM!
BUT YOU CAN BE SO MUCH *MORE!*
Y'KNOW, IT'S NOT VERY INSPIRING WHEN YOU YELL AT ME LIKE THAT!
WELL YOU'RE BEING WISHY-WASHY!
...'KAY BYE.

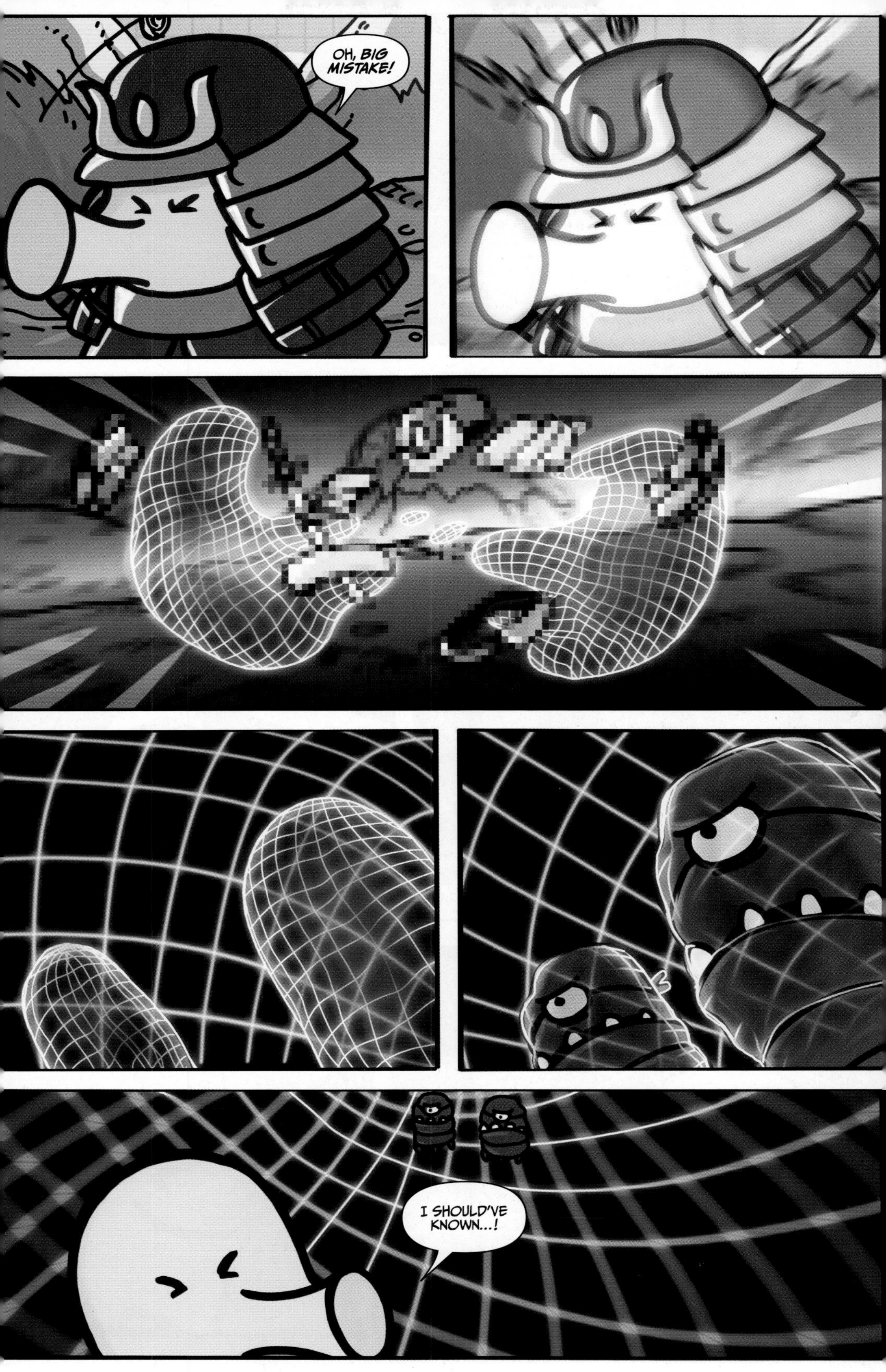
OH, BIG MISTAKE!
I SHOULD'VE KNOWN...!

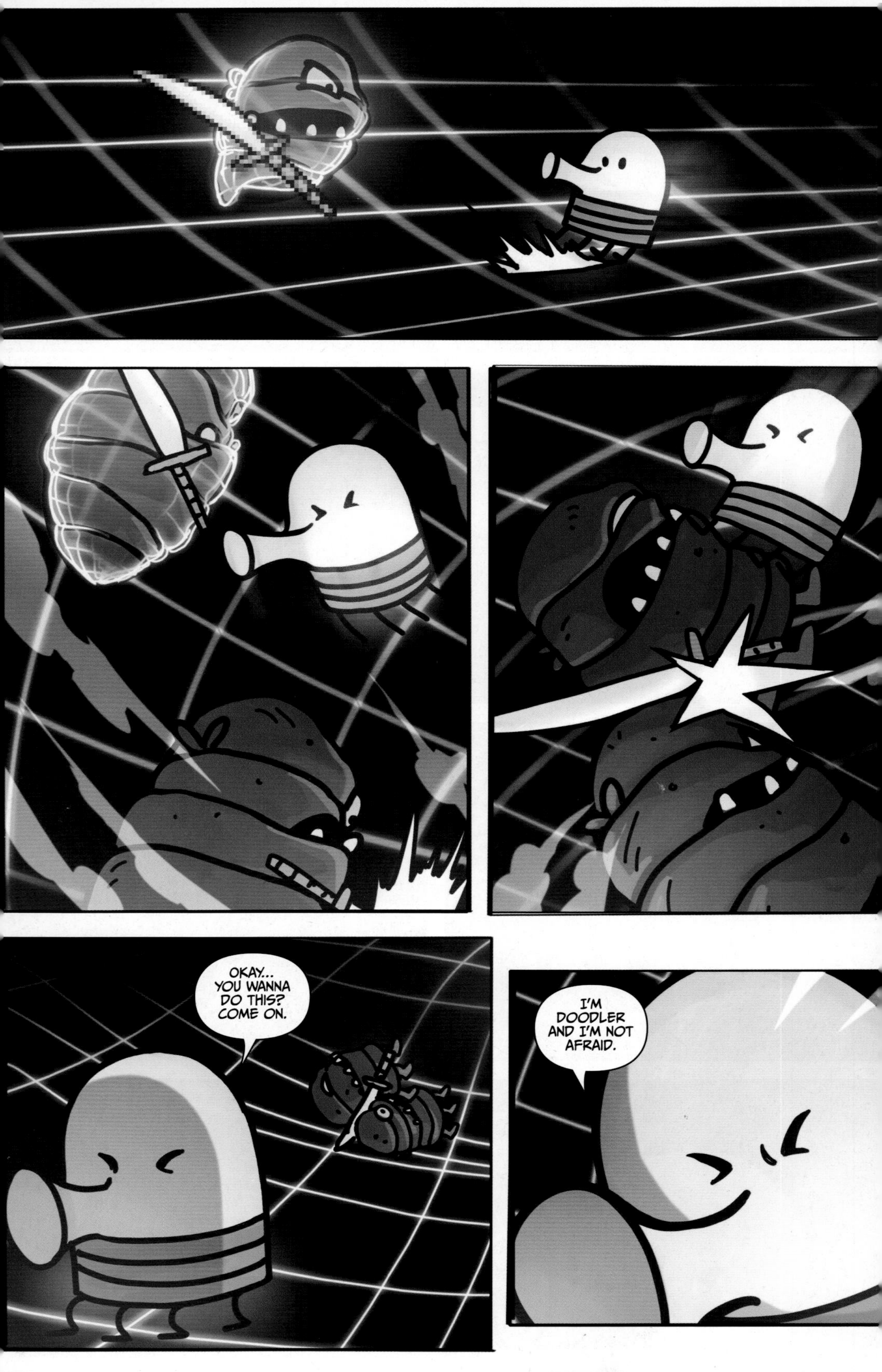
OKAY... YOU WANNA DO THIS? COME ON.
I'M DOODLER AND I'M NOT AFRAID.

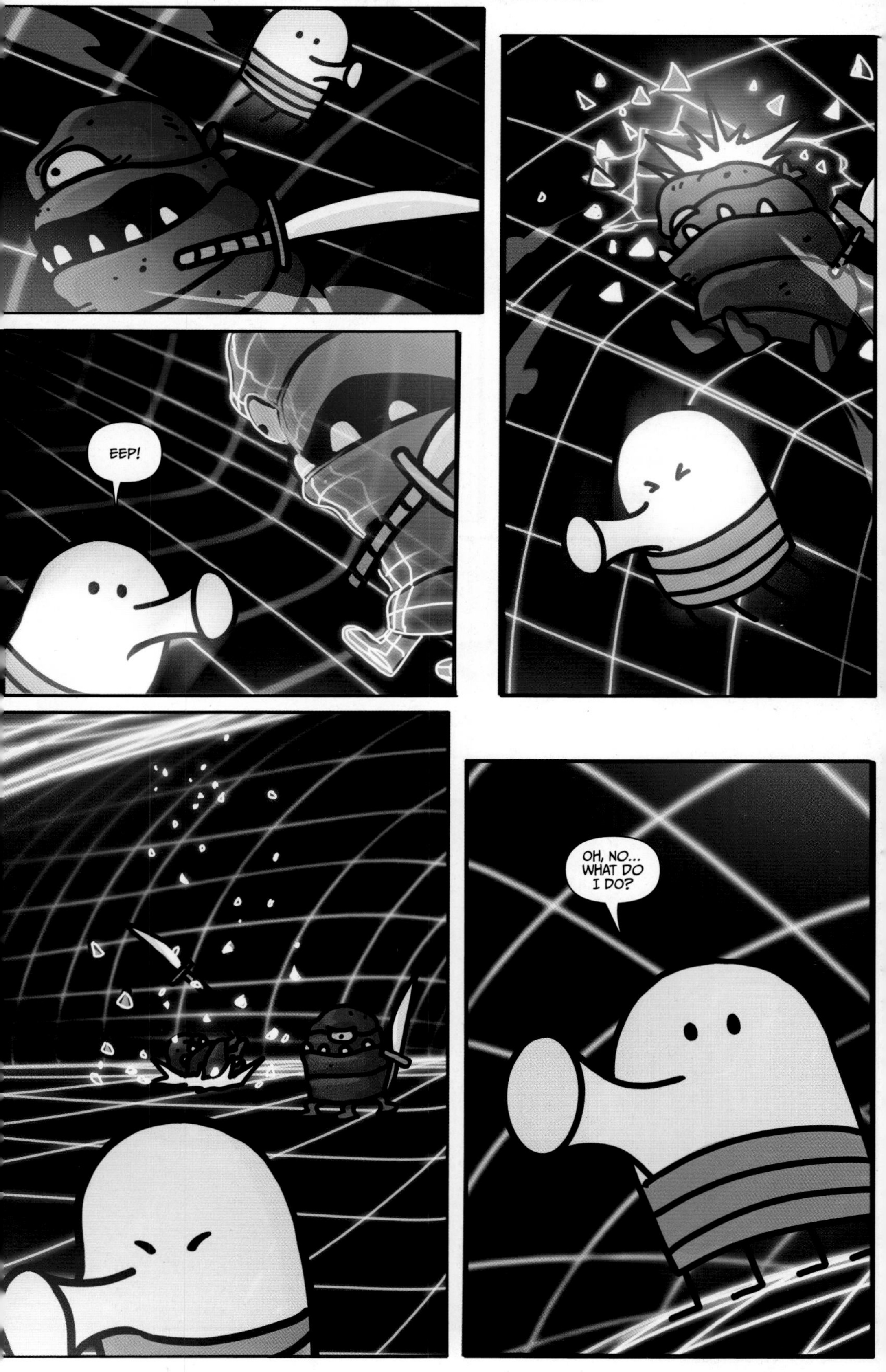
EEP!
OH, NO... WHAT DO I DO?

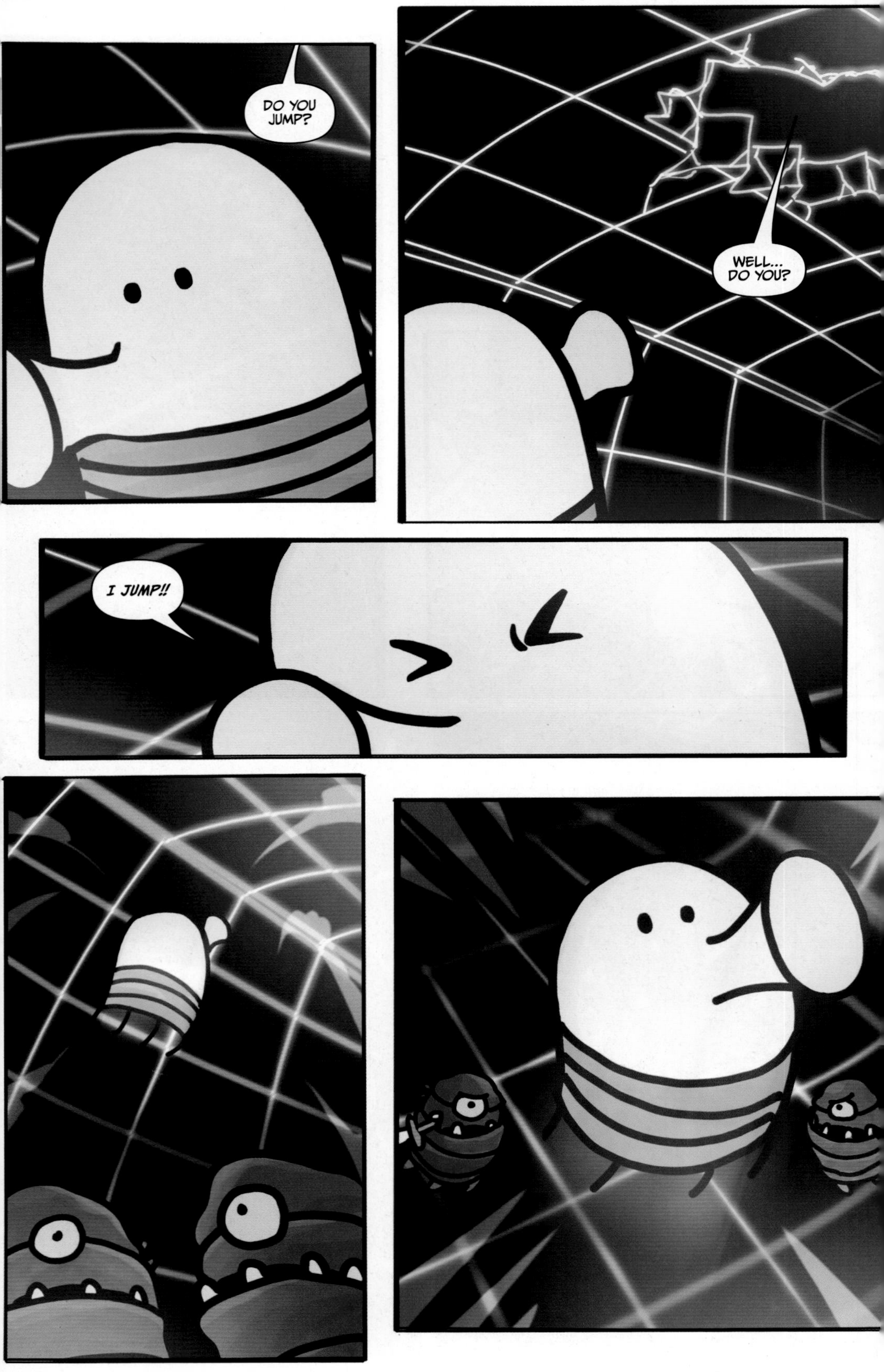
DO YOU JUMP?
WELL... DO YOU?
I JUMP!!

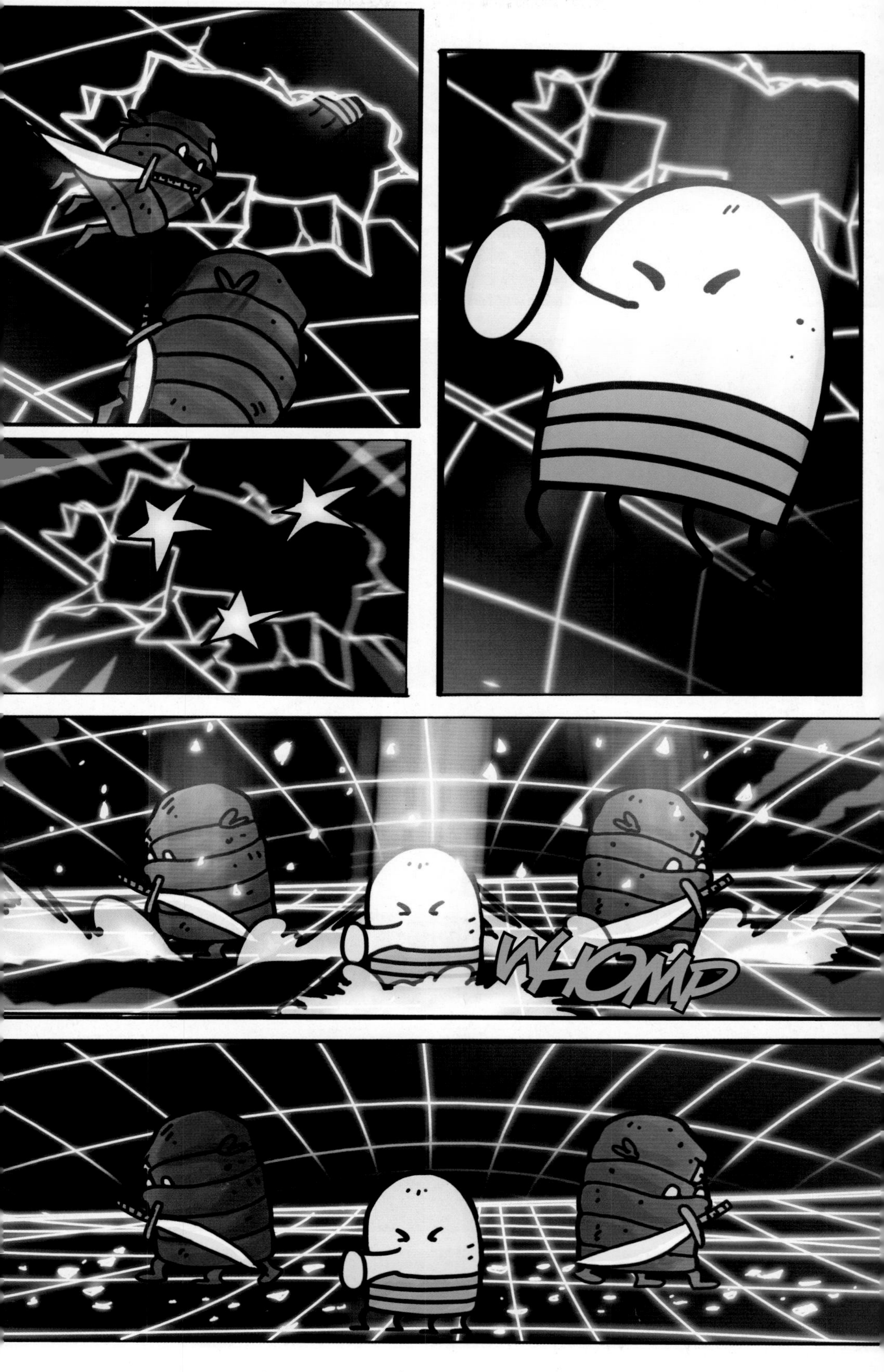
WHOMP

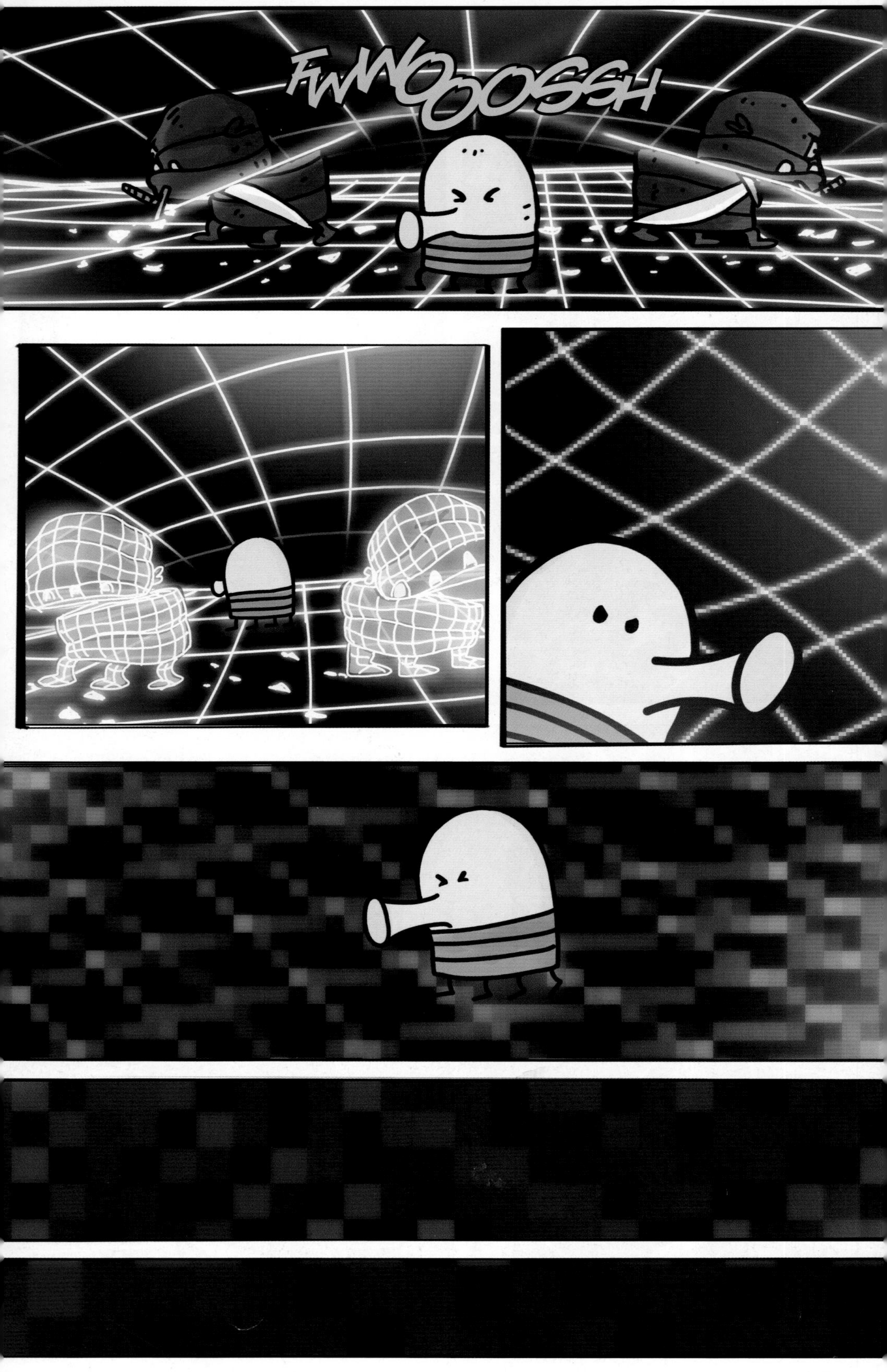
FWWOOOOSSH

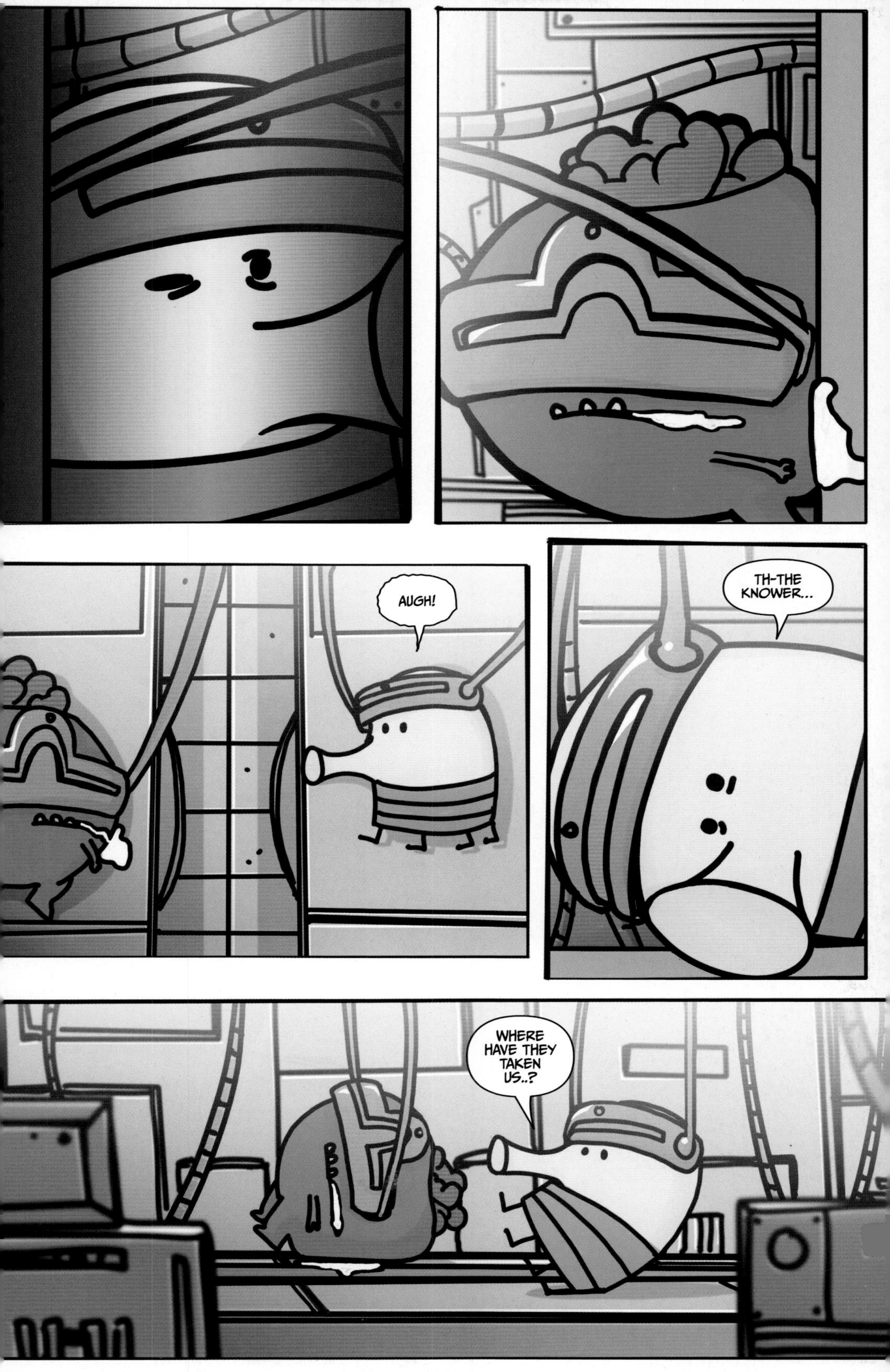
AUGH!
TH-THE KNOWER...
WHERE HAVE THEY TAKEN US..?

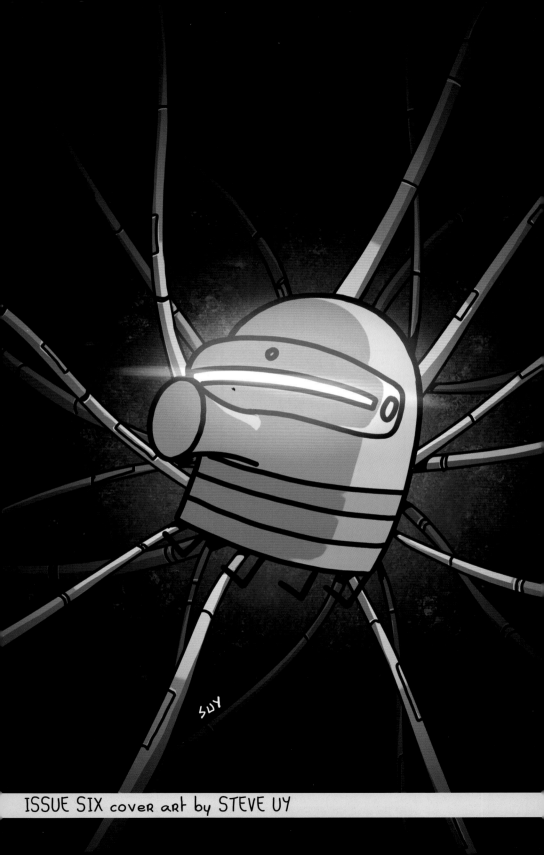

ISSUE SIX cover art by STEVE UY

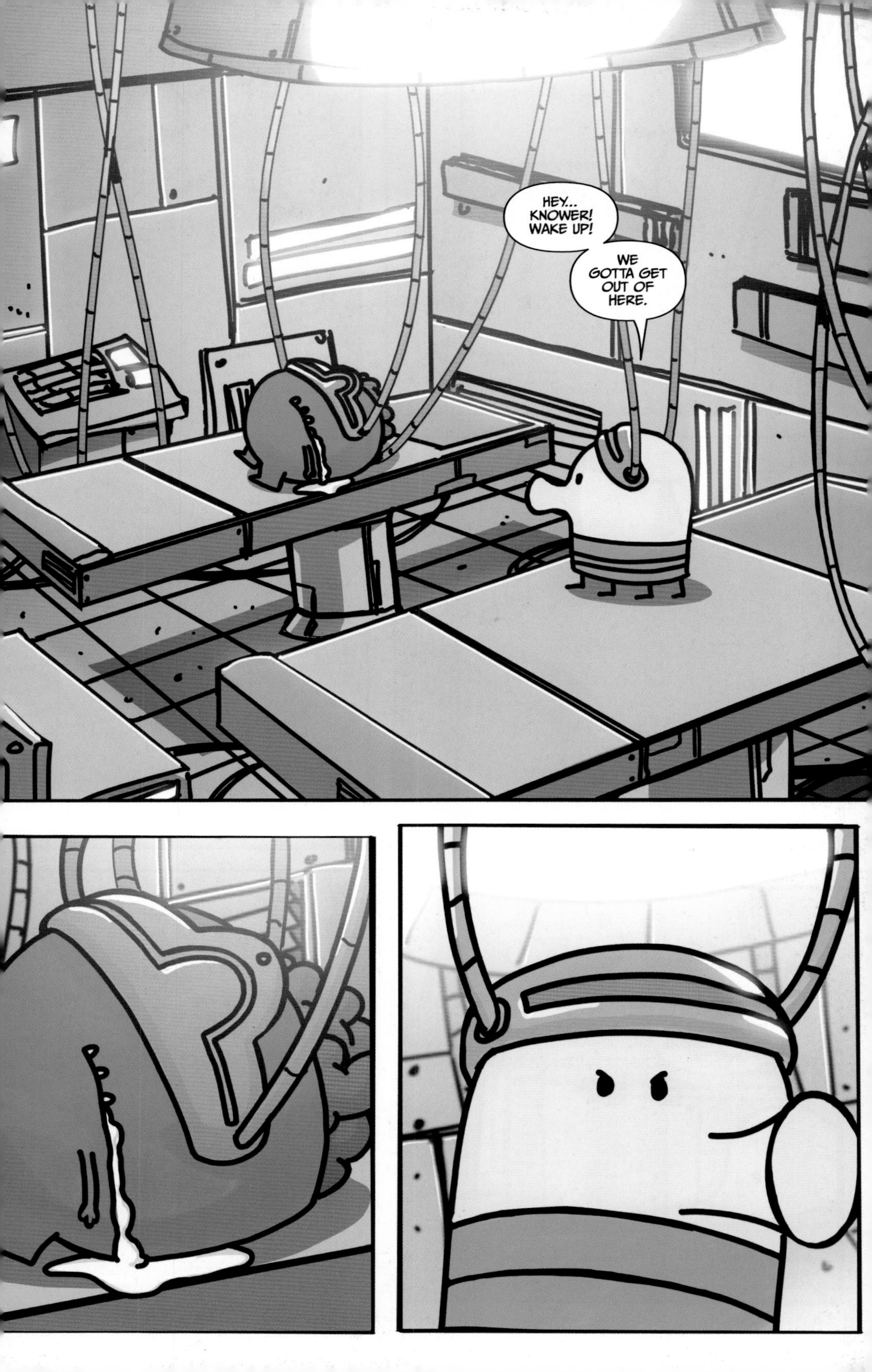
HEY... KNOWER! WAKE UP!
WE GOTTA GET OUT OF HERE.

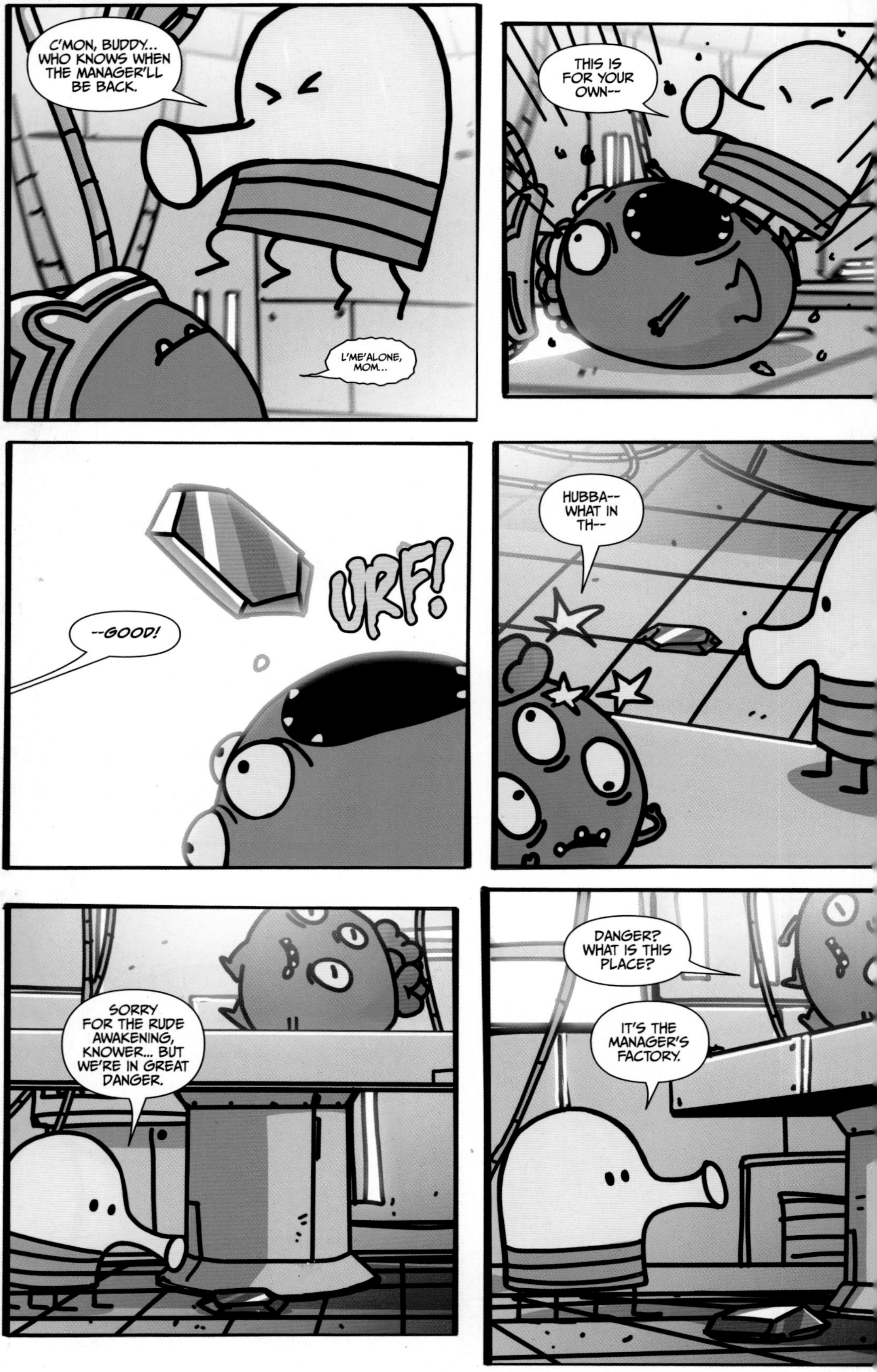
C'MON, BUDDY... WHO KNOWS WHEN THE MANAGER'LL BE BACK.
L'ME'ALONE, MOM...
THIS IS FOR YOUR OWN--
--GOOD!
URF!
HUBBA-- WHAT IN TH--
SORRY FOR THE RUDE AWAKENING, KNOWER... BUT WE'RE IN GREAT DANGER.
DANGER? WHAT IS THIS PLACE?
IT'S THE MANAGER'S FACTORY.

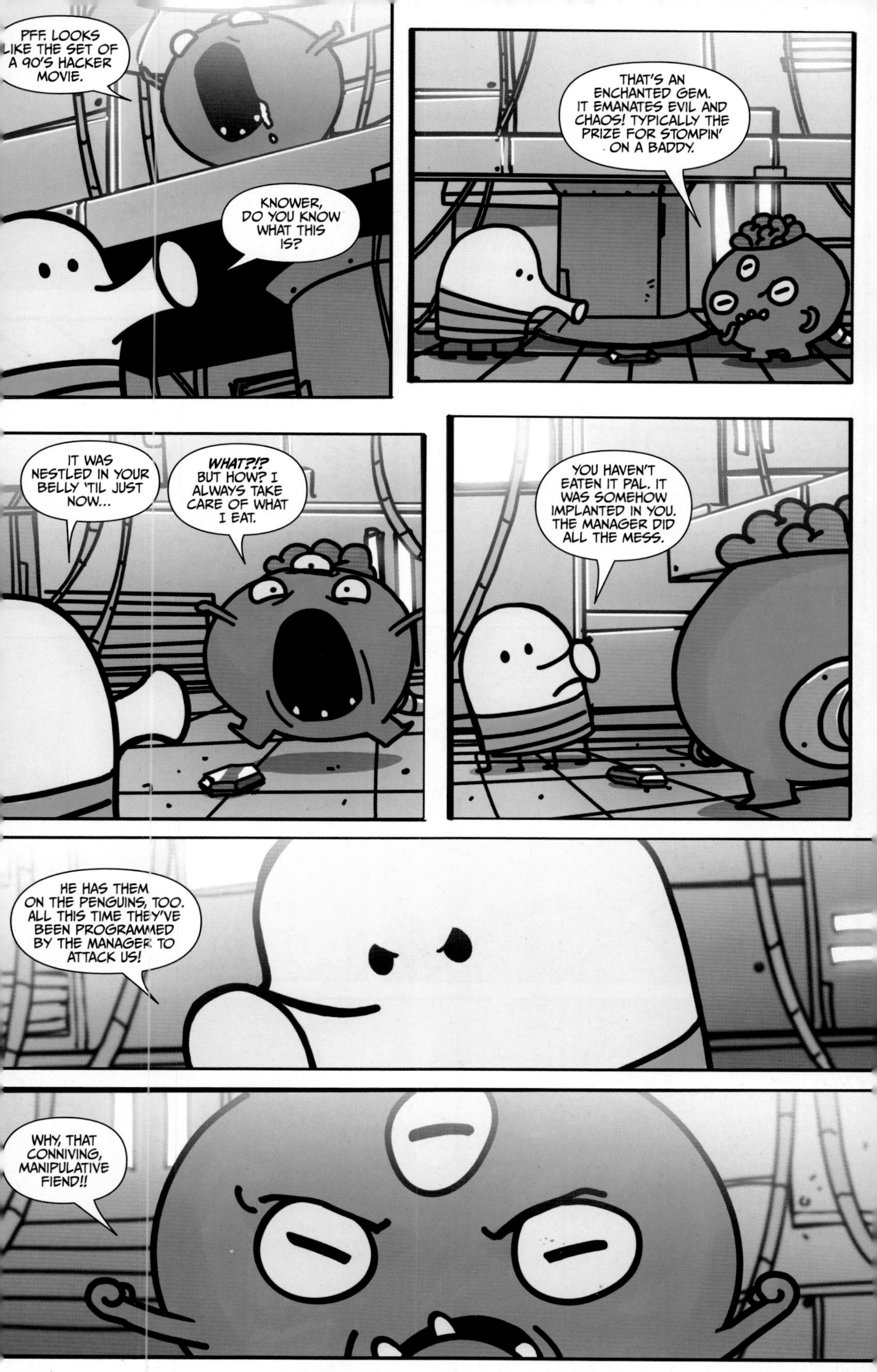
PFF. LOOKS LIKE THE SET OF A 90'S HACKER MOVIE.
KNOWER, DO YOU KNOW WHAT THIS IS?
THAT'S AN ENCHANTED GEM. IT EMANATES EVIL AND CHAOS! TYPICALLY THE PRIZE FOR STOMPIN' ON A BADDY.
IT WAS NESTLED IN YOUR BELLY 'TIL JUST NOW...
WHAT?!? BUT HOW? I ALWAYS TAKE CARE OF WHAT I EAT.
YOU HAVEN'T EATEN IT PAL. IT WAS SOMEHOW IMPLANTED IN YOU. THE MANAGER DID ALL THE MESS.
HE HAS THEM ON THE PENGUINS, TOO. ALL THIS TIME THEY'VE BEEN PROGRAMMED BY THE MANAGER TO ATTACK US!
WHY, THAT CONNIVING, MANIPULATIVE FIEND!!

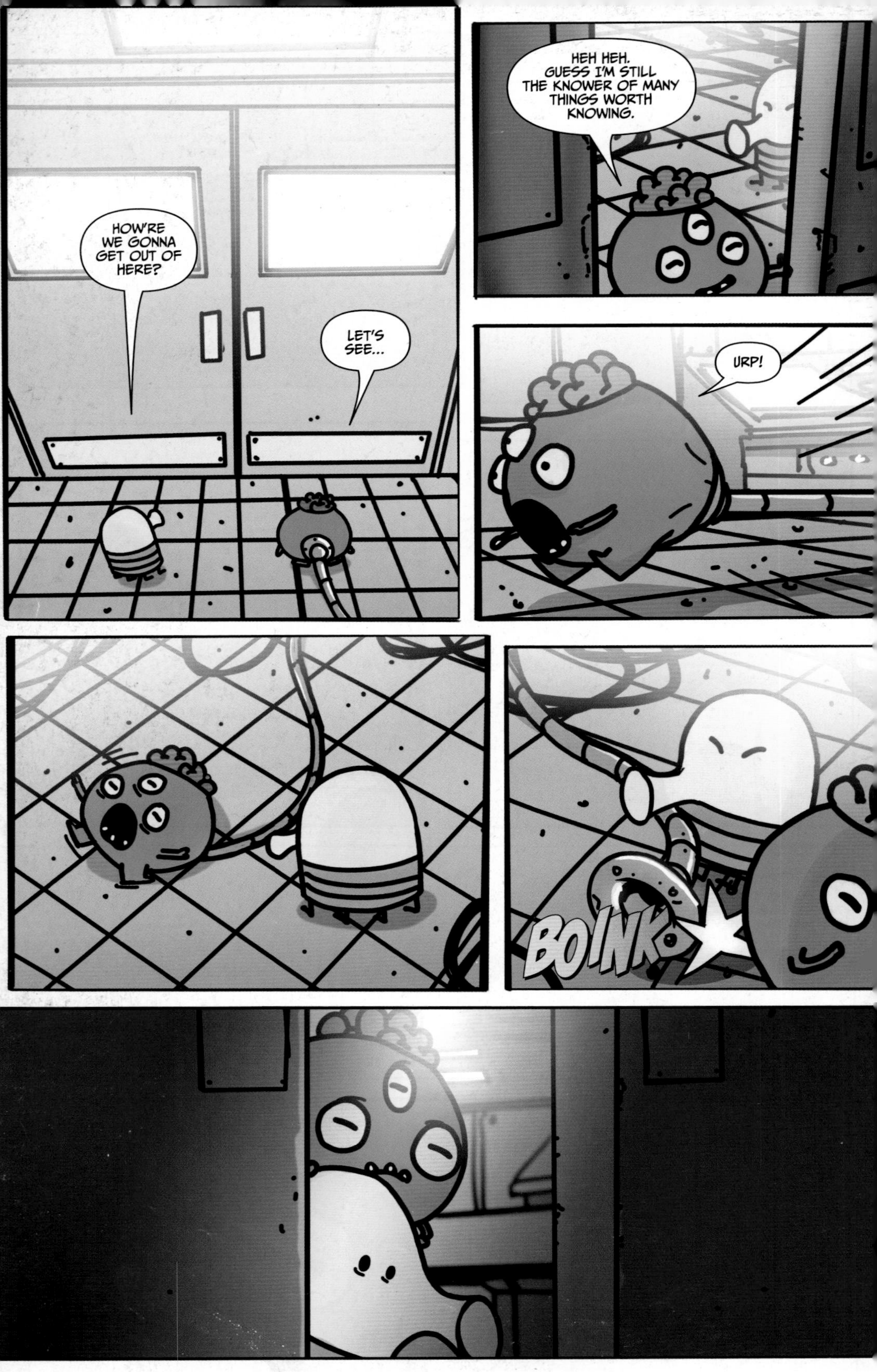
HOW'RE WE GONNA GET OUT OF HERE?
LET'S SEE...
HEH HEH. GUESS I'M STILL THE KNOWER OF MANY THINGS WORTH KNOWING.
URP!
BOINK

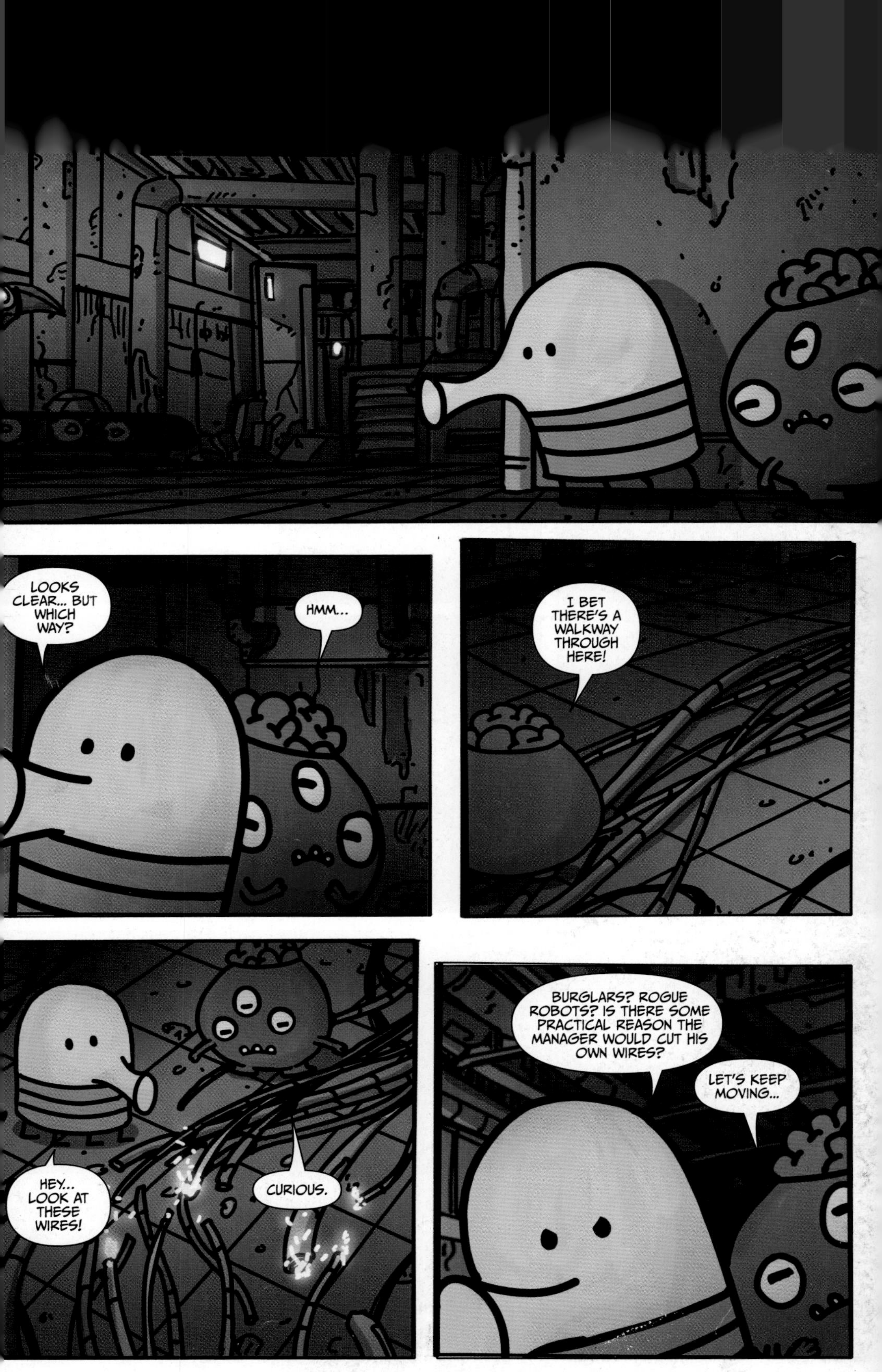
LOOKS CLEAR... BUT WHICH WAY?
HMM...
I BET THERE'S A WALKWAY THROUGH HERE!
HEY... LOOK AT THESE WIRES!
CURIOUS.
BURGLARS? ROGUE ROBOTS? IS THERE SOME PRACTICAL REASON THE MANAGER WOULD CUT HIS OWN WIRES?
LET'S KEEP MOVING...

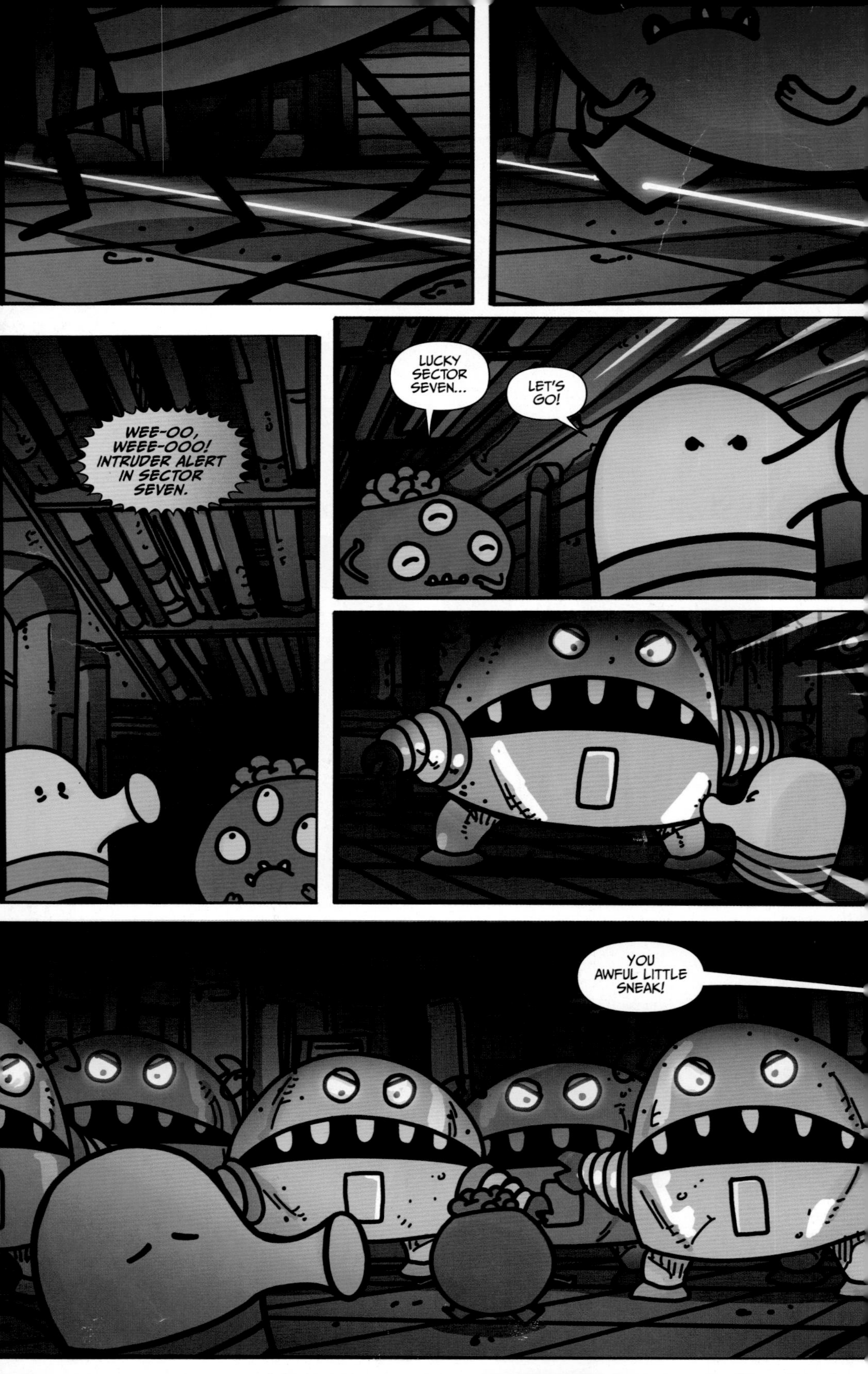
WEE-OO, WEEE-OOO! INTRUDER ALERT IN SECTOR SEVEN.
LUCKY SECTOR SEVEN...
LET'S GO!
YOU AWFUL LITTLE SNEAK!

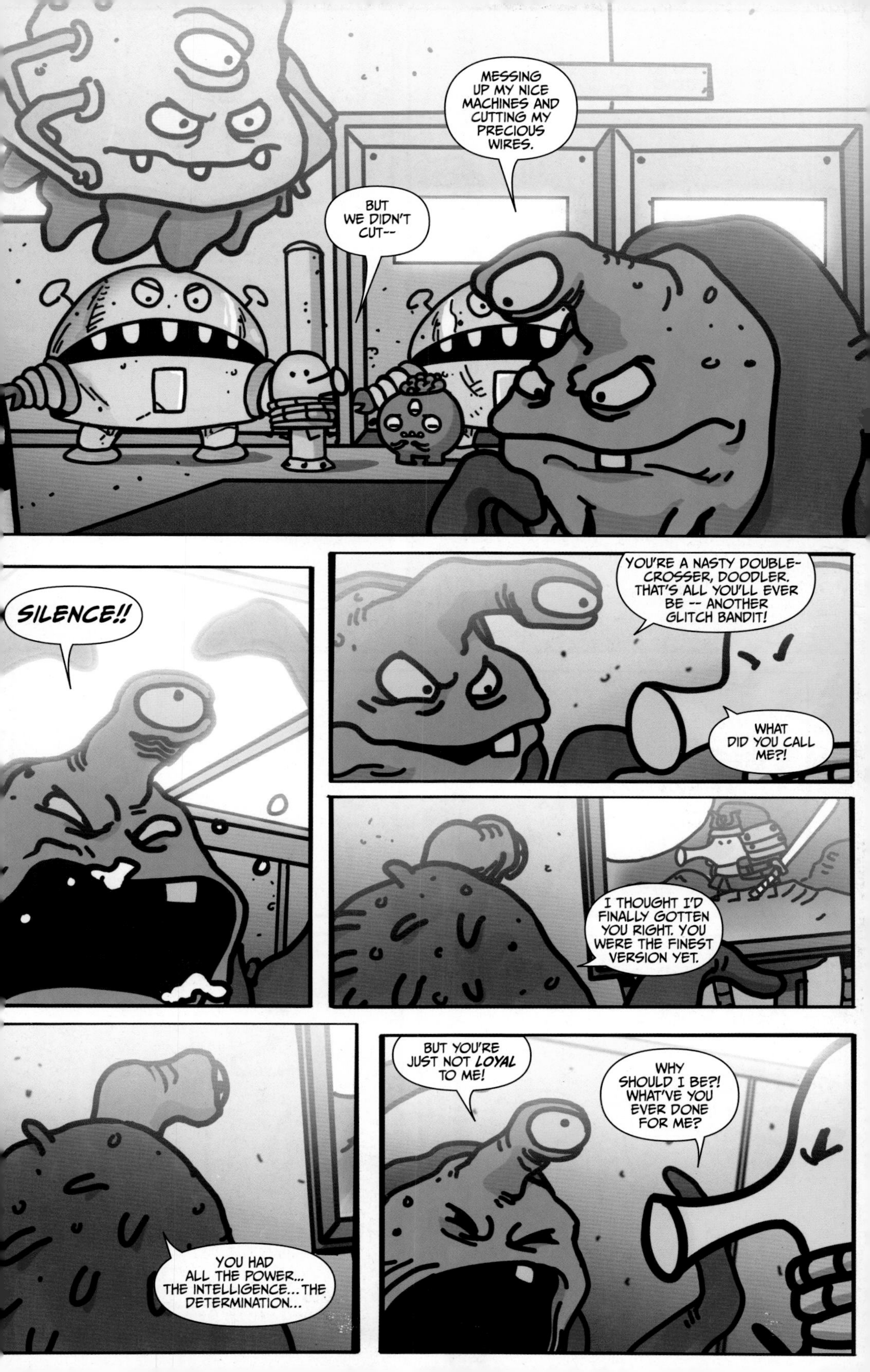
MESSING UP MY NICE MACHINES AND CUTTING MY PRECIOUS WIRES.
BUT WE DIDN'T CUT--
SILENCE!!
YOU'RE A NASTY DOUBLE-CROSSER, DOODLER. THAT'S ALL YOU'LL EVER BE -- ANOTHER GLITCH BANDIT!
WHAT DID YOU CALL ME?!
I THOUGHT I'D FINALLY GOTTEN YOU RIGHT. YOU WERE THE FINEST VERSION YET.
YOU HAD ALL THE POWER... THE INTELLIGENCE... THE DETERMINATION...
BUT YOU'RE JUST NOT LOYAL TO ME!
WHY SHOULD I BE?! WHAT'VE YOU EVER DONE FOR ME?

I CREATED YOU! GAVE YOU LIFE! SPENT YEARS AND YEARS *PERFECTING* YOU!

WHO ELSE HAS DONE *ANYTHING* FOR YOU?

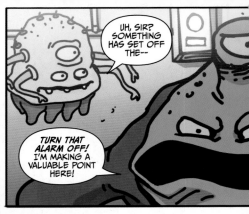

UH, SIR? SOMETHING HAS SET OFF THE--

TURN THAT ALARM OFF! I'M MAKING A VALUABLE POINT HERE!

I GAVE YOU A CHANCE TO BE THE GREATEST FIGHTER THE VIRTUAL WORLD HAS EVER KNOWN!

BUT YOU DECIDED TO GO *MERCENARY.* DIDN'T BEING ABANDONED BY YOUR FRIEND TEACH YOU A LITTLE *MATURITY?*

SIR, WE REALLY NEED TO...

SIR, WE REALLY NEED TO-- SIR, WE REALLY NEED TO--

RATTLE RATTLE RATTLE

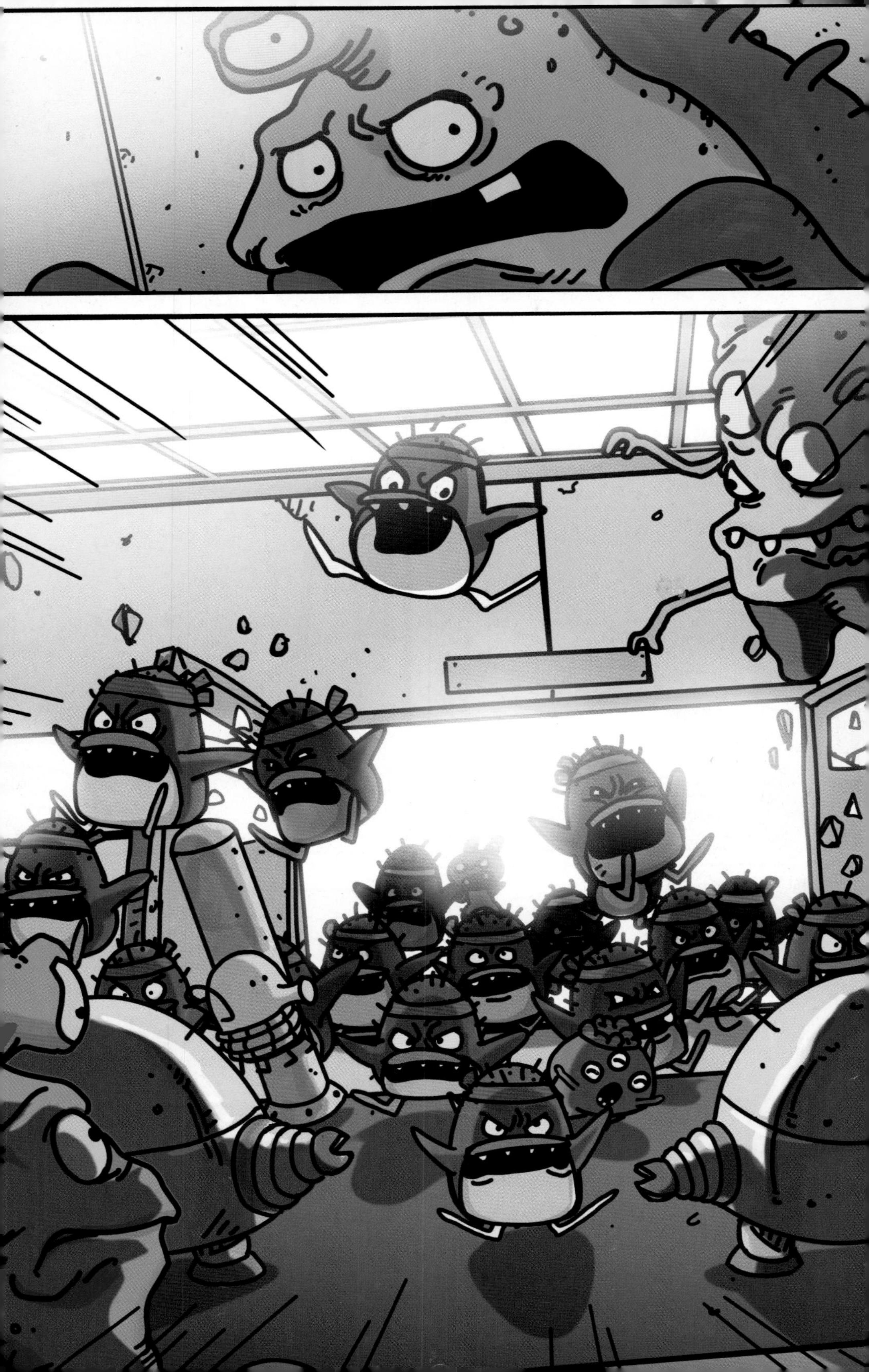

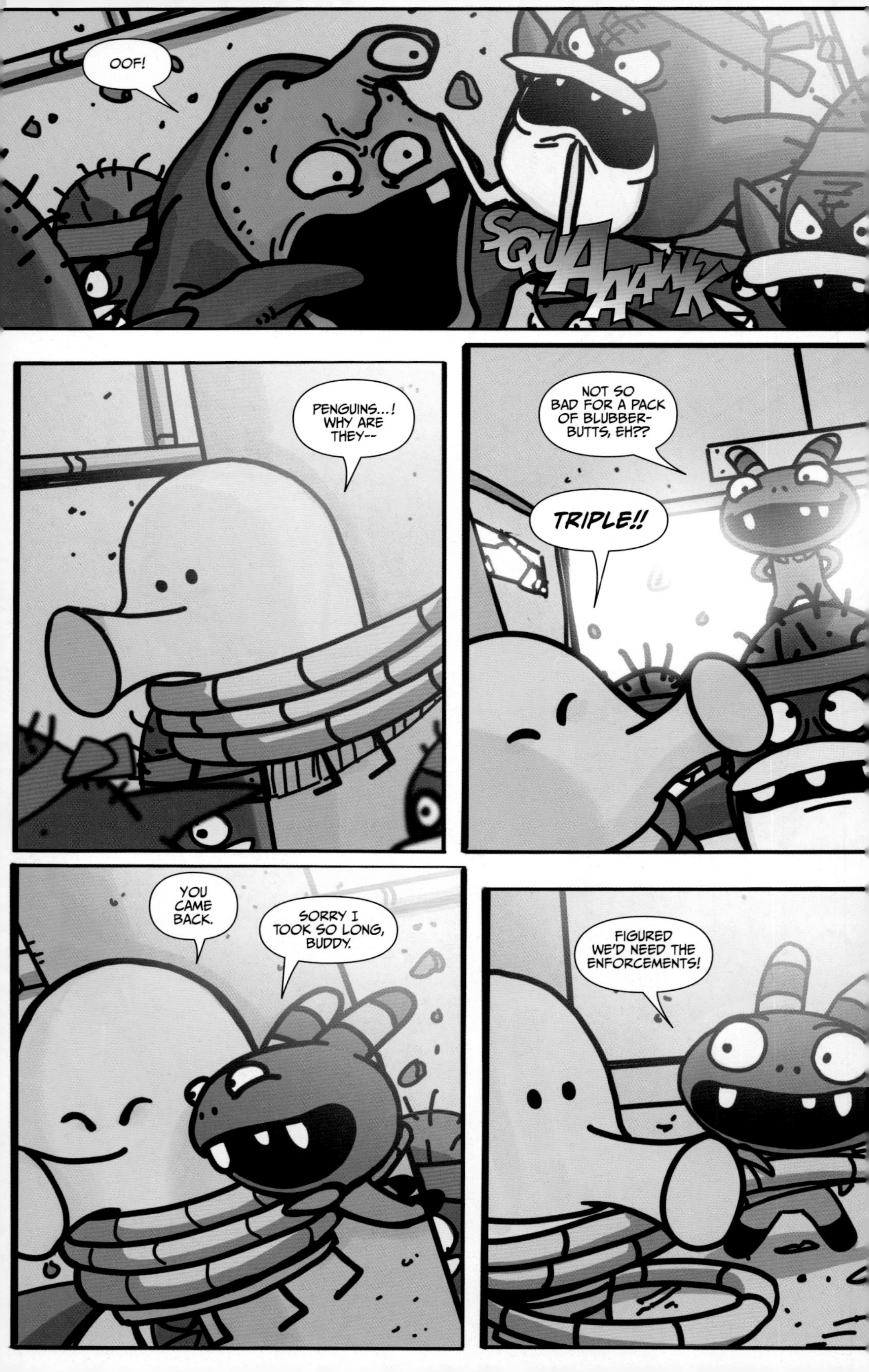
OOF!
SQUAAAAWK
PENGUINS...! WHY ARE THEY--
NOT SO BAD FOR A PACK OF BLUBBER-BUTTS, EH??
TRIPLE!!
YOU CAME BACK.
SORRY I TOOK SO LONG, BUDDY.
FIGURED WE'D NEED THE ENFORCEMENTS!

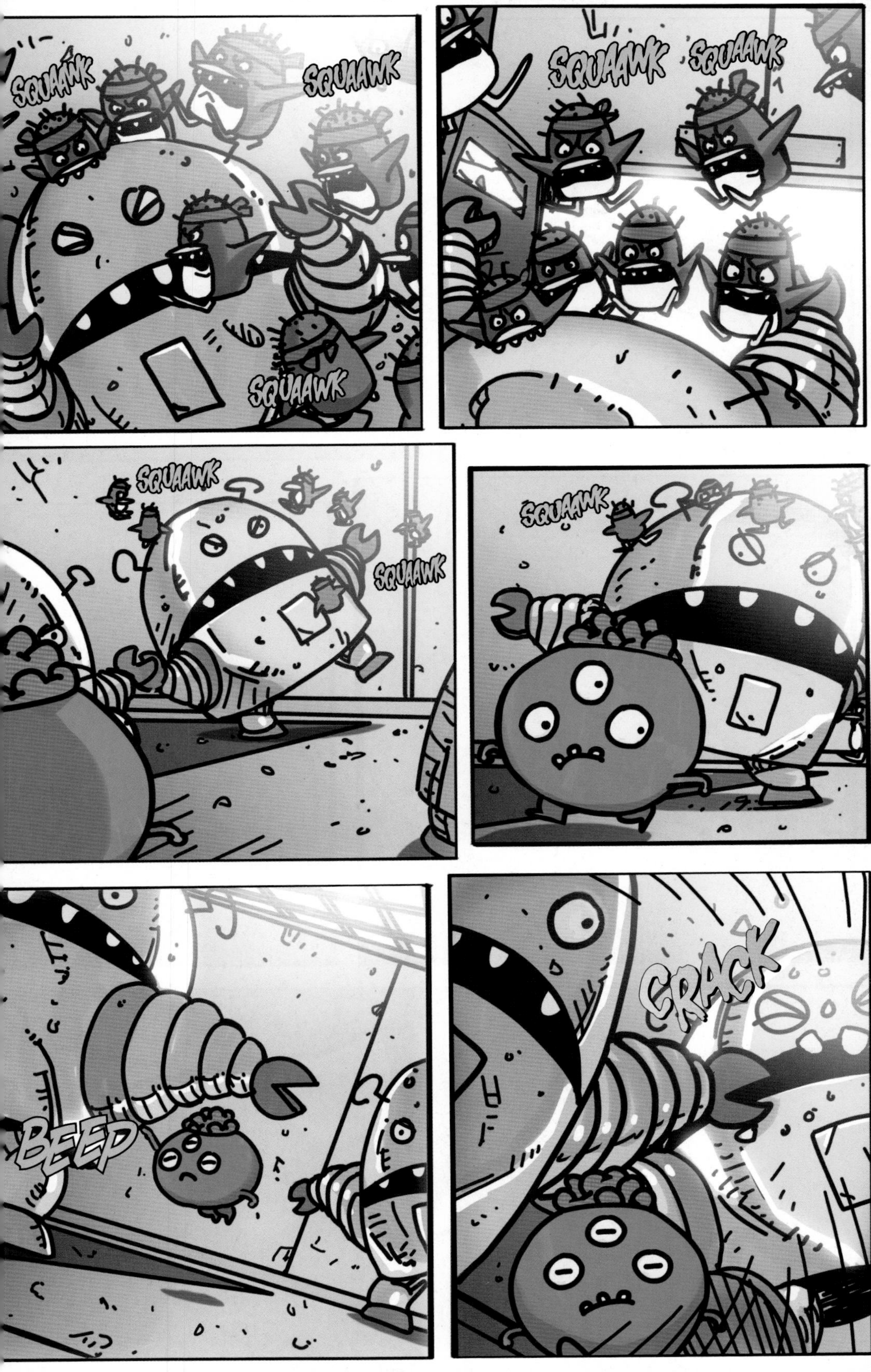
SQUAAWK
SQUAAWK
SQUAAWK
SQUAAWK
SQUAAWK
SQUAAWK
SQUAAWK
SQUAAWK
BEEP
CRACK

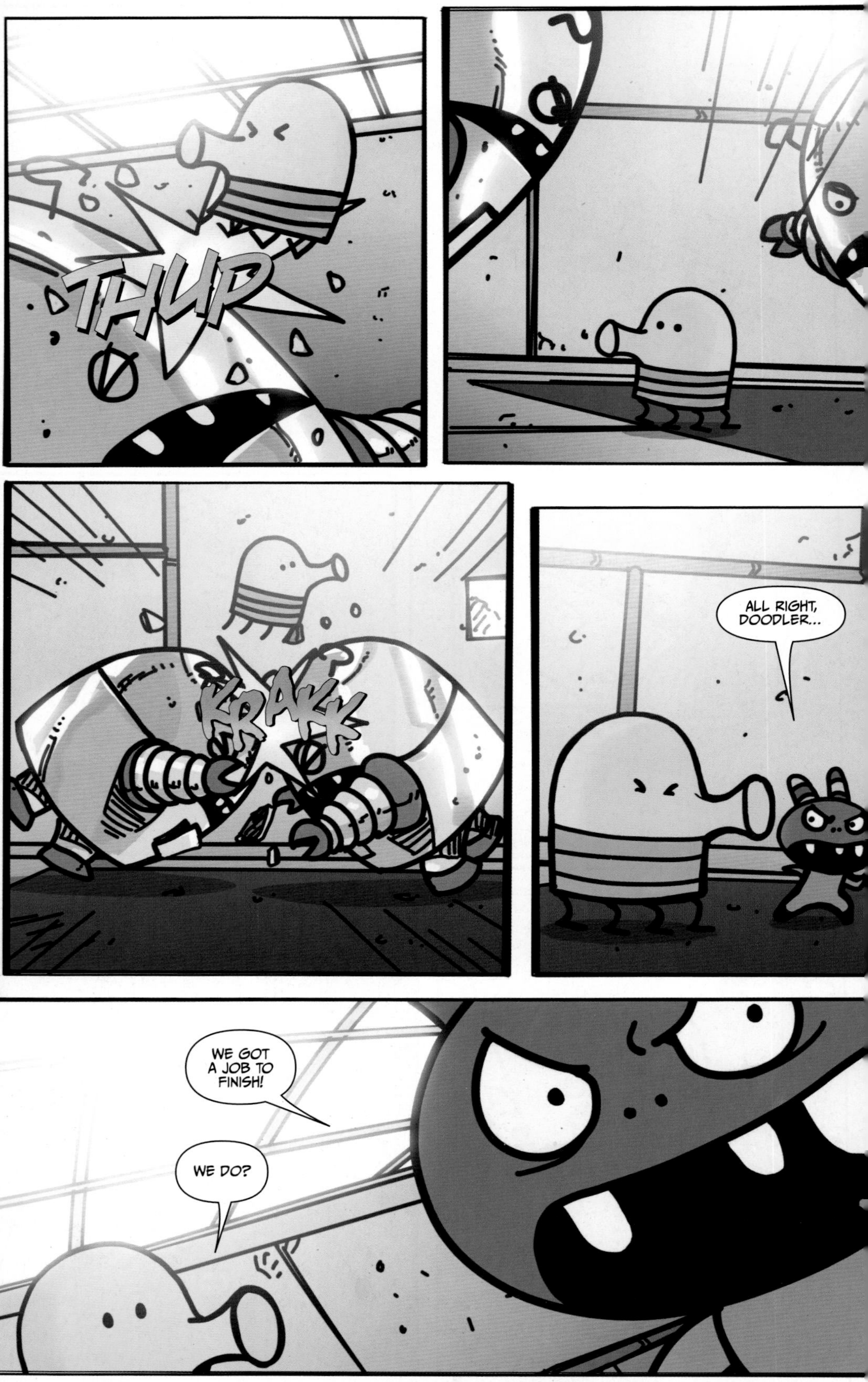
THUP
KRAKK
ALL RIGHT, DOODLER...
WE GOT A JOB TO FINISH!
WE DO?

HERE IT IS, TEAM...

SQUAAAKKK!!

SQUAKKK!

SQUAKK!

SQUAAKKK!!

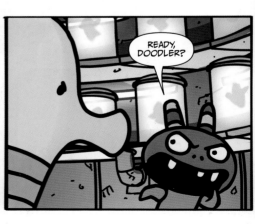

READY, DOODLER?

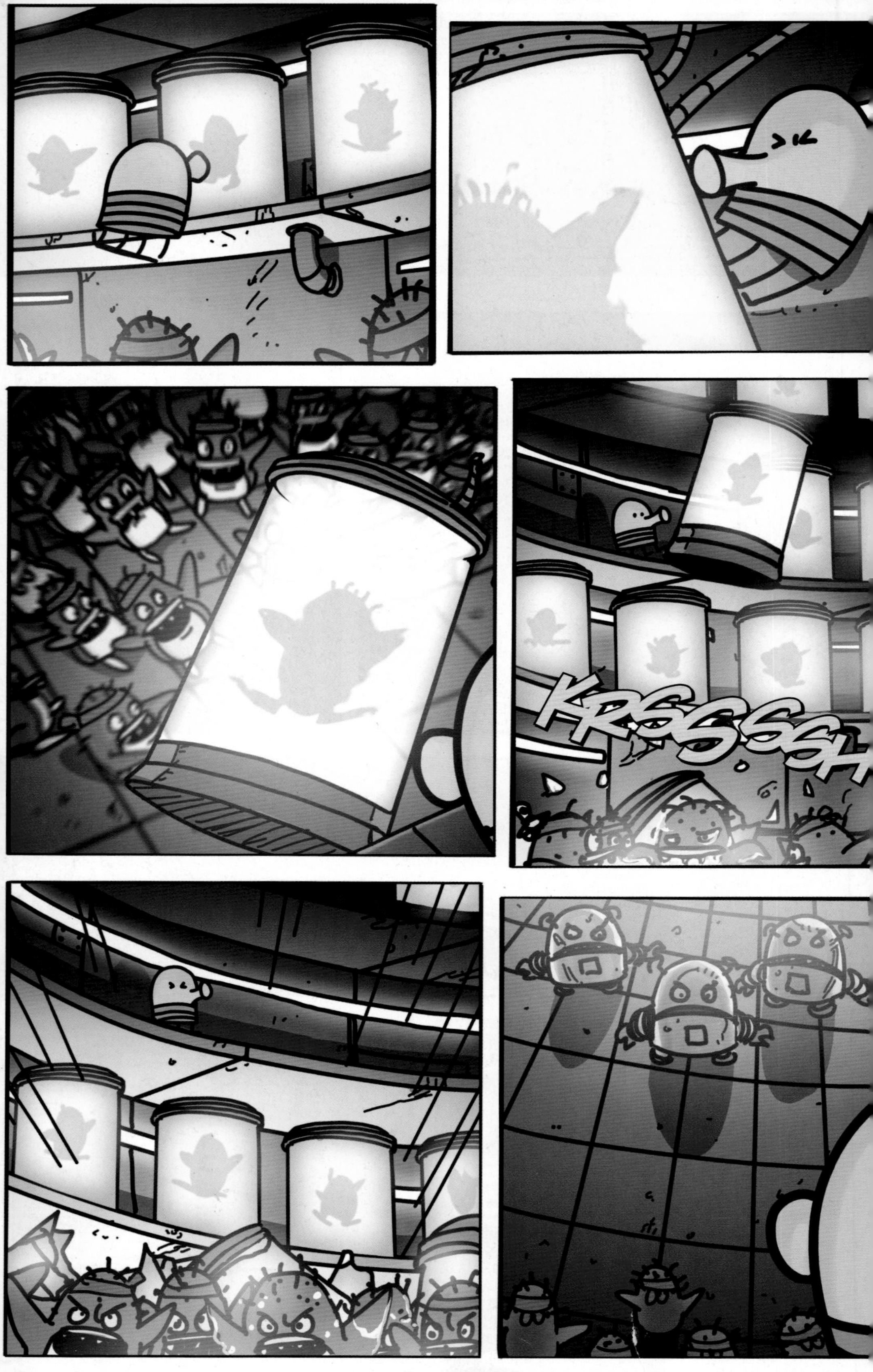
KRSSSSH

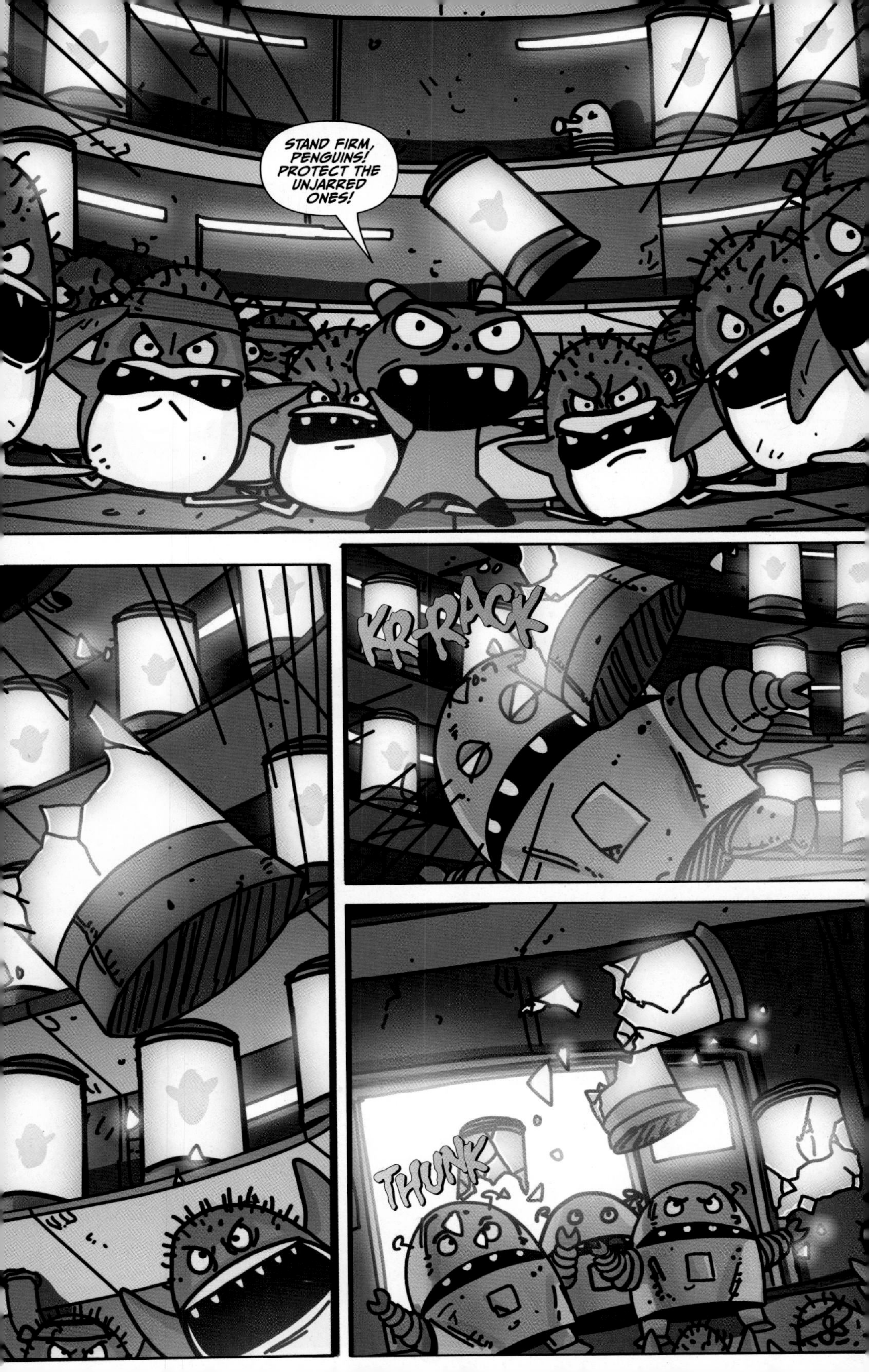

STAND FIRM, PENGUINS! PROTECT THE UNJARRED ONES!
KR-RACK
THUNK

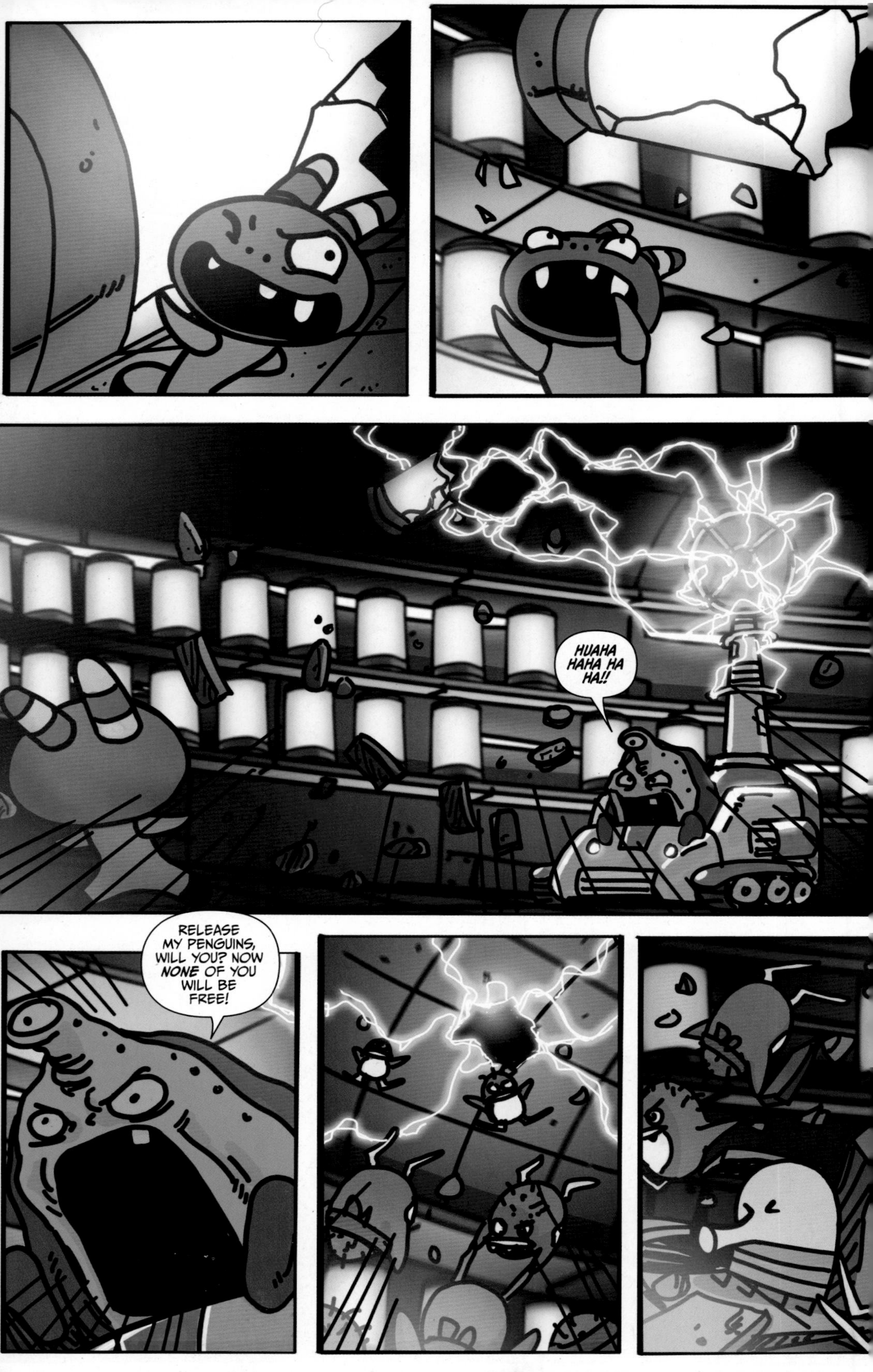
HUAHA HAHA HA HA!!
RELEASE MY PENGUINS, WILL YOU? NOW *NONE* OF YOU WILL BE FREE!

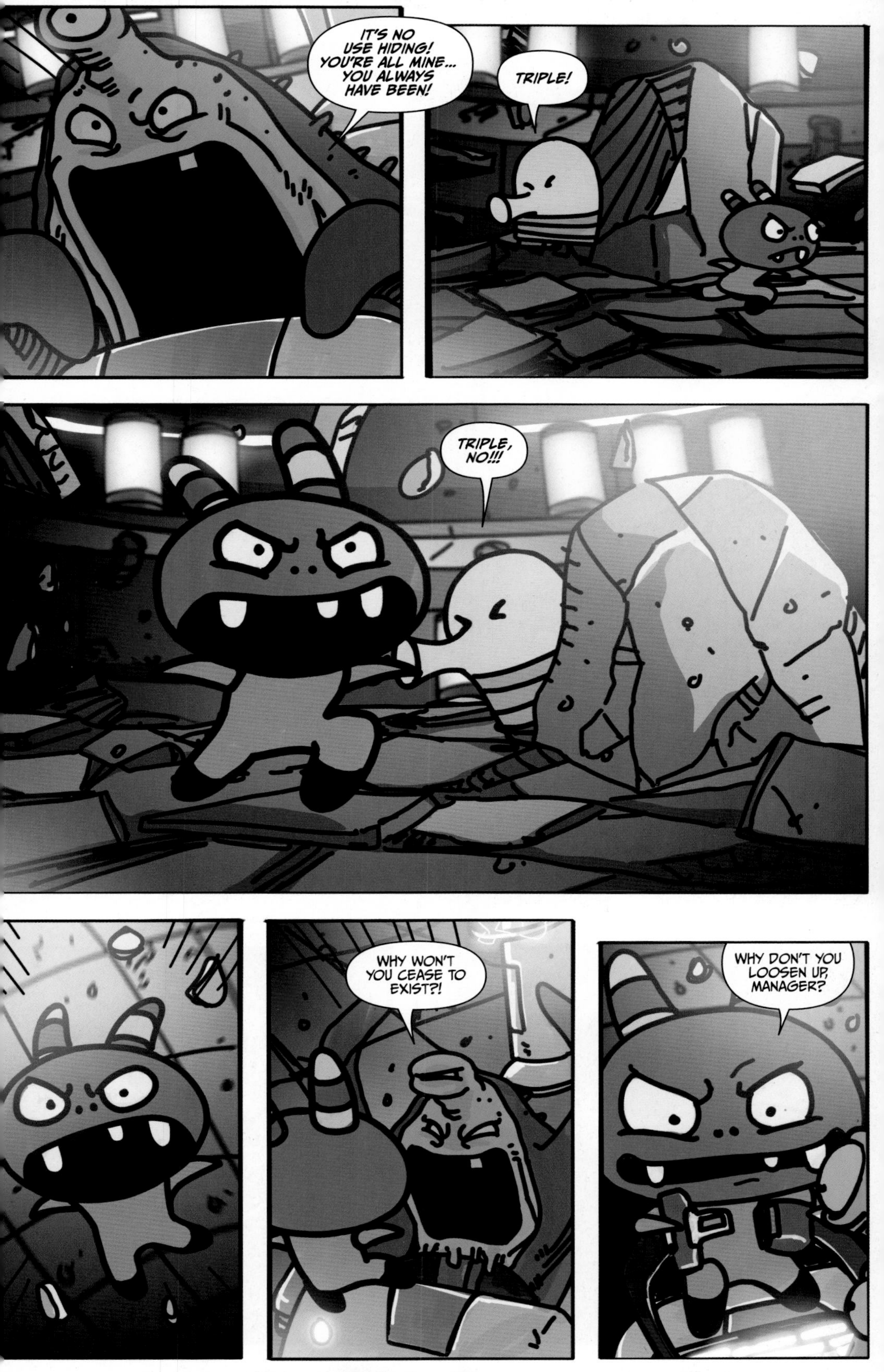
IT'S NO USE HIDING! YOU'RE ALL MINE... YOU ALWAYS HAVE BEEN!
TRIPLE!
TRIPLE, NO!!!
WHY WON'T YOU CEASE TO EXIST?!
WHY DON'T YOU LOOSEN UP, MANAGER?

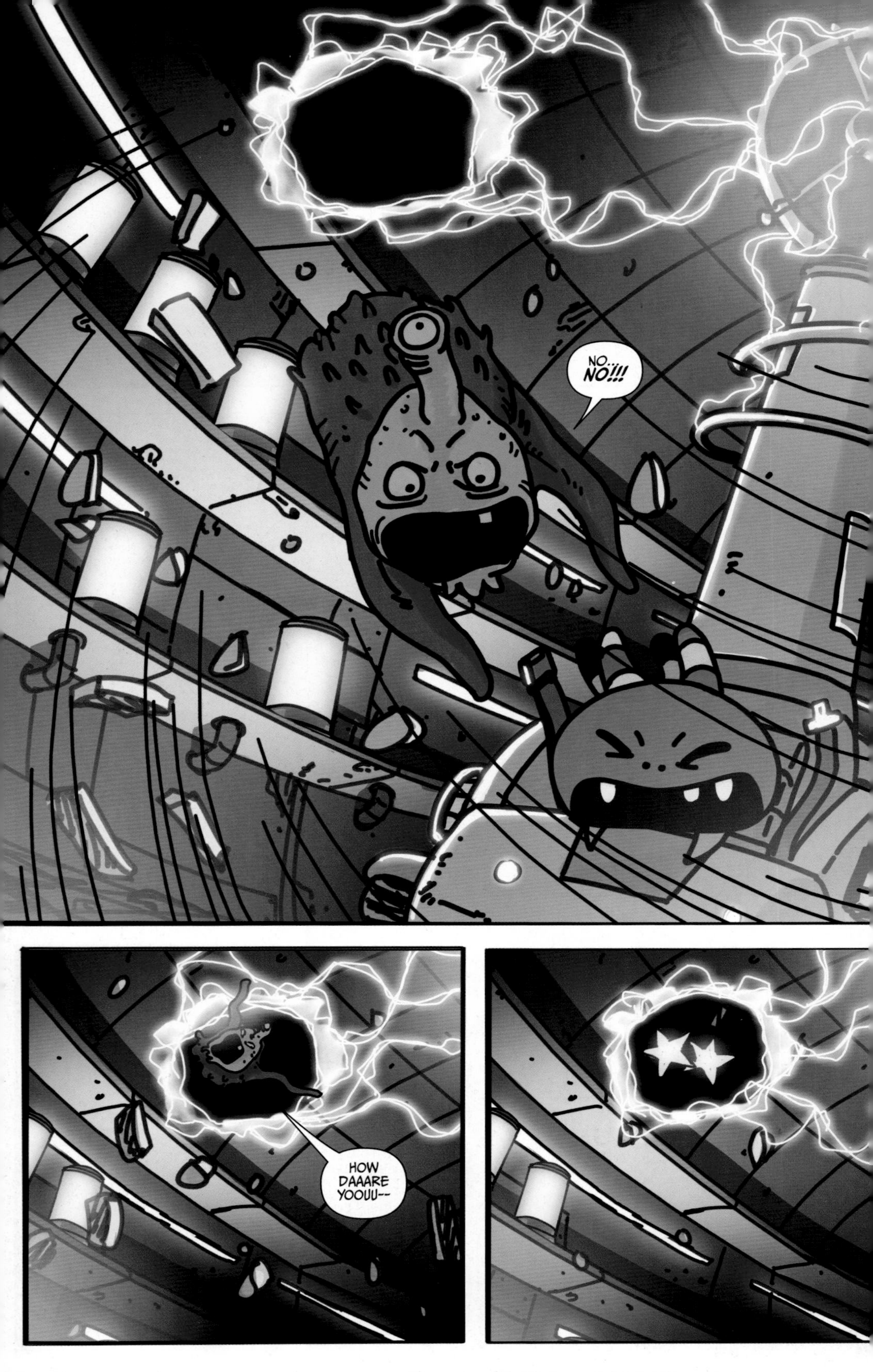
NO... NO!!!
HOW DAAARE YOOUU--

DOES THIS...COUNT AS MURDER?
HE'S ALIVE...
JUST FLOATING 'ROUND IN THE VOID.
WE'LL MAKE SURE IT STAYS THAT WAY.
GOOD RIDDANCE, YA BUM!
FORMATTING COMPLETE
SO IT WAS A LIE...
HMM?
THE PROPHECY... MY SO-CALLED DESTINY. IT WAS ALL PART OF THE MANAGER'S PLAN.

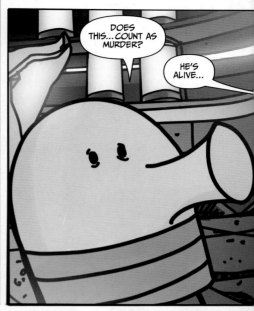

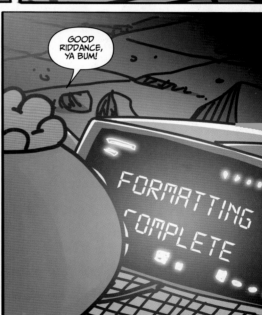

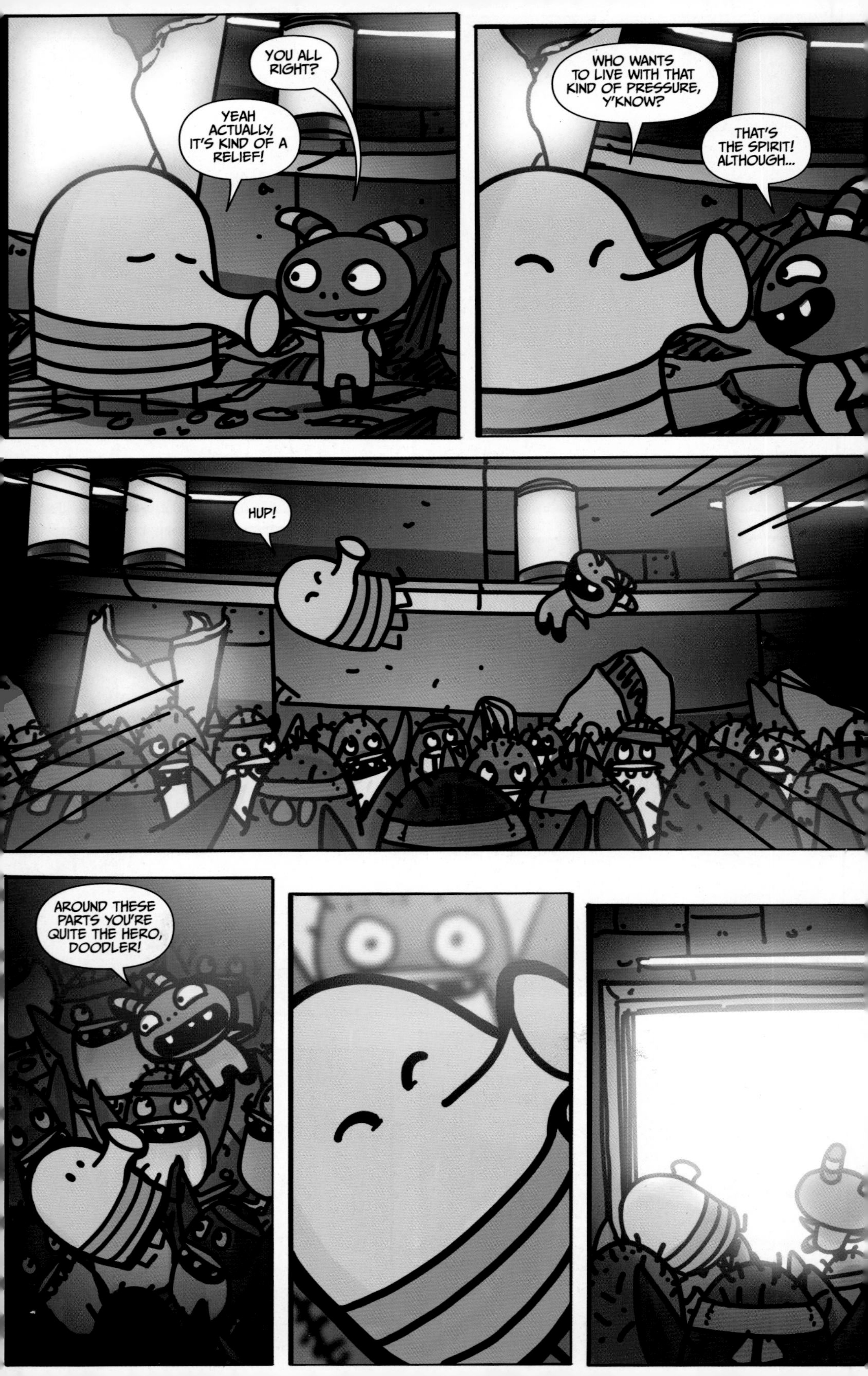
YOU ALL RIGHT?
YEAH ACTUALLY, IT'S KIND OF A RELIEF!
WHO WANTS TO LIVE WITH THAT KIND OF PRESSURE, Y'KNOW?
THAT'S THE SPIRIT! ALTHOUGH...
HUP!
AROUND THESE PARTS YOU'RE QUITE THE HERO, DOODLER!

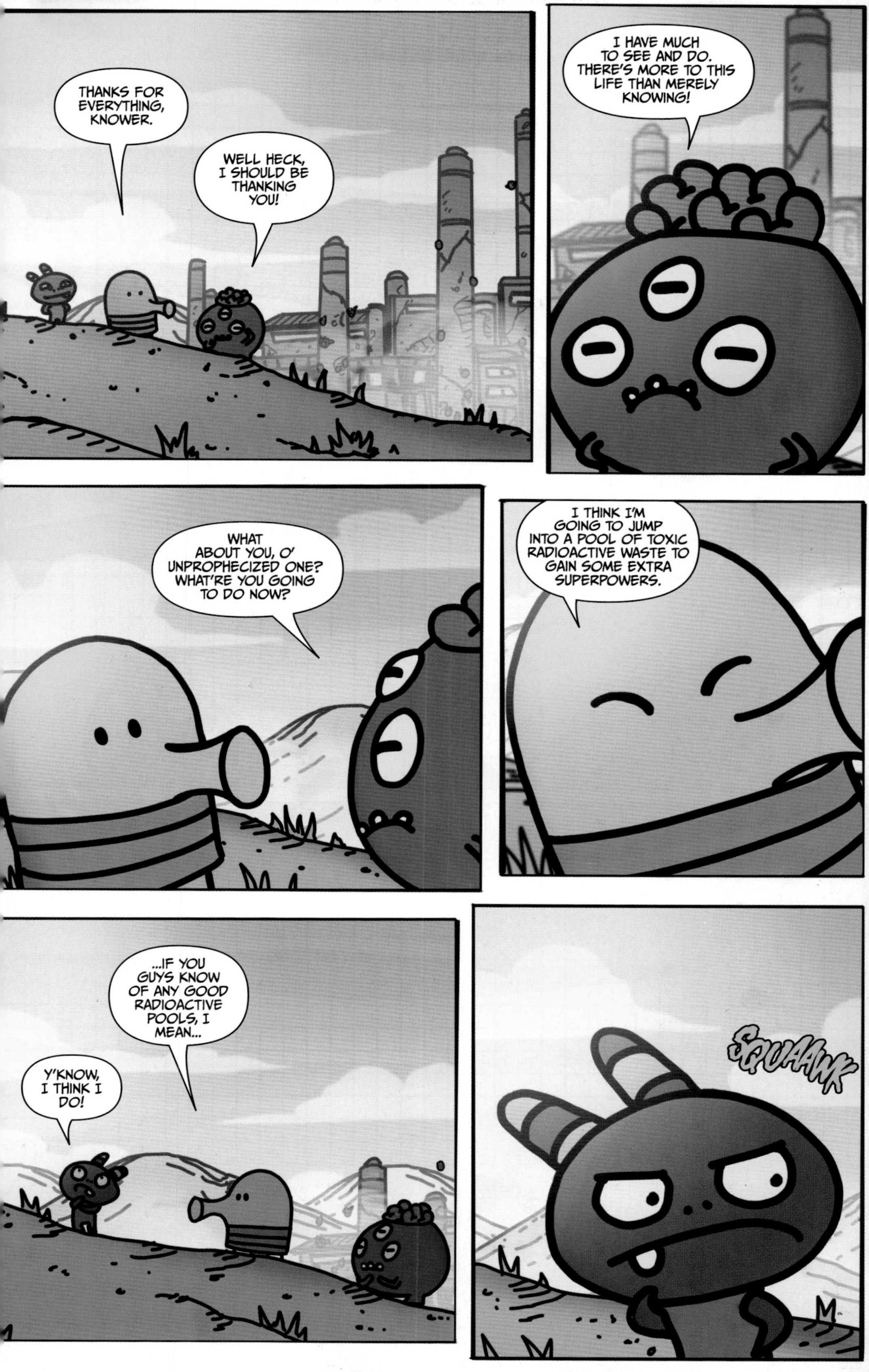
THANKS FOR EVERYTHING, KNOWER.
WELL HECK, I SHOULD BE THANKING YOU!
I HAVE MUCH TO SEE AND DO. THERE'S MORE TO THIS LIFE THAN MERELY KNOWING!
WHAT ABOUT YOU, O' UNPROPHECIZED ONE? WHAT'RE YOU GOING TO DO NOW?
I THINK I'M GOING TO JUMP INTO A POOL OF TOXIC RADIOACTIVE WASTE TO GAIN SOME EXTRA SUPERPOWERS.
...IF YOU GUYS KNOW OF ANY GOOD RADIOACTIVE POOLS, I MEAN...
Y'KNOW, I THINK I DO!
SQUAAAWK

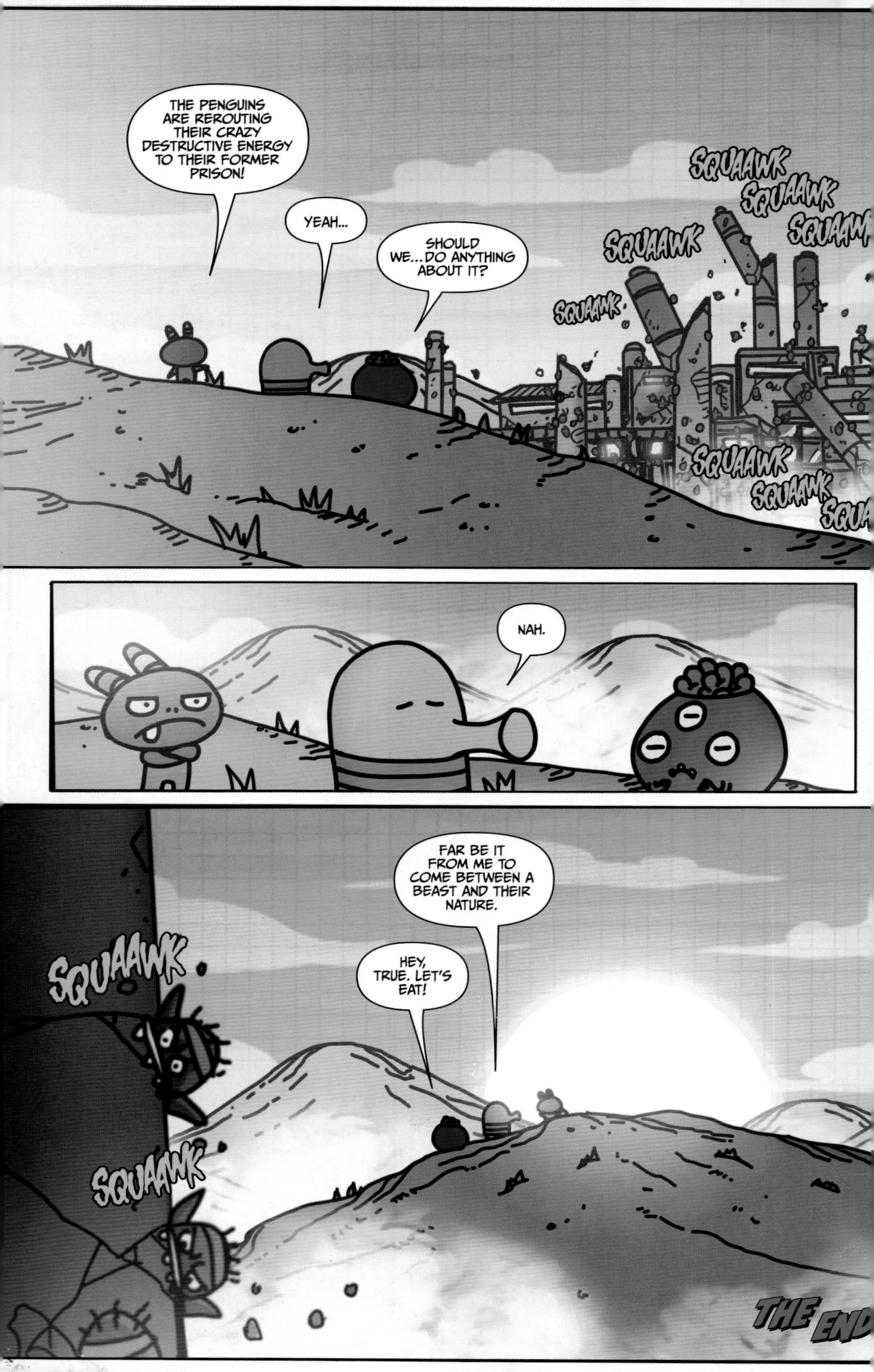
THE PENGUINS ARE REROUTING THEIR CRAZY DESTRUCTIVE ENERGY TO THEIR FORMER PRISON!
YEAH...
SHOULD WE...DO ANYTHING ABOUT IT?
SQUAAWK
SQUAAWK
SQUAAWK
SQUAAWK
SQUAAWK
SQUAAWK
NAH.
FAR BE IT FROM ME TO COME BETWEEN A BEAST AND THEIR NATURE.
HEY, TRUE. LET'S EAT!
SQUAAWK
SQUAAWK
THE END

ALTERNATE COVER GALLERY!

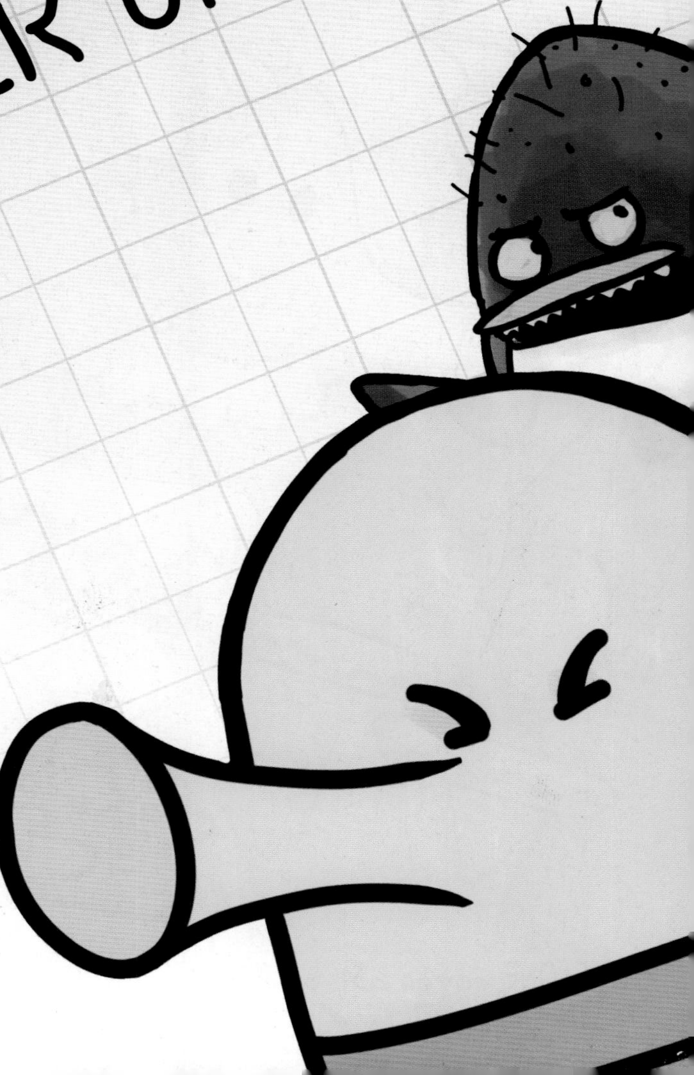

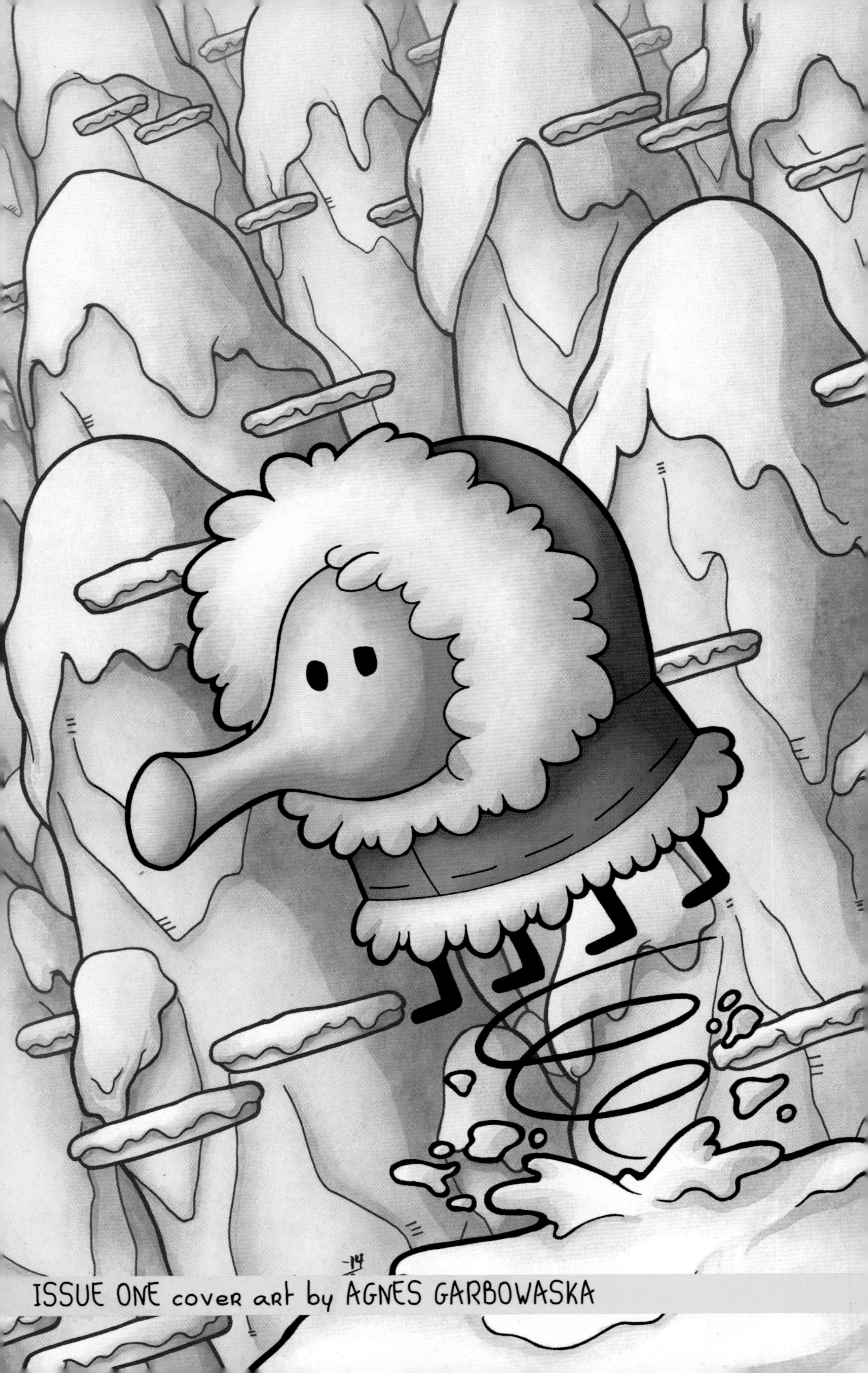

ISSUE ONE cover art by AGNES GARBOWASKA

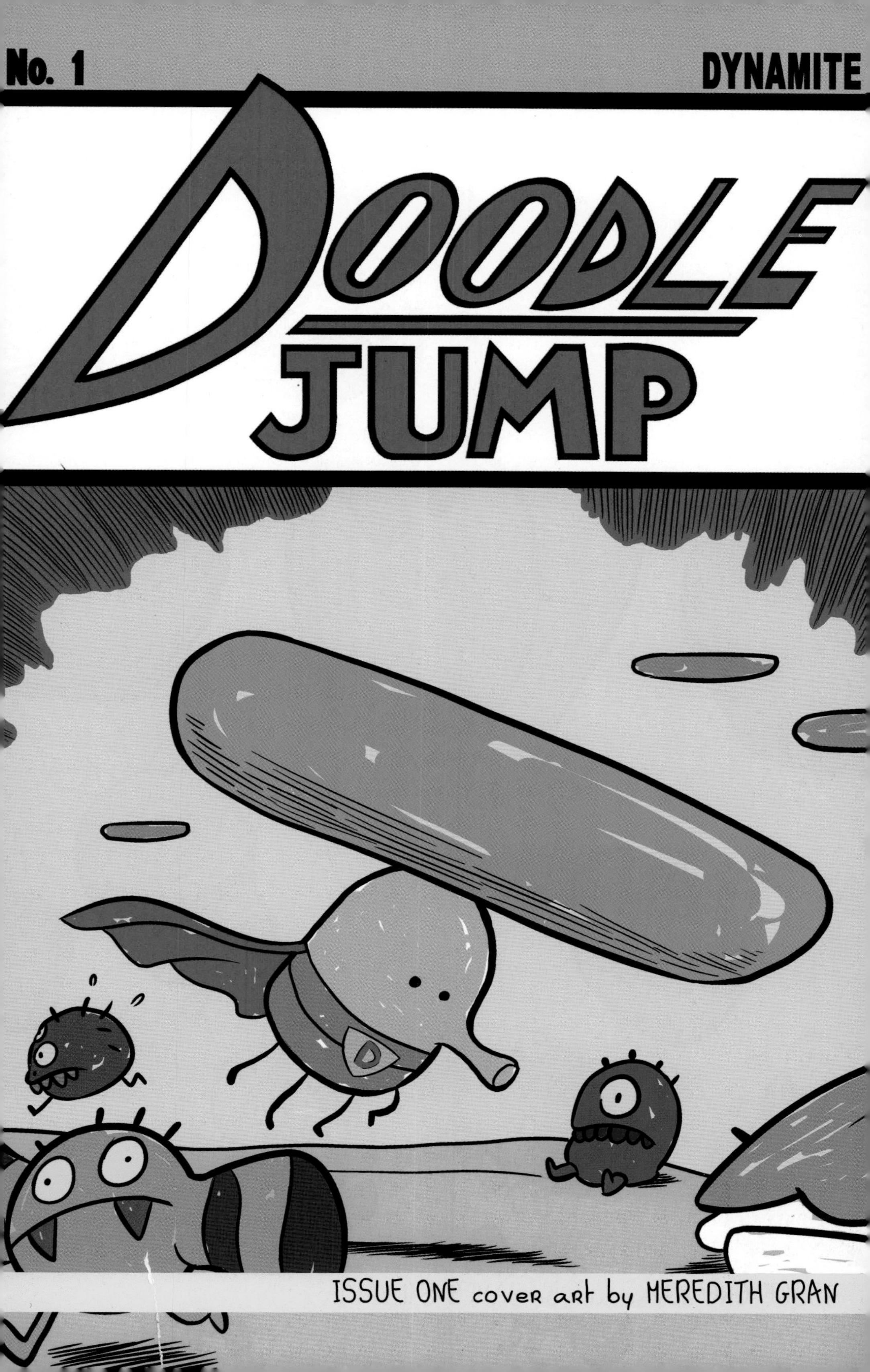
No. 1
DYNAMITE
DOODLE JUMP
ISSUE ONE cover art by MEREDITH GRAN

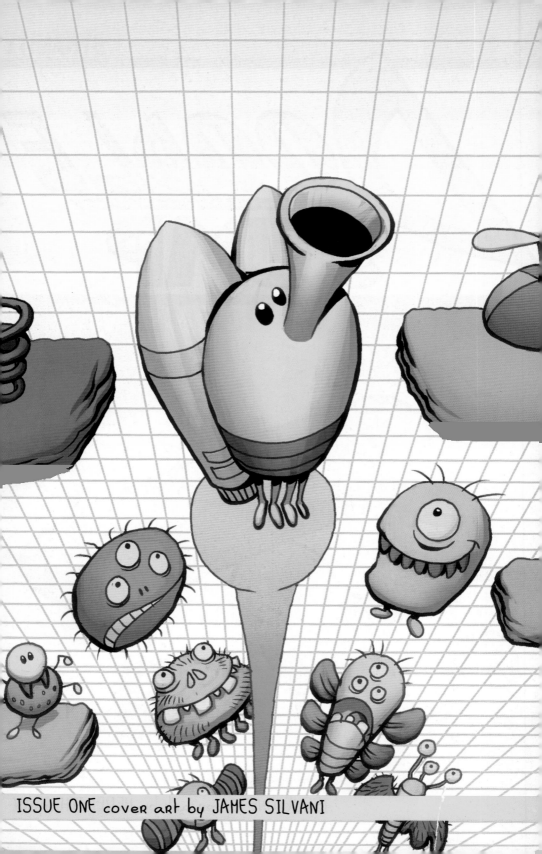

ISSUE ONE cover art by JAMES SILVANI

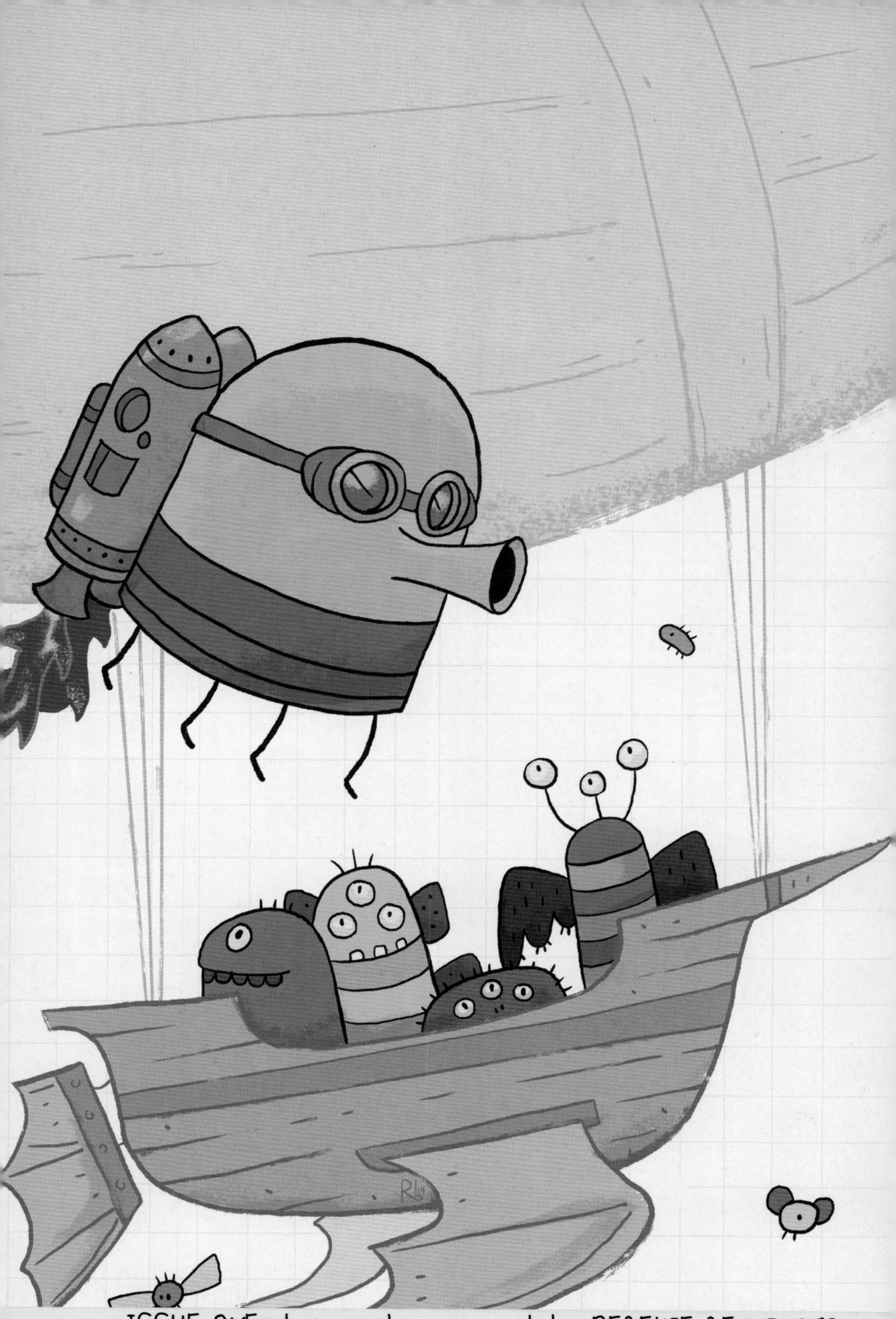

ISSUE ONE steampunk cover art by REBEKIE BENNINGTON

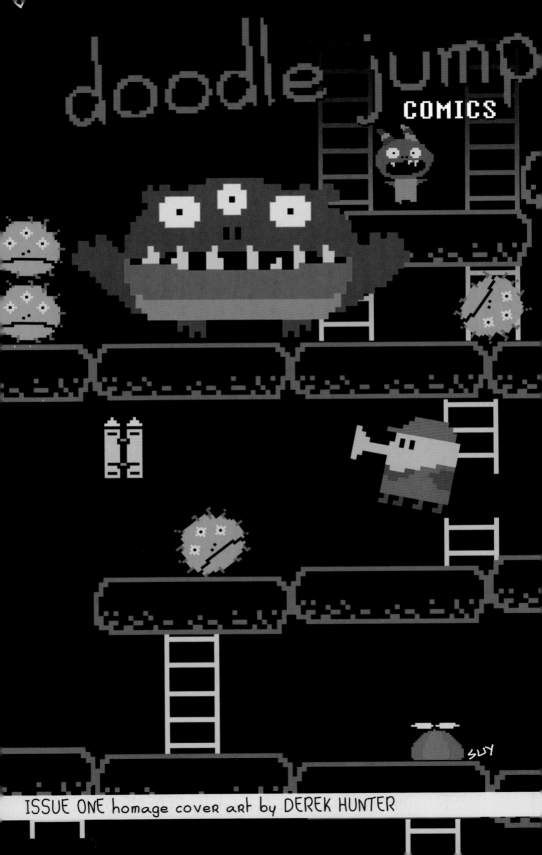

ISSUE ONE homage cover art by DEREK HUNTER

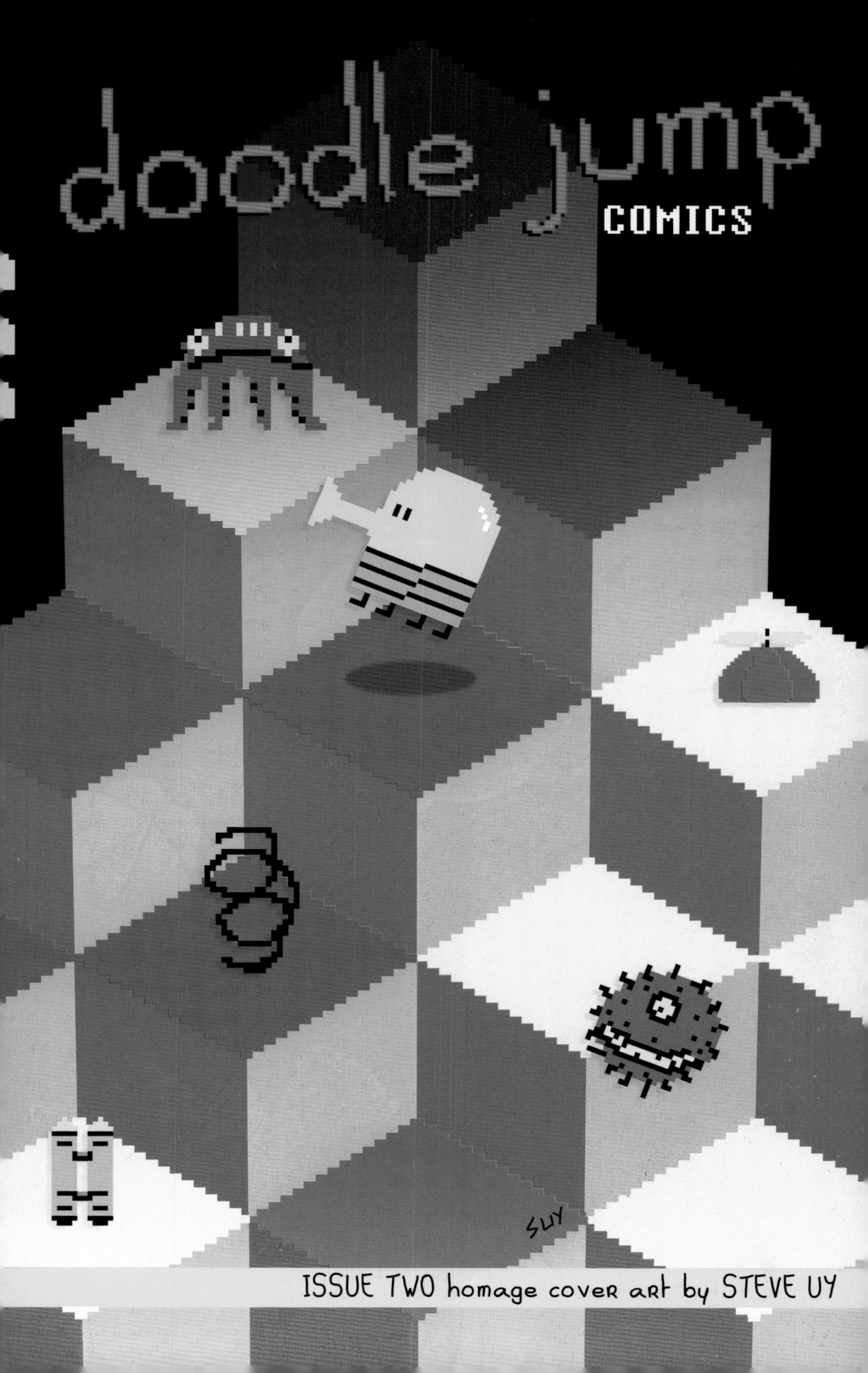
doodle jump
COMICS
SUY

ISSUE TWO homage cover art by STEVE UY

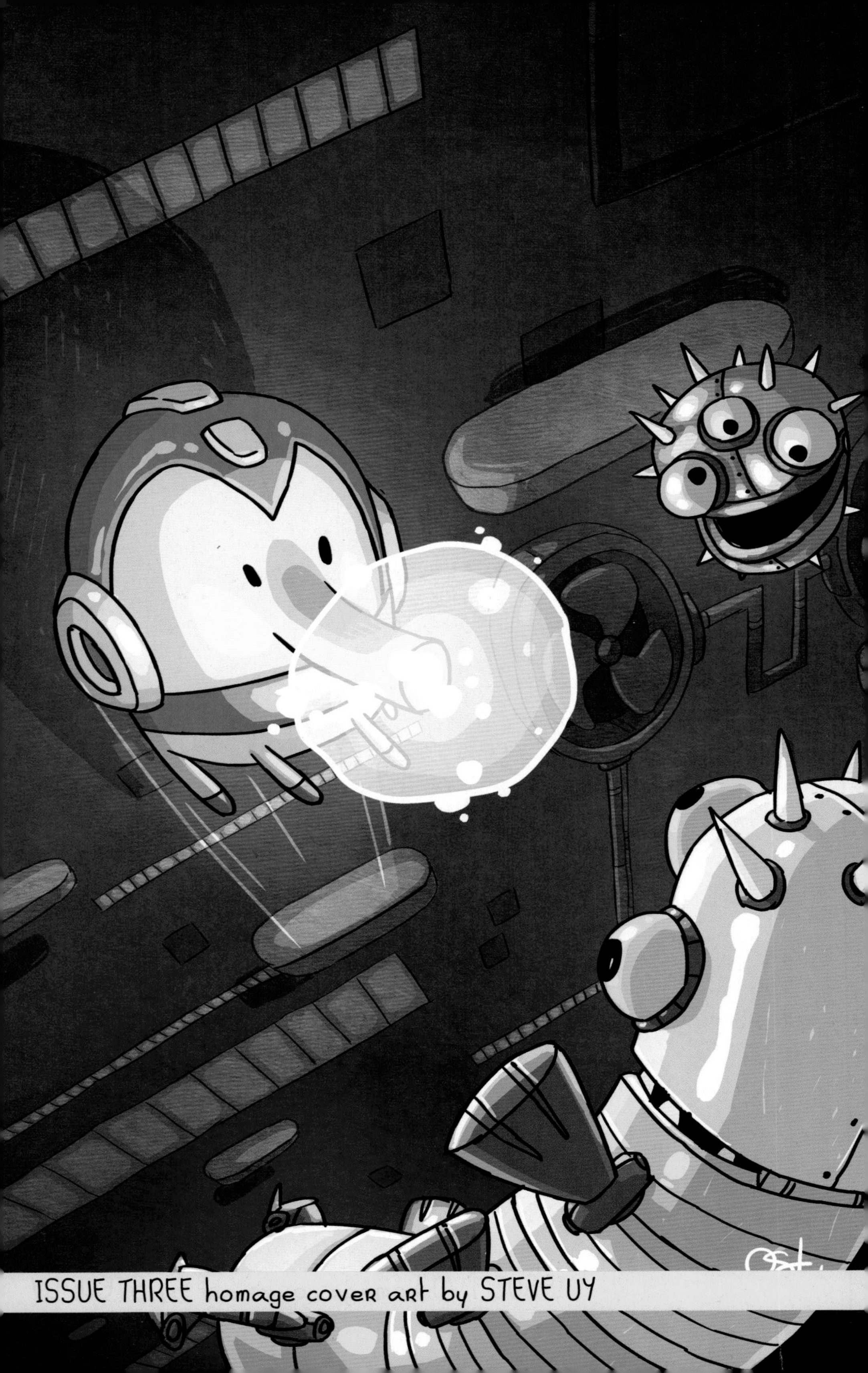

ISSUE THREE homage cover art by STEVE UY

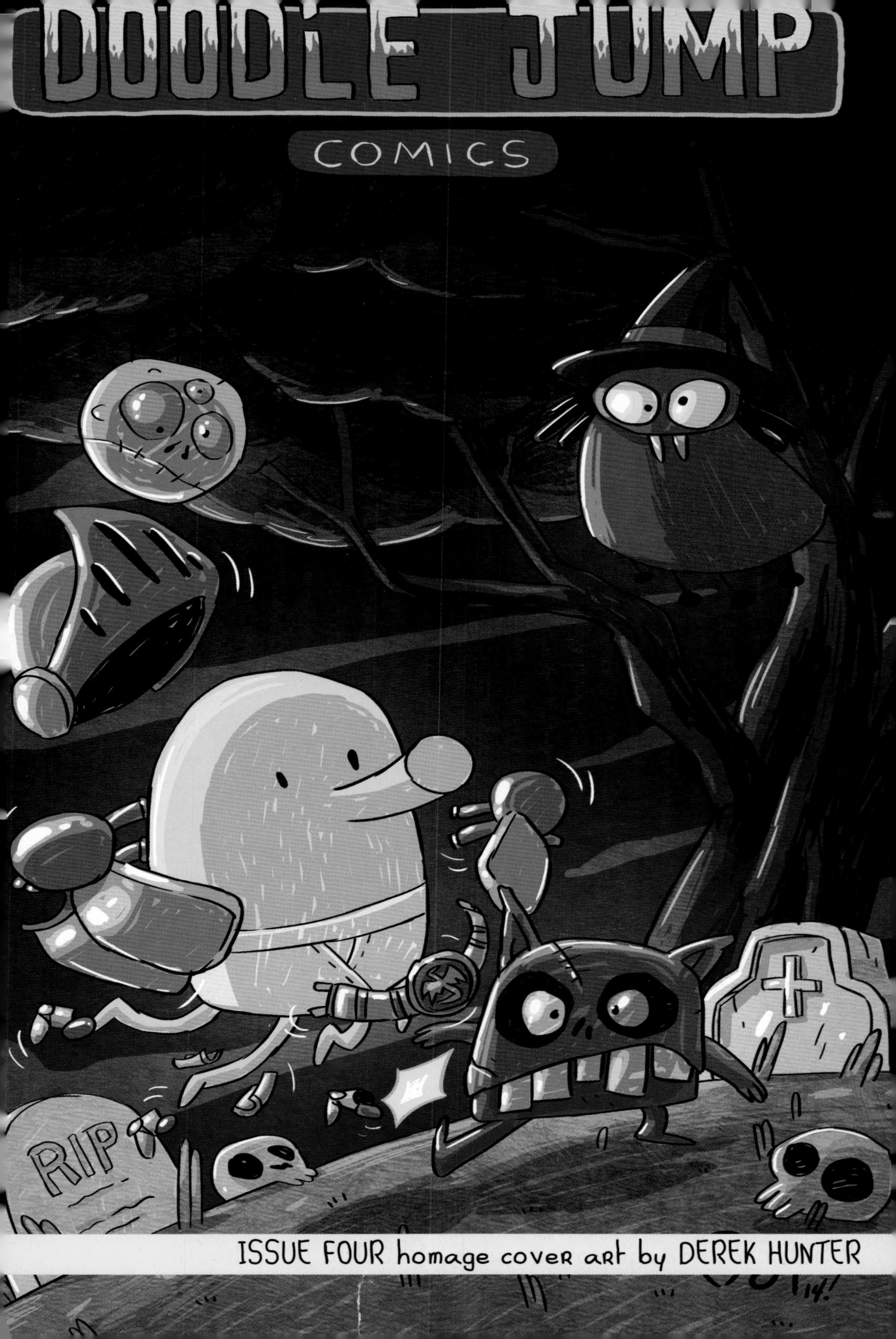
DOODLE JUMP
COMICS
RIP
ISSUE FOUR homage cover art by DEREK HUNTER

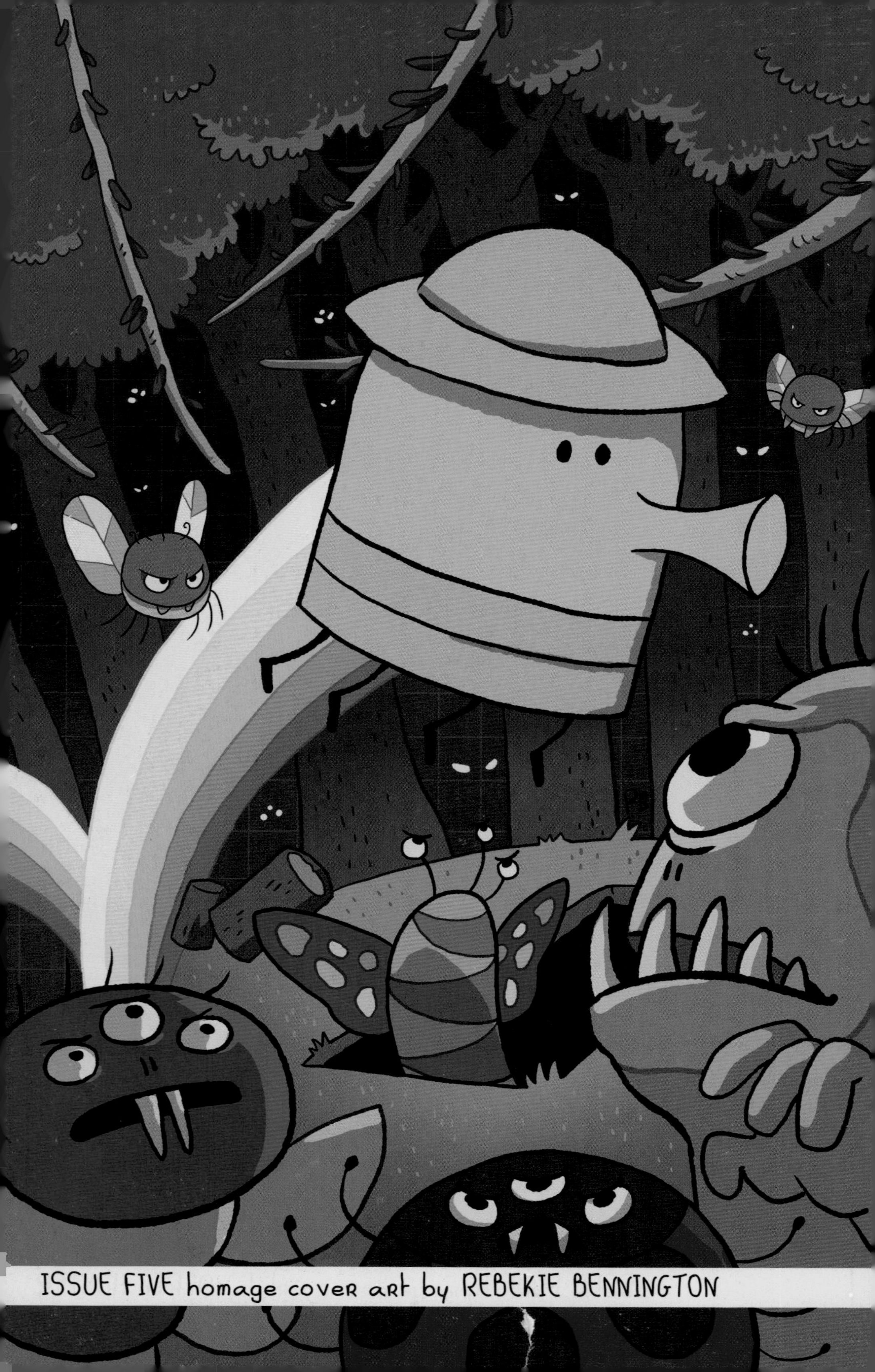

ISSUE FIVE homage cover art by REBEKIE BENNINGTON